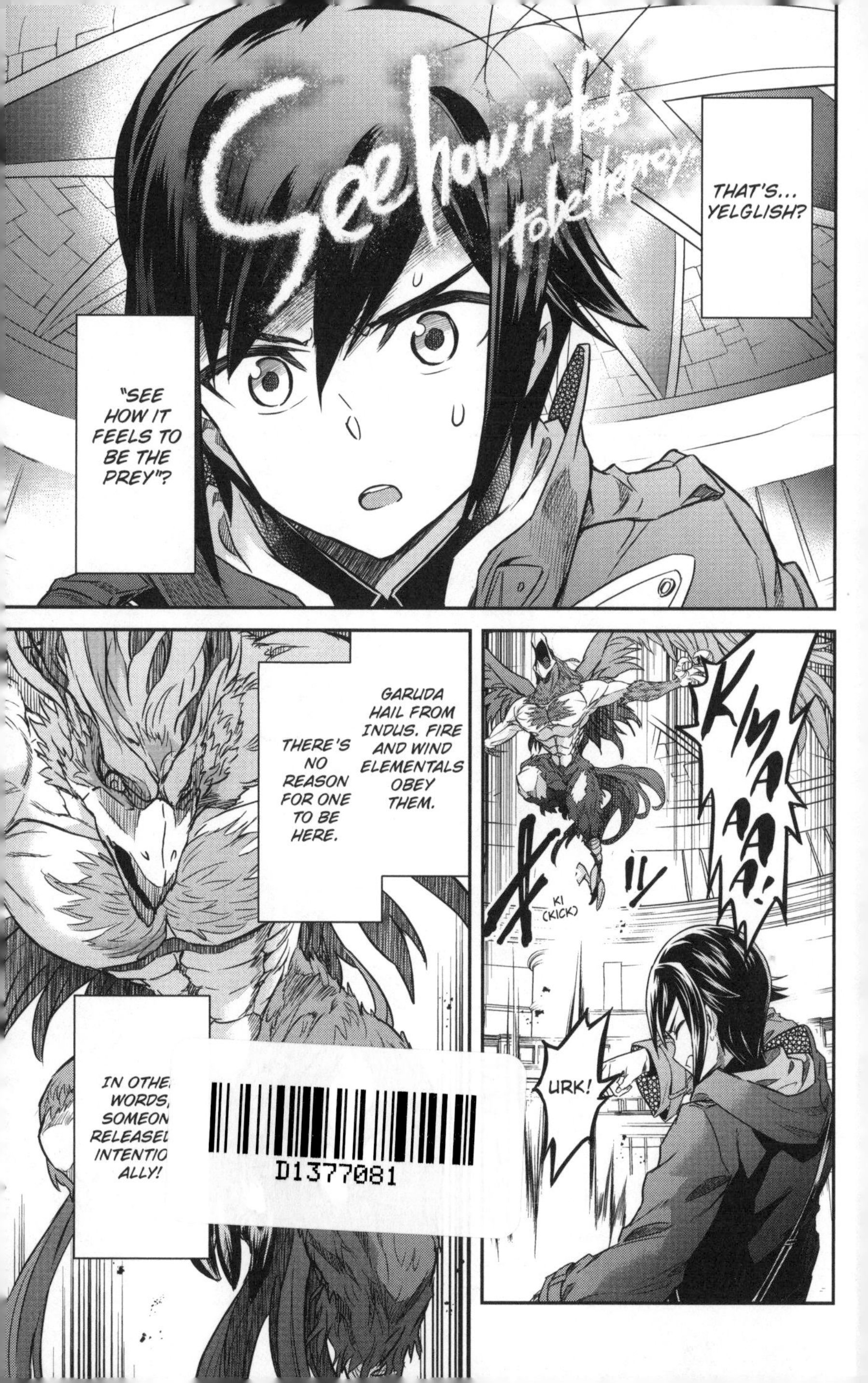
See how it feels to be the prey!?
THAT'S... YELGLISH?
"SEE HOW IT FEELS TO BE THE PREY"?
KIYAAAAAA!
KI (KICK)
!!
URK!
GARUDA HAIL FROM INDUS. FIRE AND WIND ELEMENTALS OBEY THEM.
THERE'S NO REASON FOR ONE TO BE HERE.
IN OTHE WORDS, SOMEON RELEASED INTENTIO ALLY!

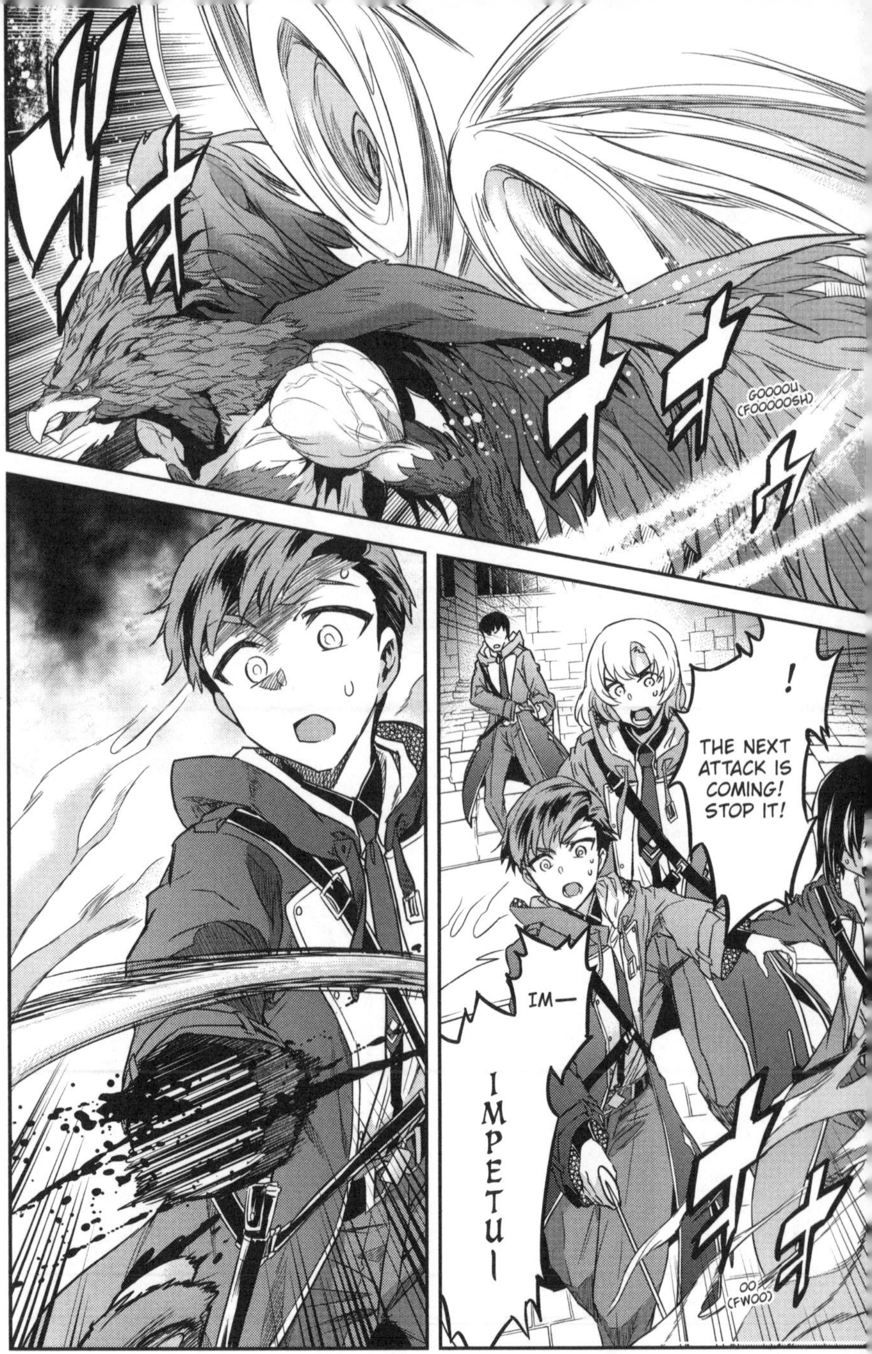
GOOOOU
(FOOOOOSH)
!
THE NEXT ATTACK IS COMING! STOP IT!
IM—
IMPETUI
OO
(FWOO)

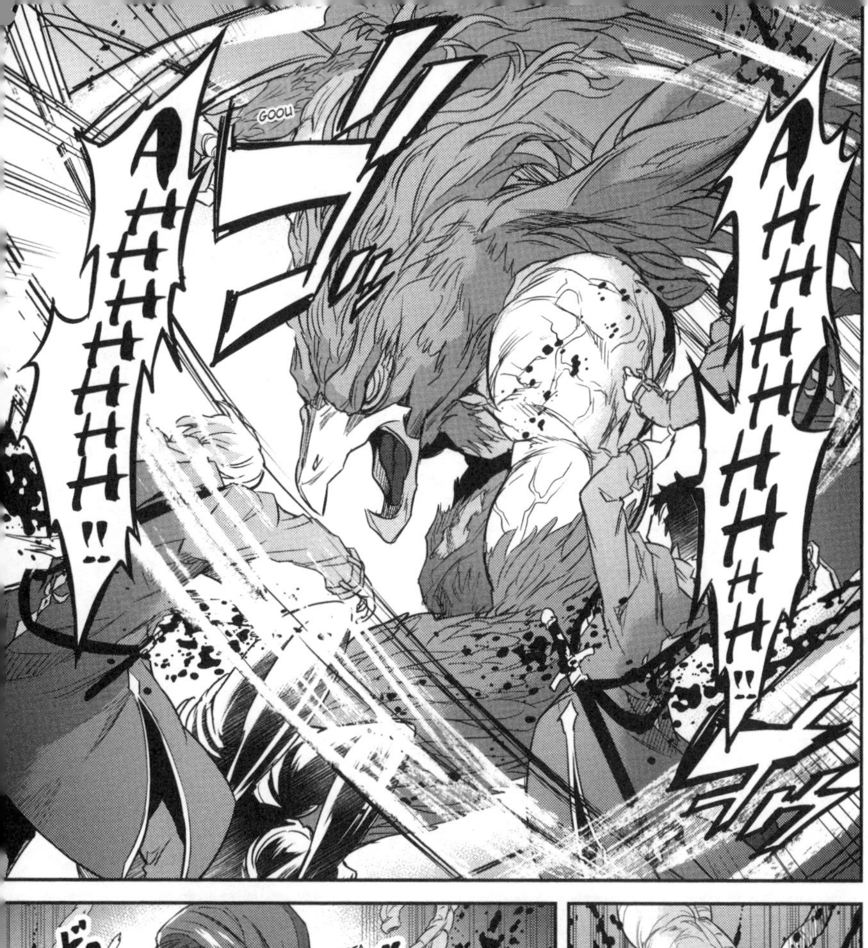
AHHHHHHHHH!!
GOOU
AHHHHHHHH!!

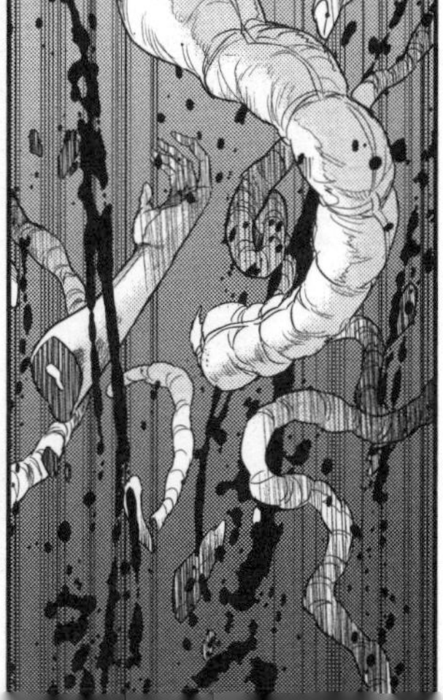

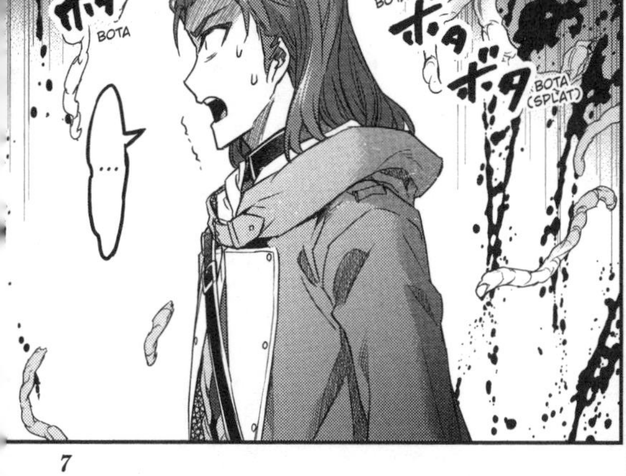
BOTA
BOTA (SPLAT)
...
BOTA

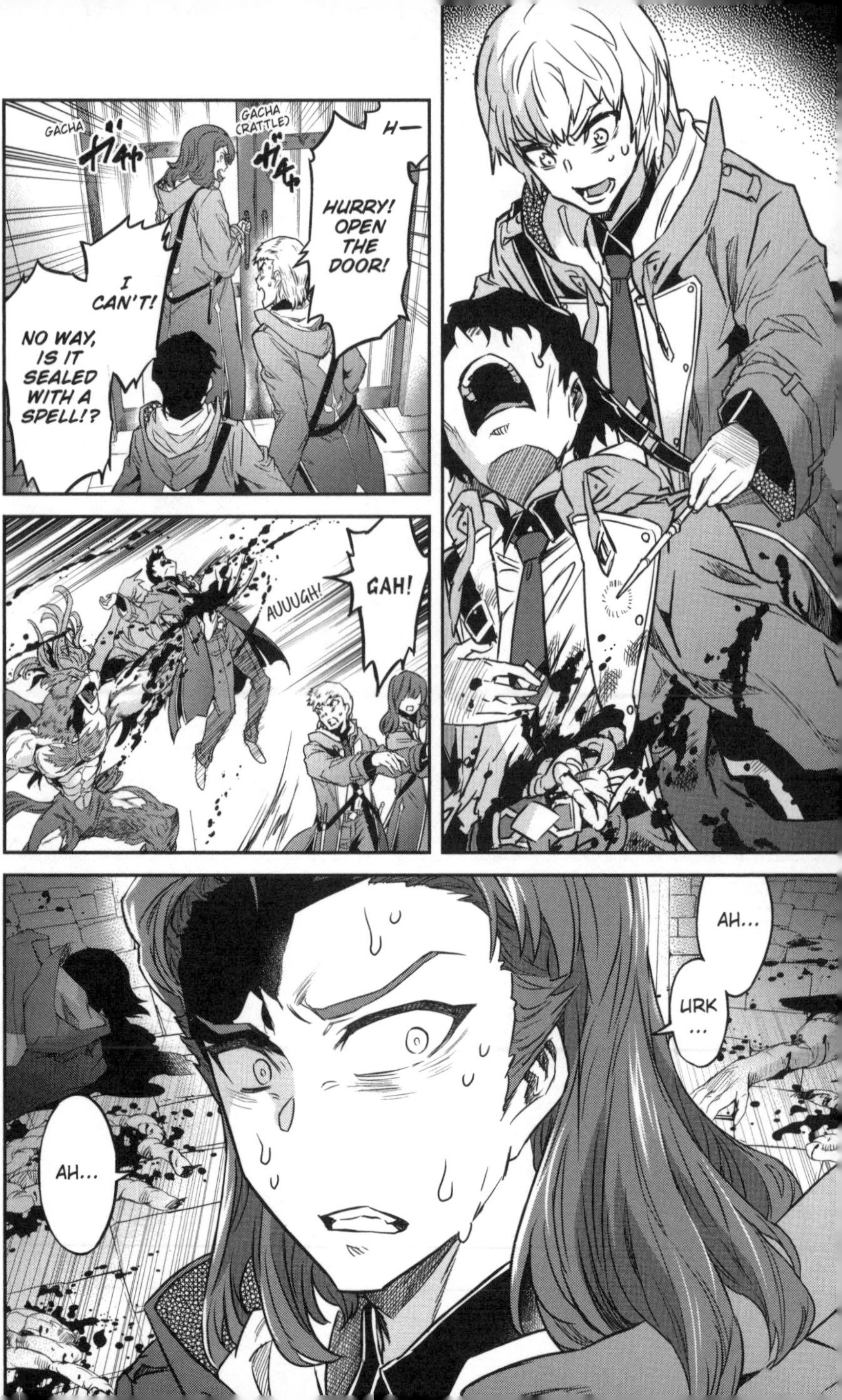
H—
GACHA (RATTLE)
GACHA
HURRY! OPEN THE DOOR!
I CAN'T!
NO WAY, IS IT SEALED WITH A SPELL!?
GAH!
AUUUGH!
AH...
URK ...
AH...

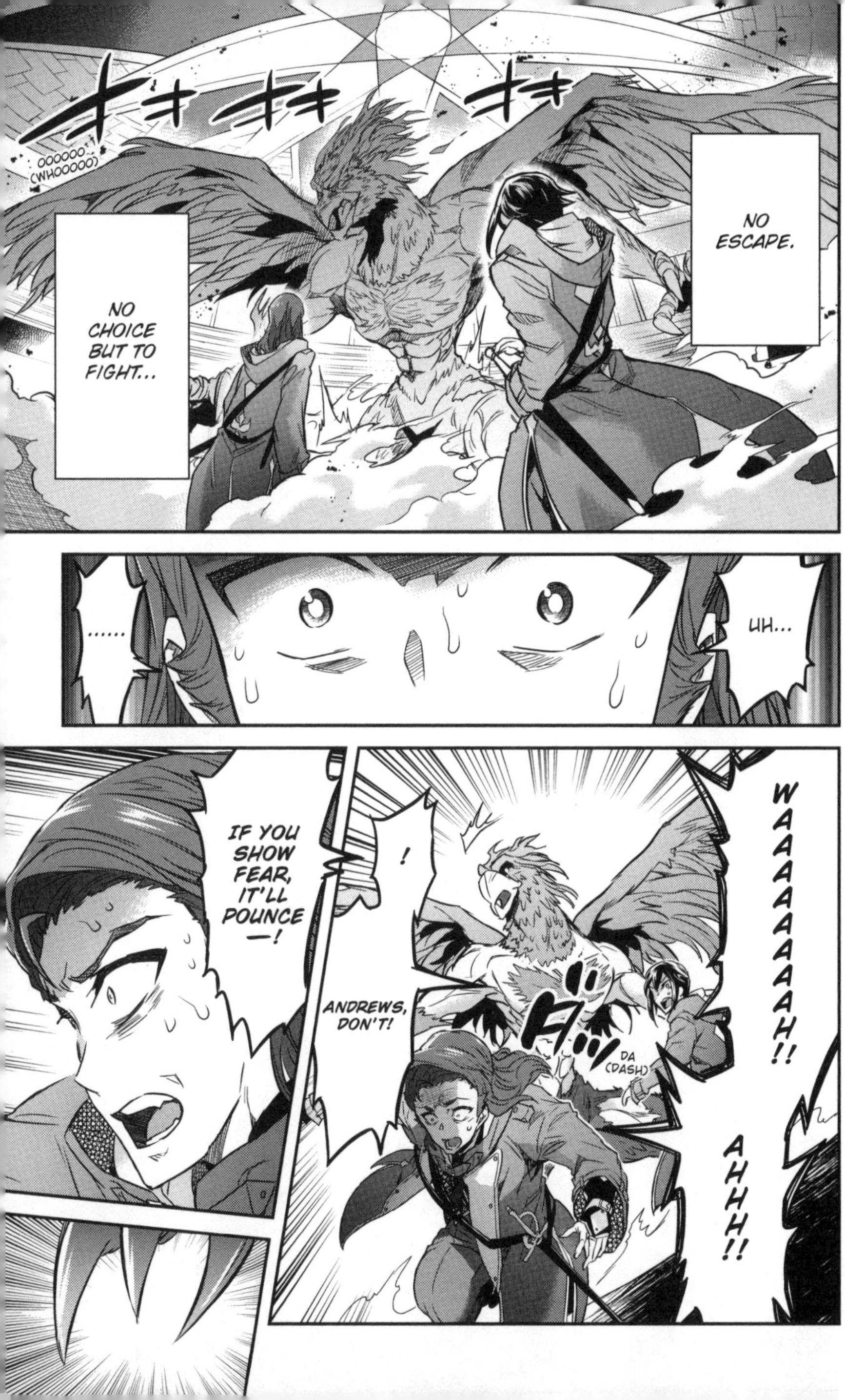
NO ESCAPE.
OOOOOO (WHOOOOO)
NO CHOICE BUT TO FIGHT...
UH...
......
WAAAAAAAAAH!!
AHHHH!!
!
DA (DASH)
ANDREWS, DON'T!
IF YOU SHOW FEAR, IT'LL POUNCE—!

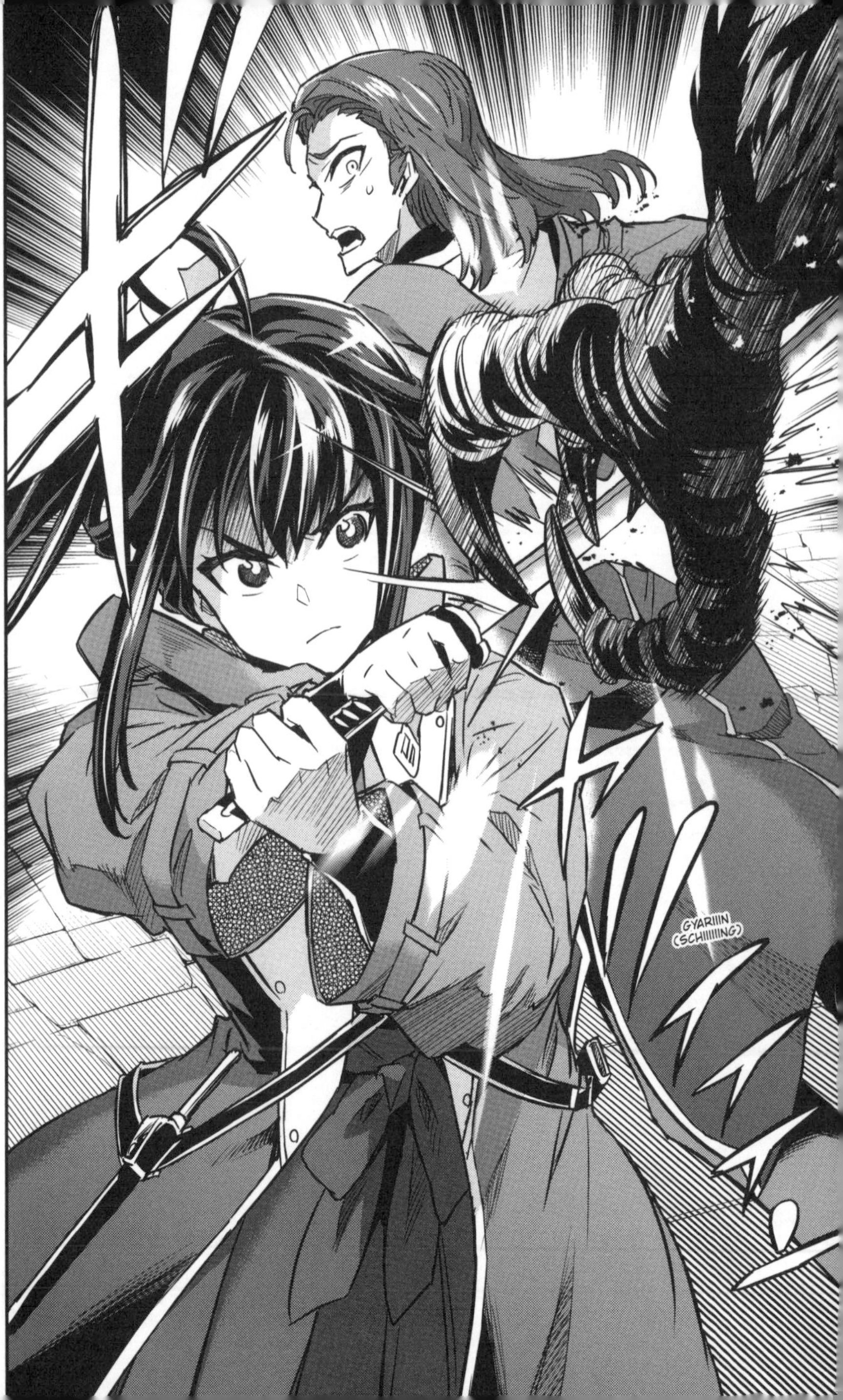
GYARIIIN
(SCHIIIIIING)

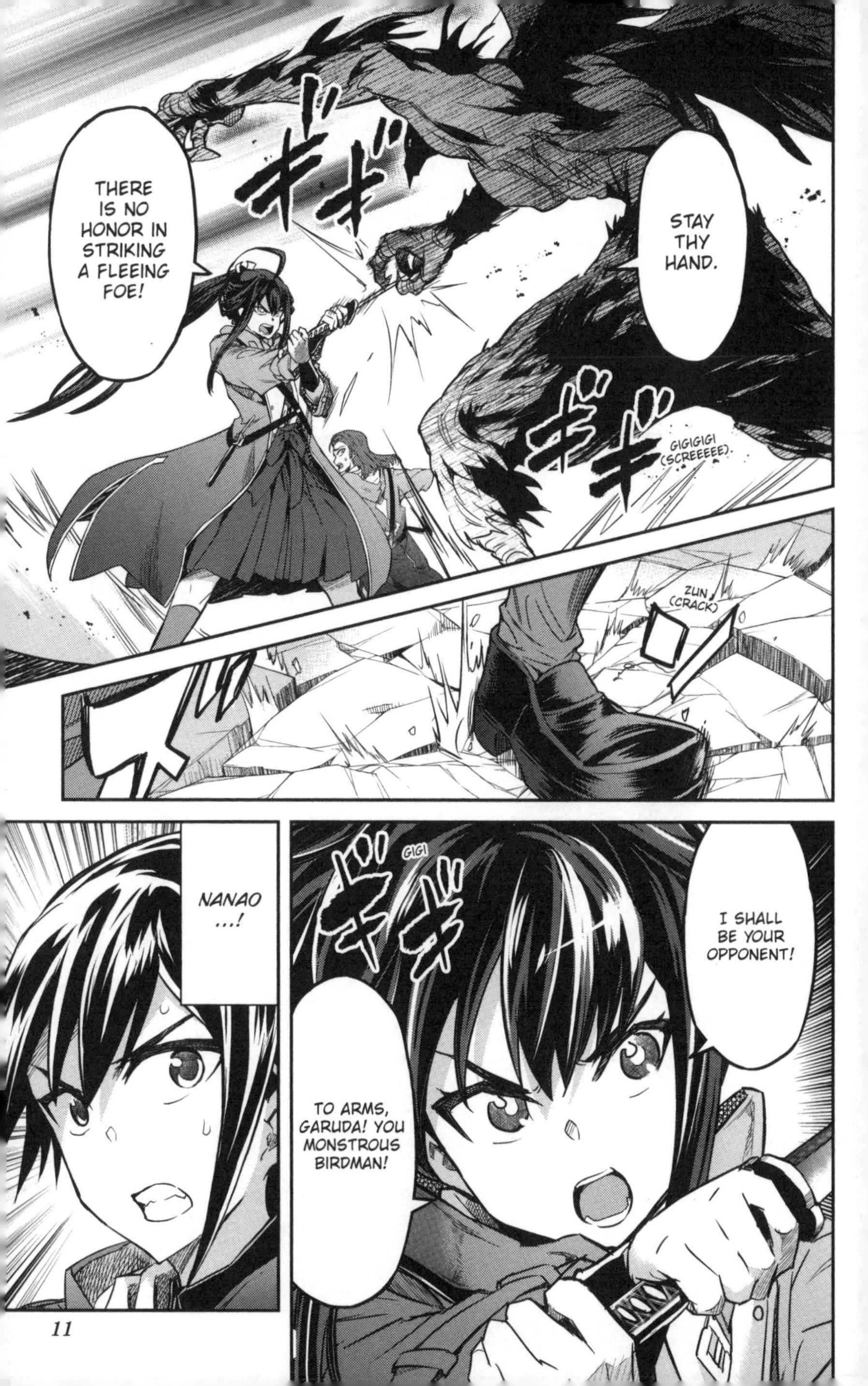
STAY THY HAND.
THERE IS NO HONOR IN STRIKING A FLEEING FOE!
GIGIGIGI (SCREEEEE)
ZUN (CRACK)
GIGI
I SHALL BE YOUR OPPONENT!
TO ARMS, GARUDA! YOU MONSTROUS BIRDMAN!
NANAO ...!

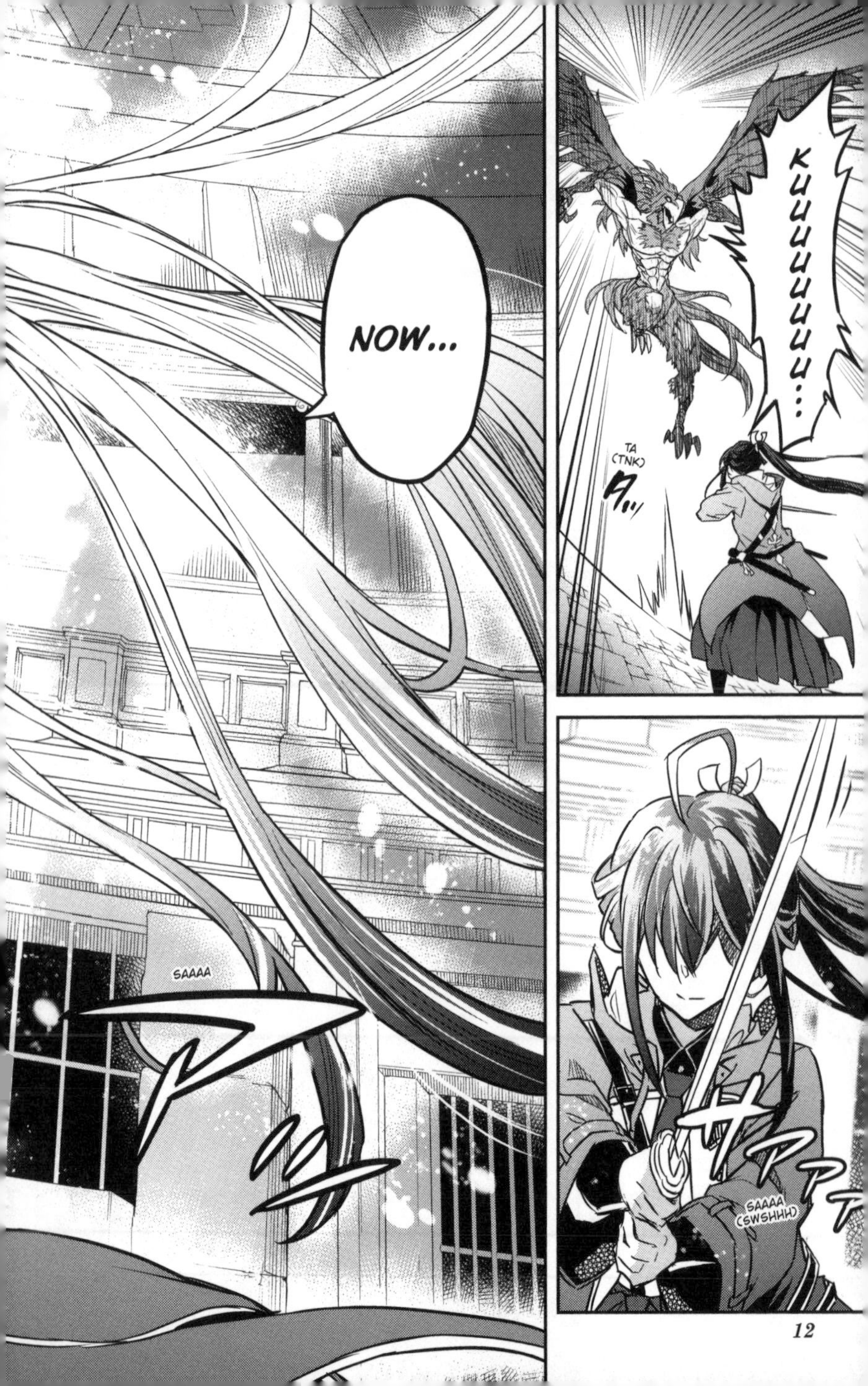
KUUUUUUUUU...
TA (TNK)
SAAAA (SWSHHH)
NOW...
SAAAA

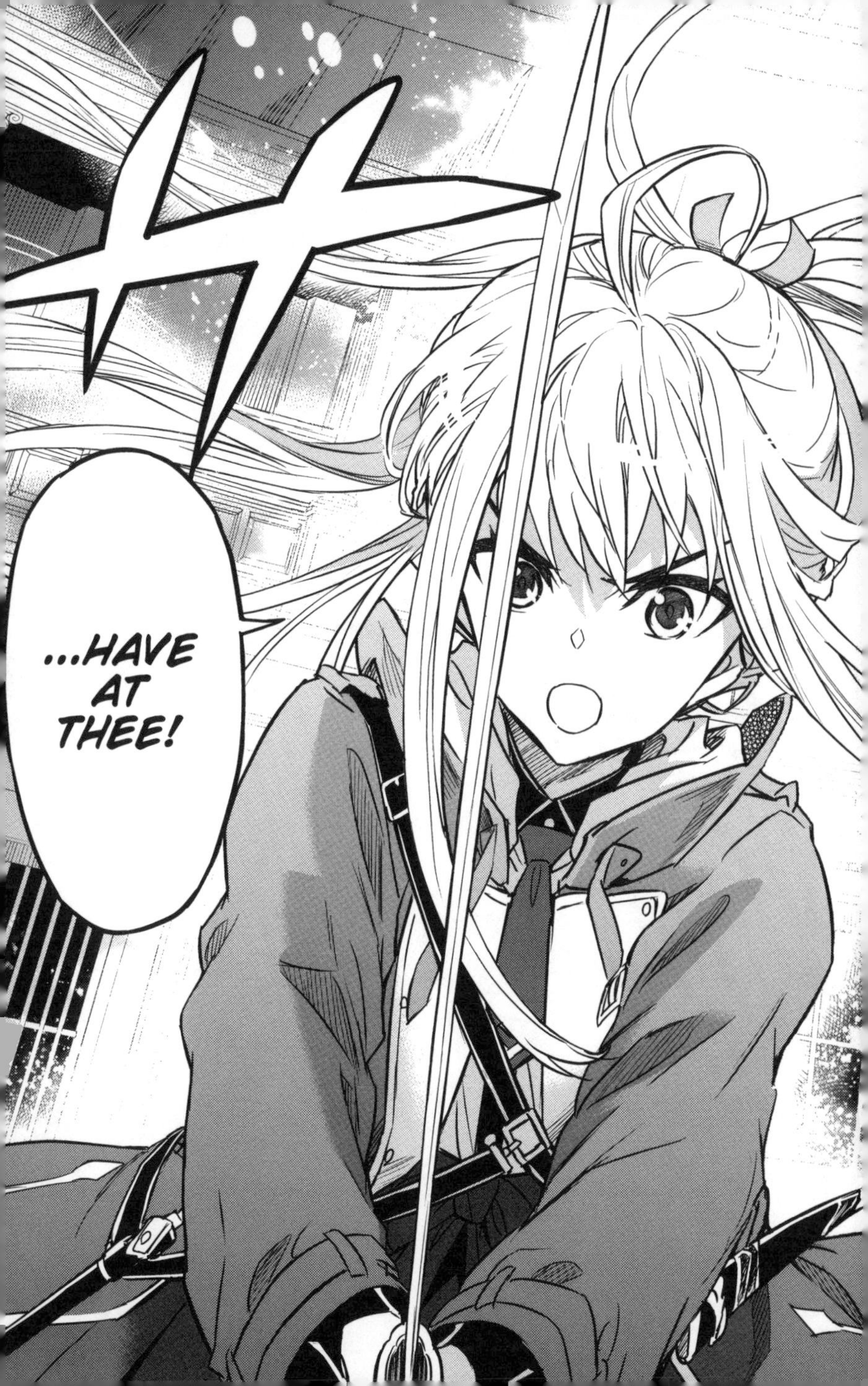
...HAVE AT THEE!

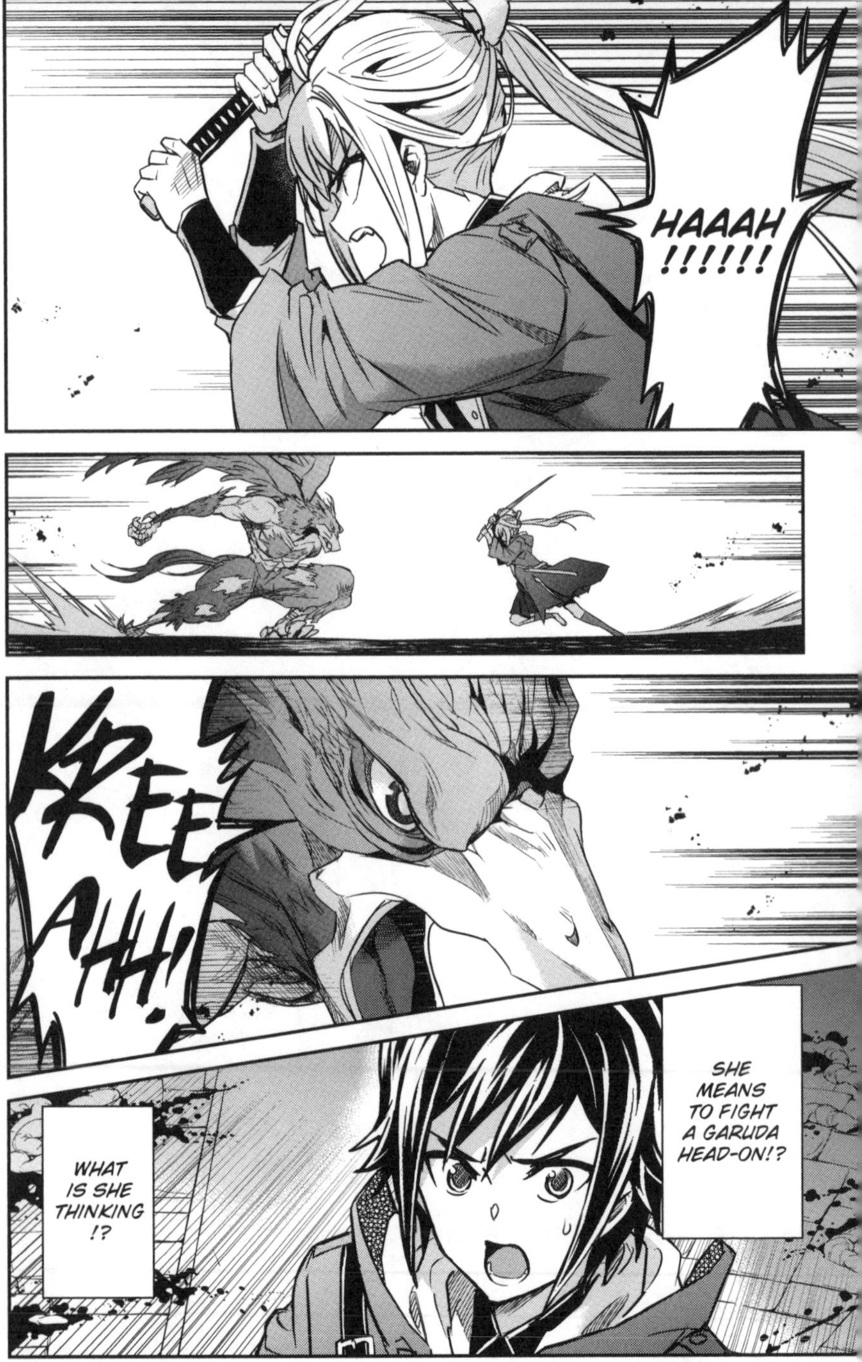
HAAAH !!!!!!
KREEEAHH!
SHE MEANS TO FIGHT A GARUDA HEAD-ON!?
WHAT IS SHE THINKING !?

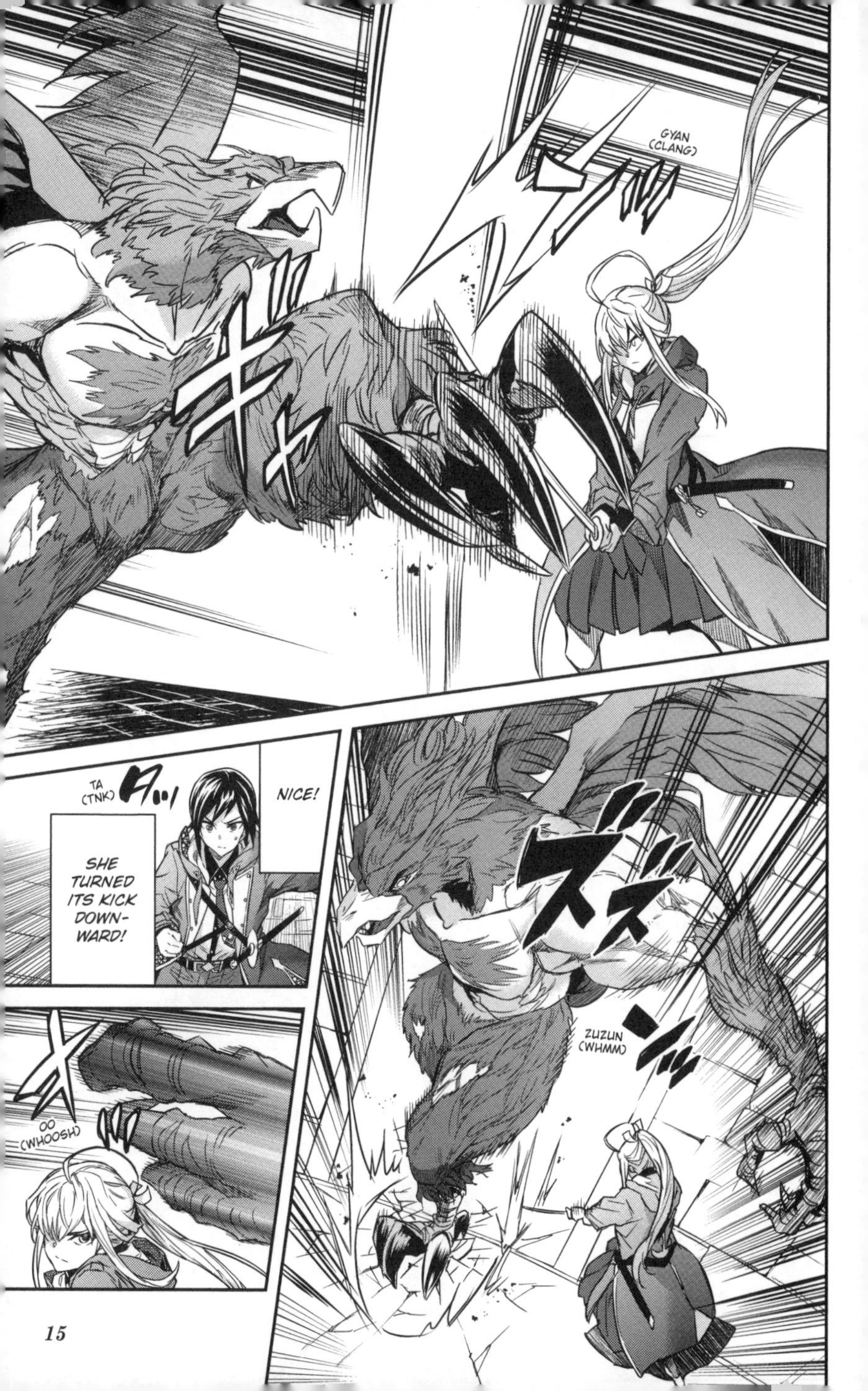
GYAN
(CLANG)
ZUZUN
(WHMM)
NICE!
TA
(TNK)
SHE TURNED ITS KICK DOWN-WARD!
OO
(WHOOSH)

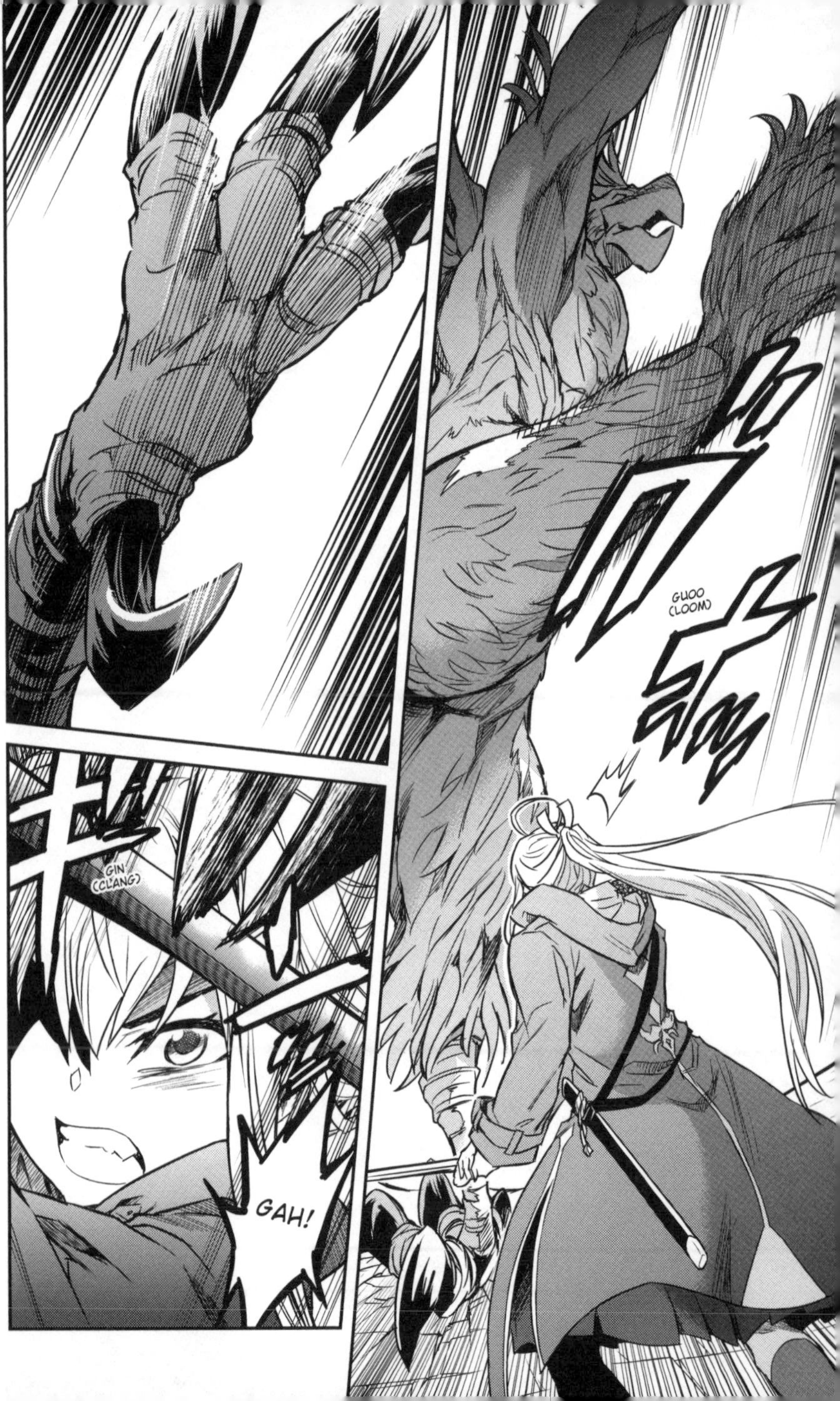
GUOO (LOOM)
GIN (CLANG)
GAH!

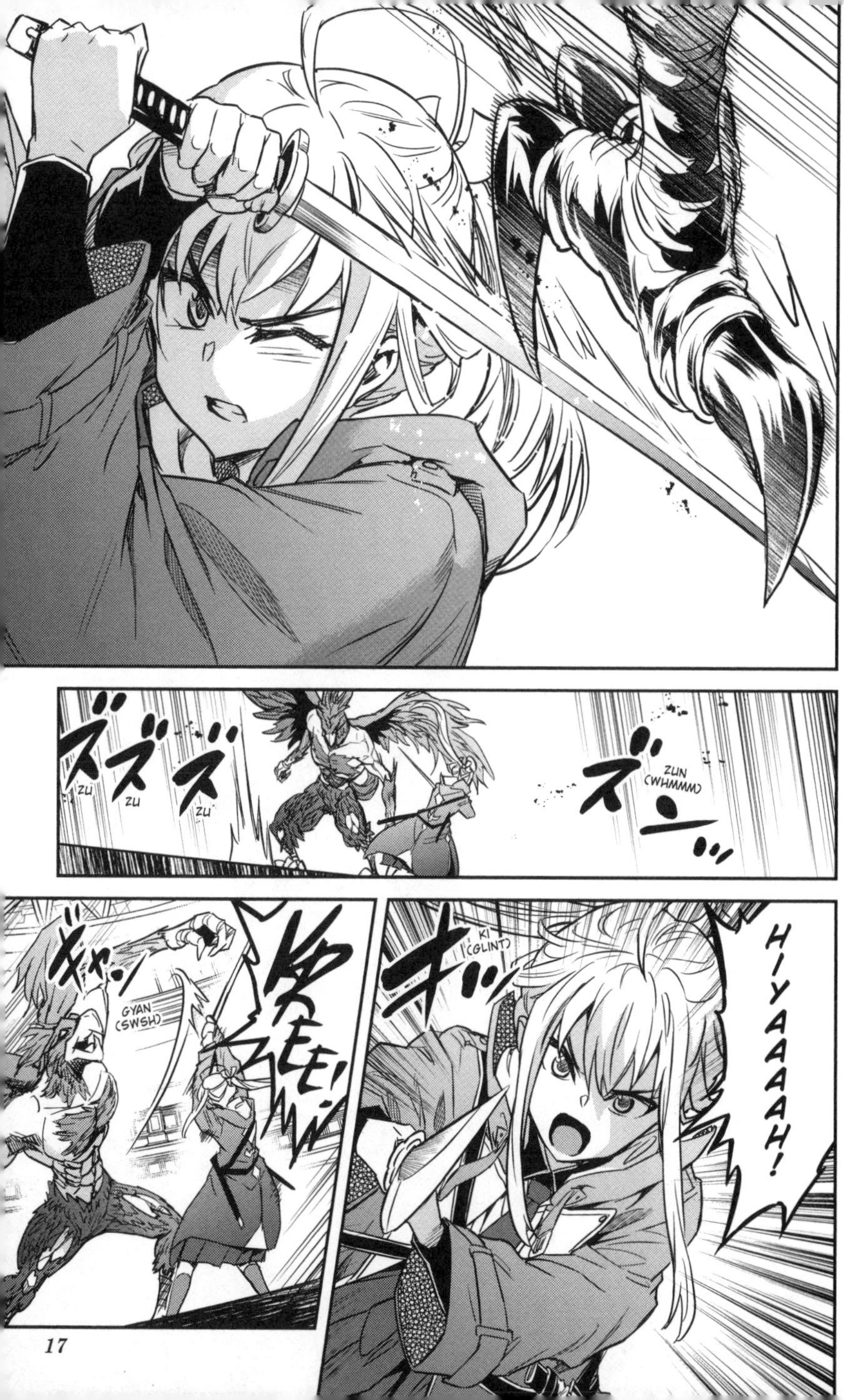

ズン
ZUN (WHMMM)
ズズズ
ZU ZU ZU
HIYAAAAAH!
キッ
KI (GLINT)
KREEE!
ギャン
GYAN (SWSH)

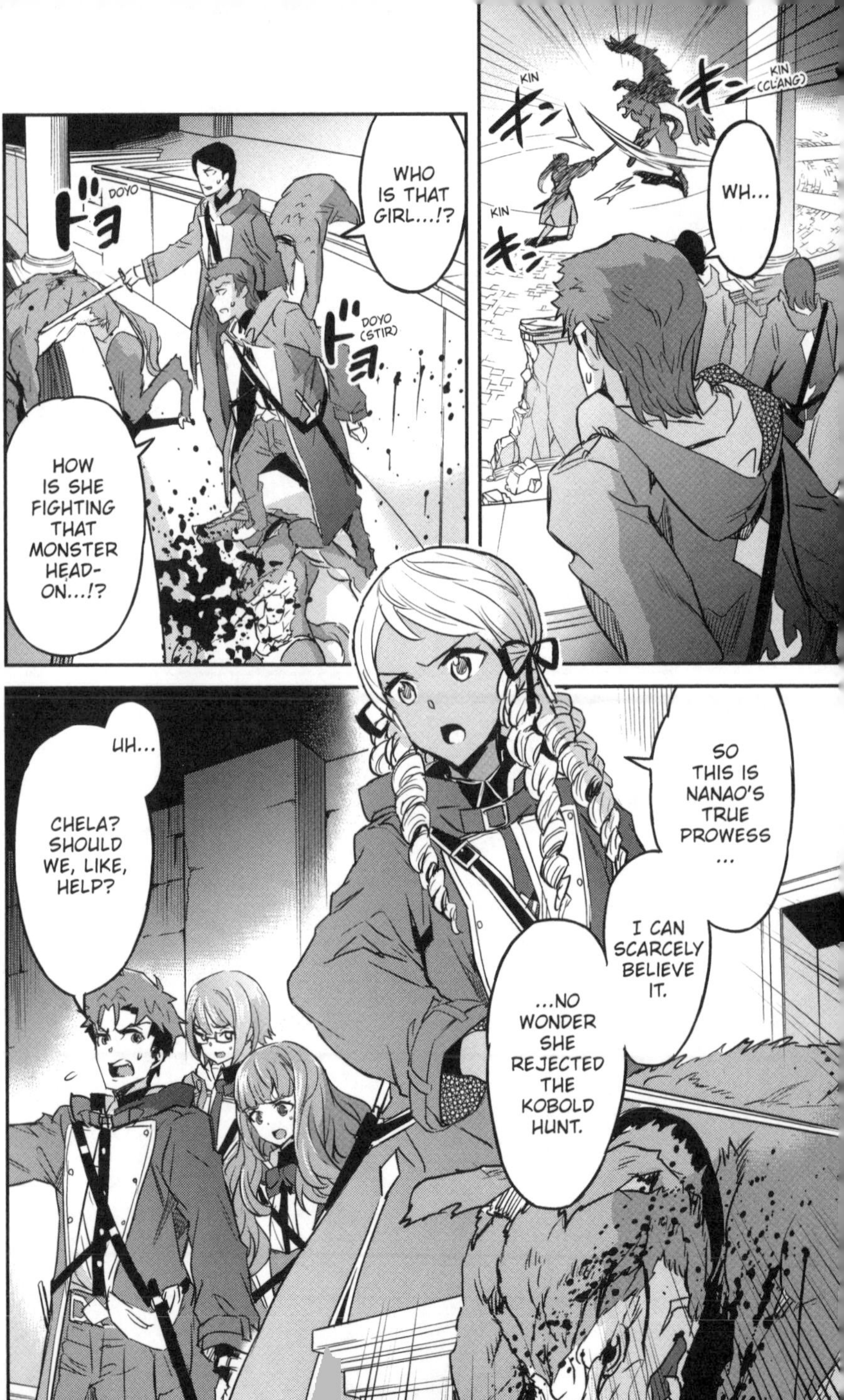
キン
KIN (CLANG)
キン
KIN
キン
KIN
WH...
WHO IS THAT GIRL...!?
ドヨ
DOYO
ドヨ
DOYO (STIR)
HOW IS SHE FIGHTING THAT MONSTER HEAD-ON...!?
SO THIS IS NANAO'S TRUE PROWESS...
I CAN SCARCELY BELIEVE IT.
...NO WONDER SHE REJECTED THE KOBOLD HUNT.
UH...
CHELA? SHOULD WE, LIKE, HELP?

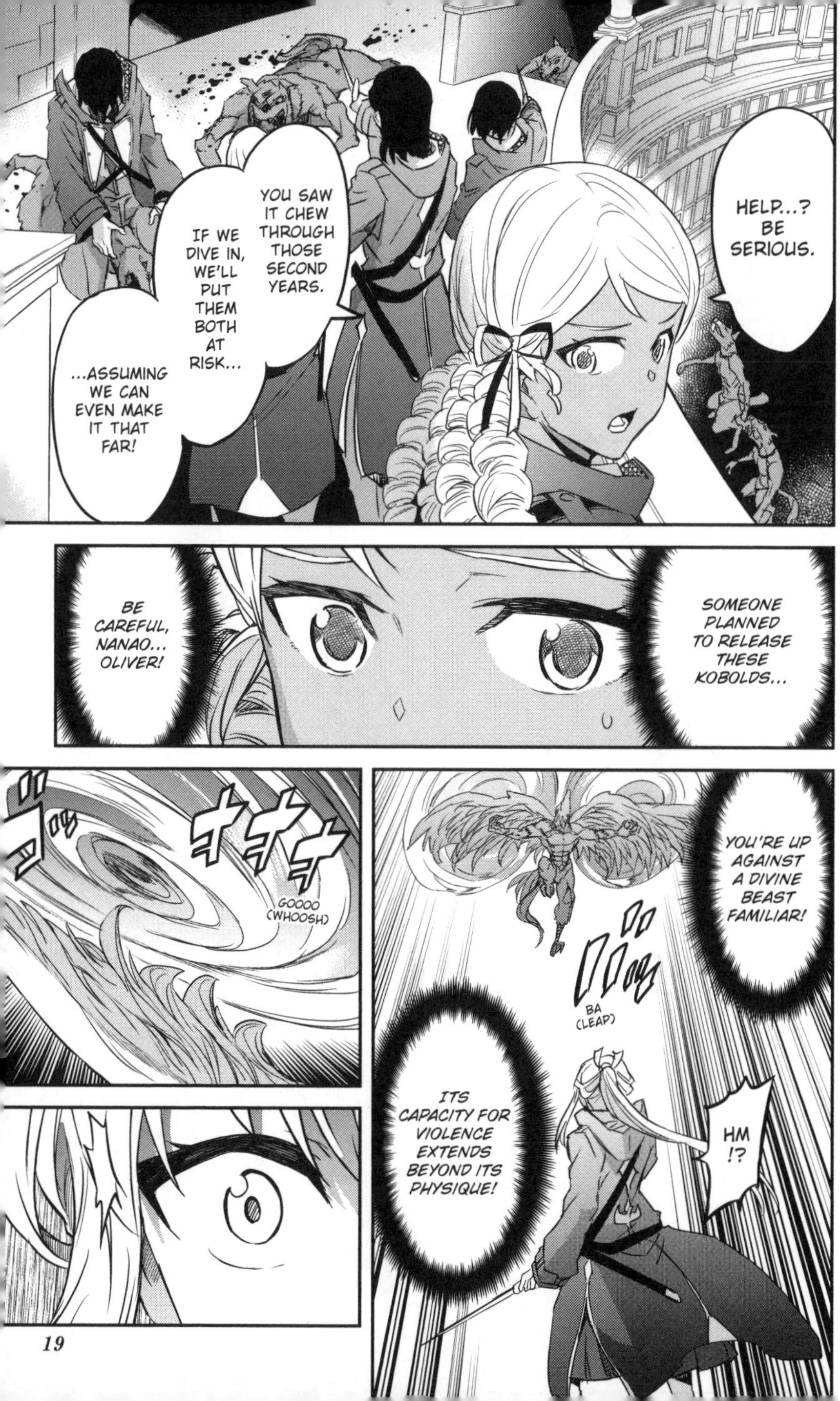
HELP...? BE SERIOUS.
YOU SAW IT CHEW THROUGH THOSE SECOND YEARS.
IF WE DIVE IN, WE'LL PUT THEM BOTH AT RISK...
...ASSUMING WE CAN EVEN MAKE IT THAT FAR!
SOMEONE PLANNED TO RELEASE THESE KOBOLDS...
BE CAREFUL, NANAO... OLIVER!
YOU'RE UP AGAINST A DIVINE BEAST FAMILIAR!
BA (LEAP)
ITS CAPACITY FOR VIOLENCE EXTENDS BEYOND ITS PHYSIQUE!
HM!?
GOOOO (WHOOSH)

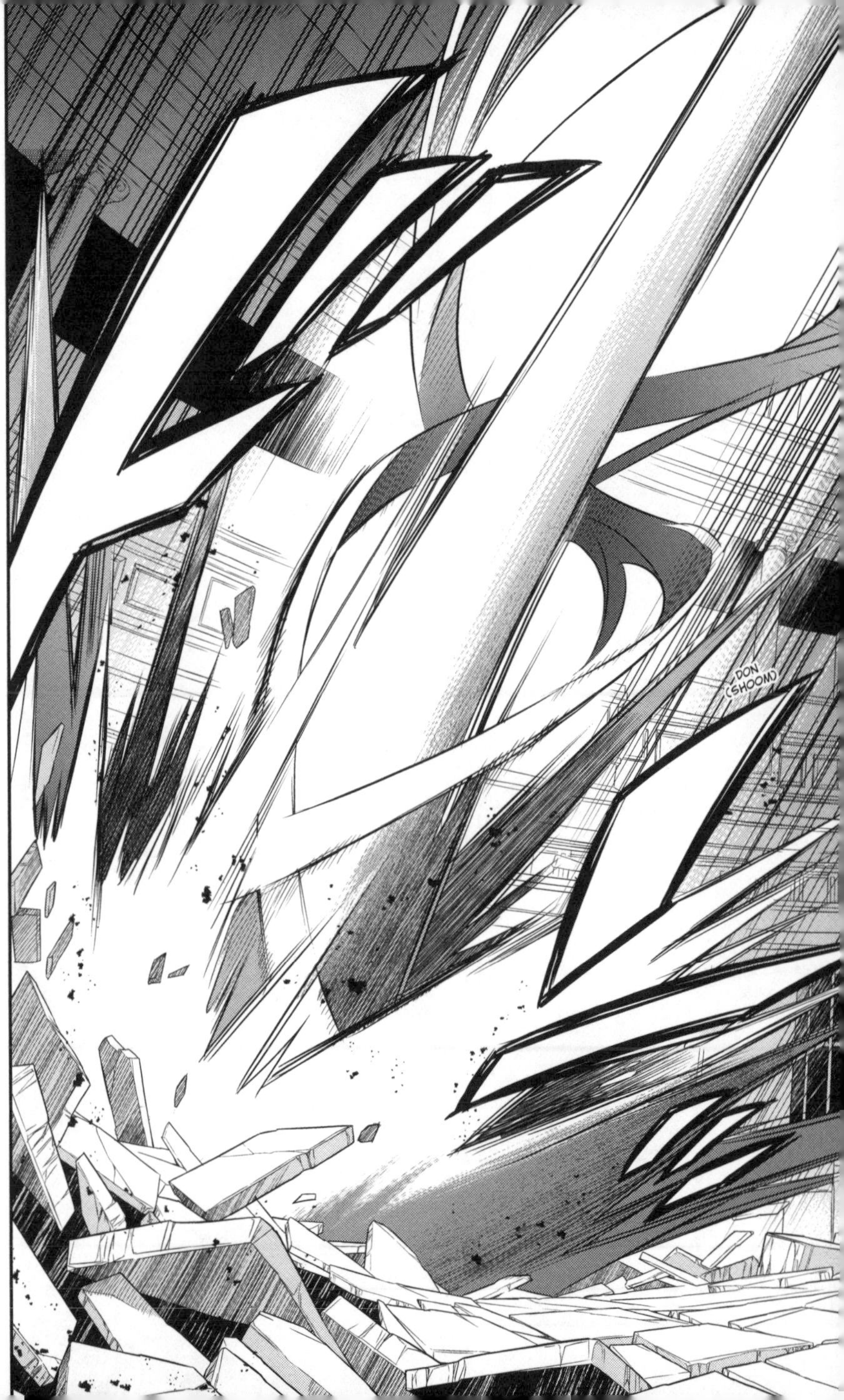
DON
(SHOOM)

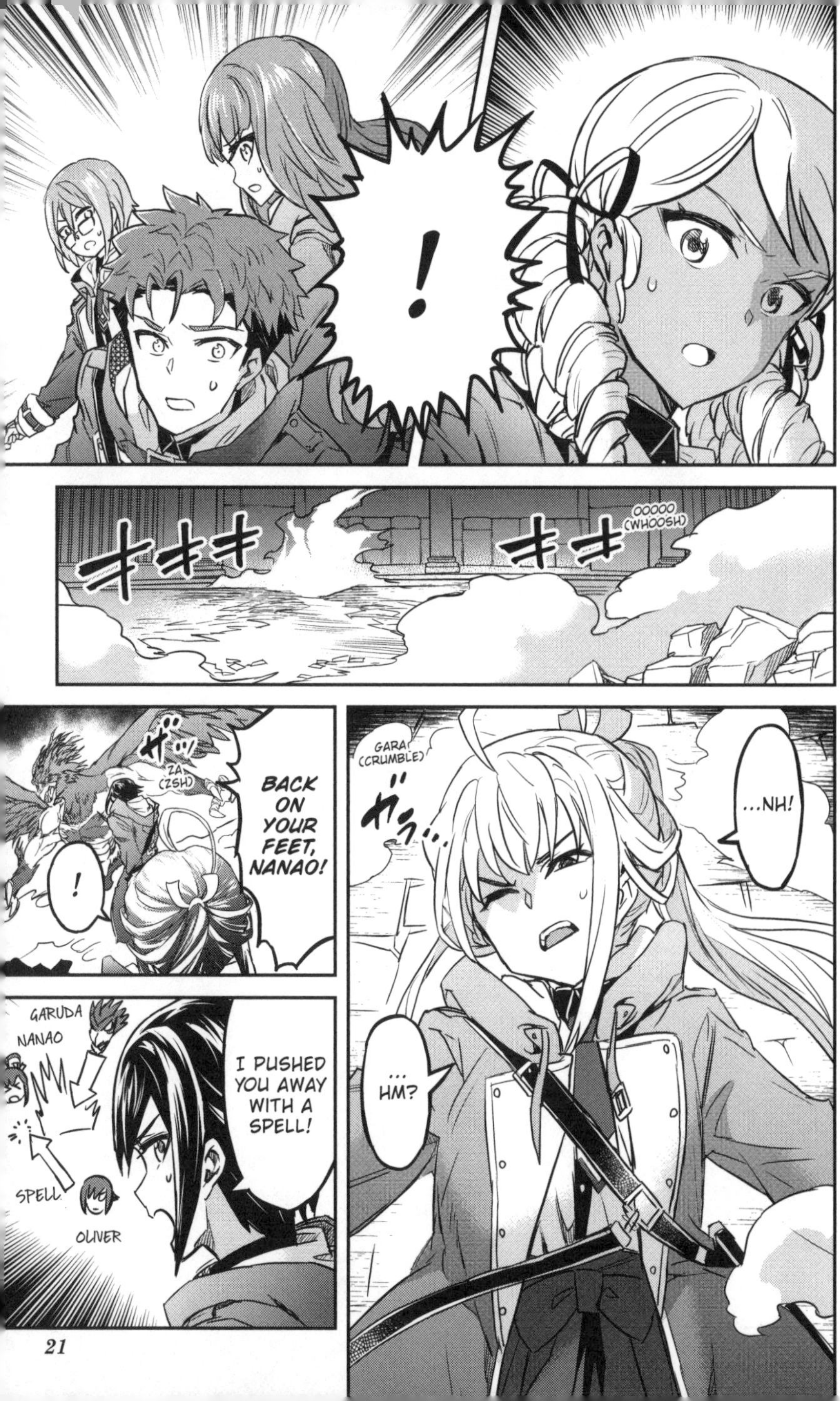
!
OOOOO (WHOOSH)
GARA (CRUMBLE)
...NH!
... HM?
ZA (ZSH)
BACK ON YOUR FEET, NANAO!
!
I PUSHED YOU AWAY WITH A SPELL!
GARUDA
NANAO
SPELL
OLIVER

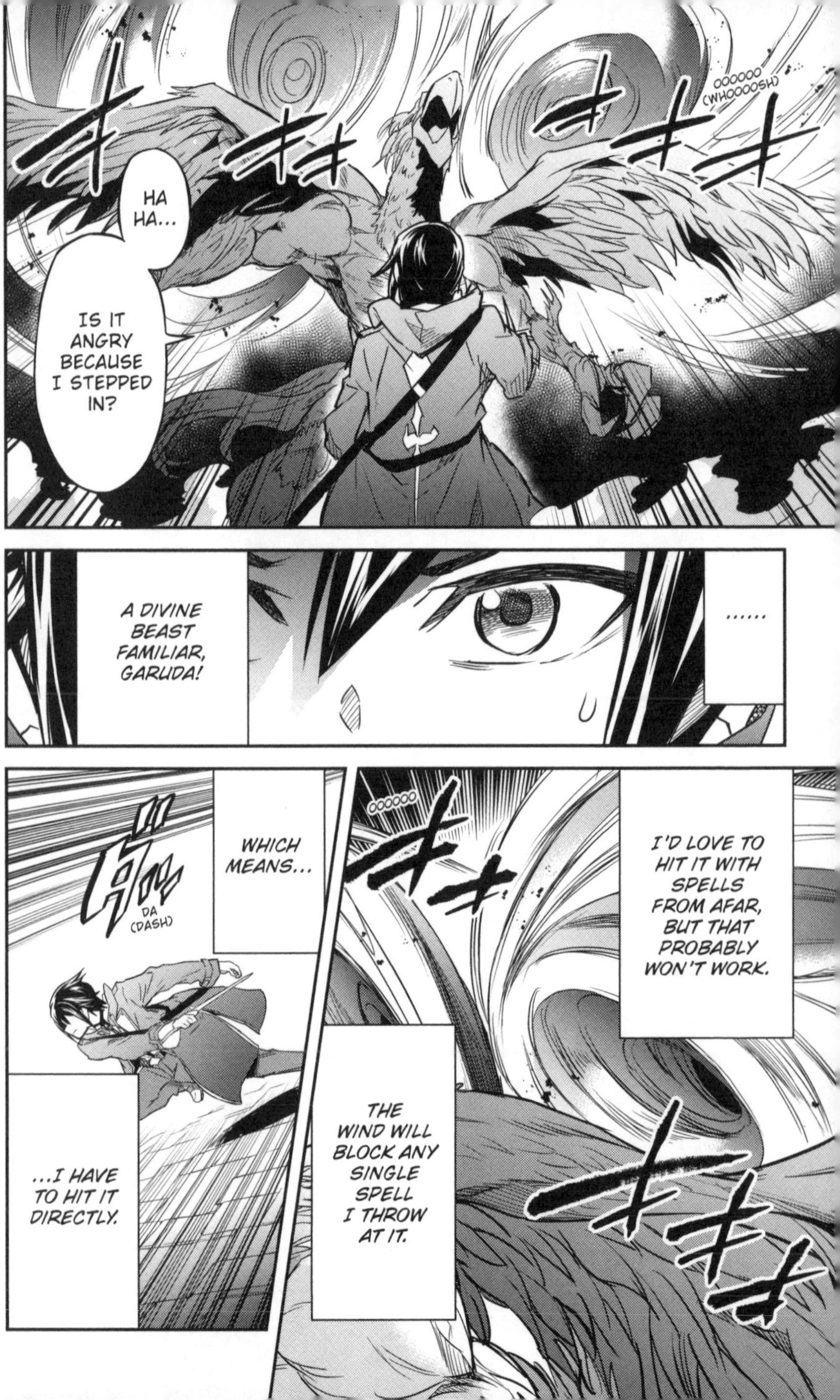
OOOOOO (WHOOOOSH)
HA HA...
IS IT ANGRY BECAUSE I STEPPED IN?
......
A DIVINE BEAST FAMILIAR, GARUDA!
I'D LOVE TO HIT IT WITH SPELLS FROM AFAR, BUT THAT PROBABLY WON'T WORK.
OOOOOO
THE WIND WILL BLOCK ANY SINGLE SPELL I THROW AT IT.
WHICH MEANS...
DA (DASH)
...I HAVE TO HIT IT DIRECTLY.

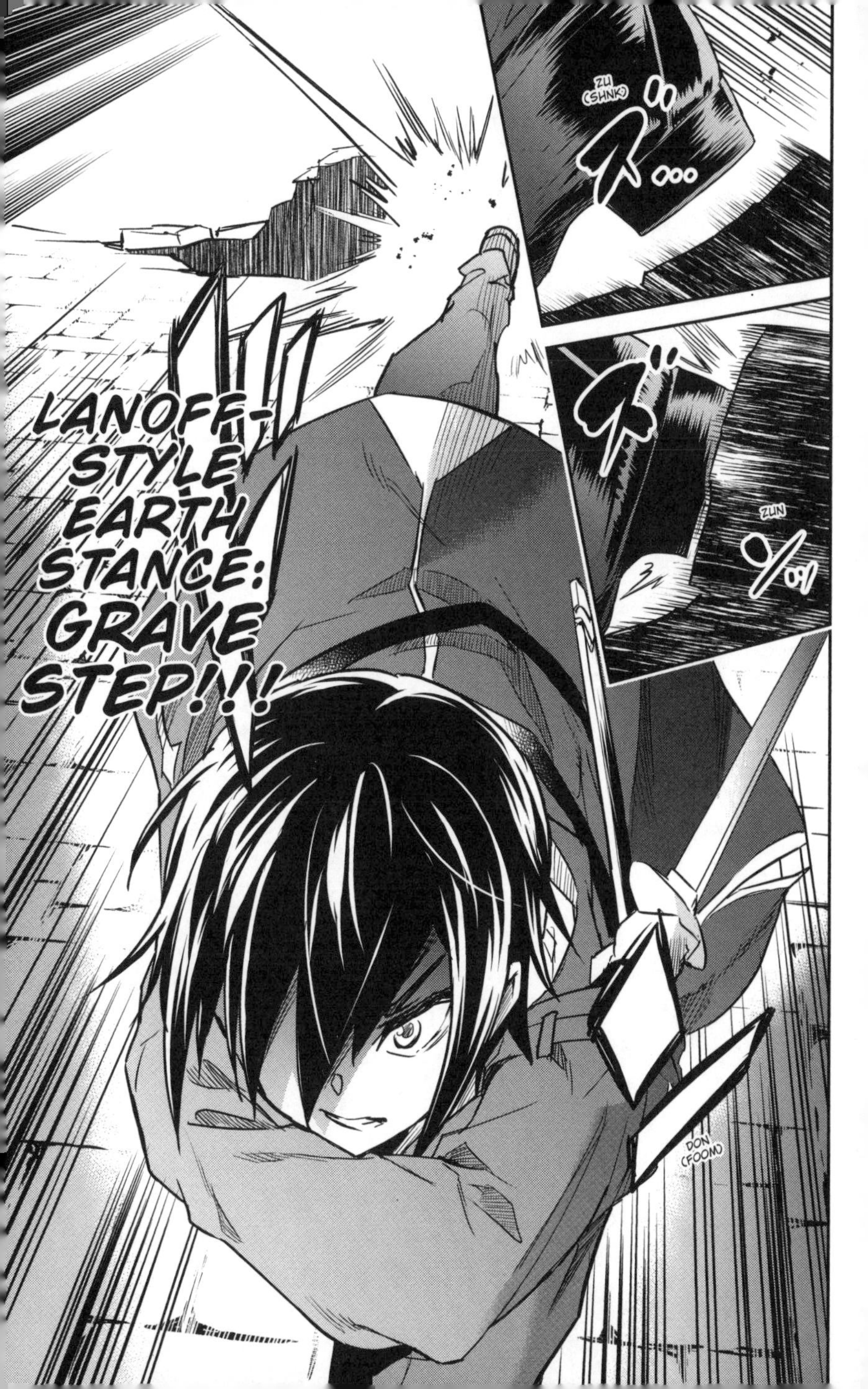
ZU (SHNK)
ZUN
LANOFF-STYLE EARTH STANCE: GRAVE STEP!!!
DON (FOOM)

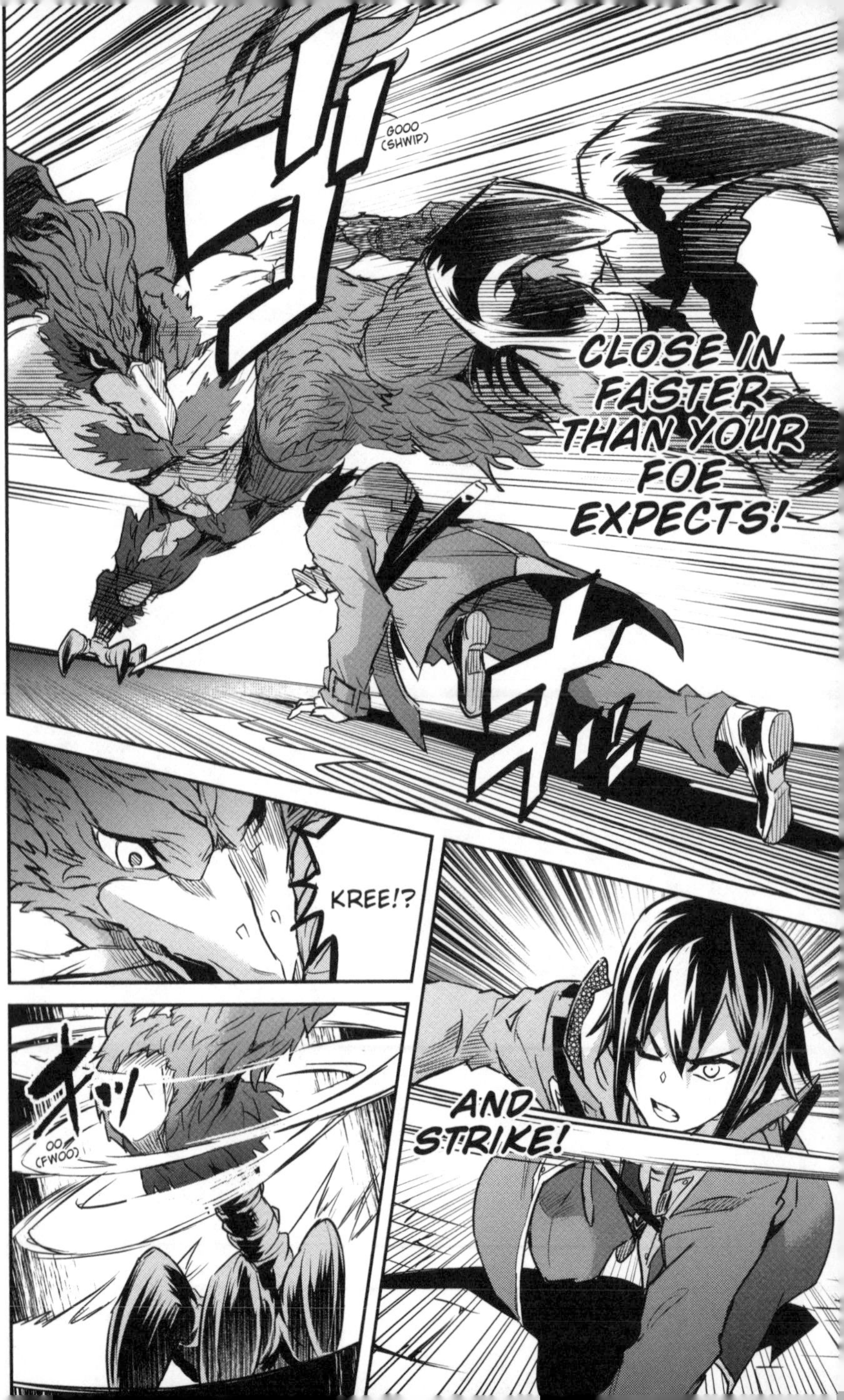
GOOO (SHWIP)
CLOSE IN FASTER THAN YOUR FOE EXPECTS!
KREE!?
AND STRIKE!
OO (FWOO)

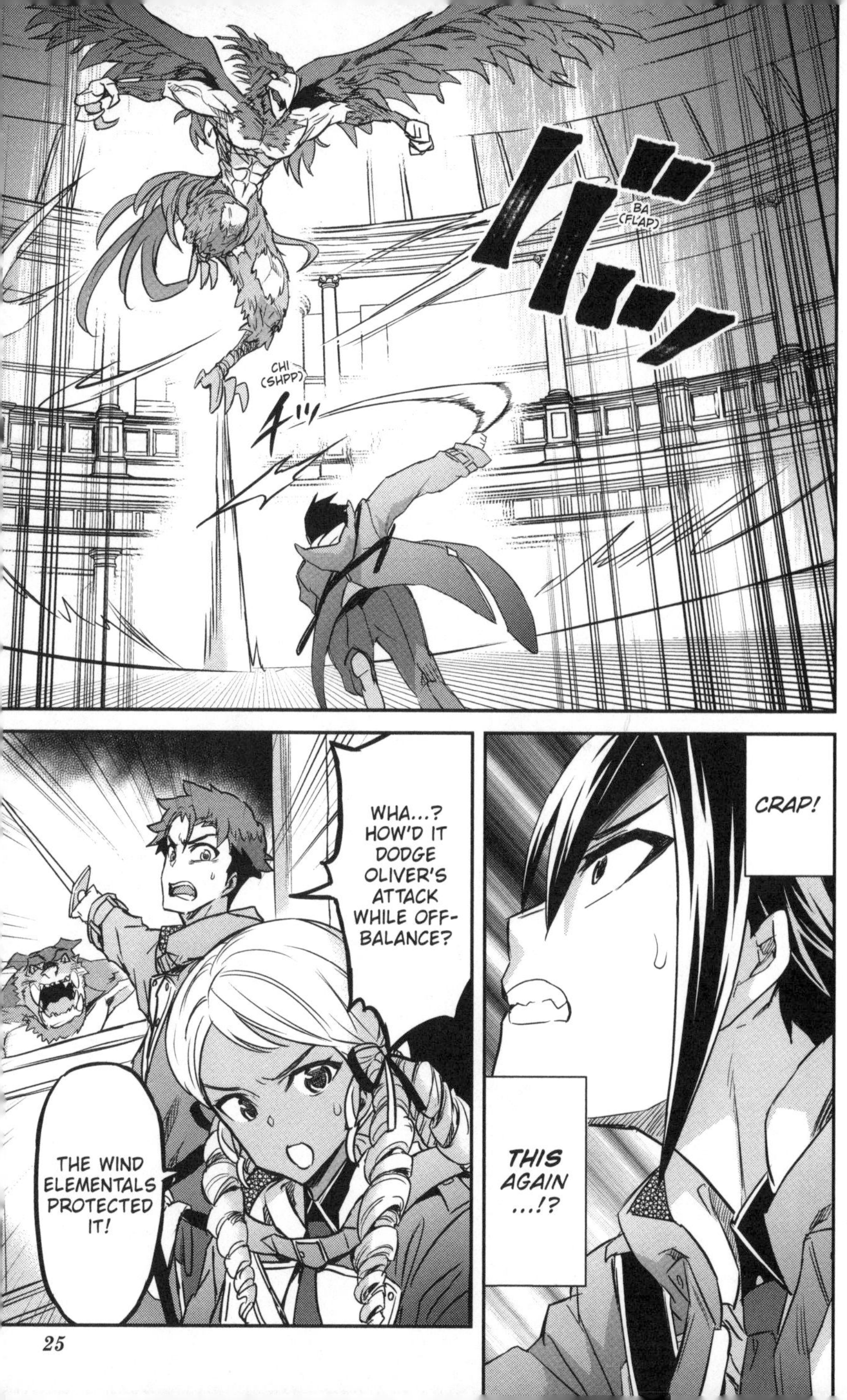
BA (FLAP)
CHI (SHPP)
CRAP!
THIS AGAIN ...!?
WHA...? HOW'D IT DODGE OLIVER'S ATTACK WHILE OFF-BALANCE?
THE WIND ELEMENTALS PROTECTED IT!

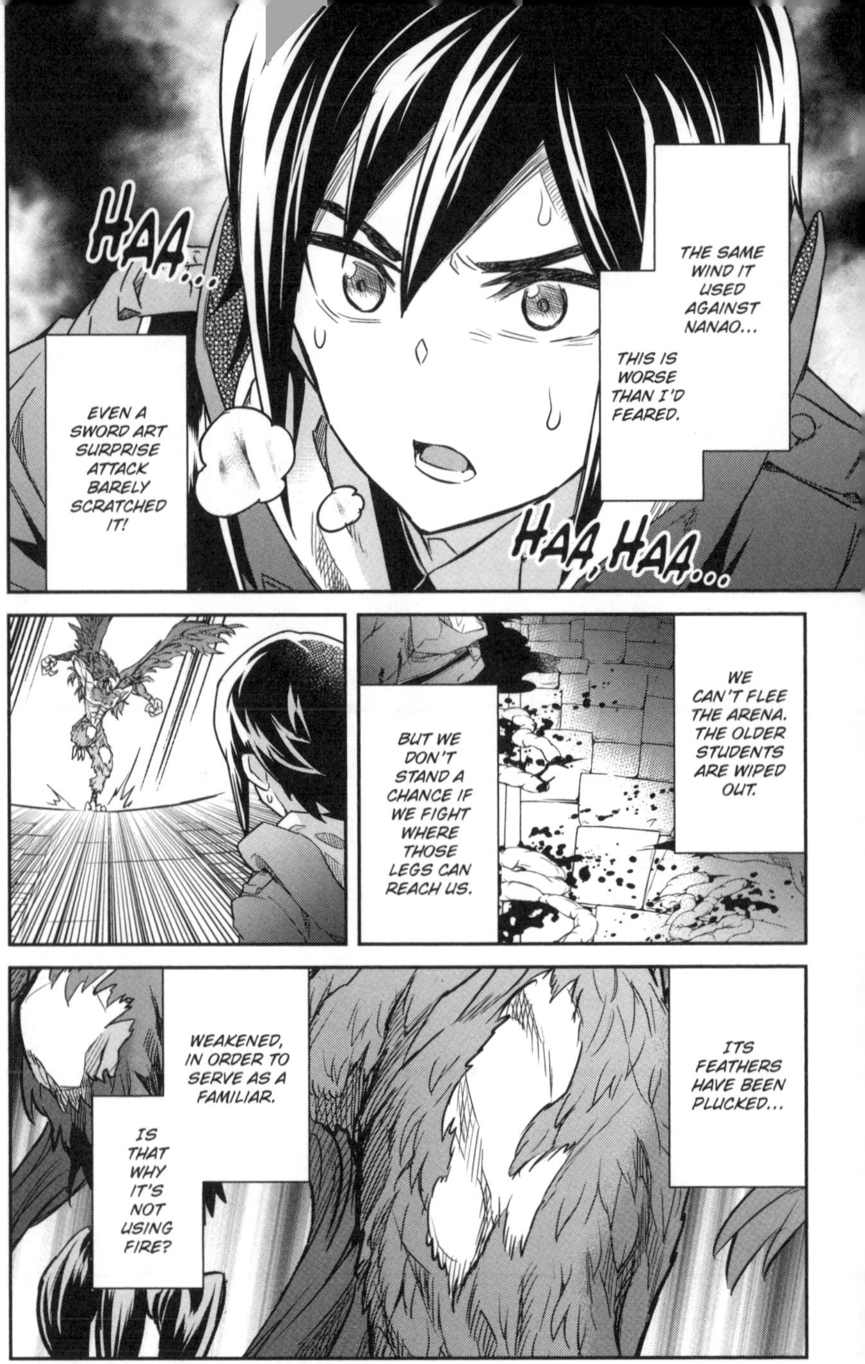
THE SAME WIND IT USED AGAINST NANAO...
THIS IS WORSE THAN I'D FEARED.
HAA...
EVEN A SWORD ART SURPRISE ATTACK BARELY SCRATCHED IT!
HAA, HAA...
WE CAN'T FLEE THE ARENA. THE OLDER STUDENTS ARE WIPED OUT.
BUT WE DON'T STAND A CHANCE IF WE FIGHT WHERE THOSE LEGS CAN REACH US.
ITS FEATHERS HAVE BEEN PLUCKED...
WEAKENED, IN ORDER TO SERVE AS A FAMILIAR.
IS THAT WHY IT'S NOT USING FIRE?

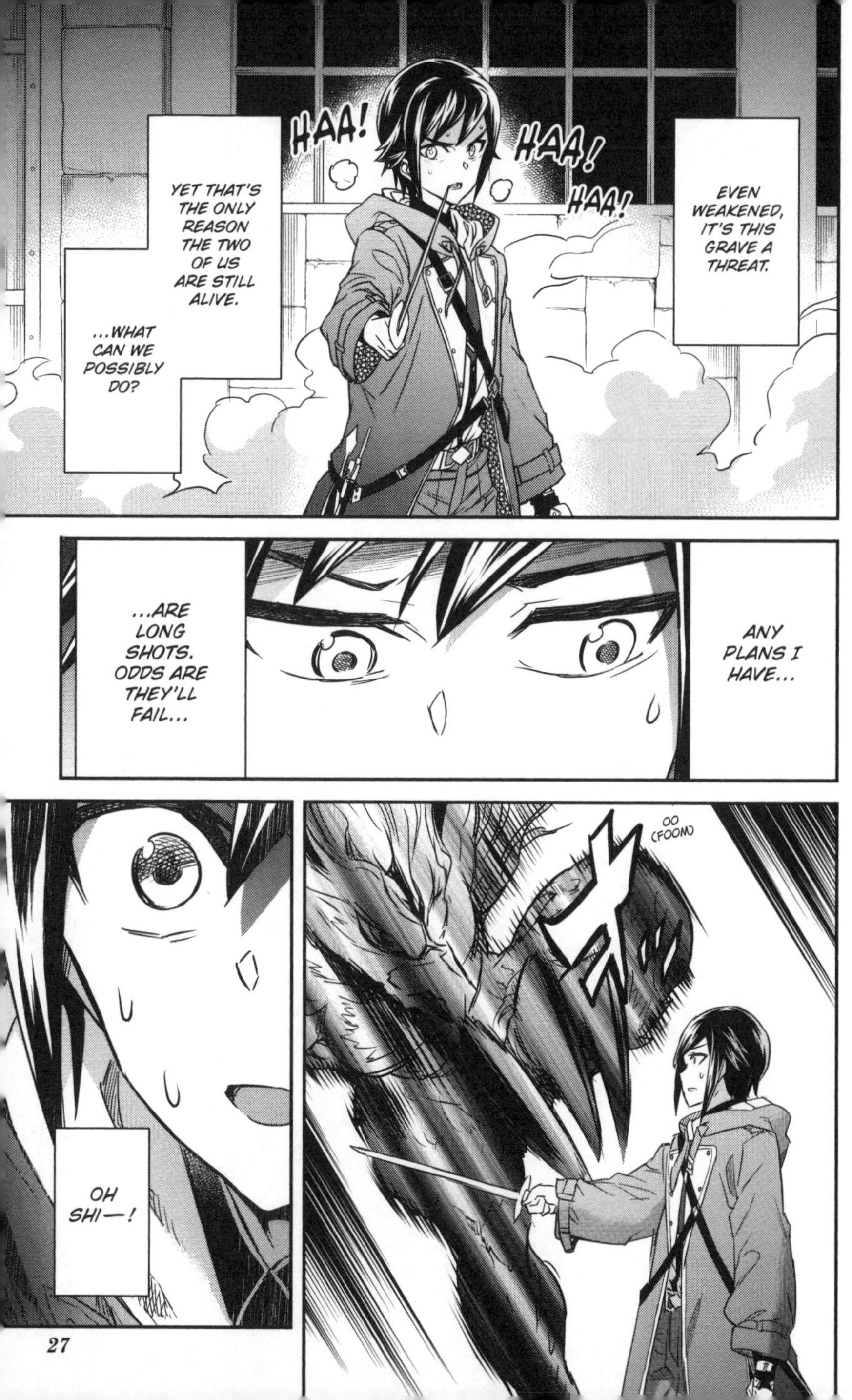
EVEN WEAKENED, IT'S THIS GRAVE A THREAT.
HAA! HAA! HAA!
YET THAT'S THE ONLY REASON THE TWO OF US ARE STILL ALIVE.
...WHAT CAN WE POSSIBLY DO?
ANY PLANS I HAVE...
...ARE LONG SHOTS. ODDS ARE THEY'LL FAIL...
OO (FOOM)
OH SHI—!

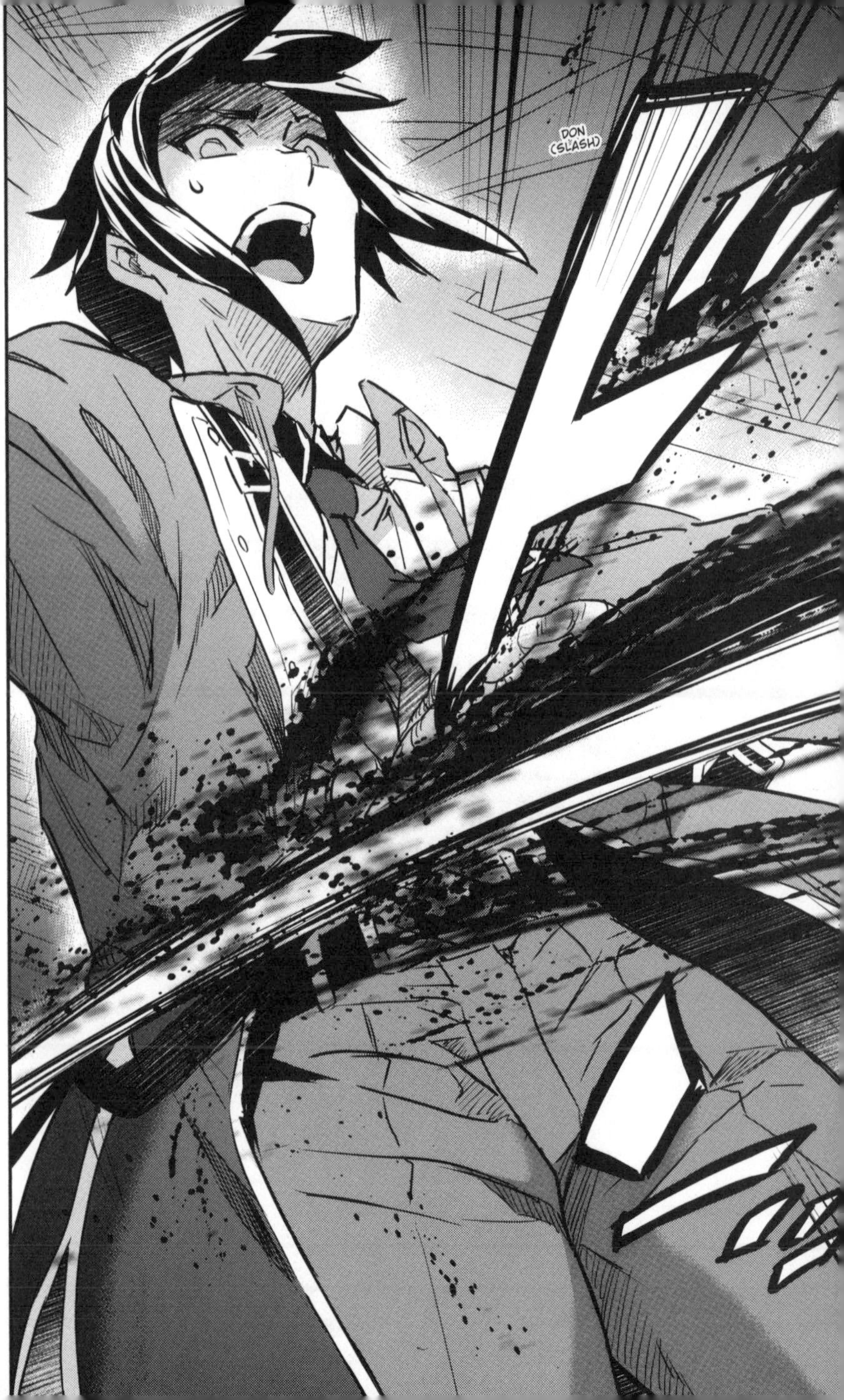
DON
(SLASH)

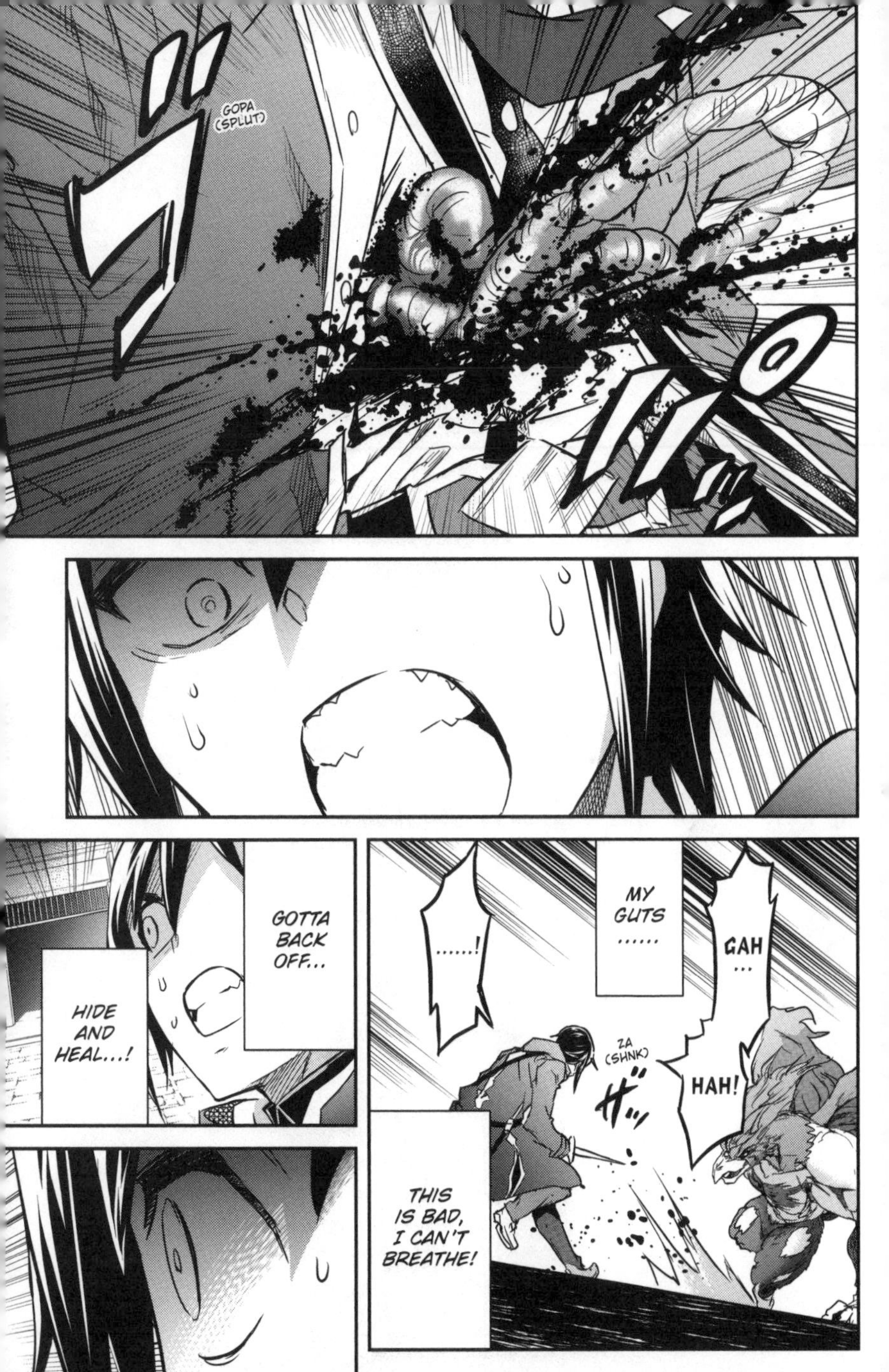
GOPA (SPLUT)
GAH...
MY GUTS......
......!
HAH!
ZA (SHNK)
THIS IS BAD, I CAN'T BREATHE!
GOTTA BACK OFF...
HIDE AND HEAL...!

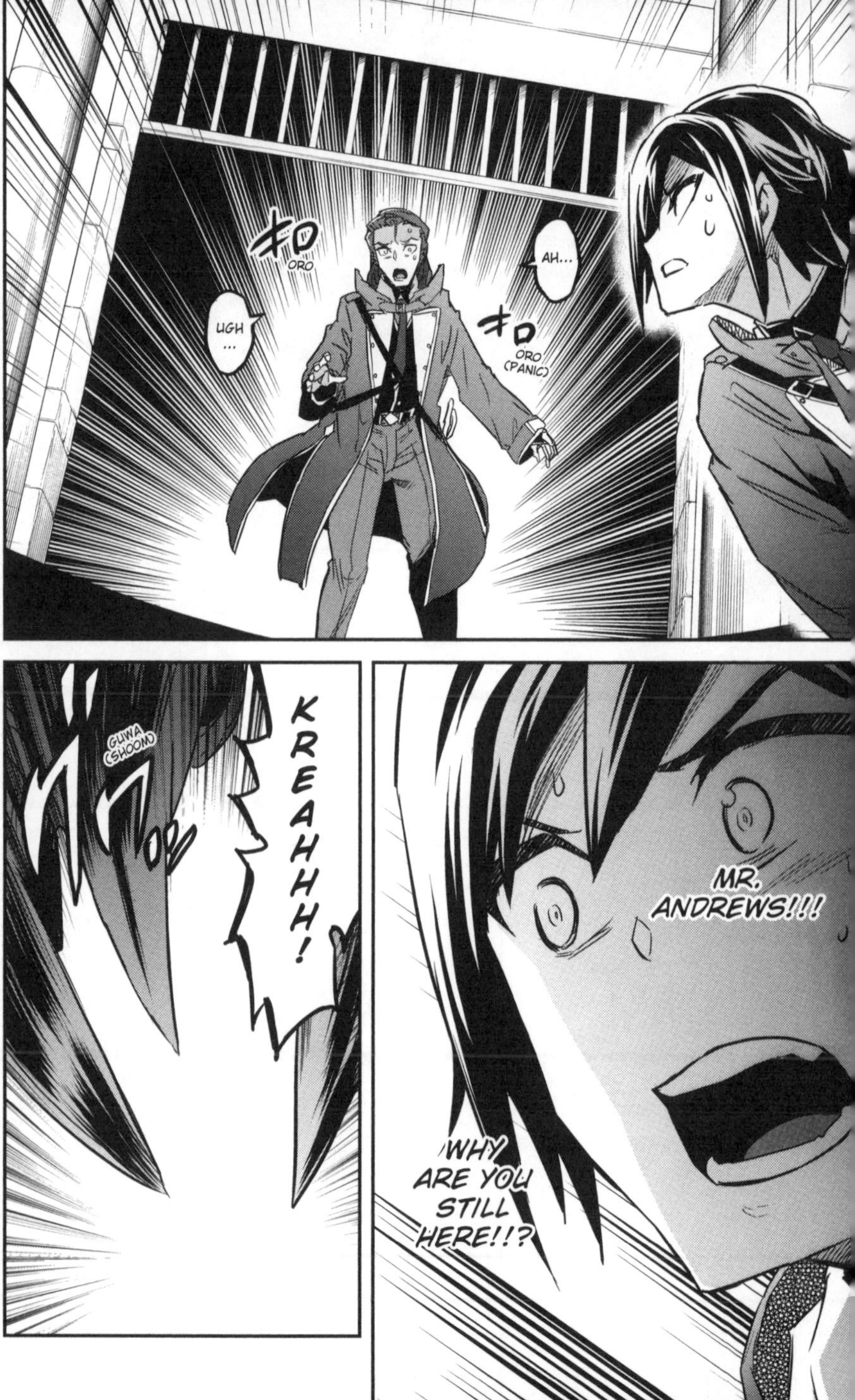
AH...
ORO
ORO (PANIC)
UGH ...
MR. ANDREWS!!!
WHY ARE YOU STILL HERE!!?
KREAHHH!
GUWA (SHOOM)

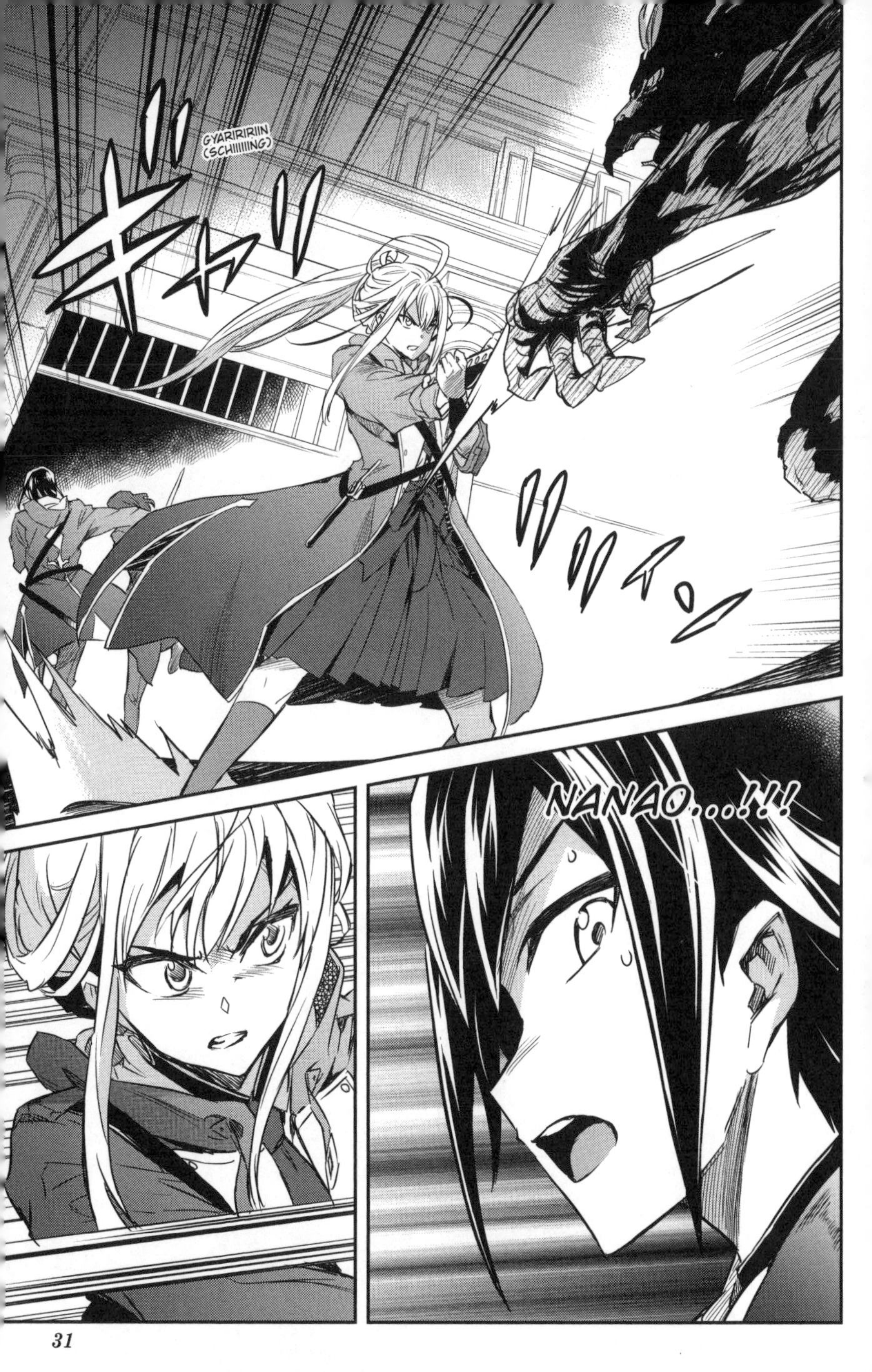
GYARIRIRIIN
(SCHIIIIIIING)
NANAO...!!!

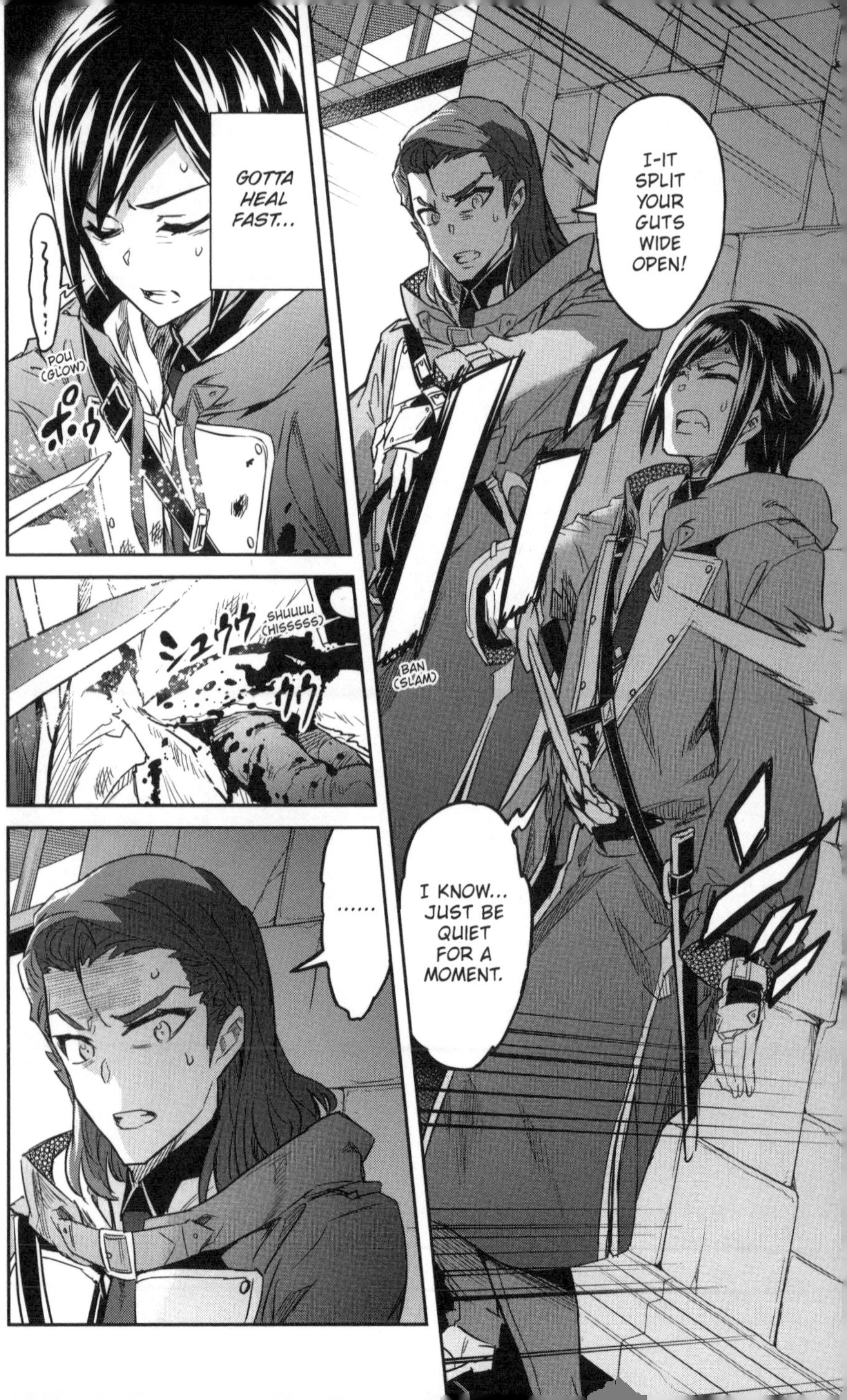
I-IT SPLIT YOUR GUTS WIDE OPEN!
BAN (SLAM)
I KNOW... JUST BE QUIET FOR A MOMENT.
GOTTA HEAL FAST...
…!
POU (GLOW)
ポゥ
SHUUUU (HISSSSS)
シュウウ
......

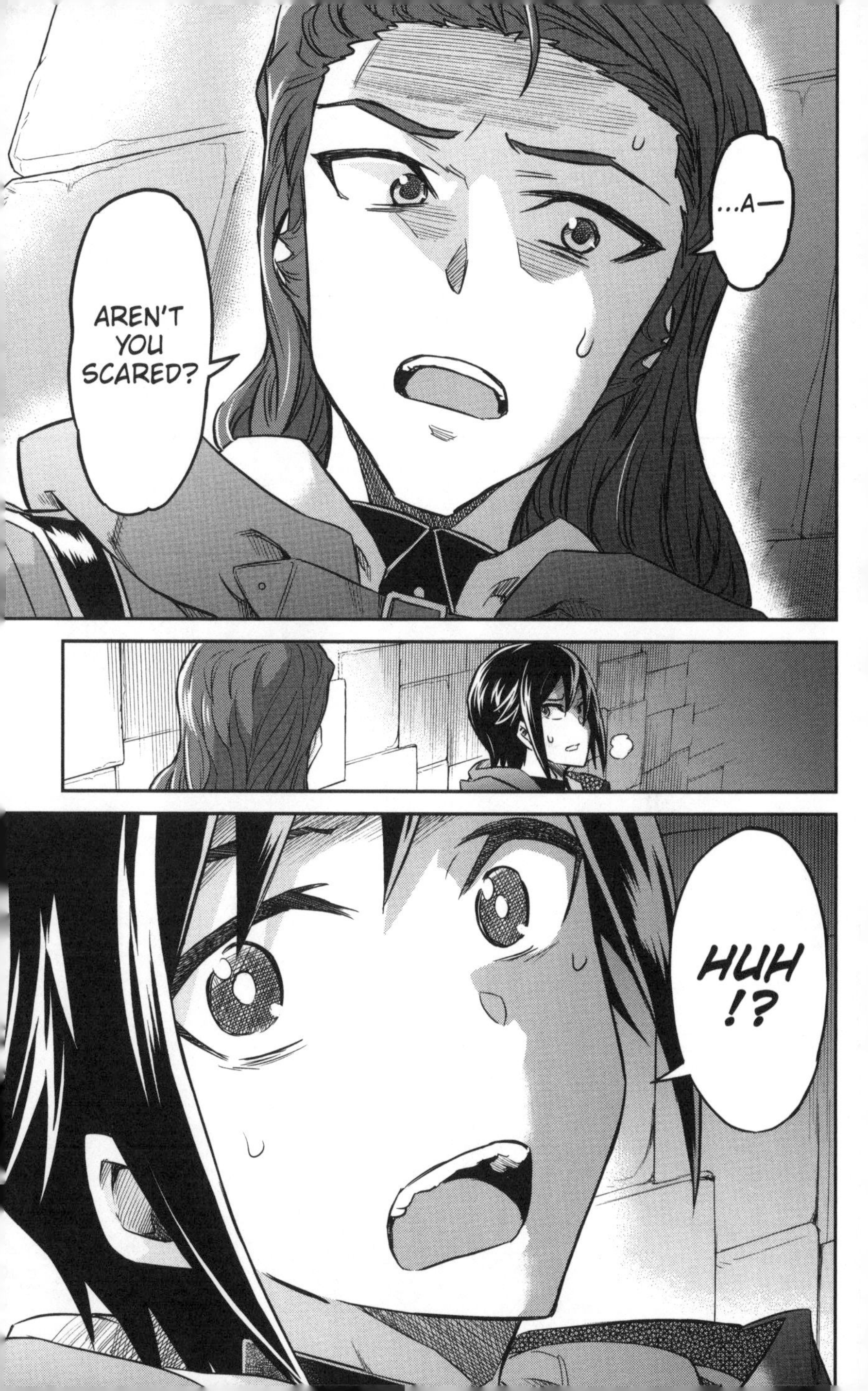
...A—
AREN'T YOU SCARED?
HUH!?

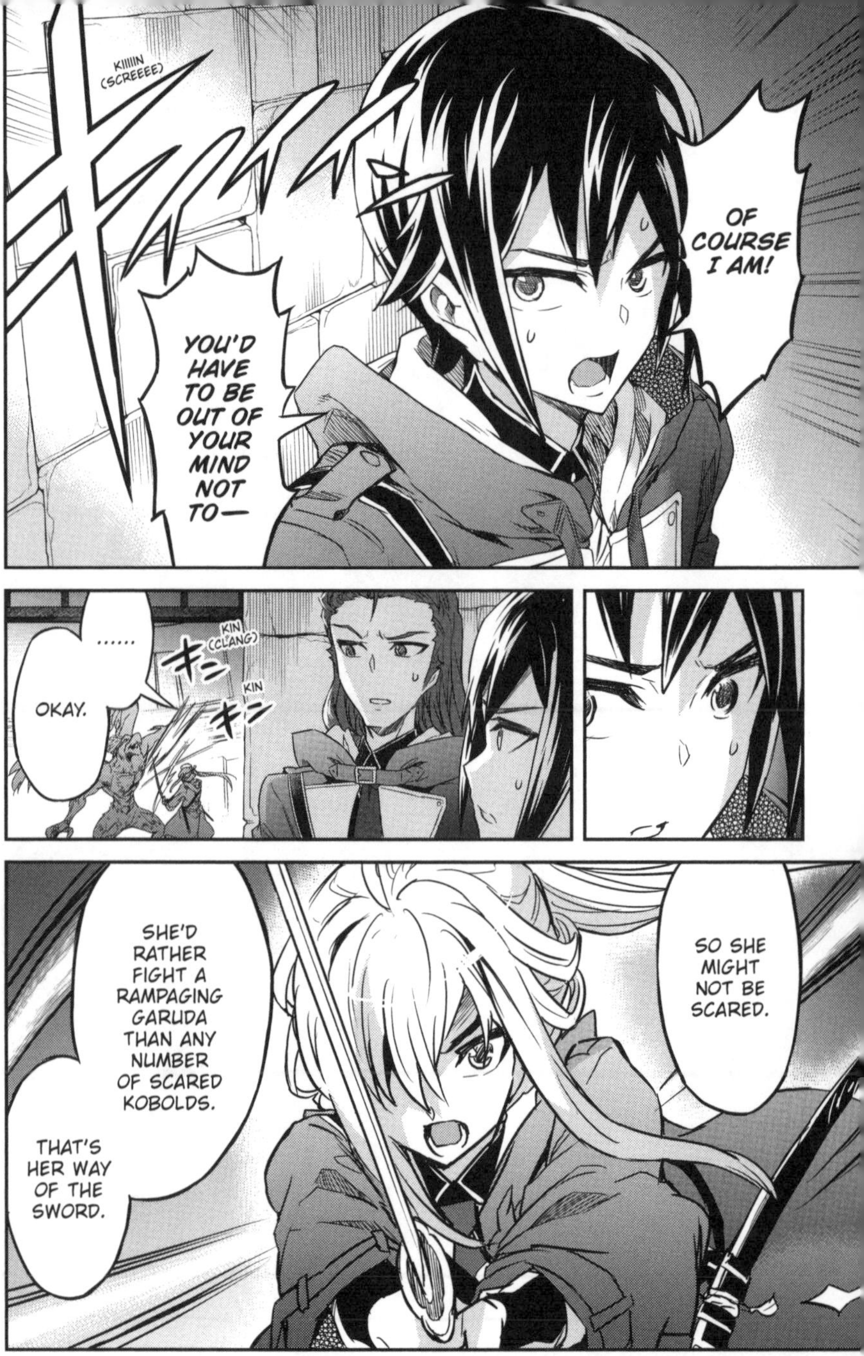
OF COURSE I AM!
YOU'D HAVE TO BE OUT OF YOUR MIND NOT TO—
KIIIIIN (SCREEEEE)
......
OKAY.
KIN (CLANG)
KIN
SO SHE MIGHT NOT BE SCARED.
SHE'D RATHER FIGHT A RAMPAGING GARUDA THAN ANY NUMBER OF SCARED KOBOLDS.
THAT'S HER WAY OF THE SWORD.

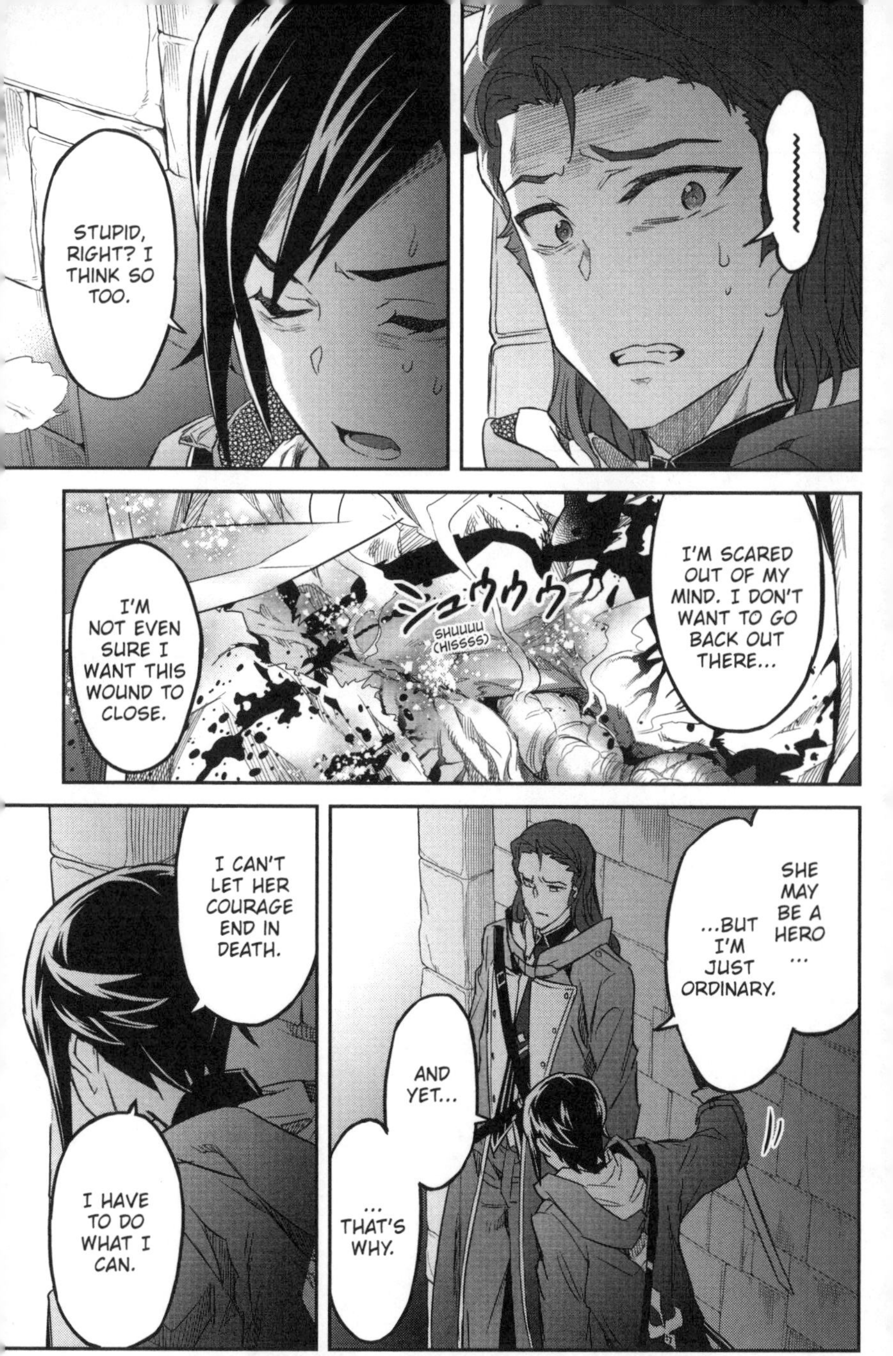
STUPID, RIGHT? I THINK SO TOO.
I'M SCARED OUT OF MY MIND. I DON'T WANT TO GO BACK OUT THERE...
シュウウウ
SHUUUU (HISSSS)
I'M NOT EVEN SURE I WANT THIS WOUND TO CLOSE.
SHE MAY BE A HERO ...
...BUT I'M JUST ORDINARY.
AND YET...
... THAT'S WHY.
I CAN'T LET HER COURAGE END IN DEATH.
I HAVE TO DO WHAT I CAN.

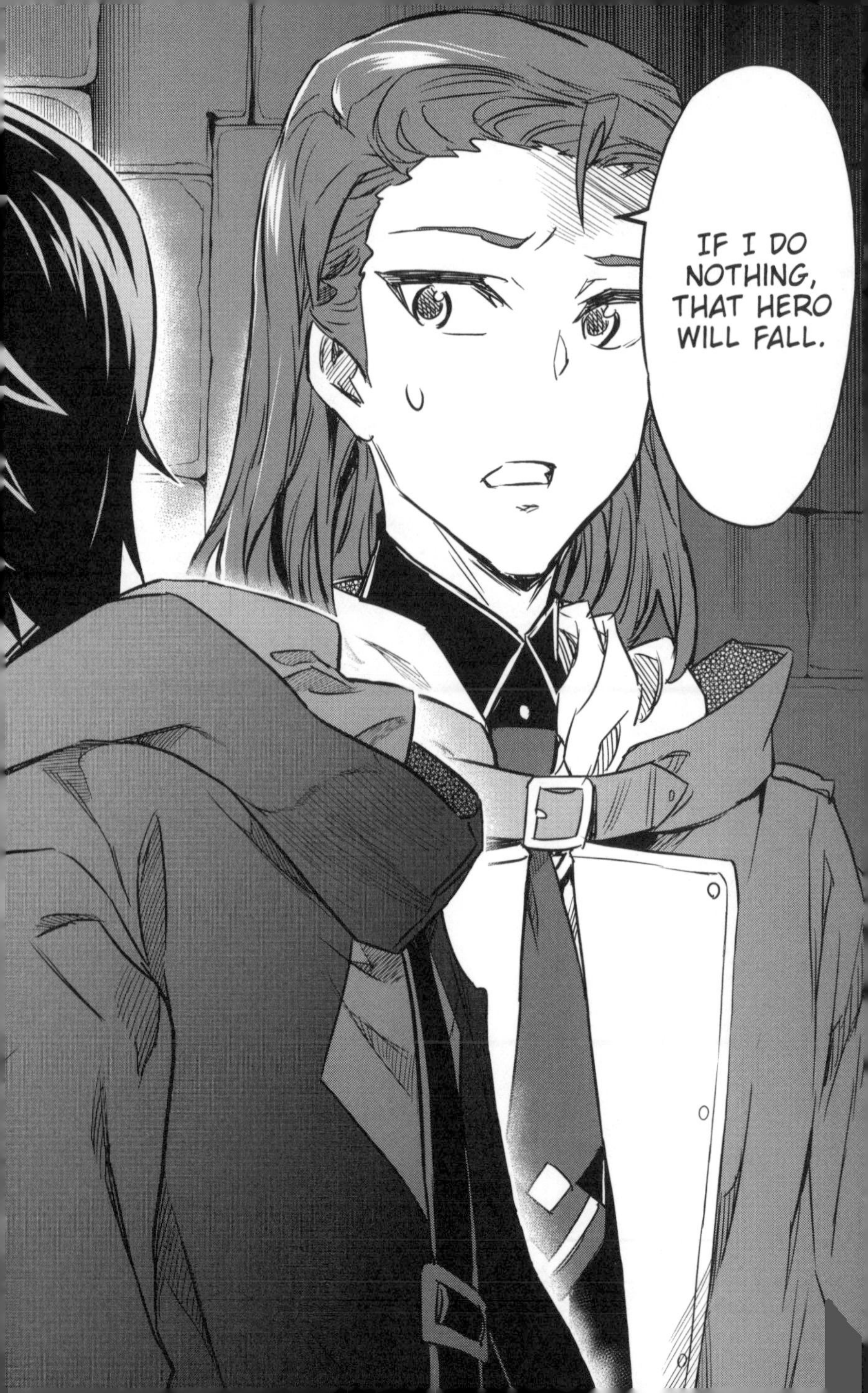
IF I DO NOTHING, THAT HERO WILL FALL.

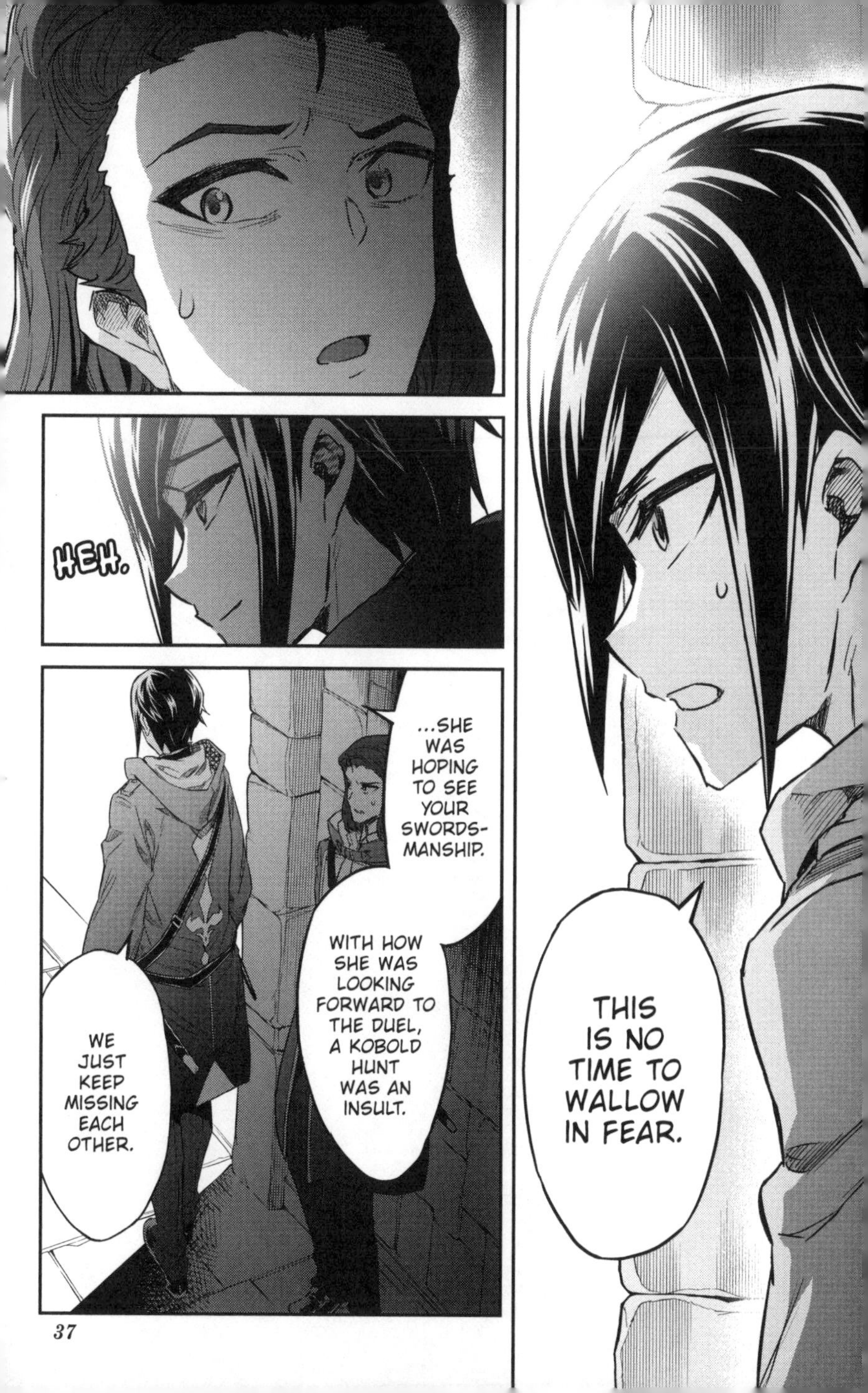
THIS IS NO TIME TO WALLOW IN FEAR.
HEH.
...SHE WAS HOPING TO SEE YOUR SWORDS-MANSHIP.
WITH HOW SHE WAS LOOKING FORWARD TO THE DUEL, A KOBOLD HUNT WAS AN INSULT.
WE JUST KEEP MISSING EACH OTHER.

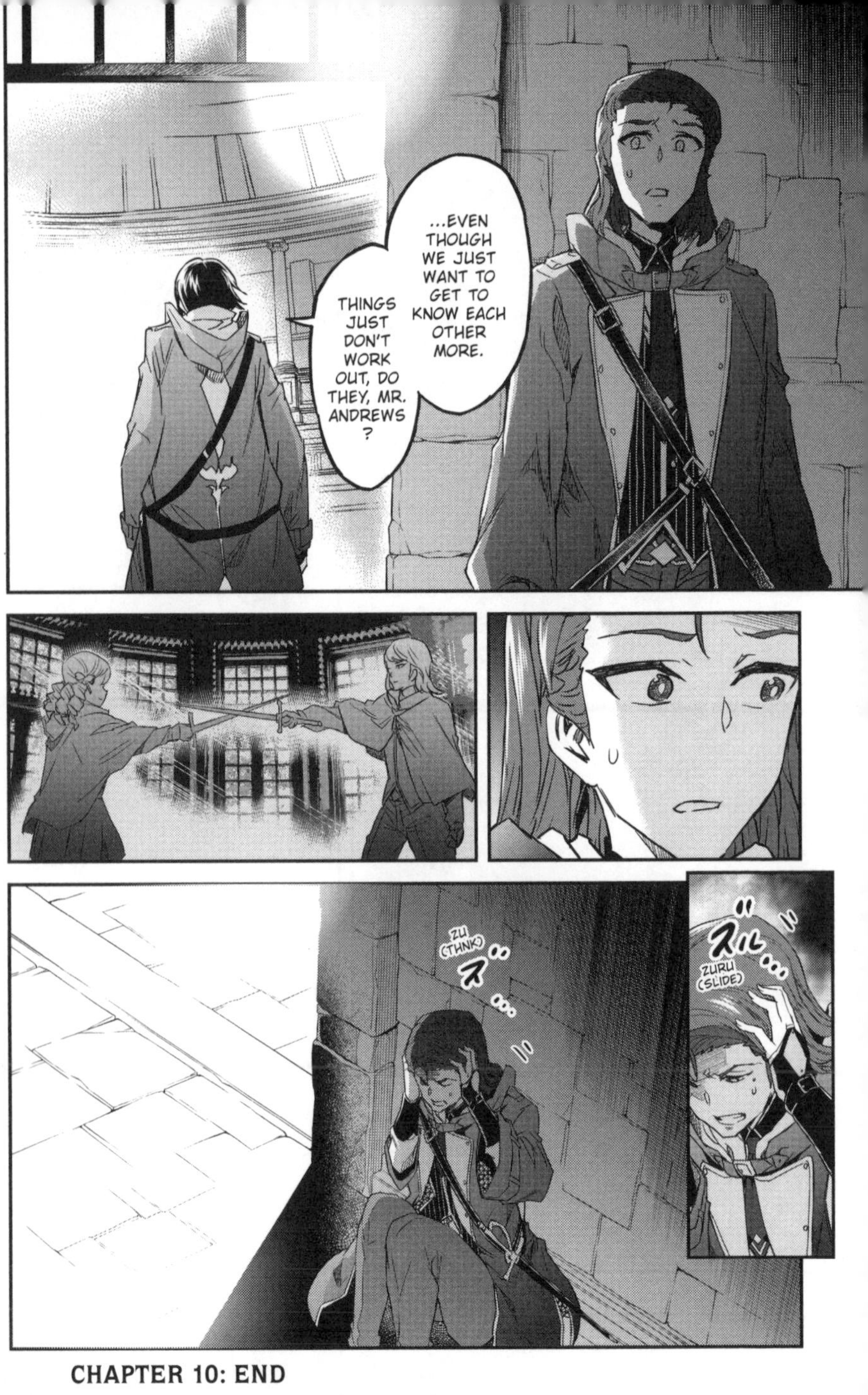
...EVEN THOUGH WE JUST WANT TO GET TO KNOW EACH OTHER MORE. THINGS JUST DON'T WORK OUT, DO THEY, MR. ANDREWS?
ズル...
ZURU (SLIDE)
ズ...
ZU (THNK)

CHAPTER 10: END

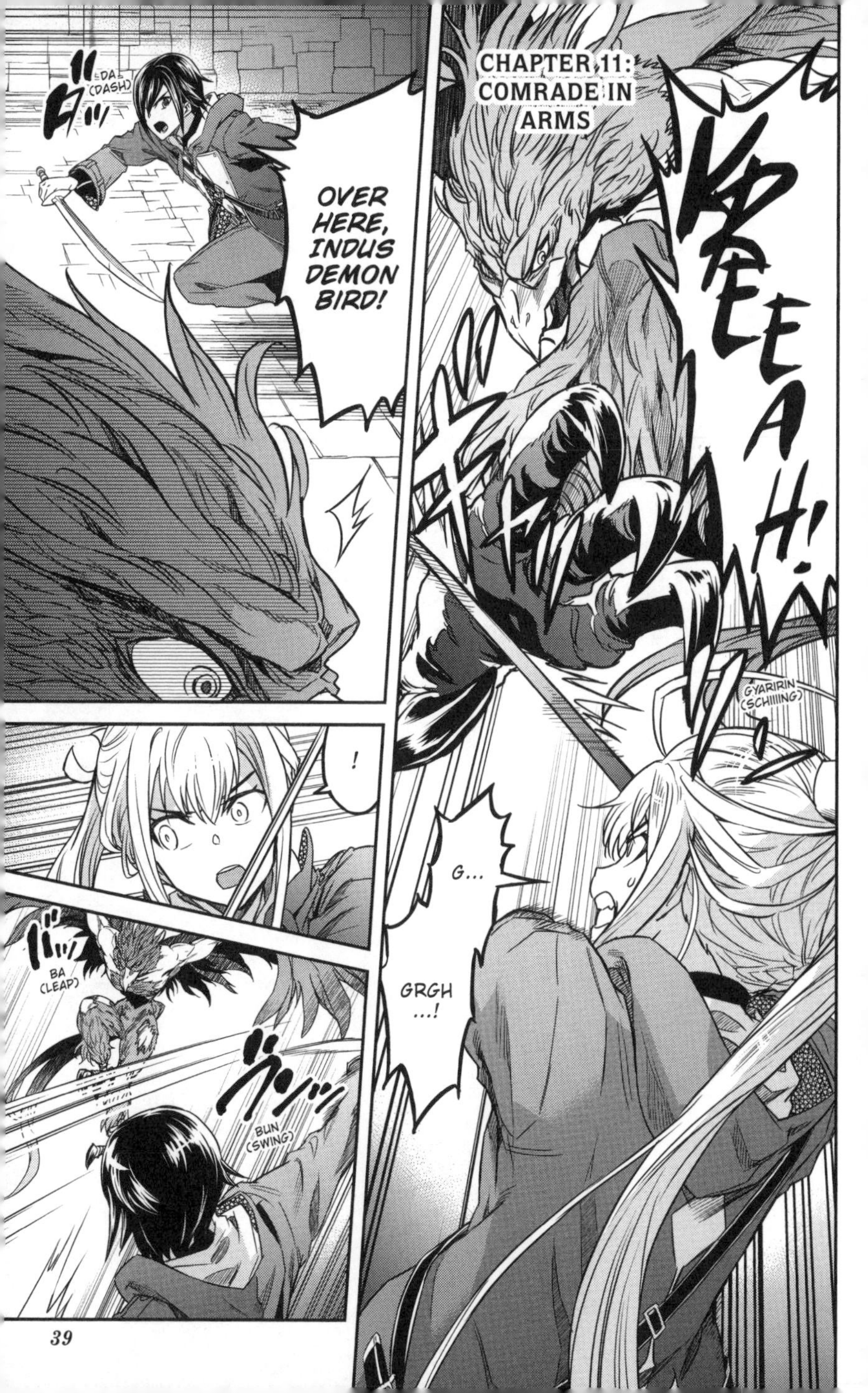
CHAPTER 11: COMRADE IN ARMS
KREEEAH!!
GYARIRIN (SCHIIIING)
G...
GRGH ...!
DA (DASH)
OVER HERE, INDUS DEMON BIRD!
!
BA (LEAP)
BUN (SWING)

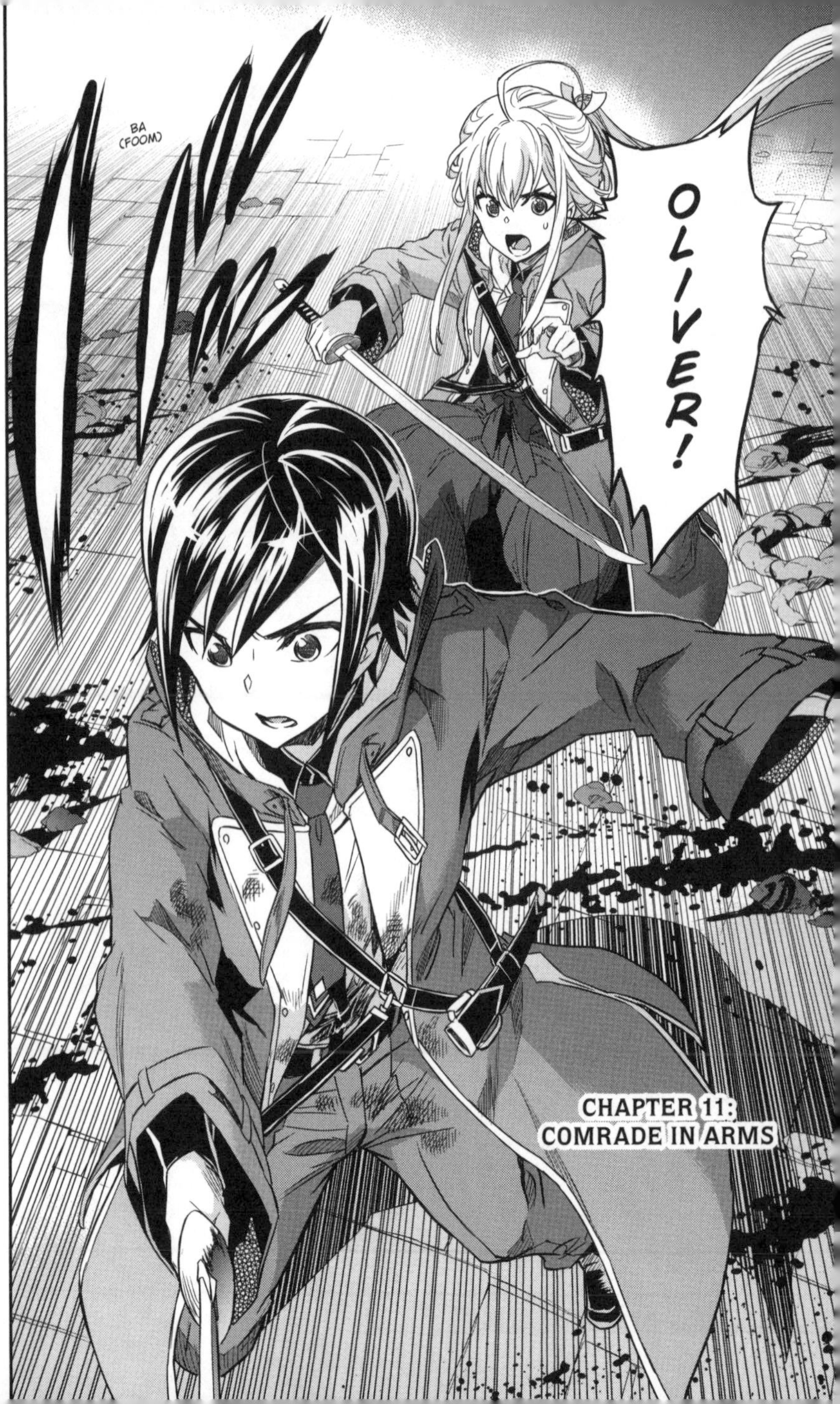
OLIVER!
BA
(FOOM)
CHAPTER 11:
COMRADE IN ARMS

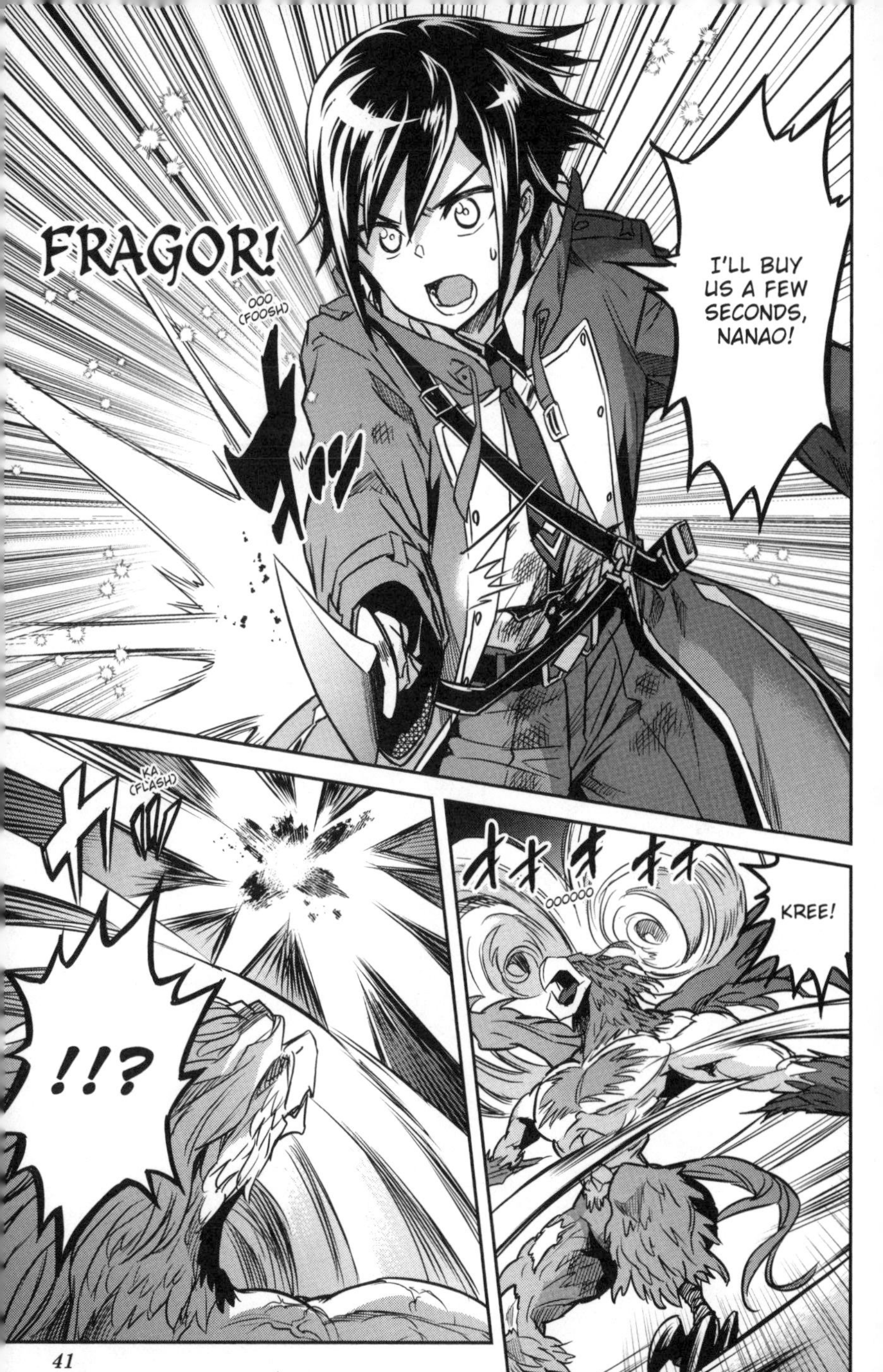
I'LL BUY US A FEW SECONDS, NANAO!
FRAGOR!
OOO (FOOSH)
KREE!
OOOOOO
KA (FLASH)
!!?

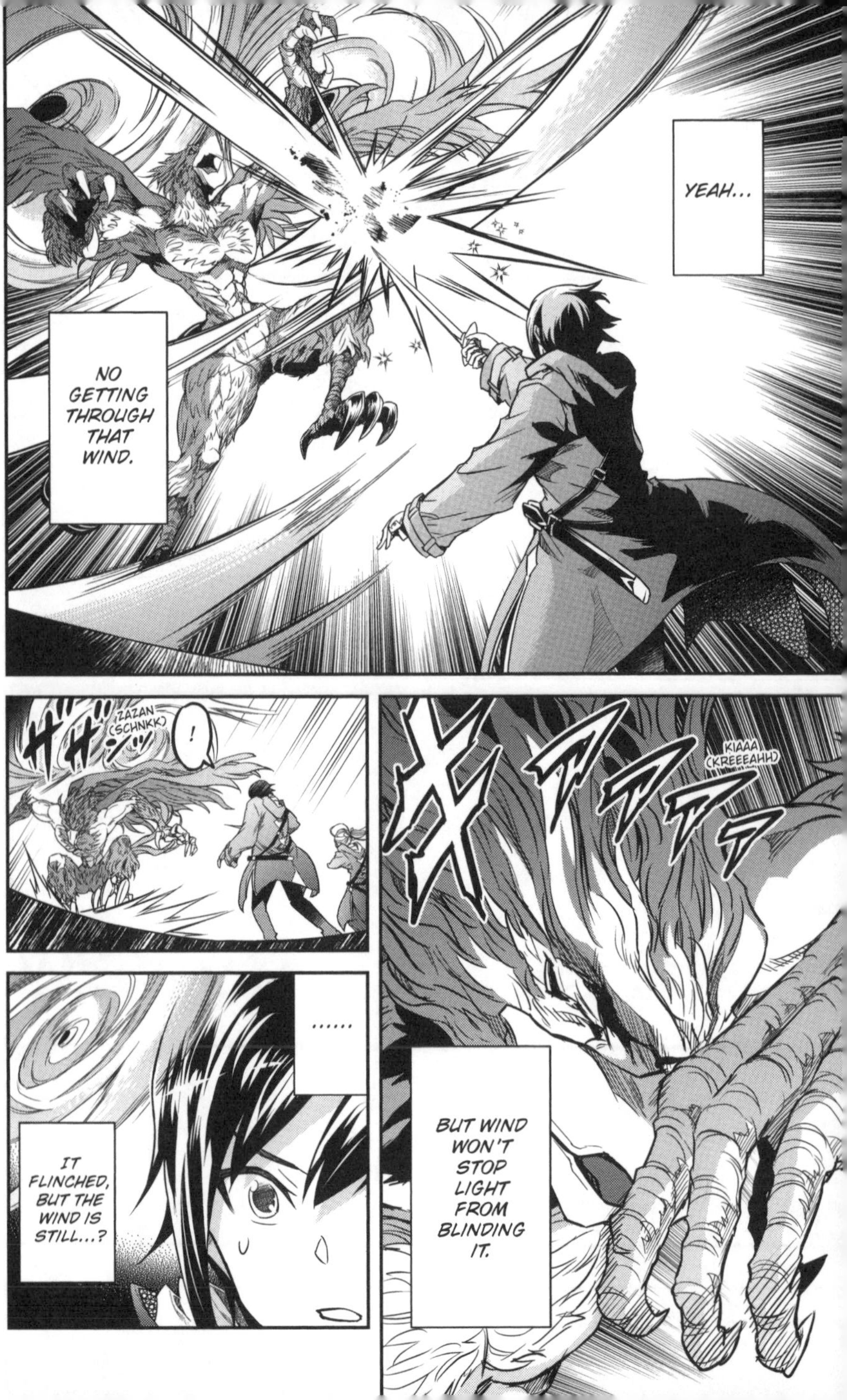

YEAH...
NO GETTING THROUGH THAT WIND.
KIAAA (KREEEAHH)
BUT WIND WON'T STOP LIGHT FROM BLINDING IT.
ZAZAN (SCHNKK)
!
......
IT FLINCHED, BUT THE WIND IS STILL...?

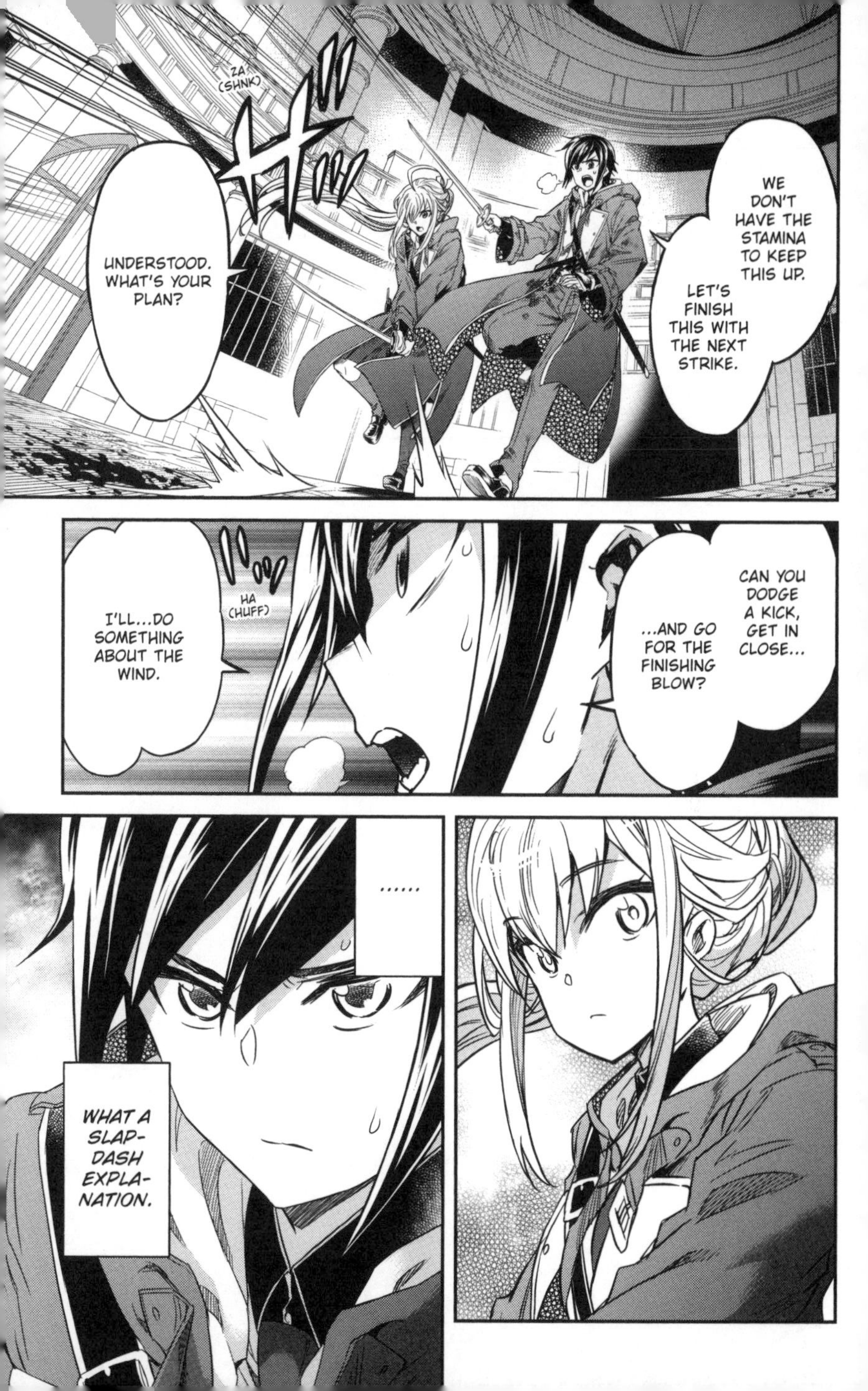
WE DON'T HAVE THE STAMINA TO KEEP THIS UP.
LET'S FINISH THIS WITH THE NEXT STRIKE.
ZA (SHNK)
UNDERSTOOD. WHAT'S YOUR PLAN?
CAN YOU DODGE A KICK, GET IN CLOSE...
...AND GO FOR THE FINISHING BLOW?
HA (HUFF)
I'LL...DO SOMETHING ABOUT THE WIND.
......
WHAT A SLAP-DASH EXPLA-NATION.

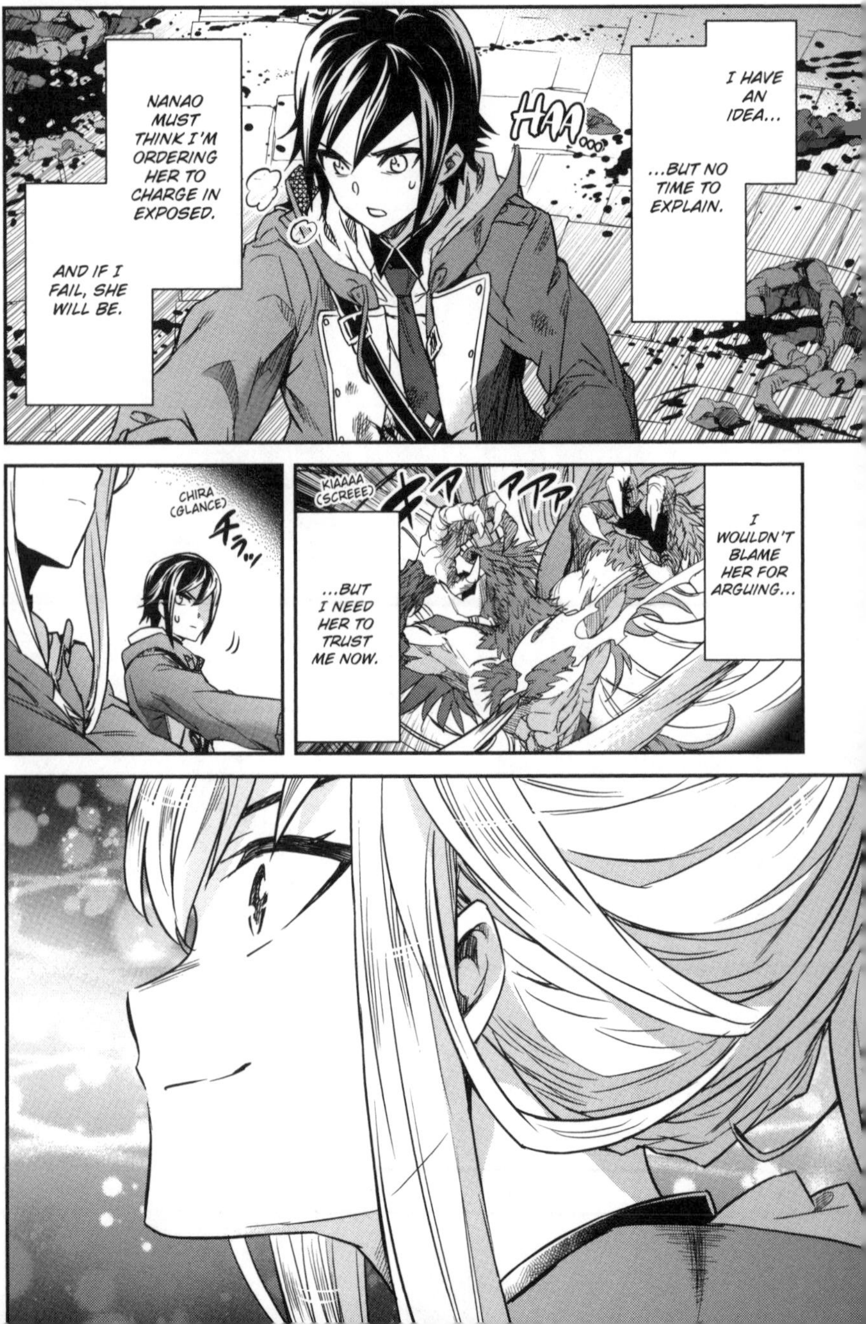
I HAVE AN IDEA...
...BUT NO TIME TO EXPLAIN.
HAA...
NANAO MUST THINK I'M ORDERING HER TO CHARGE IN EXPOSED.
AND IF I FAIL, SHE WILL BE.
I WOULDN'T BLAME HER FOR ARGUING...
KIAAAA (SCREEE)
...BUT I NEED HER TO TRUST ME NOW.
CHIRA (GLANCE)

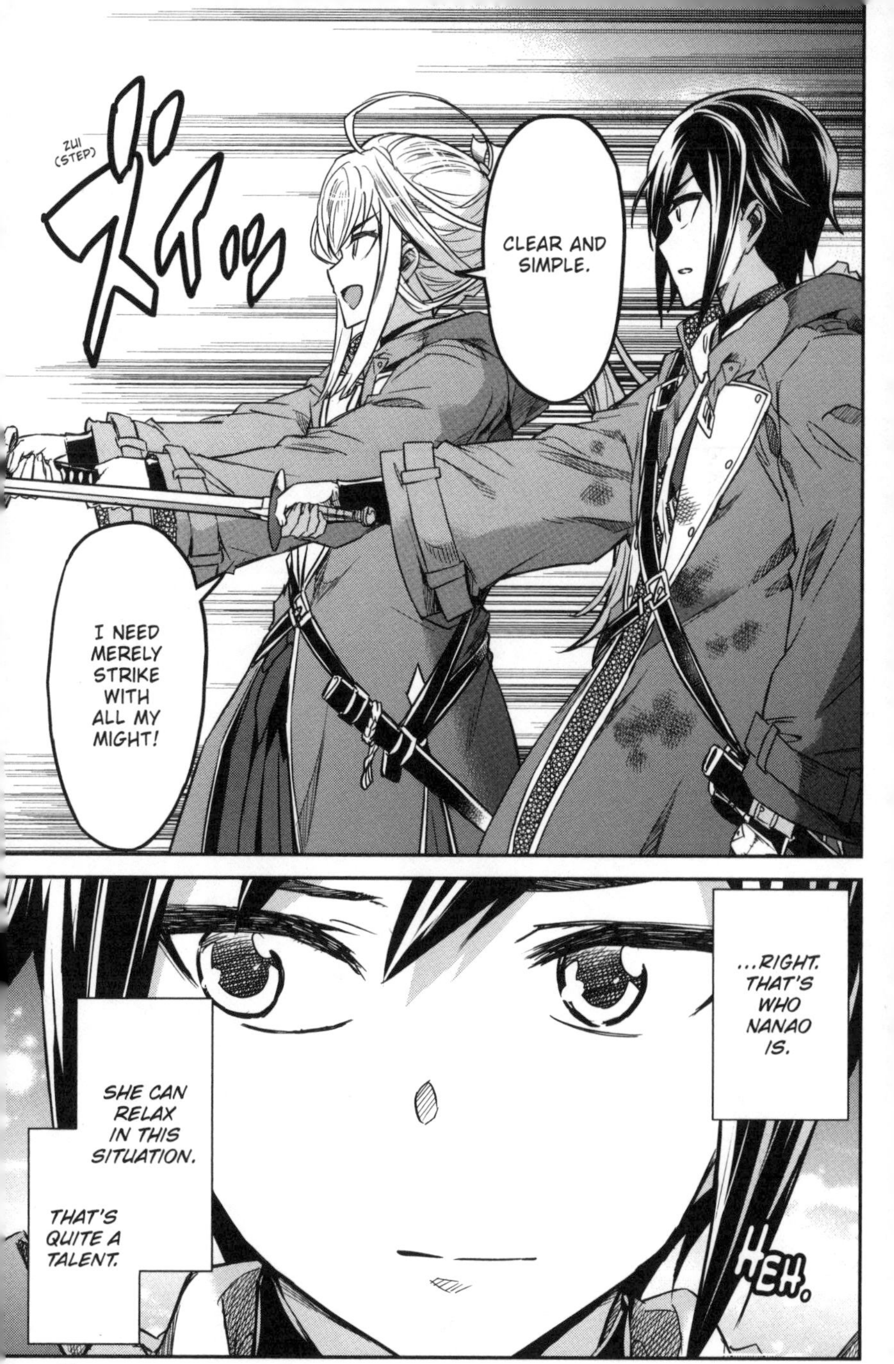
CLEAR AND SIMPLE.
ZUI (STEP)
I NEED MERELY STRIKE WITH ALL MY MIGHT!
...RIGHT. THAT'S WHO NANAO IS.
HEH.
SHE CAN RELAX IN THIS SITUATION.
THAT'S QUITE A TALENT.

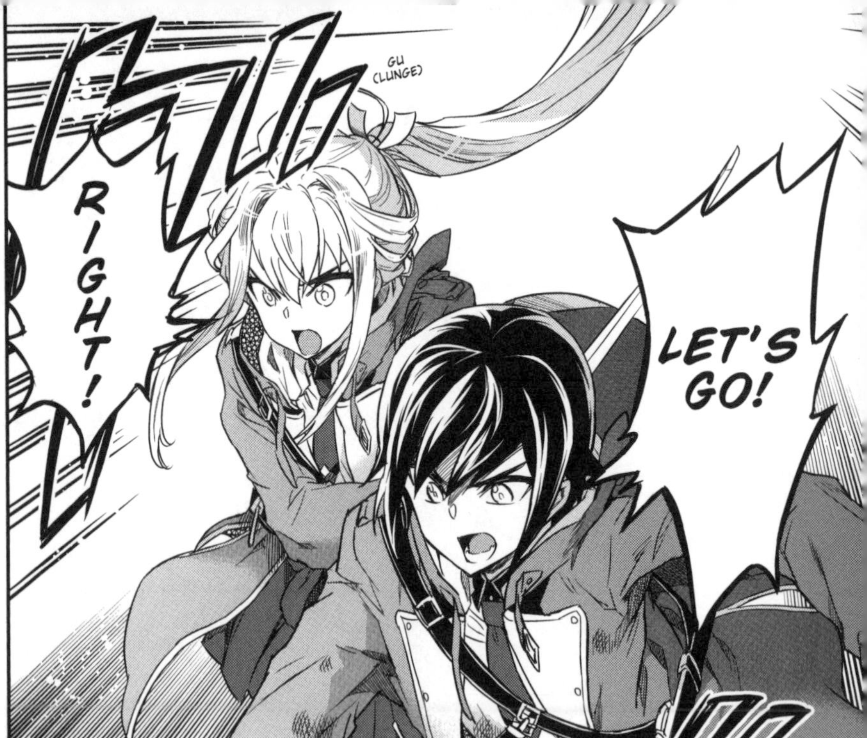
GU (LUNGE)
LET'S GO!
RIGHT!

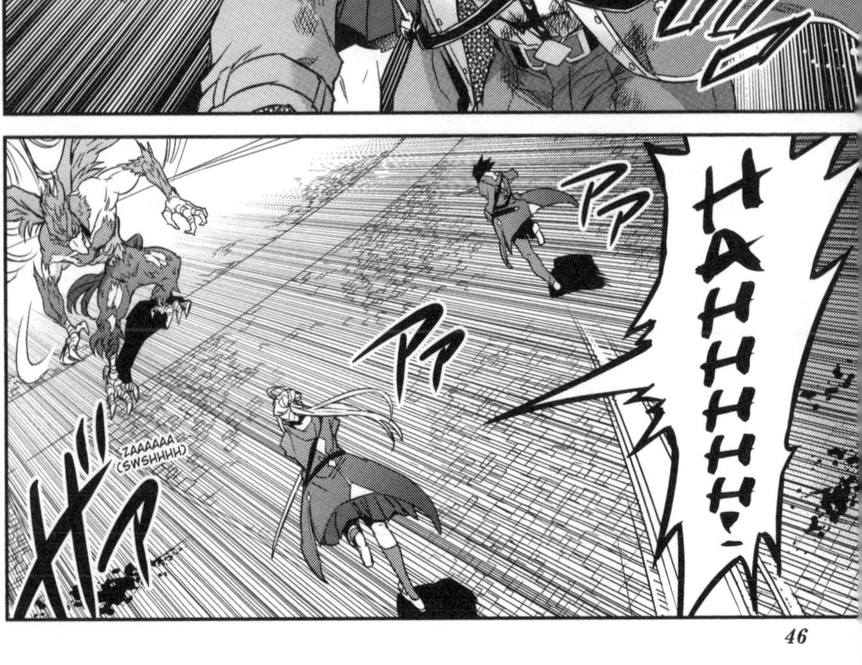
HAHHHHH!
ZAAAAAA (SWSHHHH)

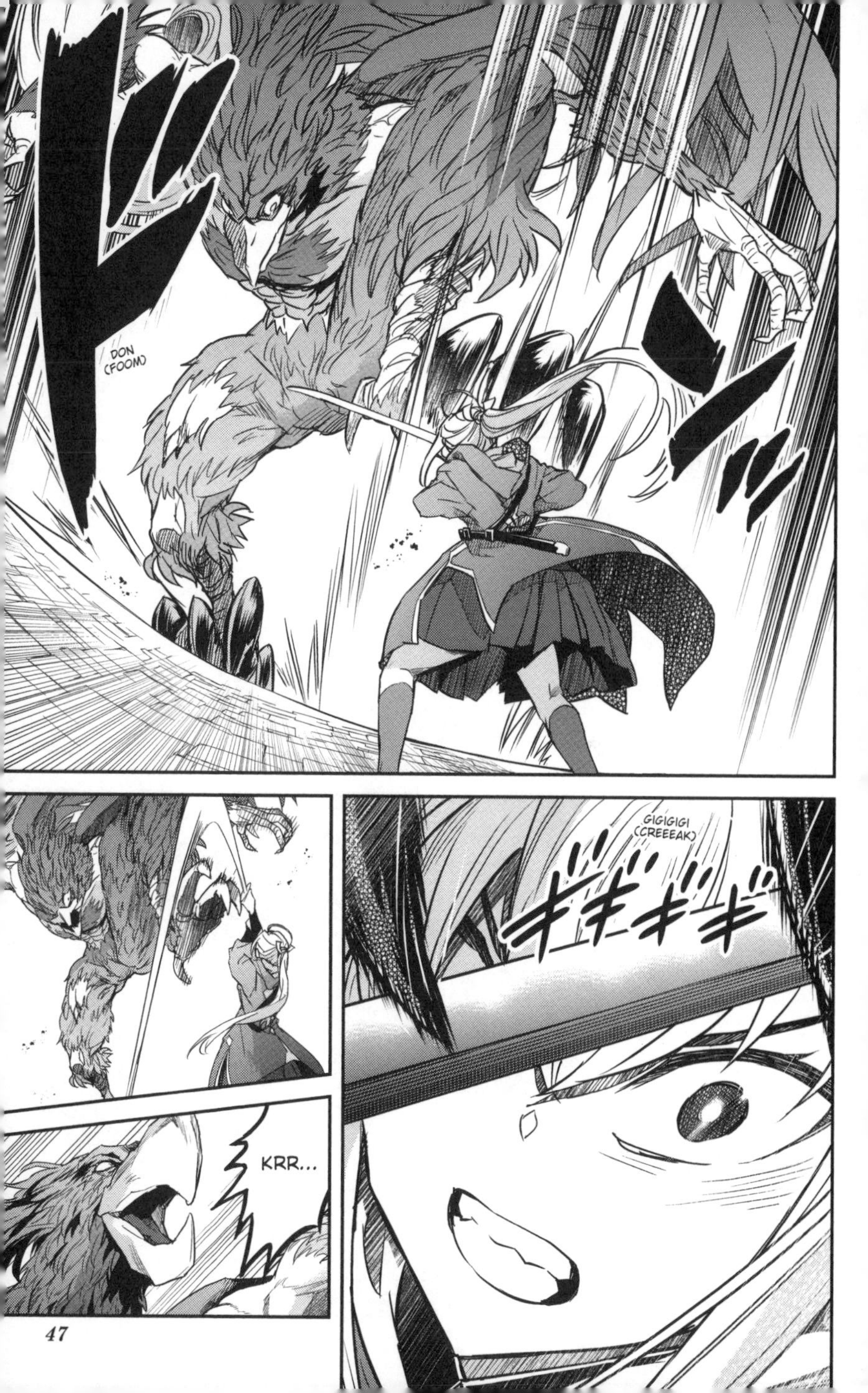
DON
(FOOM)
GIGIGIGI
(CREEEAK)
KRR...

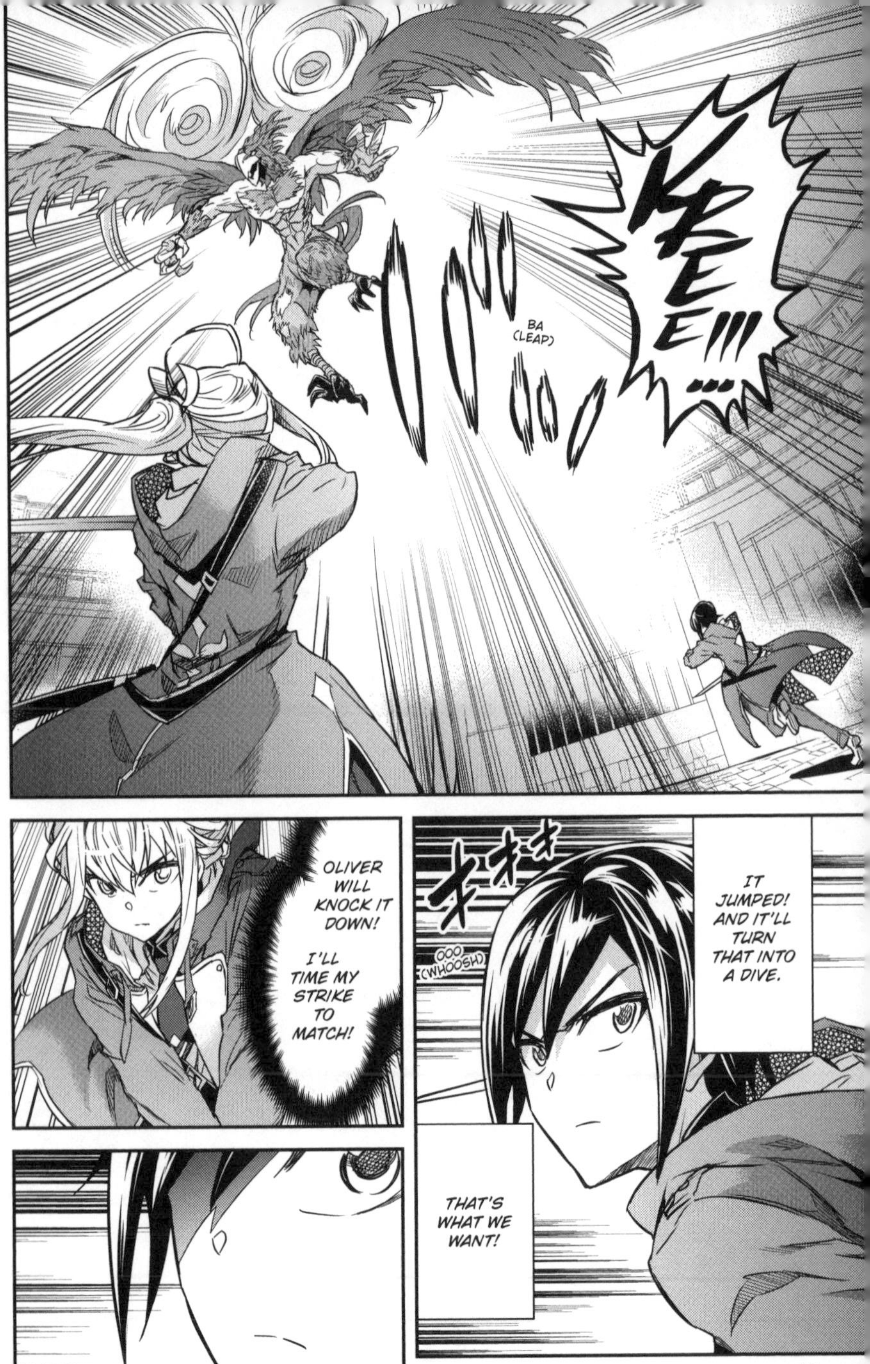
KREEE!!!
...
BA
(LEAP)
OOO
(WHOOSH)
IT JUMPED! AND IT'LL TURN THAT INTO A DIVE.
THAT'S WHAT WE WANT!
OLIVER WILL KNOCK IT DOWN!
I'LL TIME MY STRIKE TO MATCH!

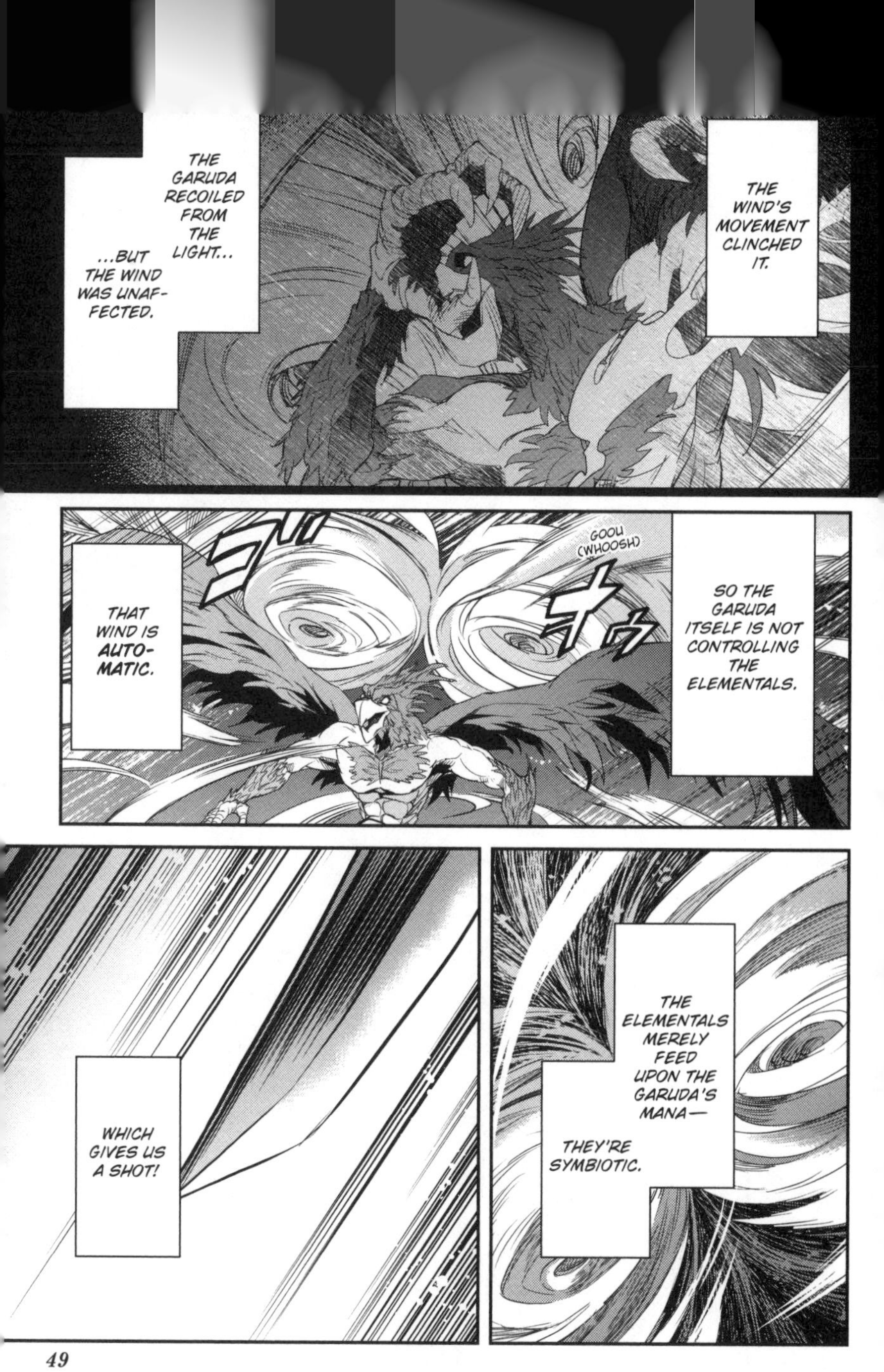
THE WIND'S MOVEMENT CLINCHED IT.
THE GARUDA RECOILED FROM THE LIGHT...
...BUT THE WIND WAS UNAFFECTED.
SO THE GARUDA ITSELF IS NOT CONTROLLING THE ELEMENTALS.
GOOU (WHOOSH)
THAT WIND IS **AUTOMATIC.**
THE ELEMENTALS MERELY FEED UPON THE GARUDA'S MANA—
THEY'RE SYMBIOTIC.
WHICH GIVES US A SHOT!

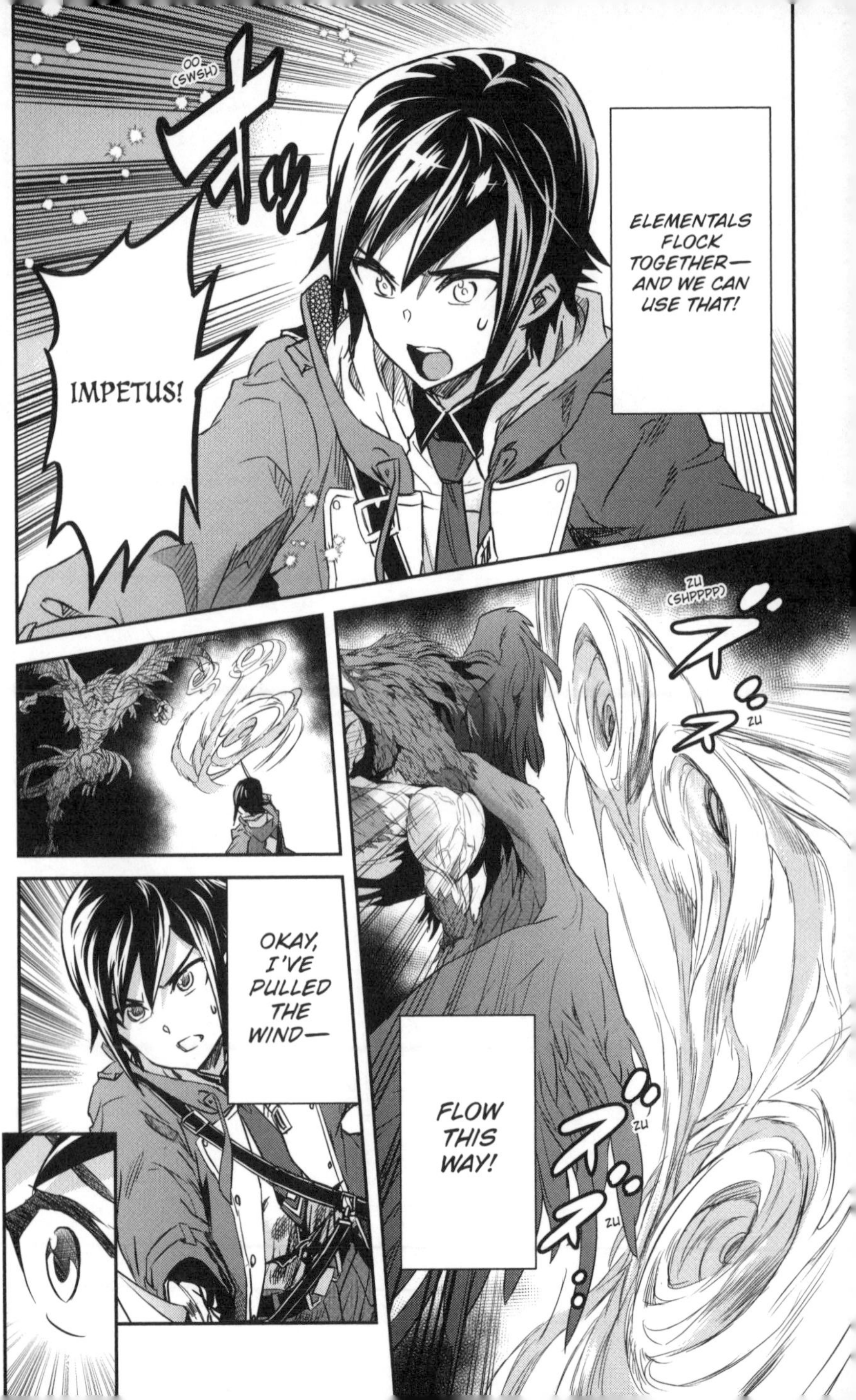

ELEMENTALS FLOCK TOGETHER—AND WE CAN USE THAT!
OO (SWSH)
IMPETUS!
ZU (SHPPPP)
ZU
OKAY, I'VE PULLED THE WIND—
FLOW THIS WAY!
ZU
ZU

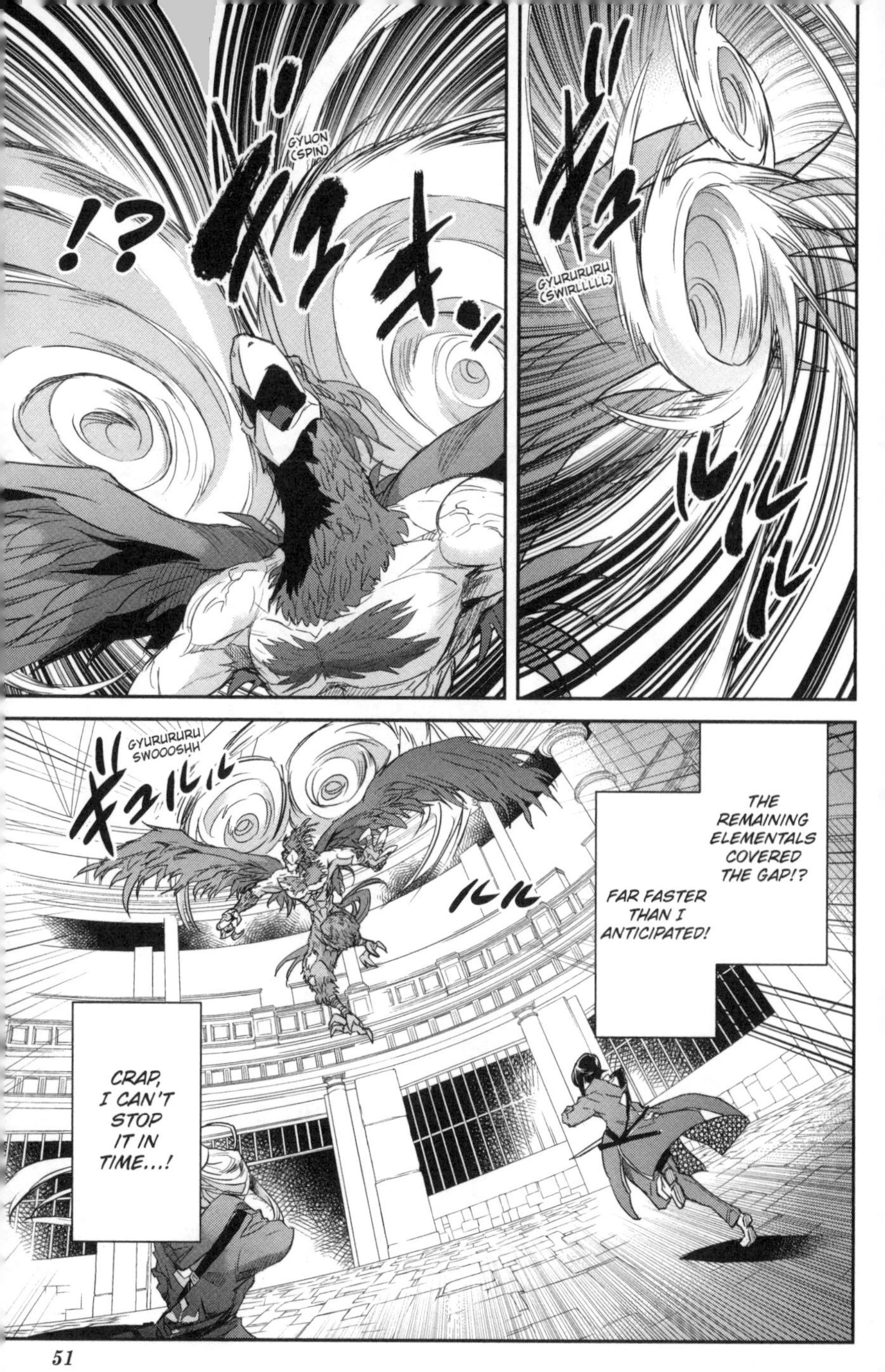
GYURURURU (SWIRLLLLL)
GYUON (SPIN)
!?
THE REMAINING ELEMENTALS COVERED THE GAP!?
FAR FASTER THAN I ANTICIPATED!
GYURURURU SWOOOSHH
CRAP, I CAN'T STOP IT IN TIME...!

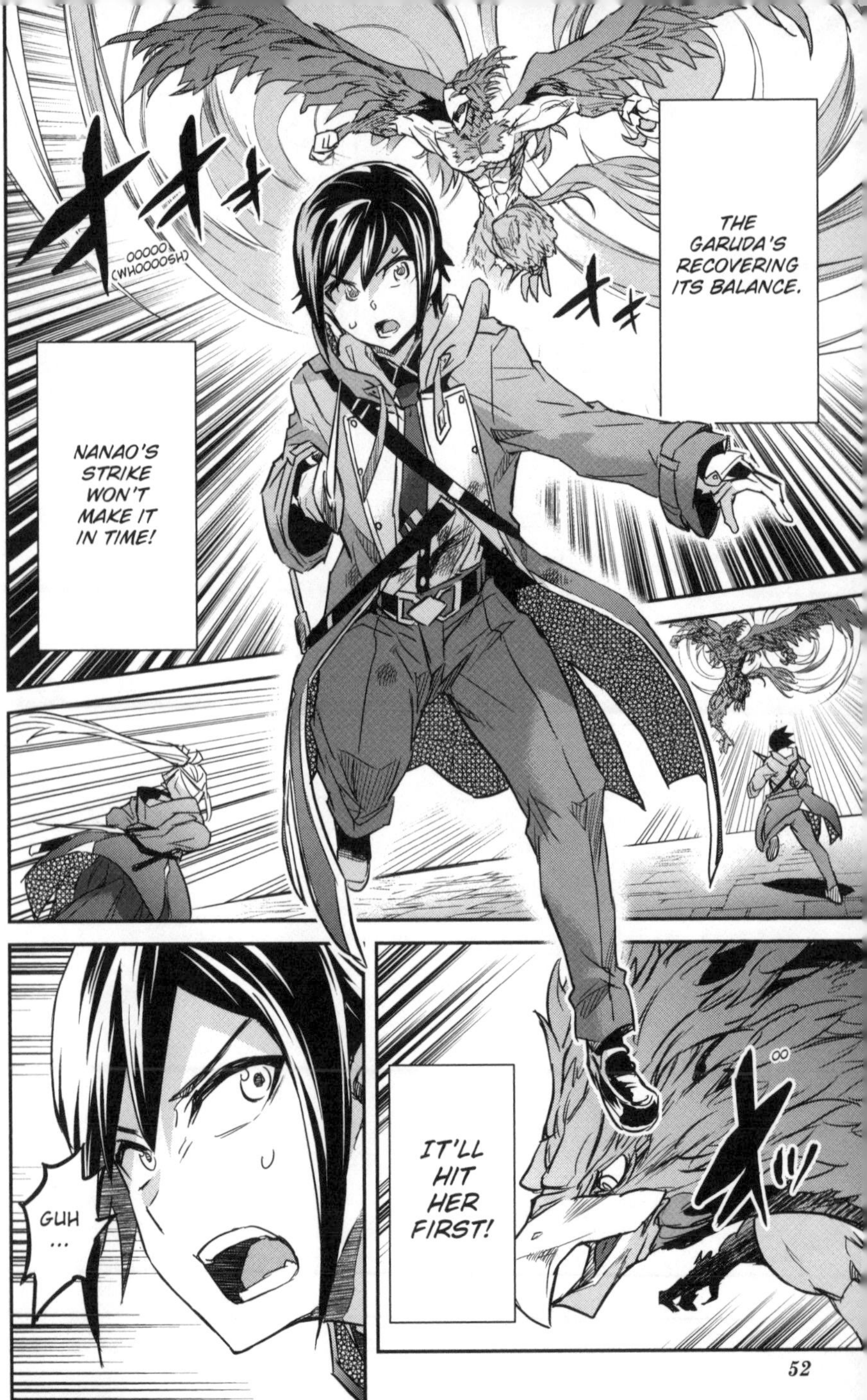
THE GARUDA'S RECOVERING ITS BALANCE.
OOOOO (WHOOOOSH)
NANAO'S STRIKE WON'T MAKE IT IN TIME!
IT'LL HIT HER FIRST!
GUH ...

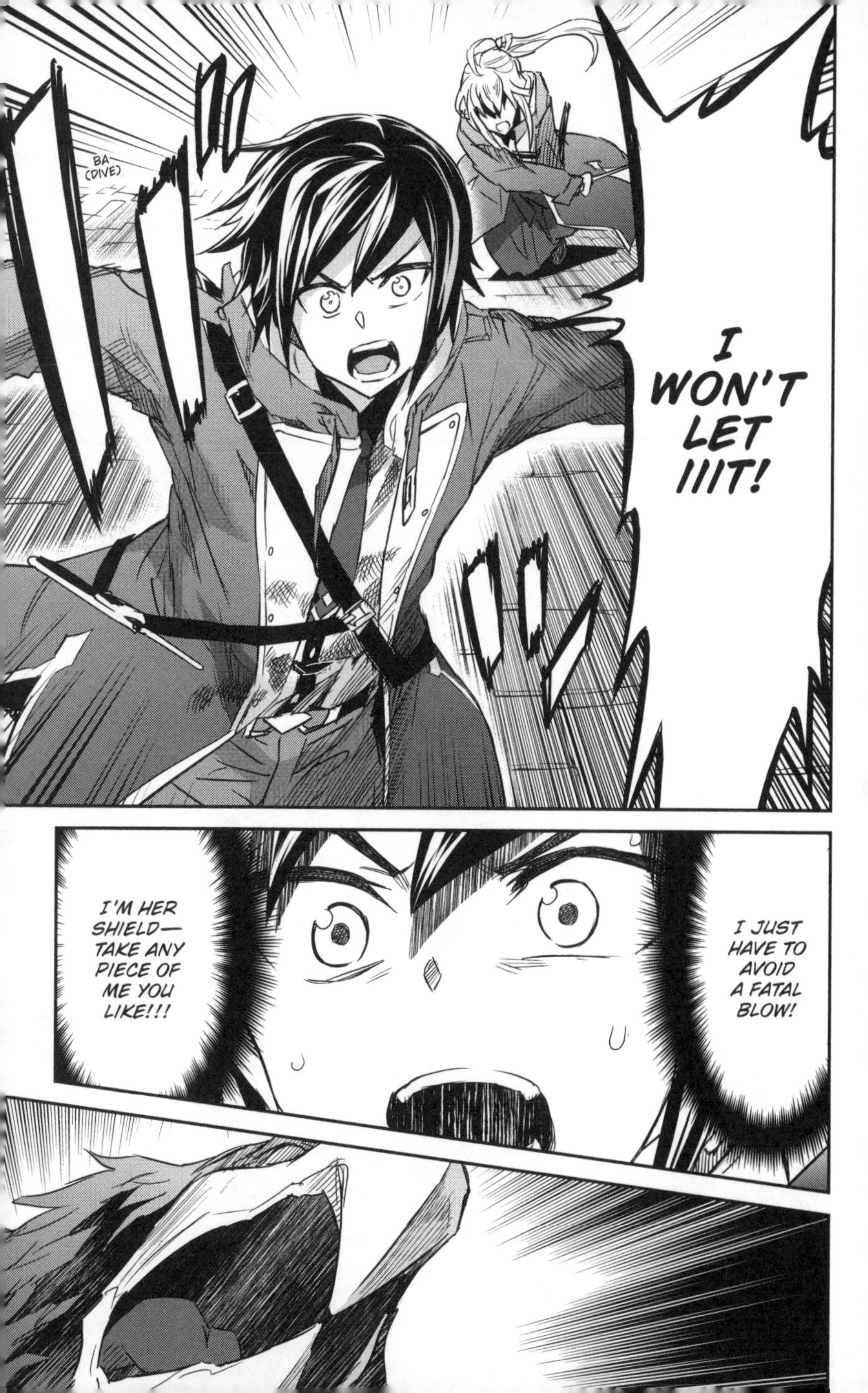
I WON'T LET IIIT!
BA (DIVE)
I JUST HAVE TO AVOID A FATAL BLOW!
I'M HER SHIELD— TAKE ANY PIECE OF ME YOU LIKE!!!

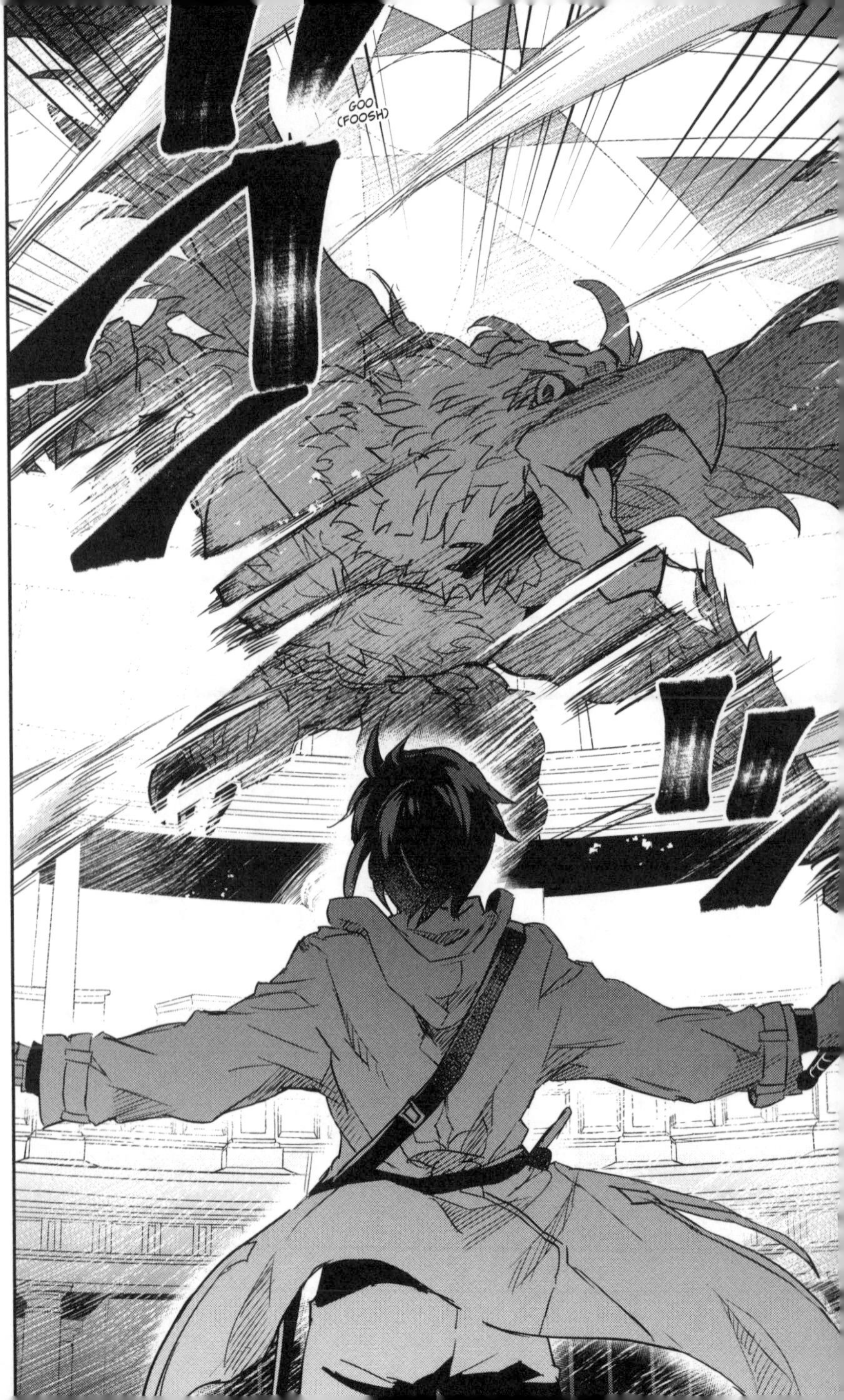
GOO
(FOOSH)

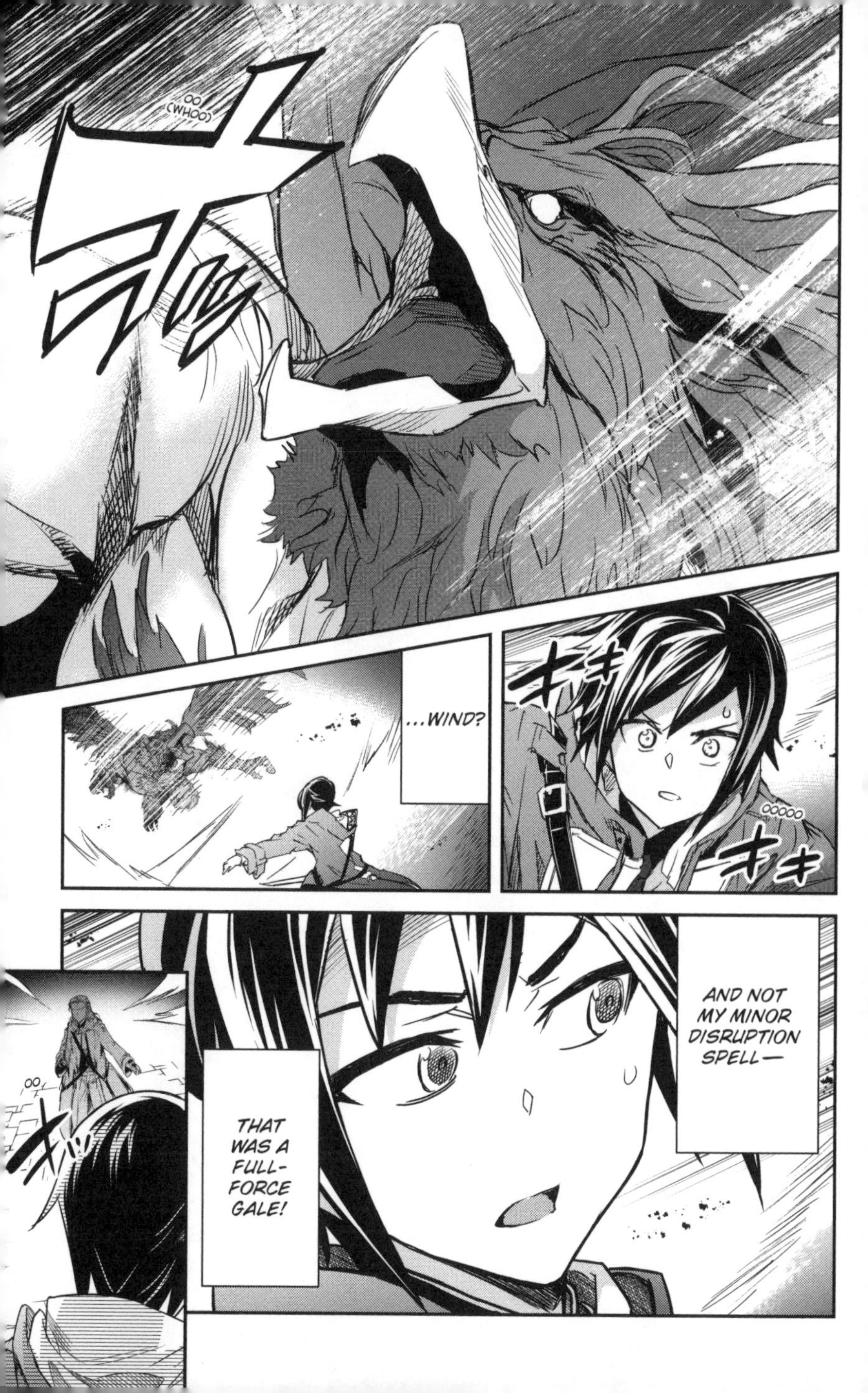
OO
(WHOO)
OOOOO
...WIND?
AND NOT MY MINOR DISRUPTION SPELL—
THAT WAS A FULL-FORCE GALE!
OO

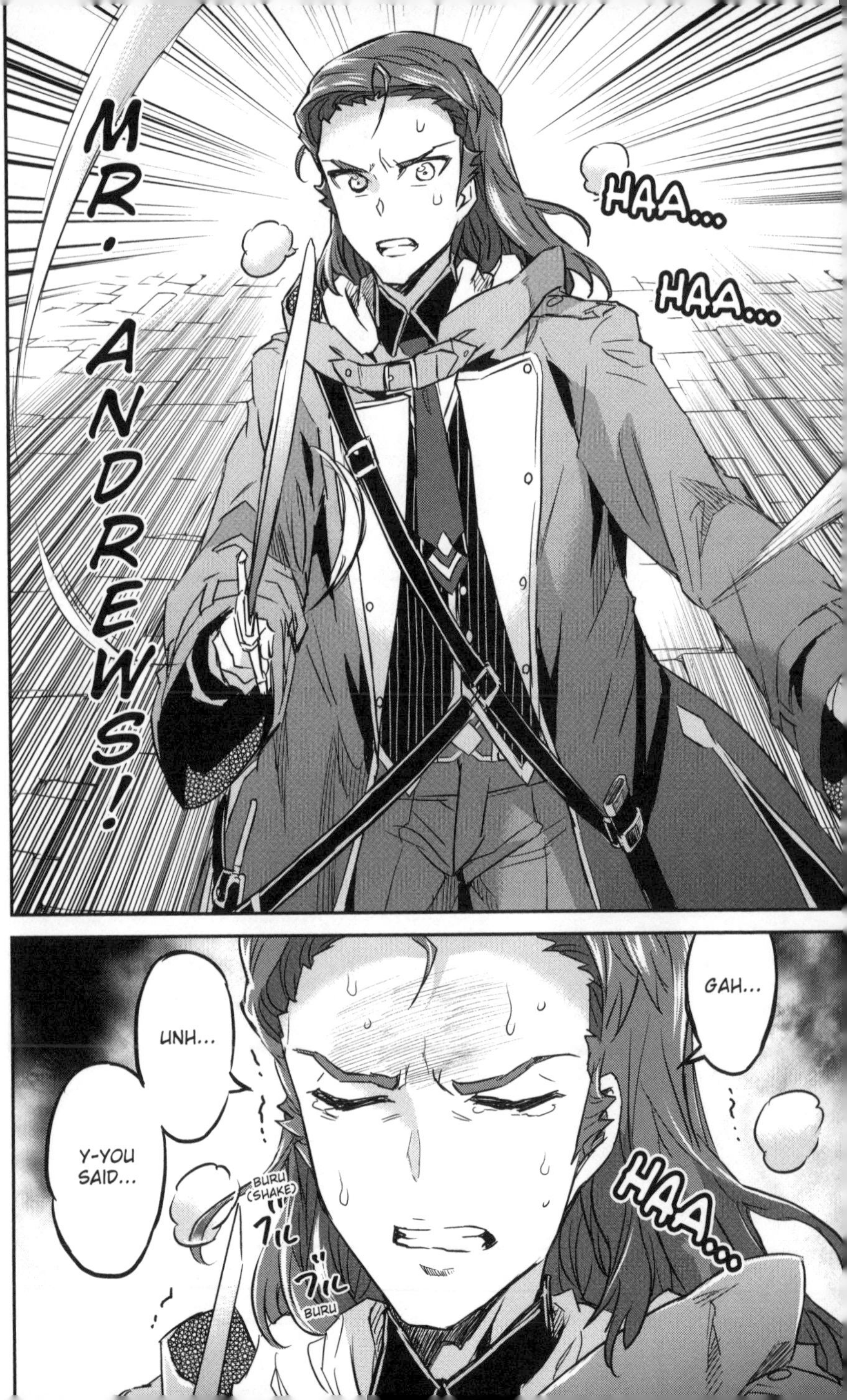
HAA...
HAA...
MR. ANDREWS!
GAH...
HAA...
BURU (SHAKE)
BURU
UNH...
Y-YOU SAID...

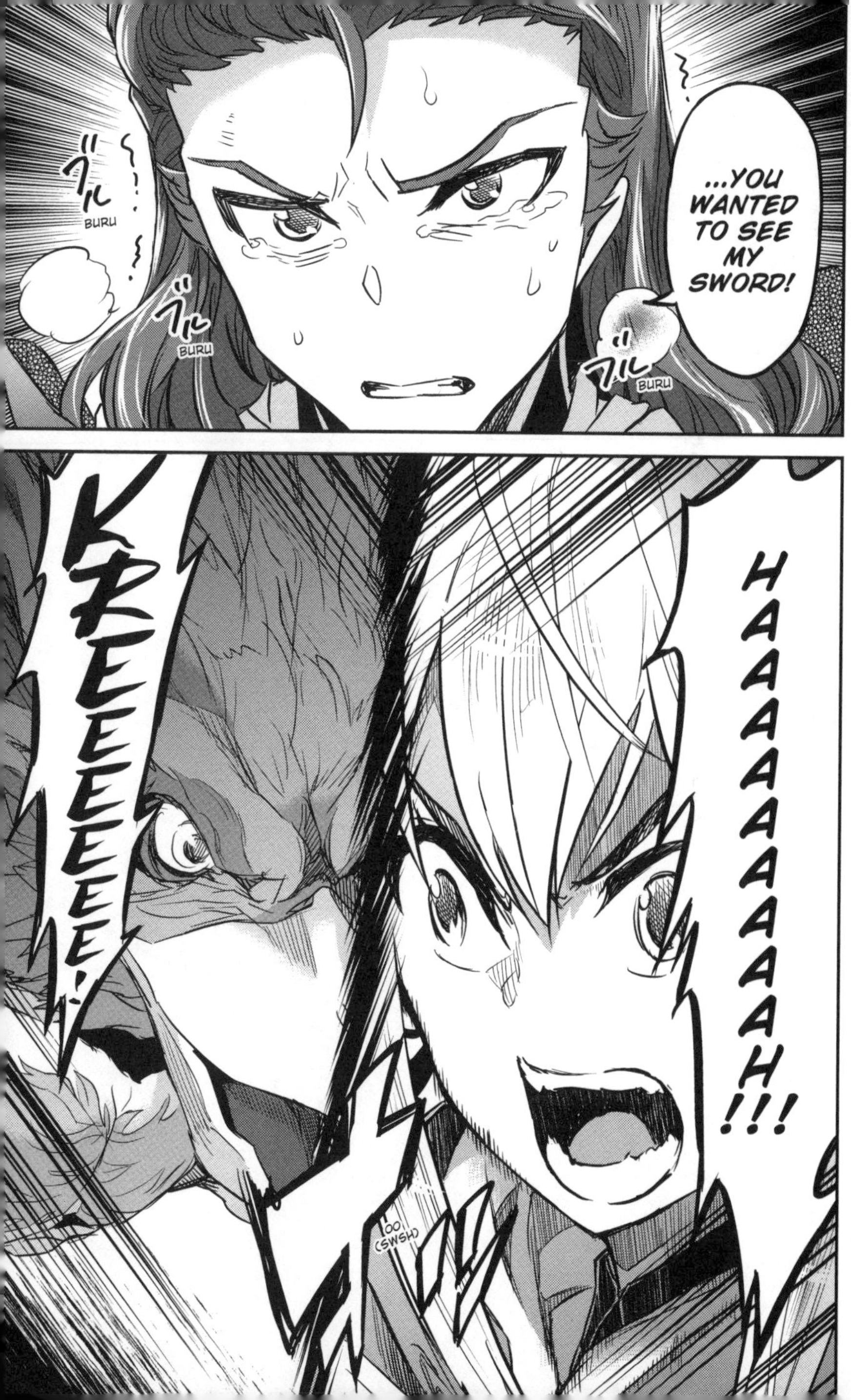

...YOU WANTED TO SEE MY SWORD!
ブル BURU
ブル BURU
ブル BURU
HAAAAAAAAAH!!!
KREEEEEEEEEE!
(SWSH)

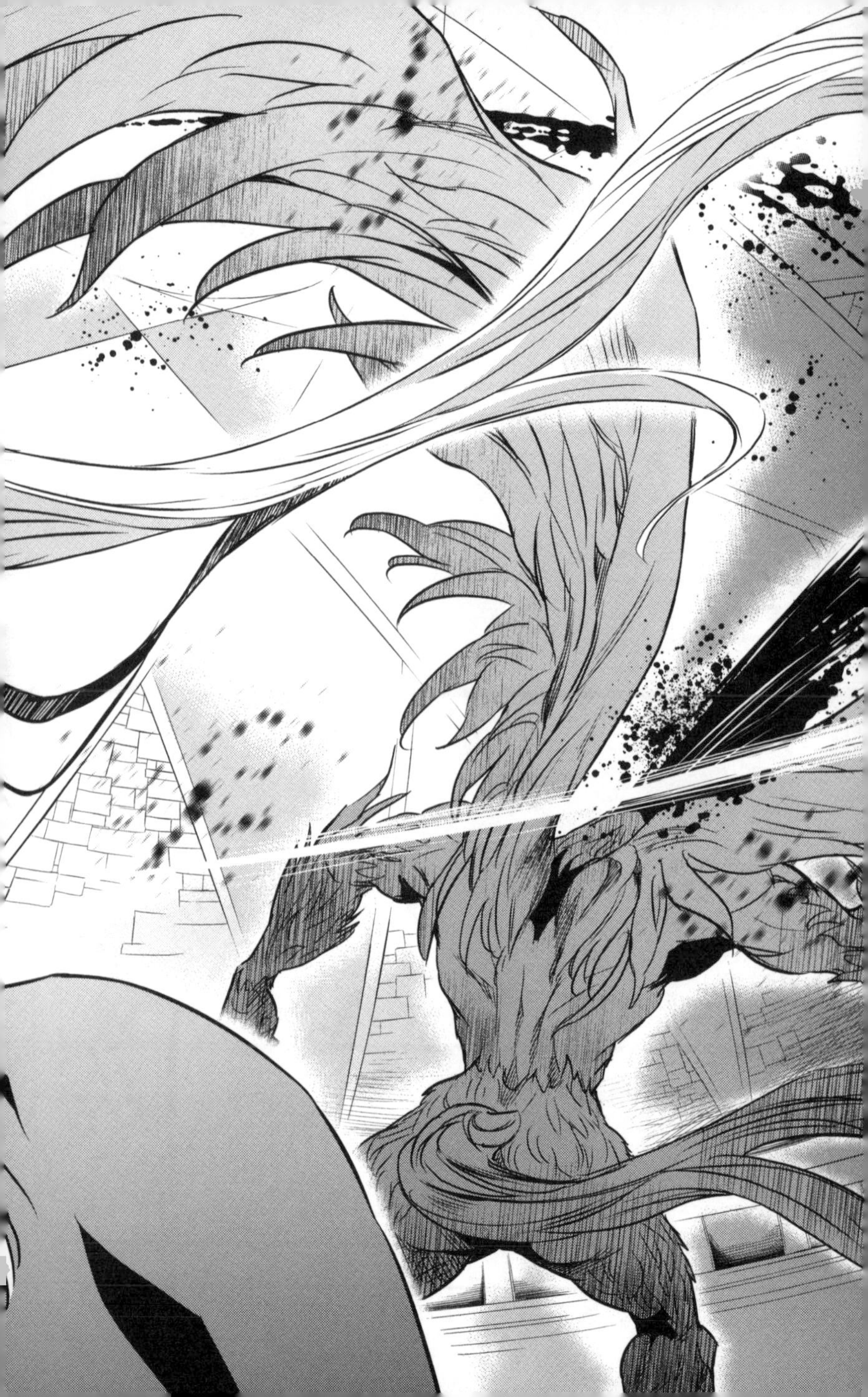

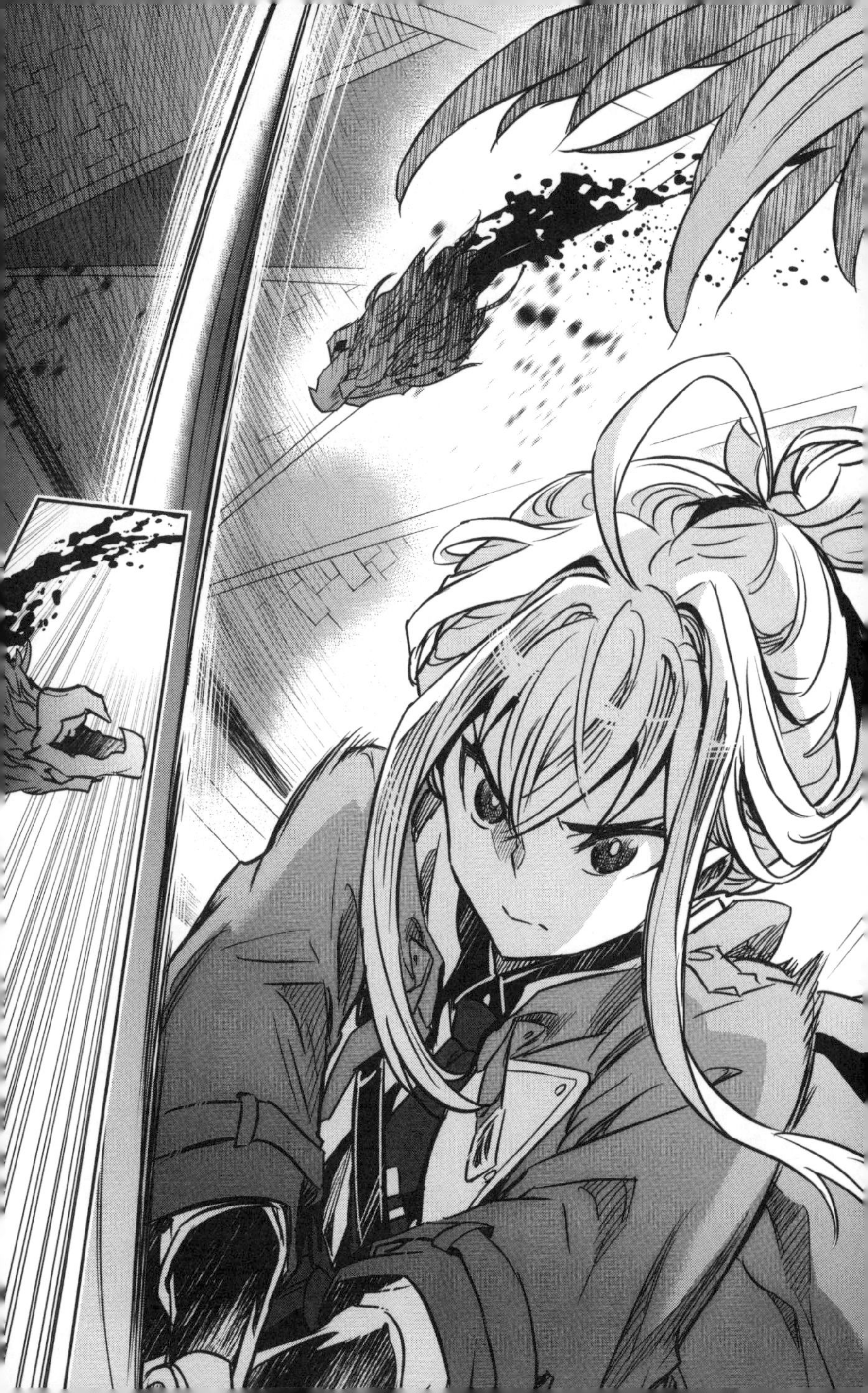

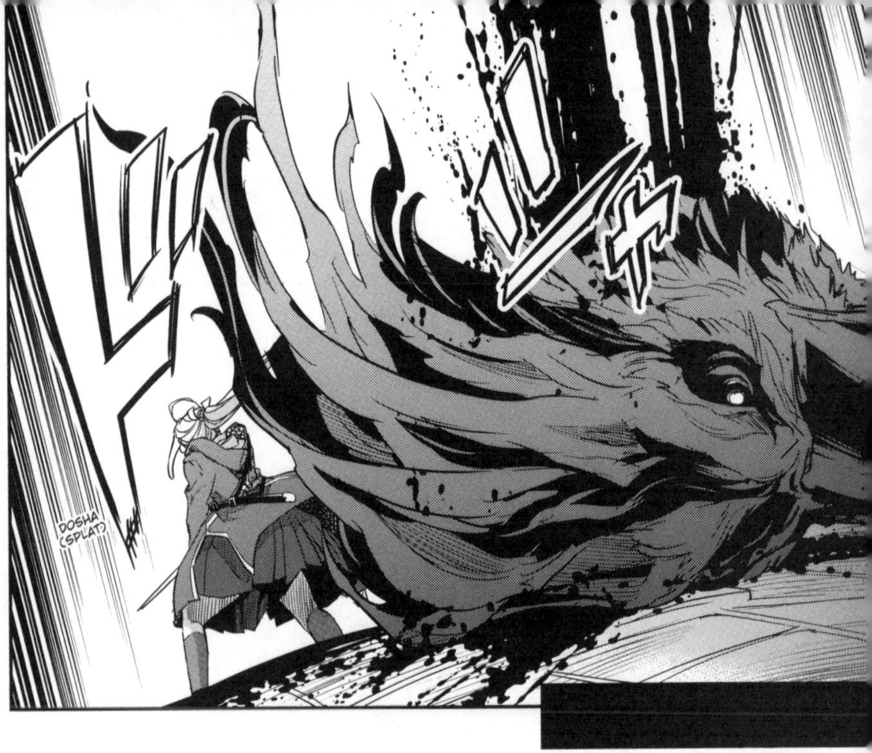
DOSHA (SPLAT)

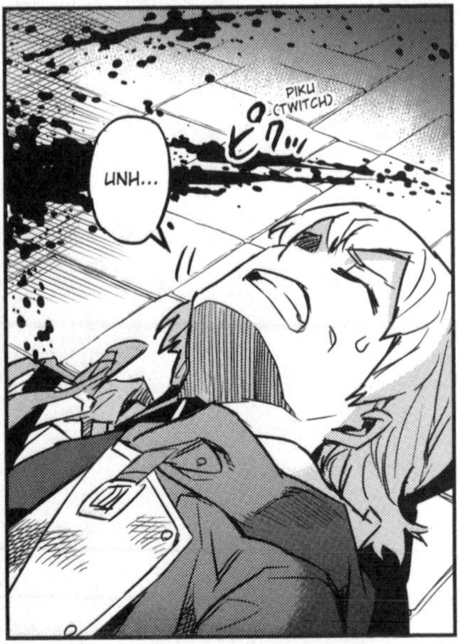
PIKU (TWITCH)
UNH...

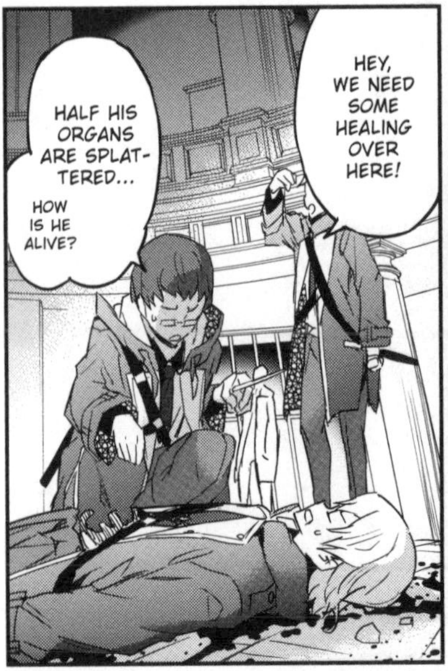
HEY, WE NEED SOME HEALING OVER HERE!
HALF HIS ORGANS ARE SPLAT-TERED...
HOW IS HE ALIVE?

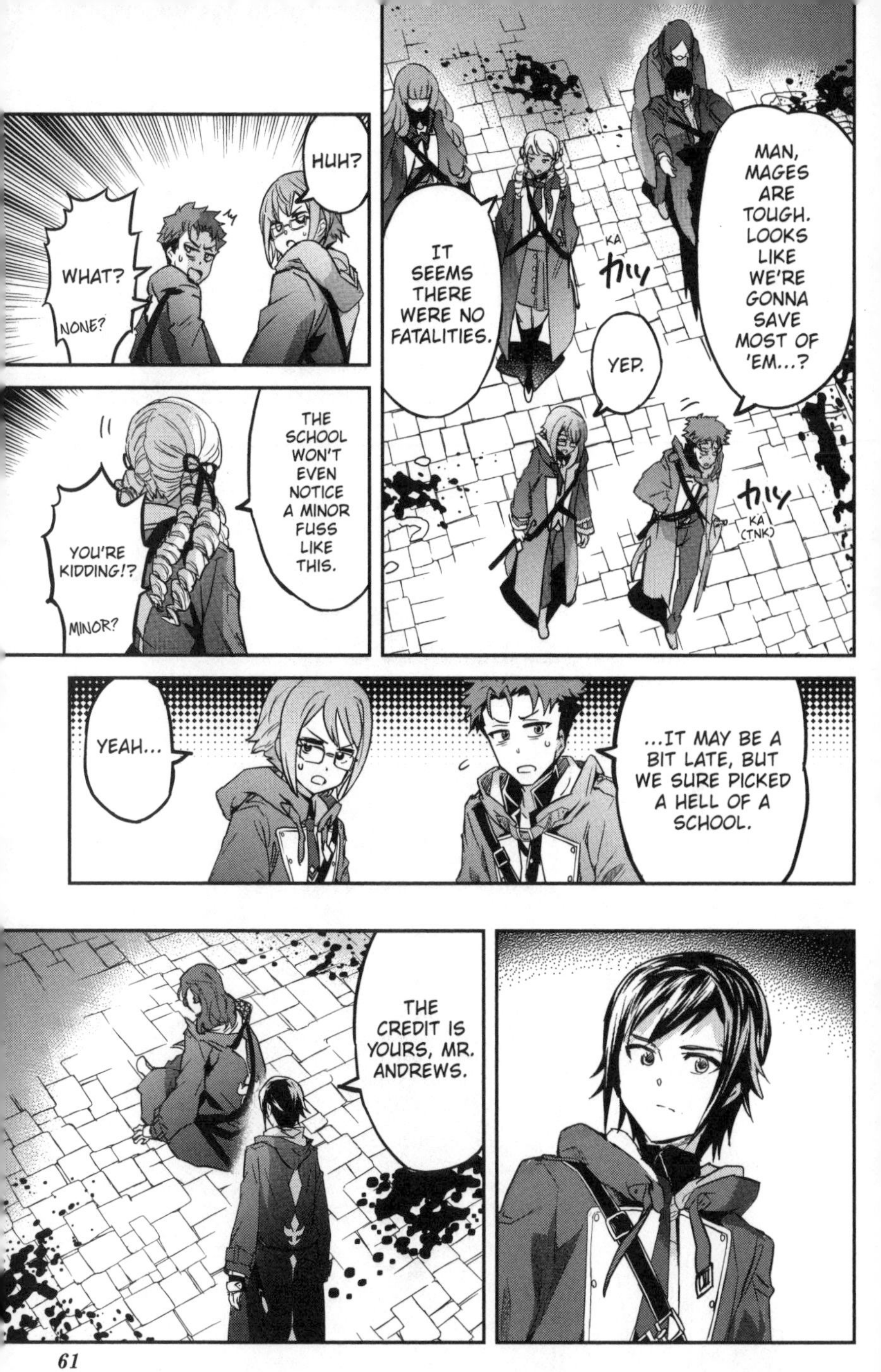
MAN, MAGES ARE TOUGH. LOOKS LIKE WE'RE GONNA SAVE MOST OF 'EM...?
KA
IT SEEMS THERE WERE NO FATALITIES.
YEP.
KA (TNK)
HUH?
WHAT?
NONE?
THE SCHOOL WON'T EVEN NOTICE A MINOR FUSS LIKE THIS.
YOU'RE KIDDING!?
MINOR?
...IT MAY BE A BIT LATE, BUT WE SURE PICKED A HELL OF A SCHOOL.
YEAH...
THE CREDIT IS YOURS, MR. ANDREWS.

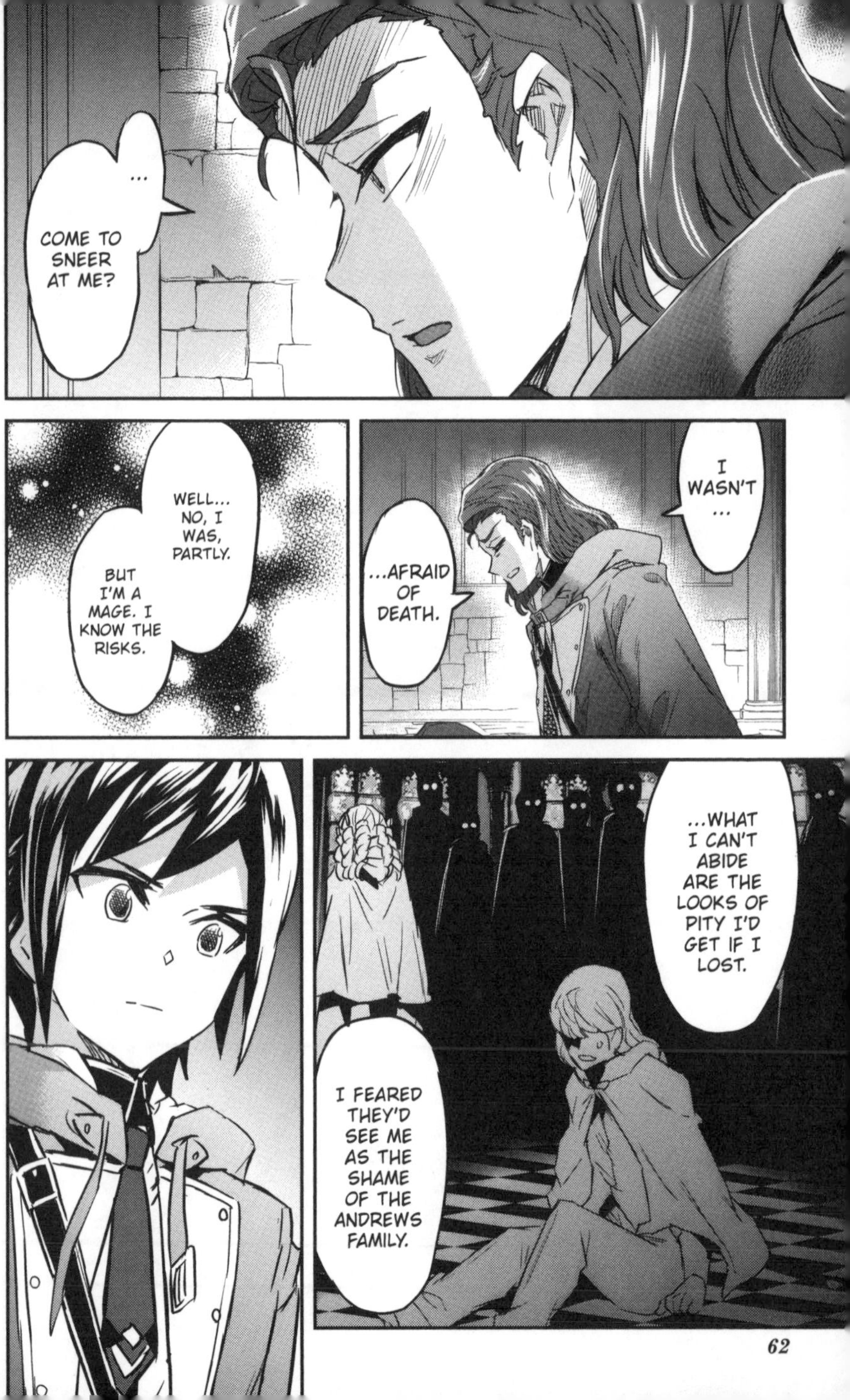
...
COME TO SNEER AT ME?
I WASN'T ...
...AFRAID OF DEATH.
WELL... NO, I WAS, PARTLY.
BUT I'M A MAGE. I KNOW THE RISKS.
...WHAT I CAN'T ABIDE ARE THE LOOKS OF PITY I'D GET IF I LOST.
I FEARED THEY'D SEE ME AS THE SHAME OF THE ANDREWS FAMILY.

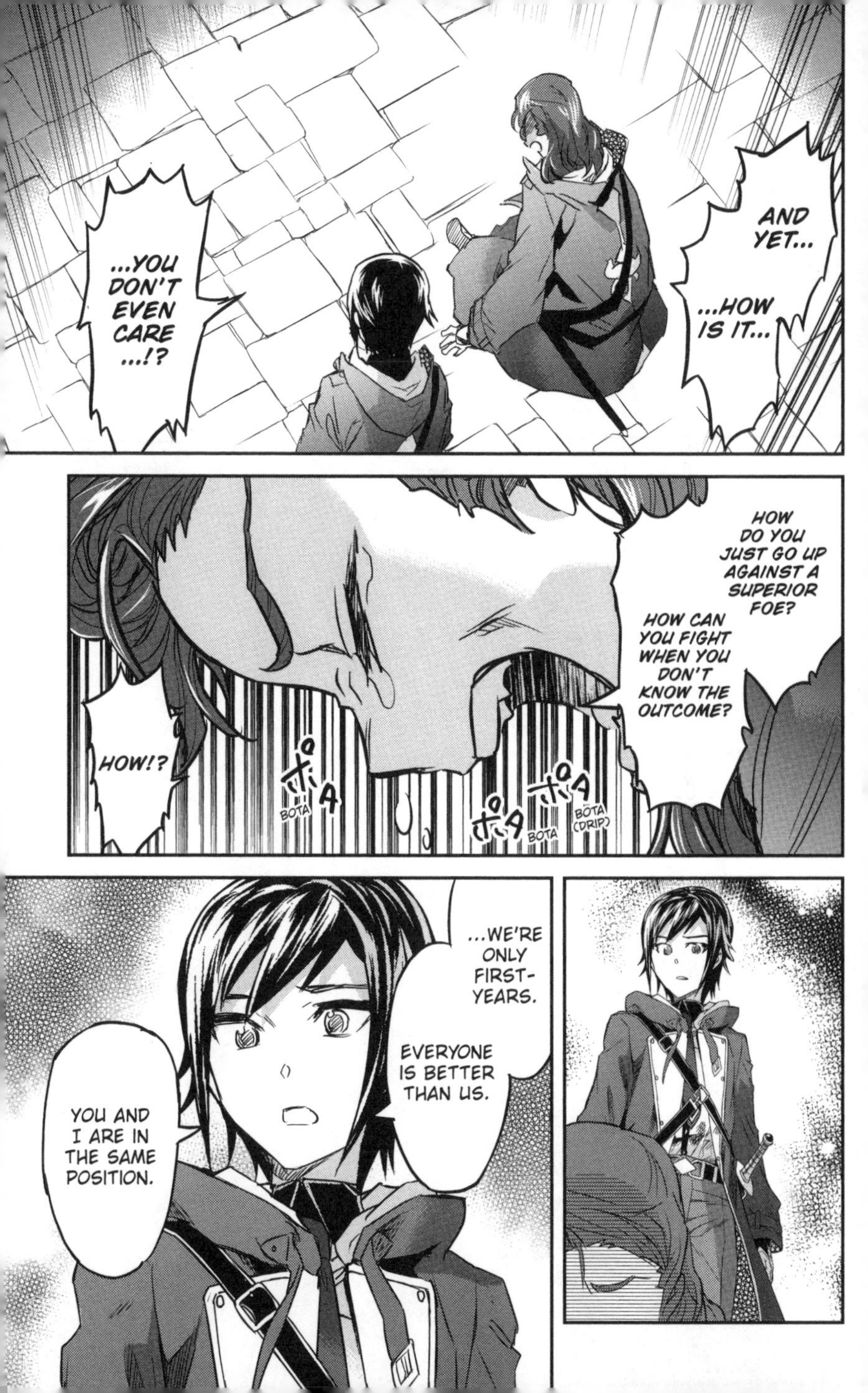
AND YET...
...HOW IS IT...
...YOU DON'T EVEN CARE ...!?
HOW DO YOU JUST GO UP AGAINST A SUPERIOR FOE?
HOW CAN YOU FIGHT WHEN YOU DON'T KNOW THE OUTCOME?
HOW!?
BÖTA (DRIP)
BOTA
BOTA
BOTA
...WE'RE ONLY FIRST-YEARS.
EVERYONE IS BETTER THAN US.
YOU AND I ARE IN THE SAME POSITION.

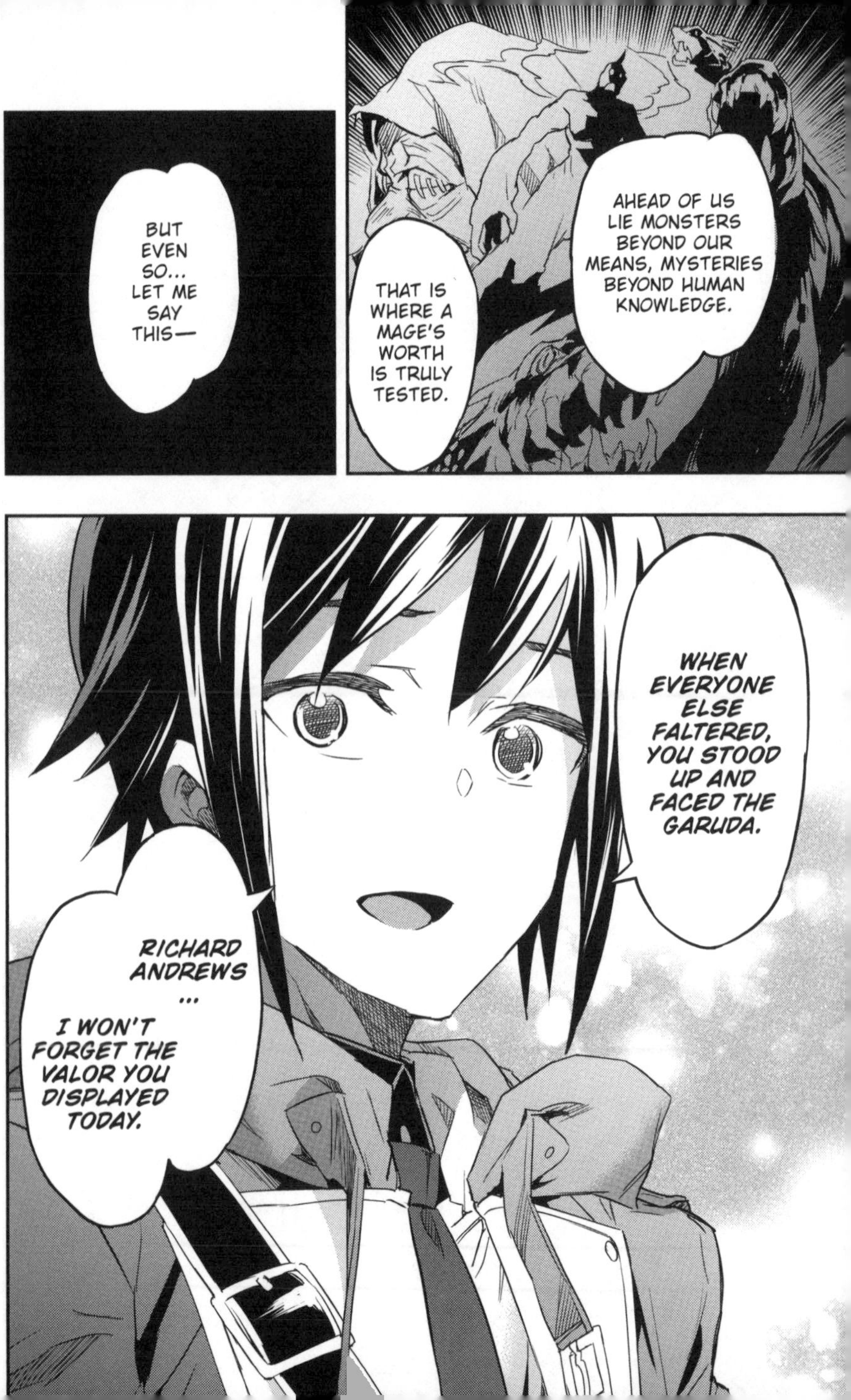
AHEAD OF US LIE MONSTERS BEYOND OUR MEANS, MYSTERIES BEYOND HUMAN KNOWLEDGE.
THAT IS WHERE A MAGE'S WORTH IS TRULY TESTED.
BUT EVEN SO... LET ME SAY THIS—
WHEN EVERYONE ELSE FALTERED, YOU STOOD UP AND FACED THE GARUDA.
RICHARD ANDREWS... I WON'T FORGET THE VALOR YOU DISPLAYED TODAY.

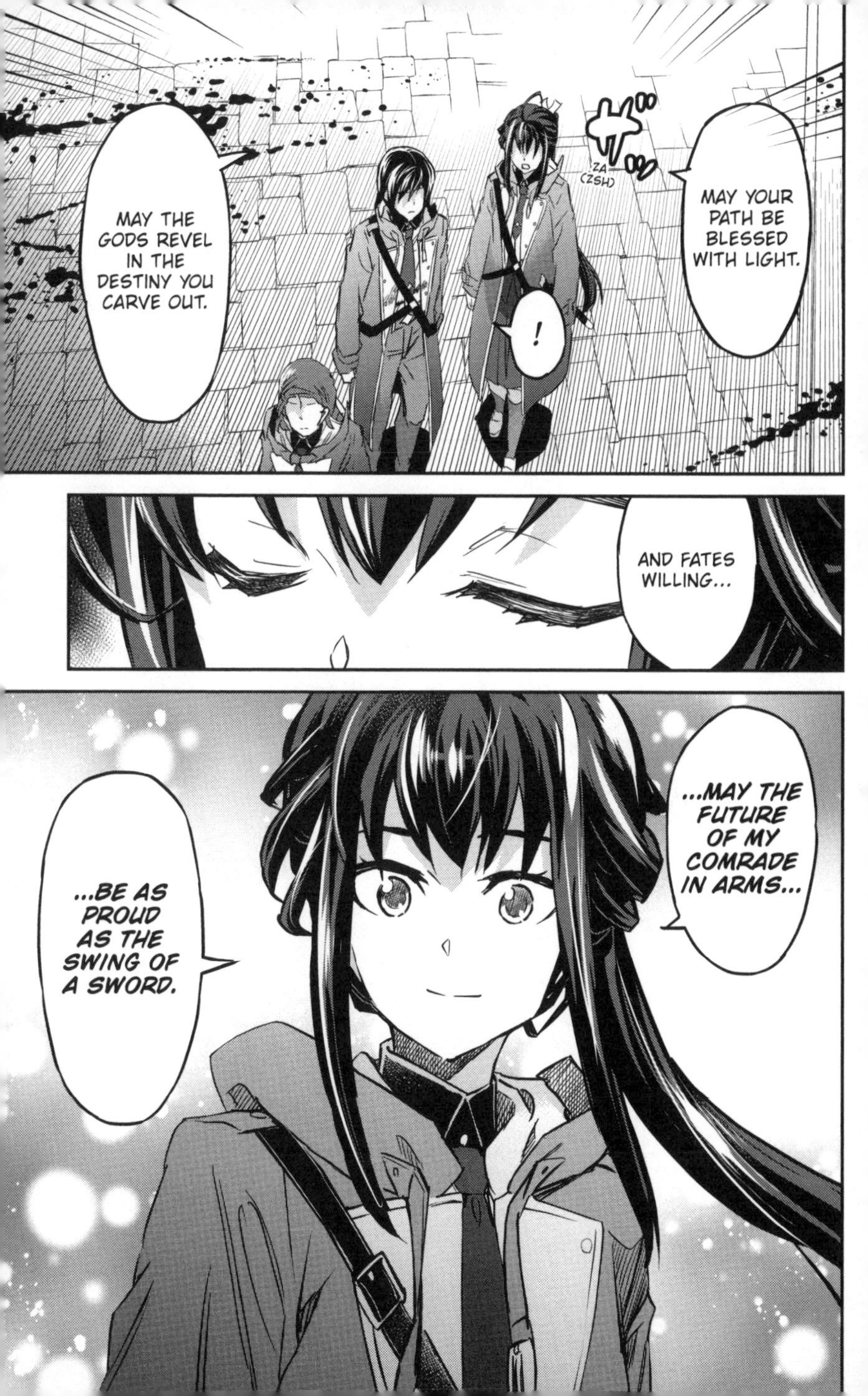
MAY YOUR PATH BE BLESSED WITH LIGHT.
ZA (ZSH)
!
MAY THE GODS REVEL IN THE DESTINY YOU CARVE OUT.
AND FATES WILLING...
...MAY THE FUTURE OF MY COMRADE IN ARMS...
...BE AS PROUD AS THE SWING OF A SWORD.

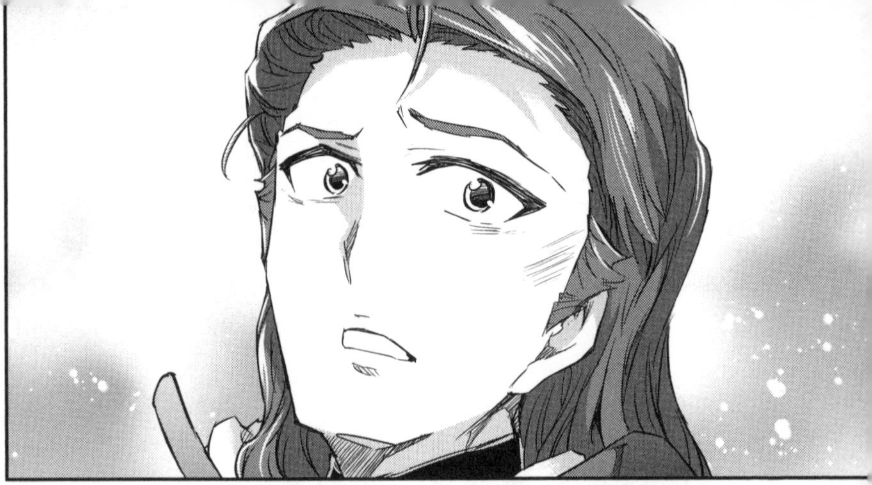

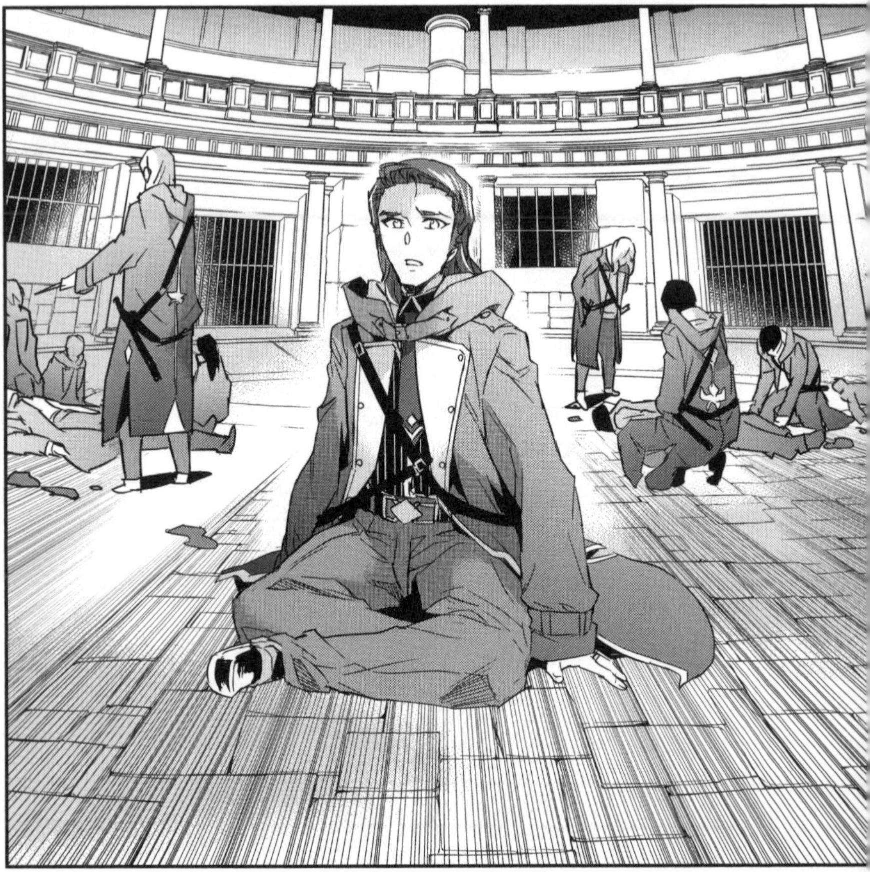

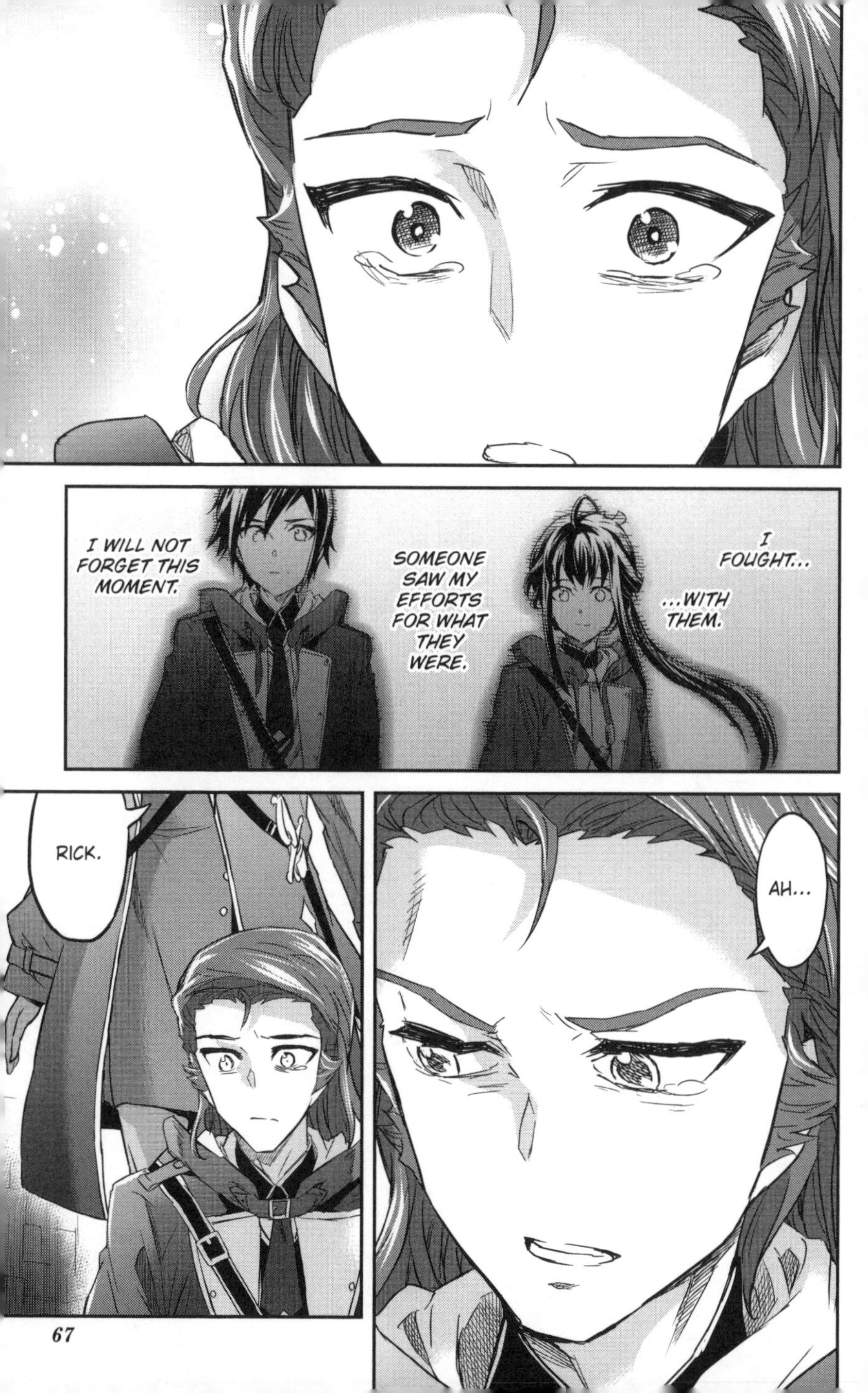
I FOUGHT...
...WITH THEM.
SOMEONE SAW MY EFFORTS FOR WHAT THEY WERE.
I WILL NOT FORGET THIS MOMENT.
AH...
RICK.

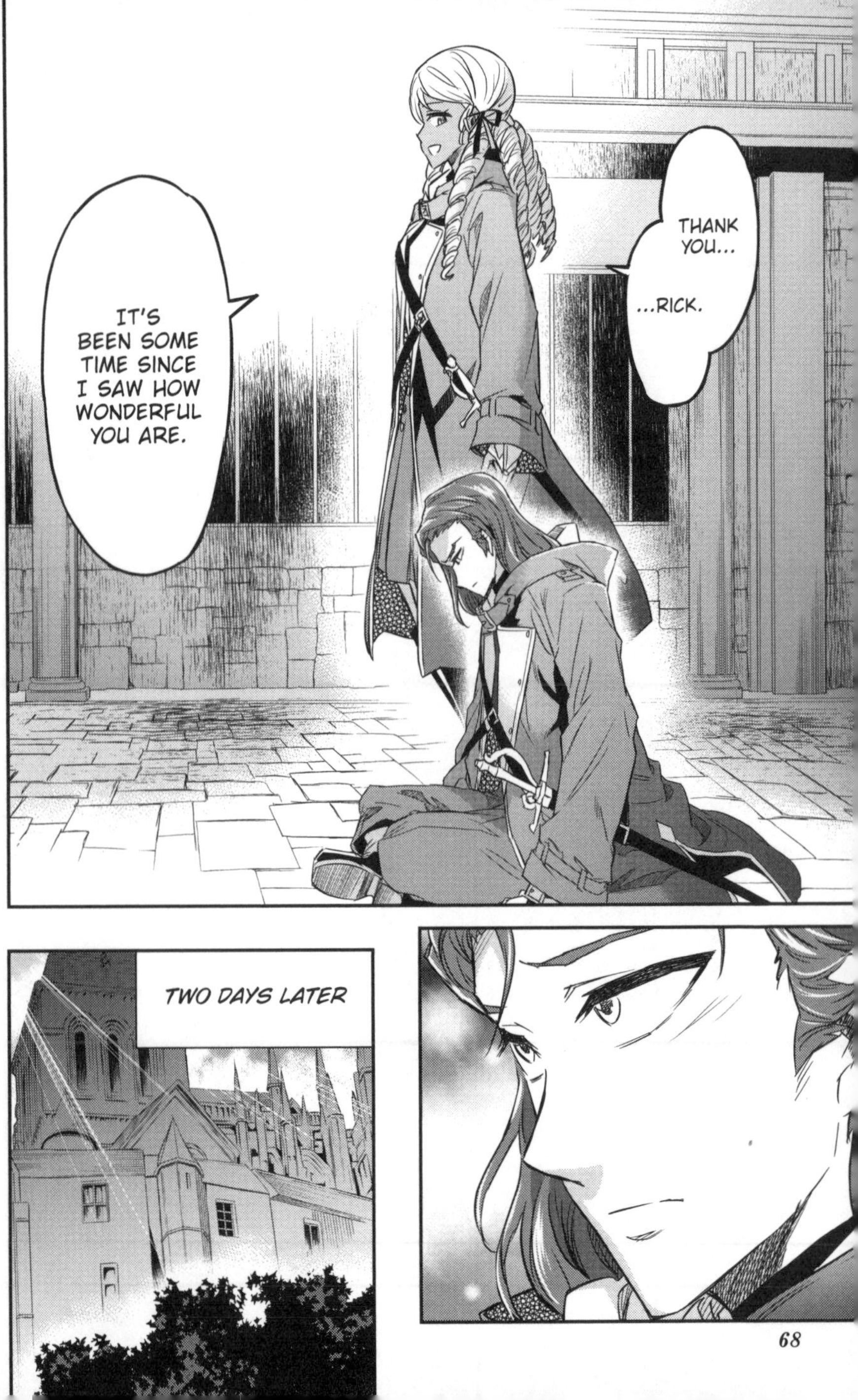
THANK YOU...
...RICK.
IT'S BEEN SOME TIME SINCE I SAW HOW WONDERFUL YOU ARE.
TWO DAYS LATER

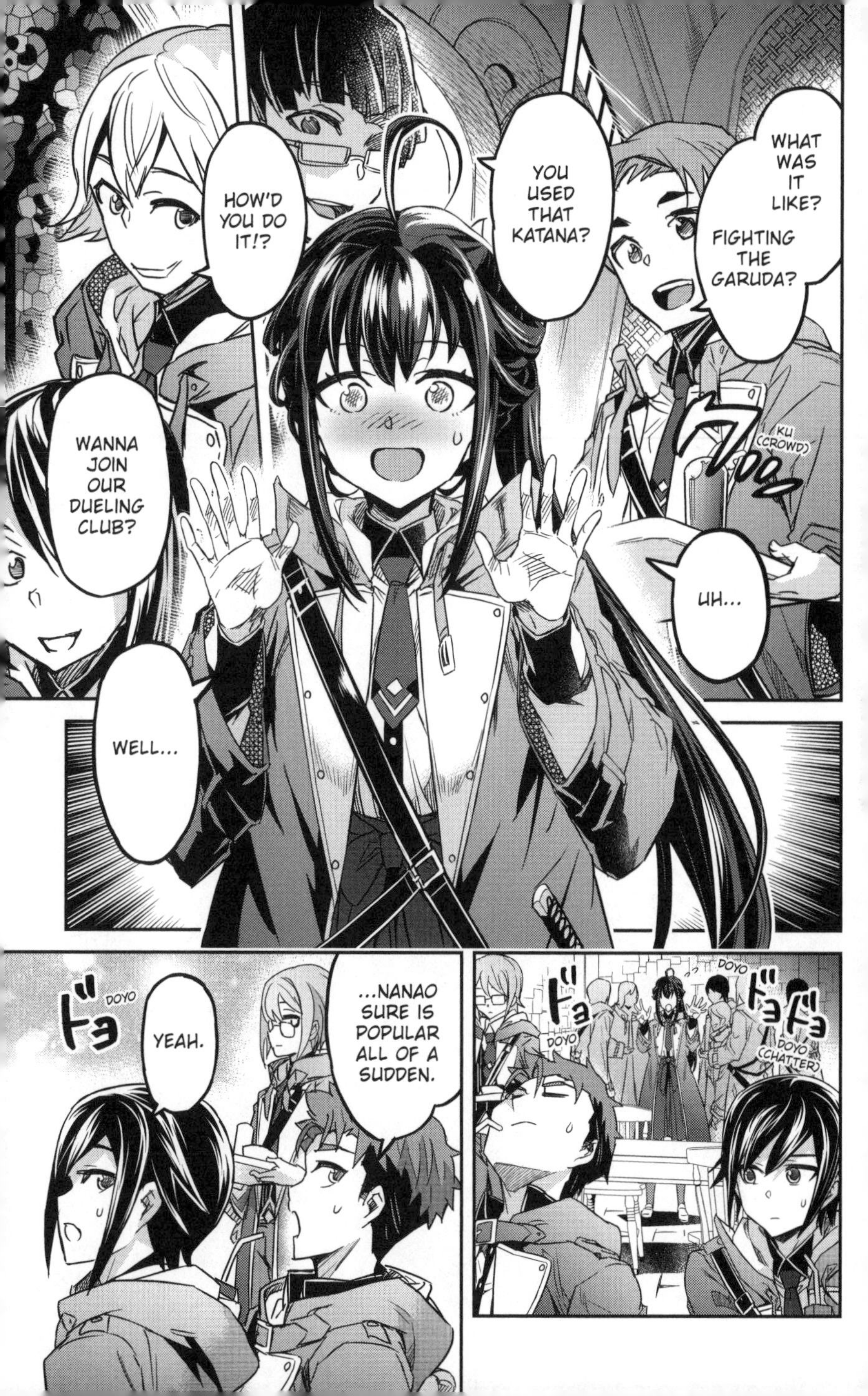
WHAT WAS IT LIKE?
FIGHTING THE GARUDA?
YOU USED THAT KATANA?
HOW'D YOU DO IT!?
WANNA JOIN OUR DUELING CLUB?
KU (CROWD)
UH...
WELL...
DOYO
DOYO
DOYO (CHATTER)
...NANAO SURE IS POPULAR ALL OF A SUDDEN.
YEAH.
DOYO

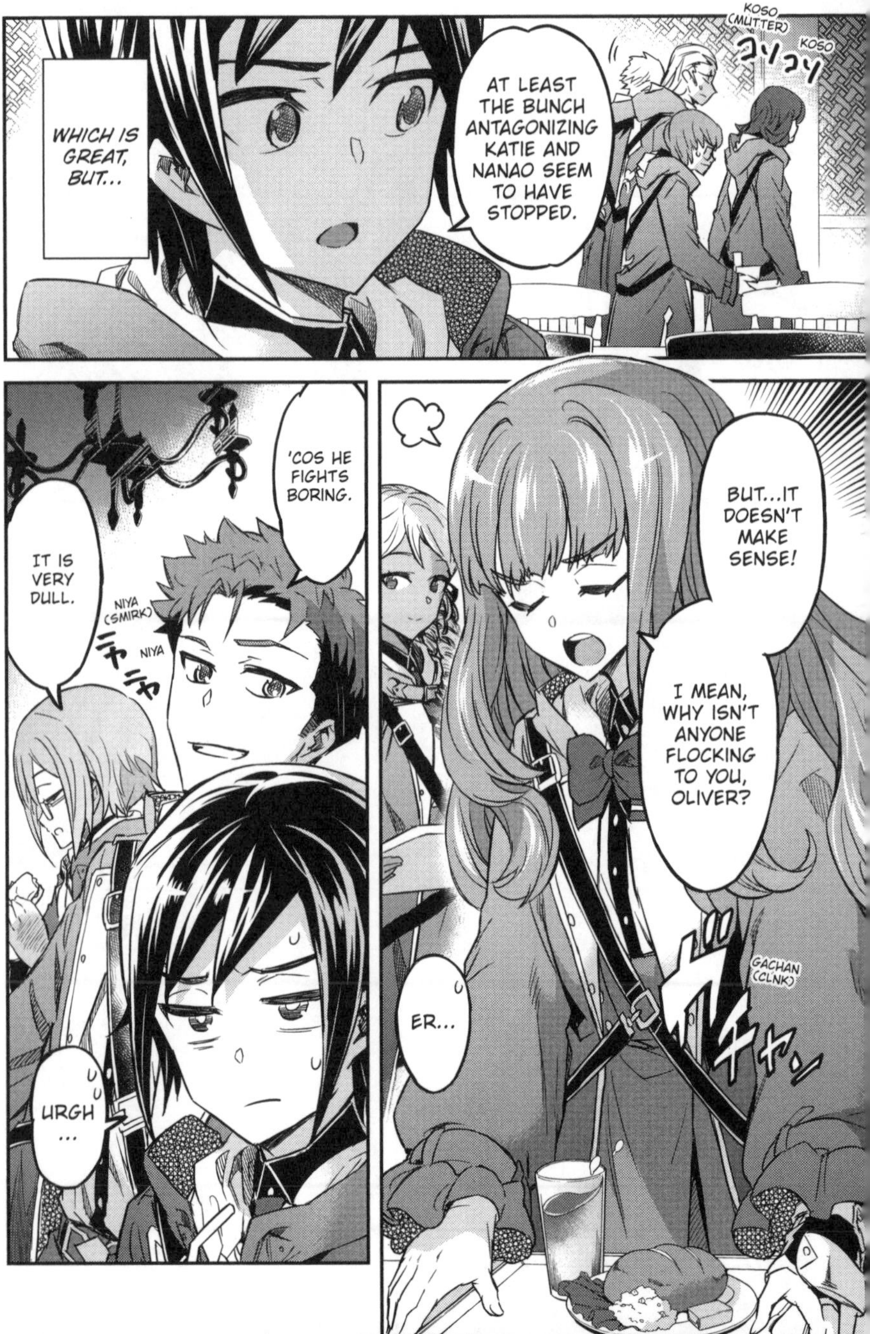
KOSO (MUTTER) KOSO
AT LEAST THE BUNCH ANTAGONIZING KATIE AND NANAO SEEM TO HAVE STOPPED.
WHICH IS GREAT, BUT...
BUT...IT DOESN'T MAKE SENSE!
I MEAN, WHY ISN'T ANYONE FLOCKING TO YOU, OLIVER?
GACHAN (CLNK)
ER...
'COS HE FIGHTS BORING.
IT IS VERY DULL.
NIYA (SMIRK) NIYA
URGH...

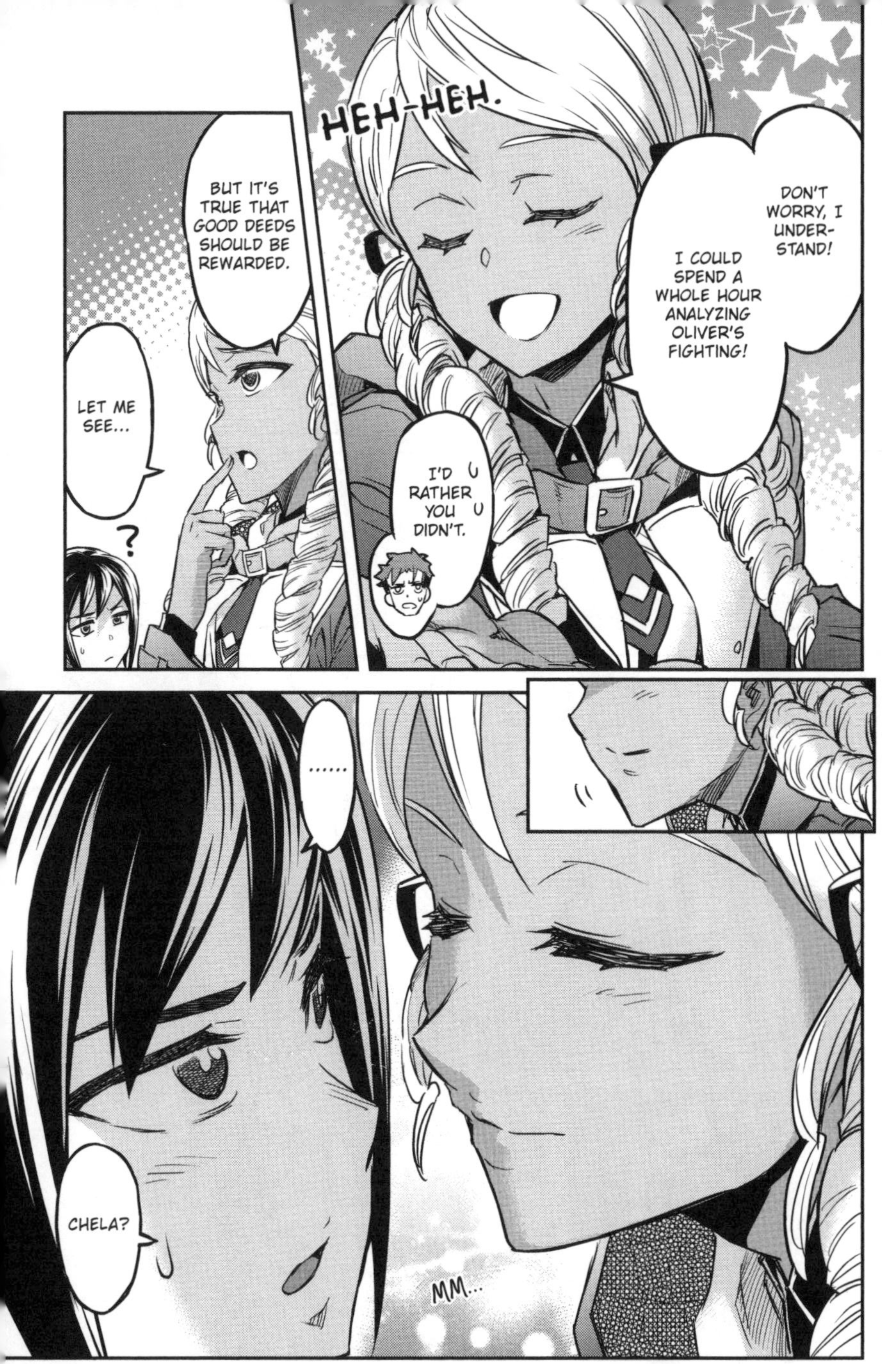
HEH-HEH.
DON'T WORRY, I UNDERSTAND!
I COULD SPEND A WHOLE HOUR ANALYZING OLIVER'S FIGHTING!
I'D RATHER YOU DIDN'T.
BUT IT'S TRUE THAT GOOD DEEDS SHOULD BE REWARDED.
LET ME SEE...
?
......
CHELA?
MM...

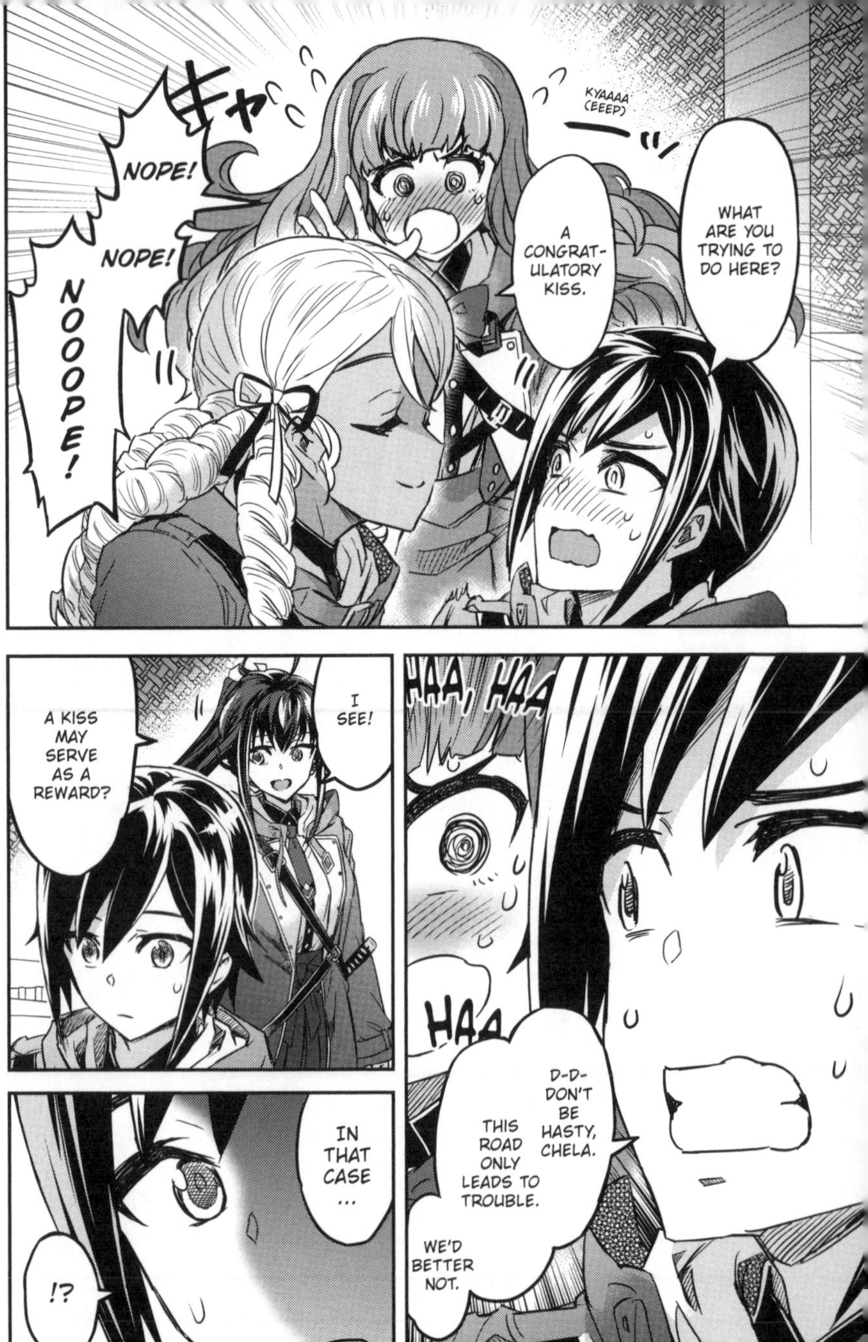
WHAT ARE YOU TRYING TO DO HERE?
A CONGRAT-ULATORY KISS.
KYAAAA (EEEP)
キャ
NOPE!
NOPE!
NOOOOPE!
HAA, HAA
HAA
D-D-DON'T BE HASTY, CHELA.
THIS ROAD ONLY LEADS TO TROUBLE.
WE'D BETTER NOT.
I SEE!
A KISS MAY SERVE AS A REWARD?
IN THAT CASE ...
!?

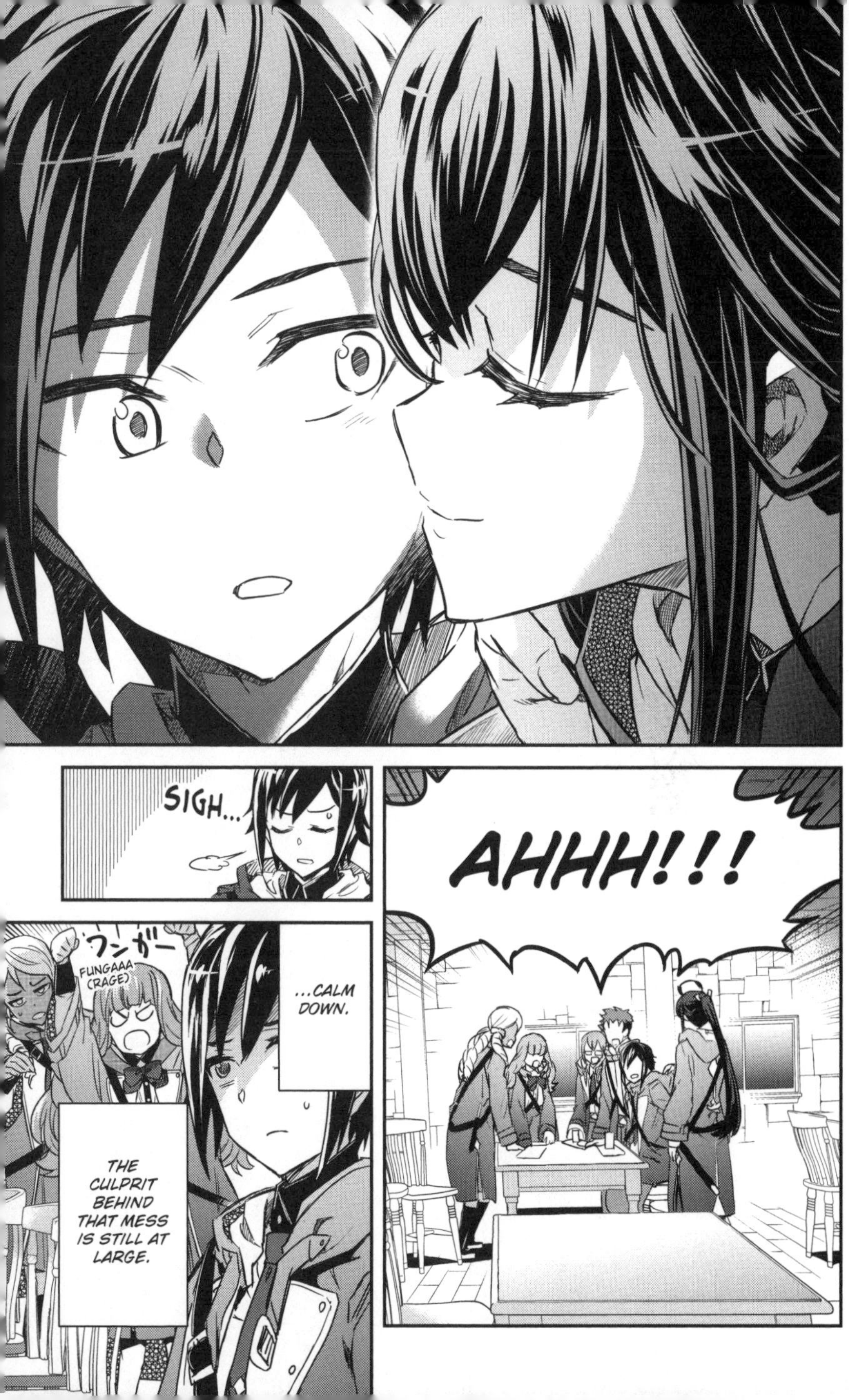
AHHH!!!
SIGH...
...CALM DOWN.
フンガー
FUNGAAA (RAGE)
THE CULPRIT BEHIND THAT MESS IS STILL AT LARGE.

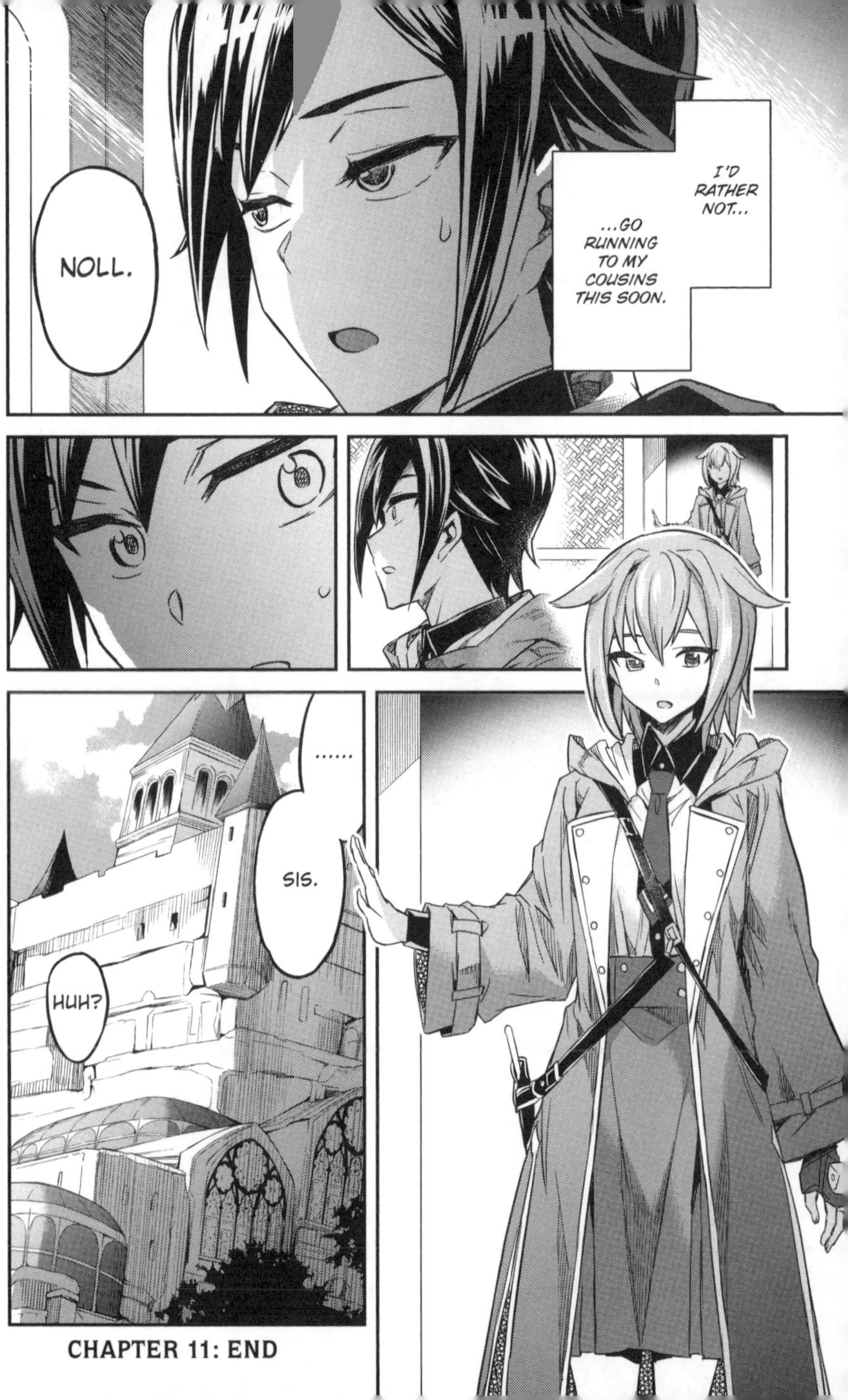
I'D RATHER NOT...
...GO RUNNING TO MY COUSINS THIS SOON.
NOLL.
......
SIS.
HUH?

CHAPTER 11: END

Reign of the Seven Spellblades

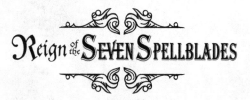

Early Character File 01

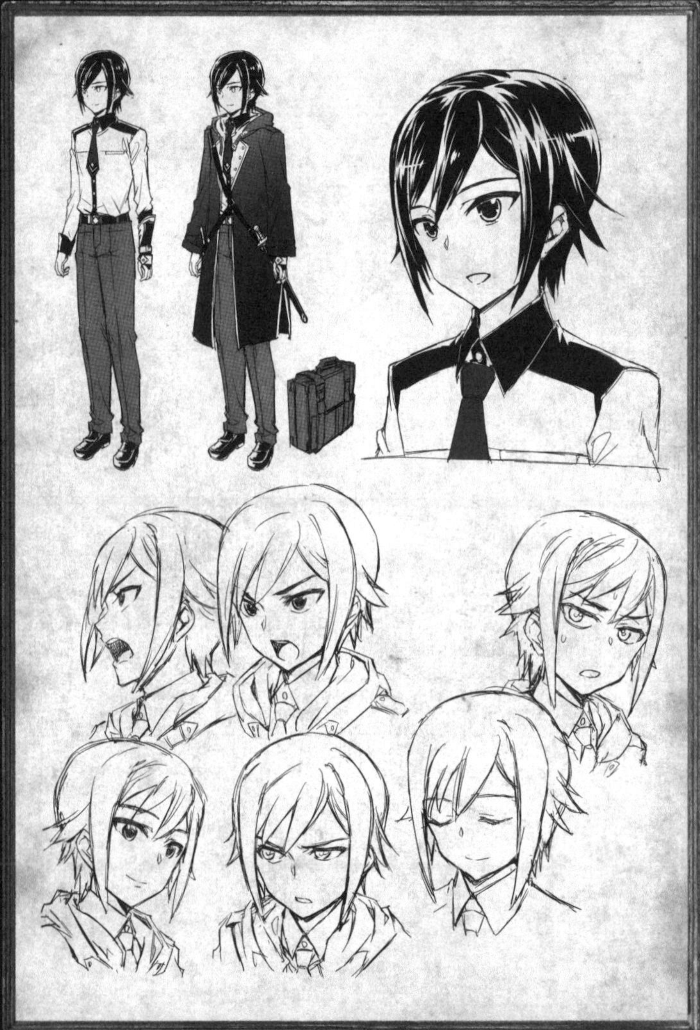

EARLY CHARACTER FILE 01

| Oliver Horn |

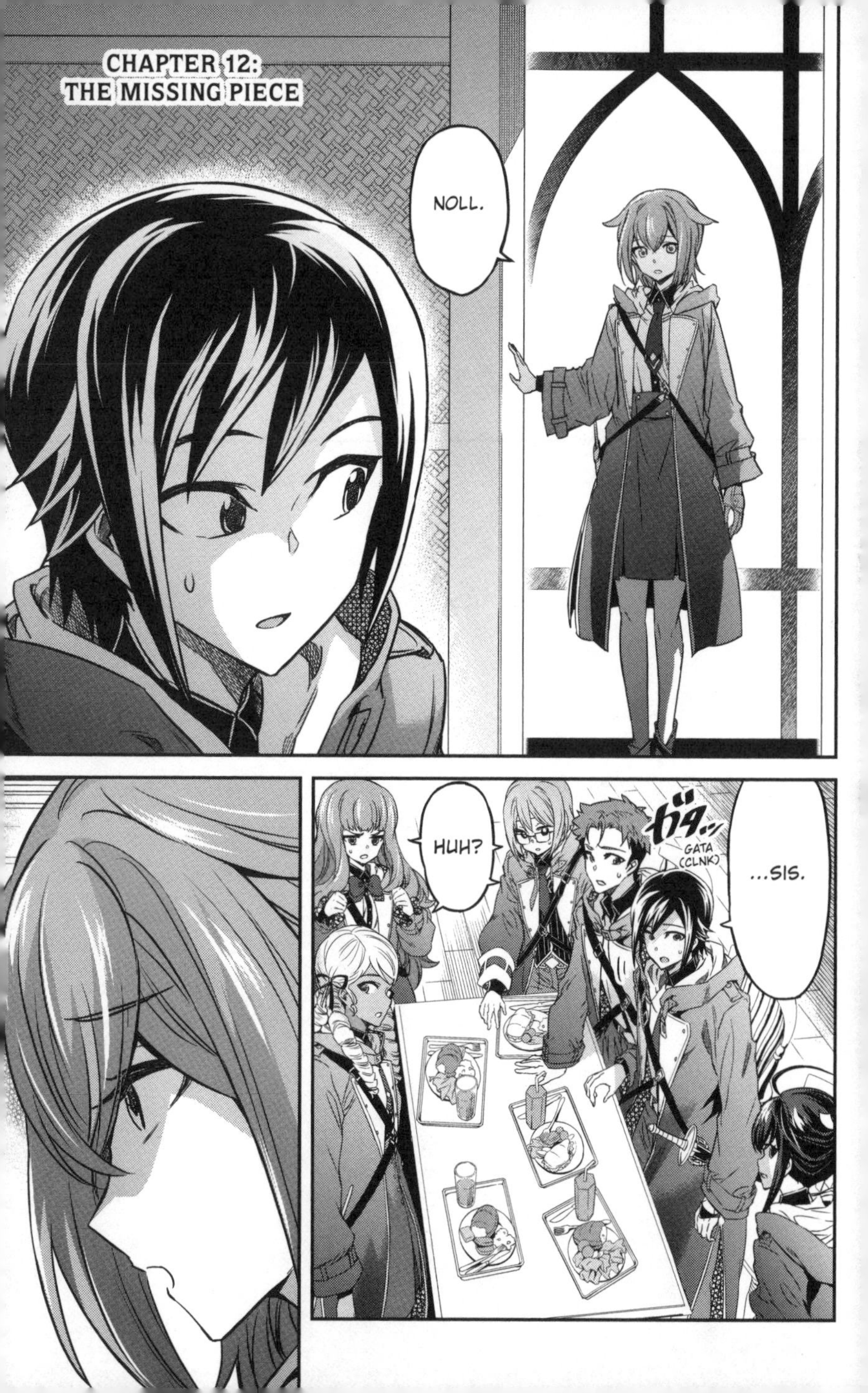
CHAPTER 12: THE MISSING PIECE
NOLL.
...SIS.
ガタッ
GATA (CLNK)
HUH?

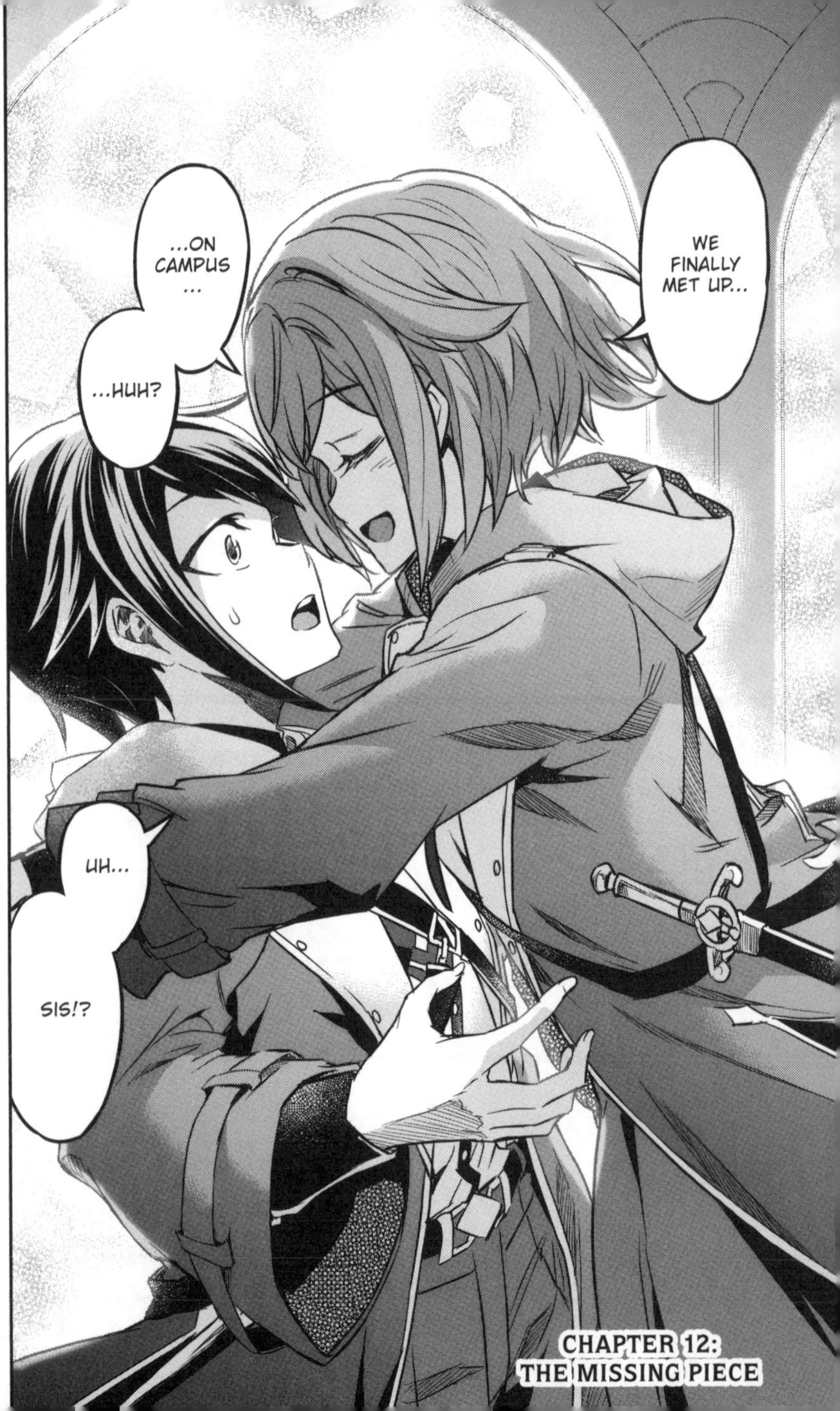
WE FINALLY MET UP...
...ON CAMPUS ...
...HUH?
UH...
SIS!?

CHAPTER 12: THE MISSING PIECE

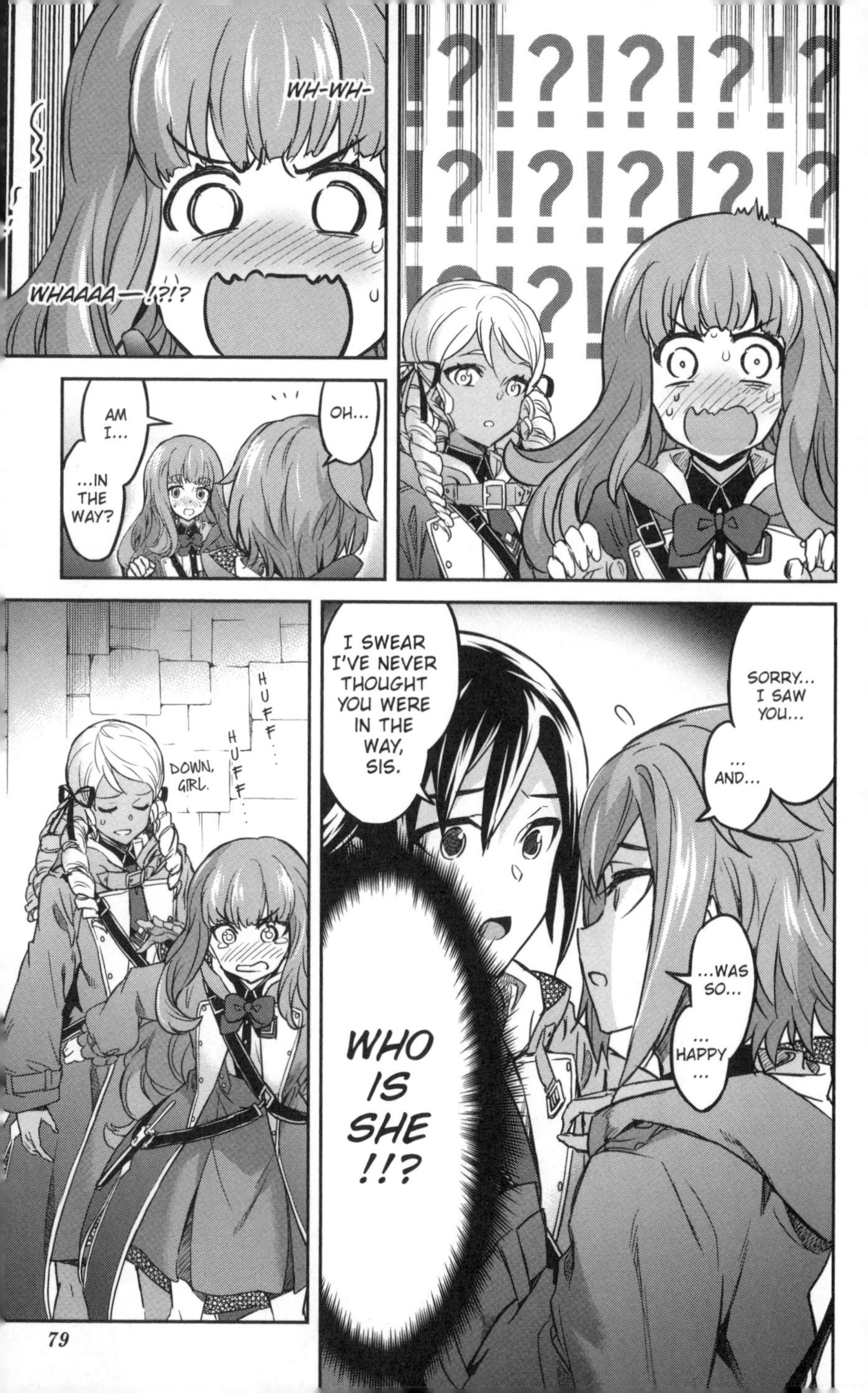
!?!?!?!?!?
!?!?!?!?!?
!?!?!
WH-WH-
WHAAAA—!?!?
OH...
AM I...
...IN THE WAY?
SORRY... I SAW YOU...
... AND...
...WAS SO...
... HAPPY ...
I SWEAR I'VE NEVER THOUGHT YOU WERE IN THE WAY, SIS.
WHO IS SHE !!?
HUFF...
HUFF...
DOWN, GIRL.

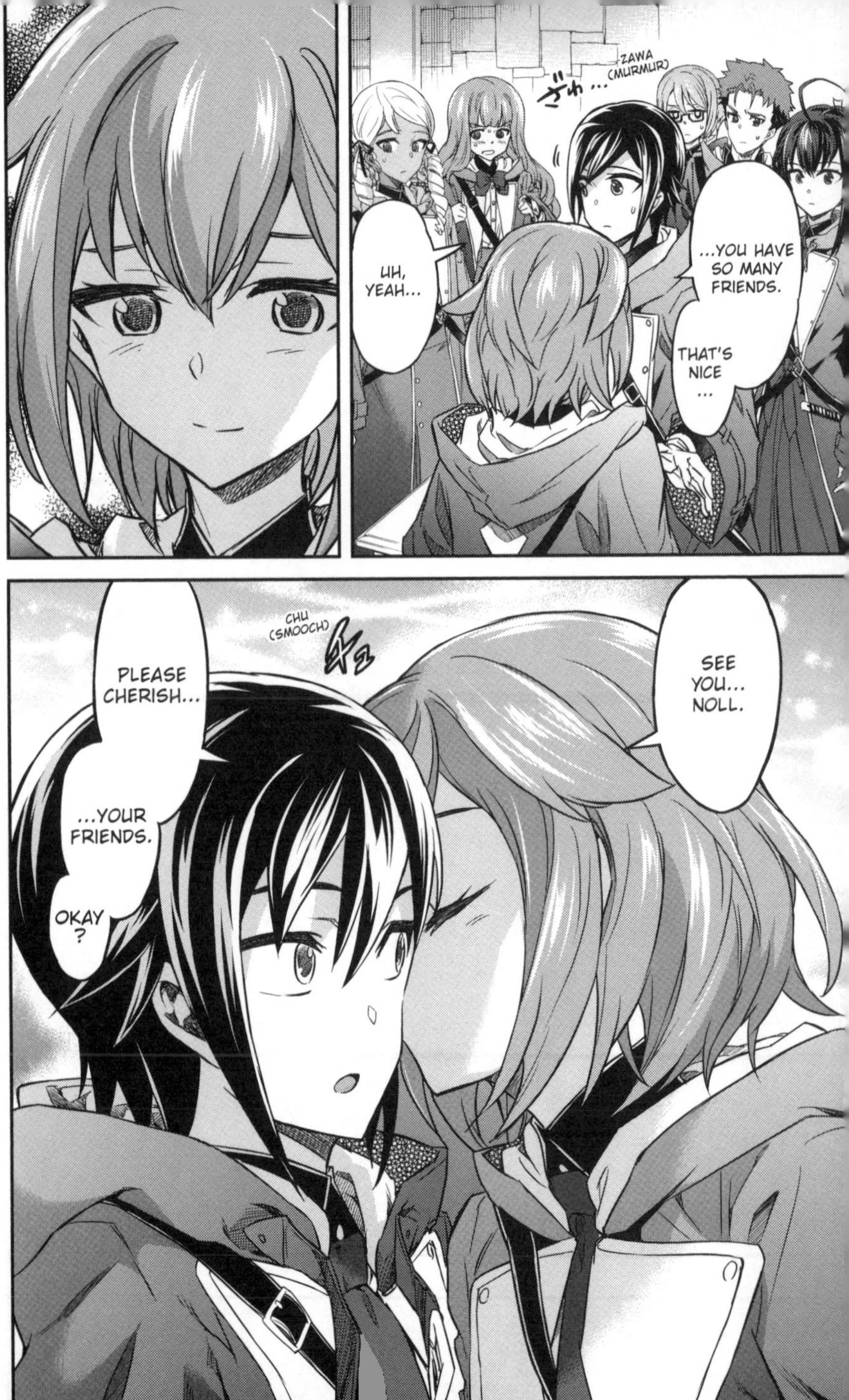
ZAWA (MURMUR)
...YOU HAVE SO MANY FRIENDS.
THAT'S NICE...
UH, YEAH...
SEE YOU... NOLL.
CHU (SMOOCH)
PLEASE CHERISH...
...YOUR FRIENDS.
OKAY?

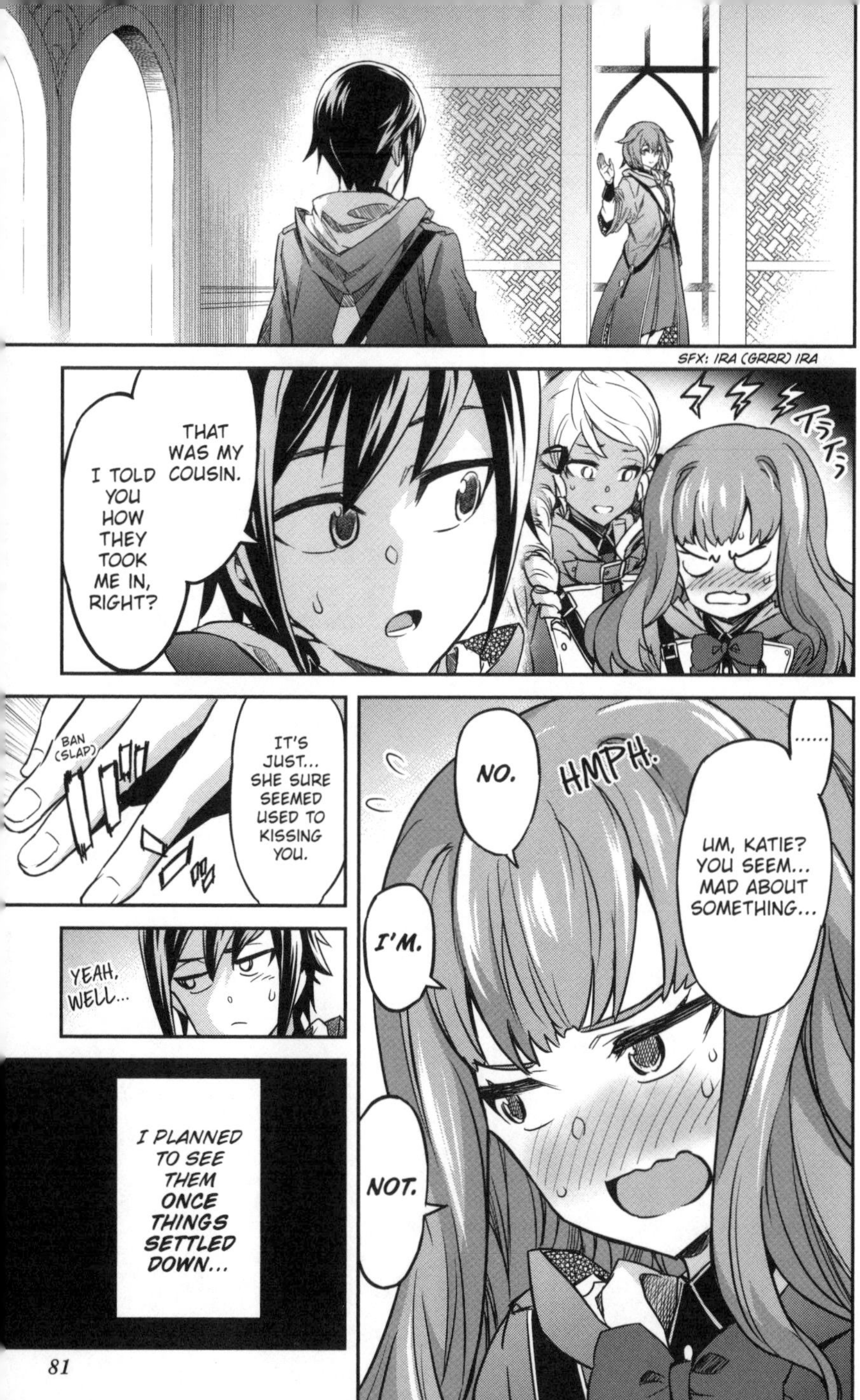
SFX: IRA (GRRR) IRA
THAT WAS MY COUSIN.
I TOLD YOU HOW THEY TOOK ME IN, RIGHT?
......
UM, KATIE? YOU SEEM... MAD ABOUT SOMETHING...
HMPH.
NO.
I'M.
NOT.
IT'S JUST... SHE SURE SEEMED USED TO KISSING YOU.
BAN (SLAP)
YEAH, WELL...
I PLANNED TO SEE THEM ONCE THINGS SETTLED DOWN...

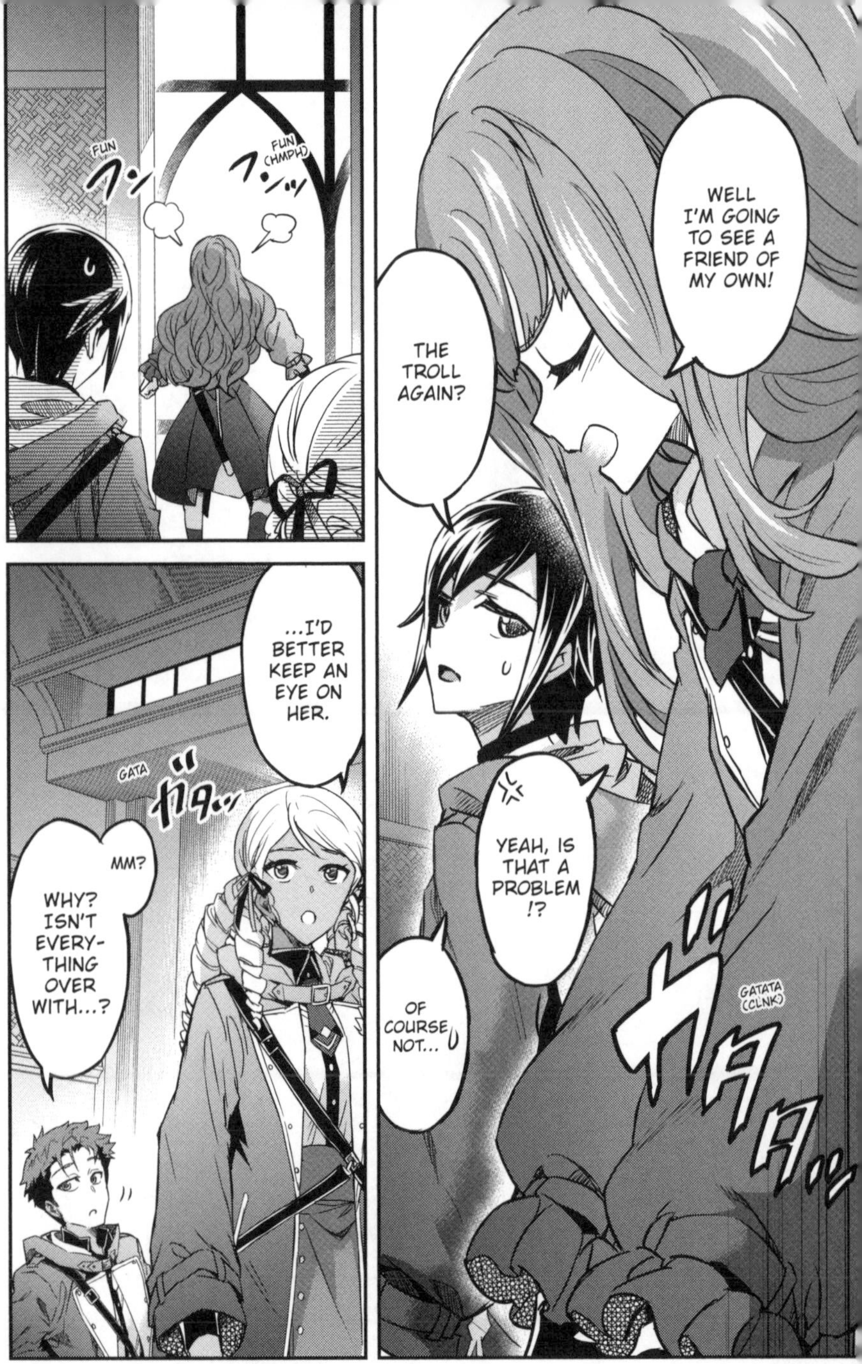
WELL I'M GOING TO SEE A FRIEND OF MY OWN!
THE TROLL AGAIN?
YEAH, IS THAT A PROBLEM !?
OF COURSE NOT...
GATATA (CLINK)
FUN (HMPH)
FUN
...I'D BETTER KEEP AN EYE ON HER.
GATA
MM?
WHY? ISN'T EVERY-THING OVER WITH...?

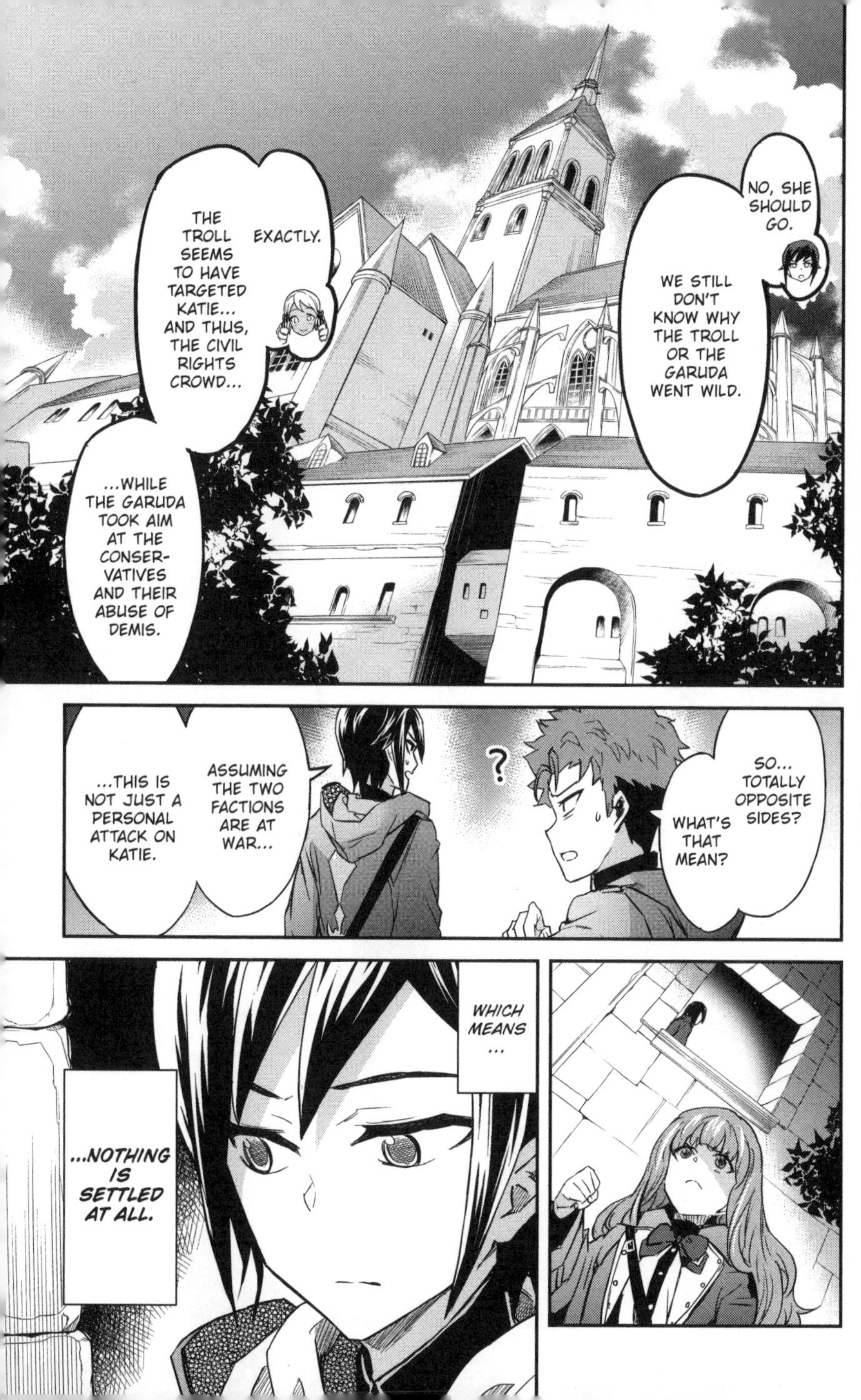
NO, SHE SHOULD GO.
WE STILL DON'T KNOW WHY THE TROLL OR THE GARUDA WENT WILD.
EXACTLY.
THE TROLL SEEMS TO HAVE TARGETED KATIE... AND THUS, THE CIVIL RIGHTS CROWD...
...WHILE THE GARUDA TOOK AIM AT THE CONSER-VATIVES AND THEIR ABUSE OF DEMIS.
SO... TOTALLY OPPOSITE SIDES?
WHAT'S THAT MEAN?
?
ASSUMING THE TWO FACTIONS ARE AT WAR...
...THIS IS NOT JUST A PERSONAL ATTACK ON KATIE.
WHICH MEANS...
...NOTHING IS SETTLED AT ALL.

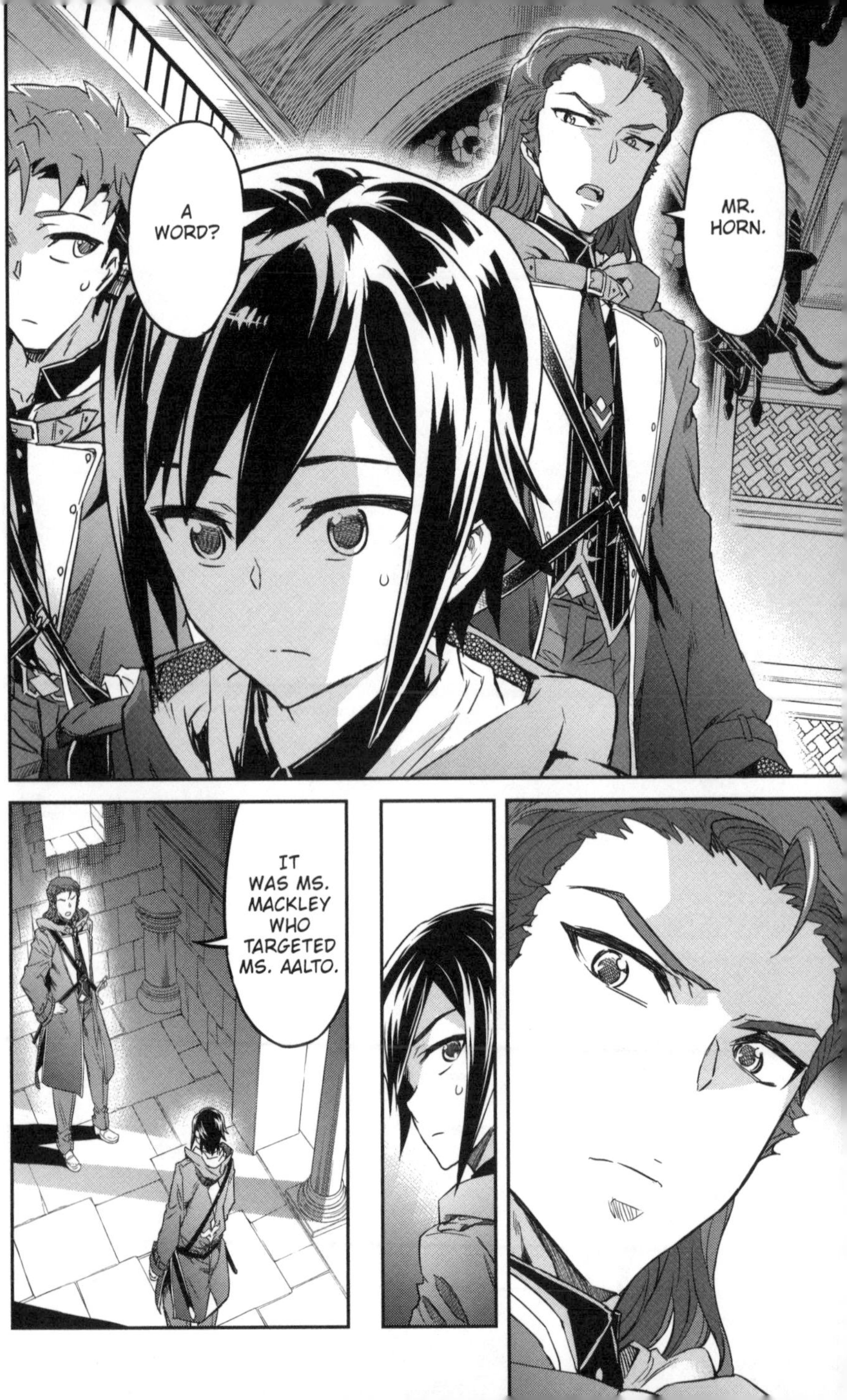
MR. HORN.
A WORD?
IT WAS MS. MACKLEY WHO TARGETED MS. AALTO.

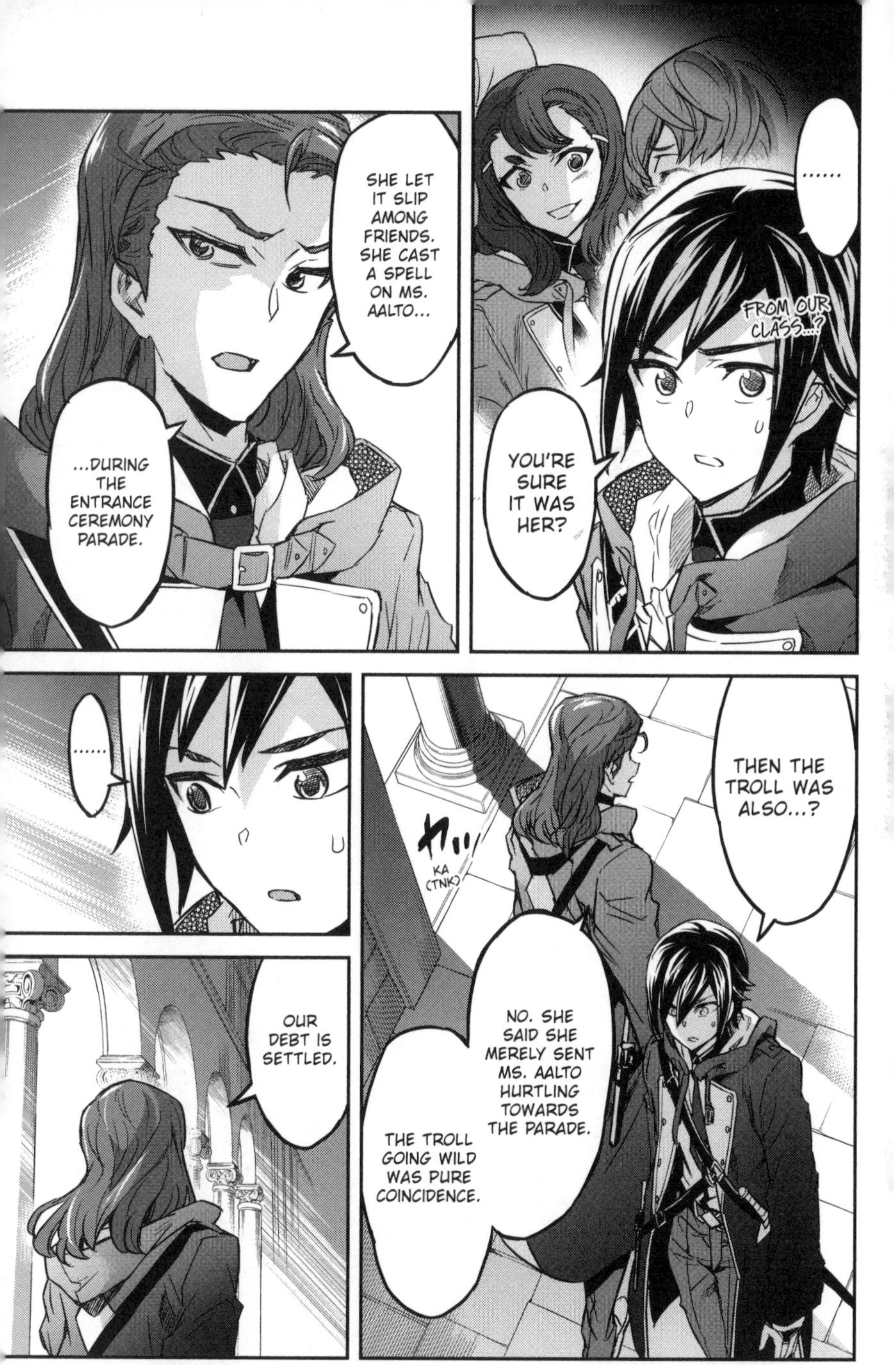
......
FROM OUR CLASS...?
YOU'RE SURE IT WAS HER?
SHE LET IT SLIP AMONG FRIENDS. SHE CAST A SPELL ON MS. AALTO...
...DURING THE ENTRANCE CEREMONY PARADE.
THEN THE TROLL WAS ALSO...?
KA (TNK)
NO. SHE SAID SHE MERELY SENT MS. AALTO HURTLING TOWARDS THE PARADE.
THE TROLL GOING WILD WAS PURE COINCIDENCE.
......
OUR DEBT IS SETTLED.

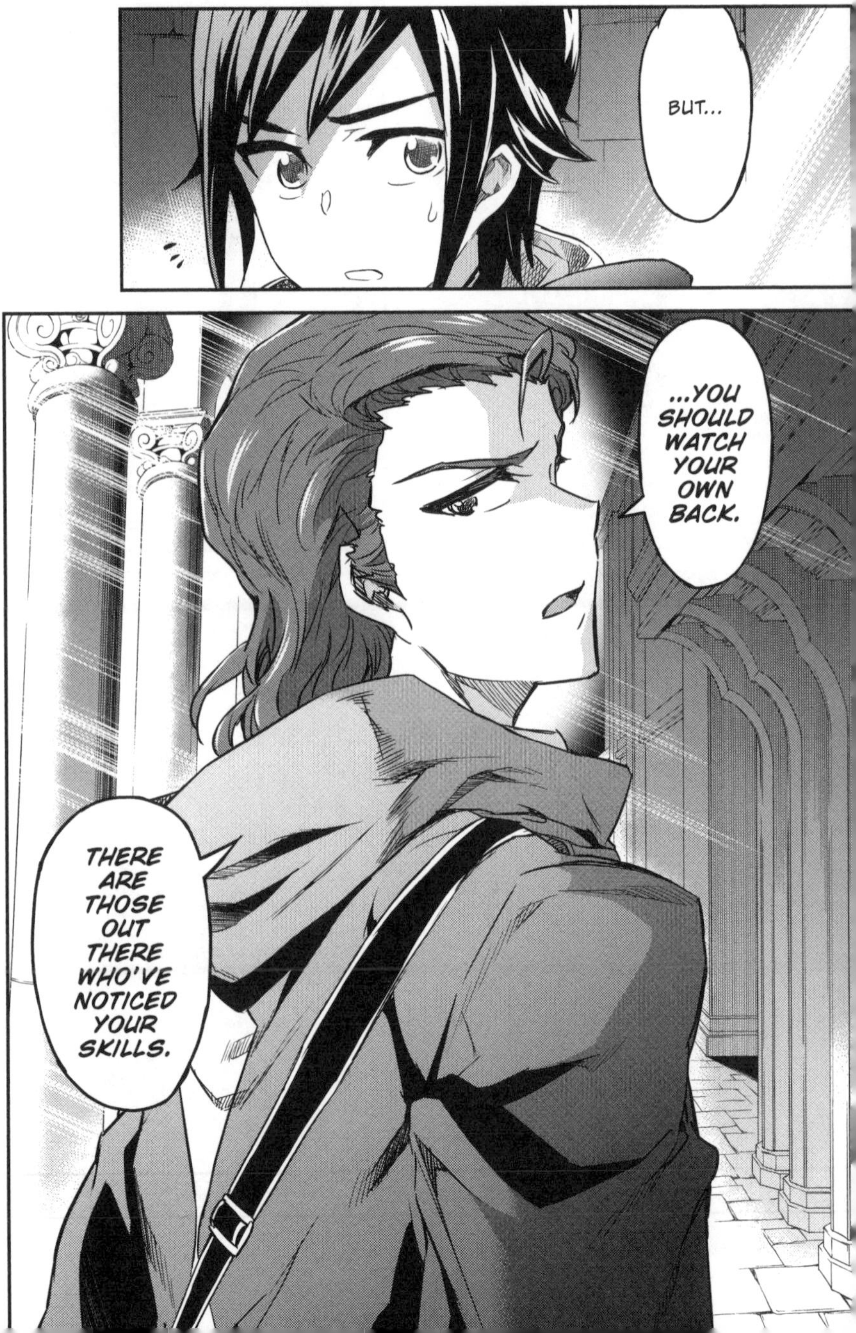
BUT...
...YOU SHOULD WATCH YOUR OWN BACK.
THERE ARE THOSE OUT THERE WHO'VE NOTICED YOUR SKILLS.

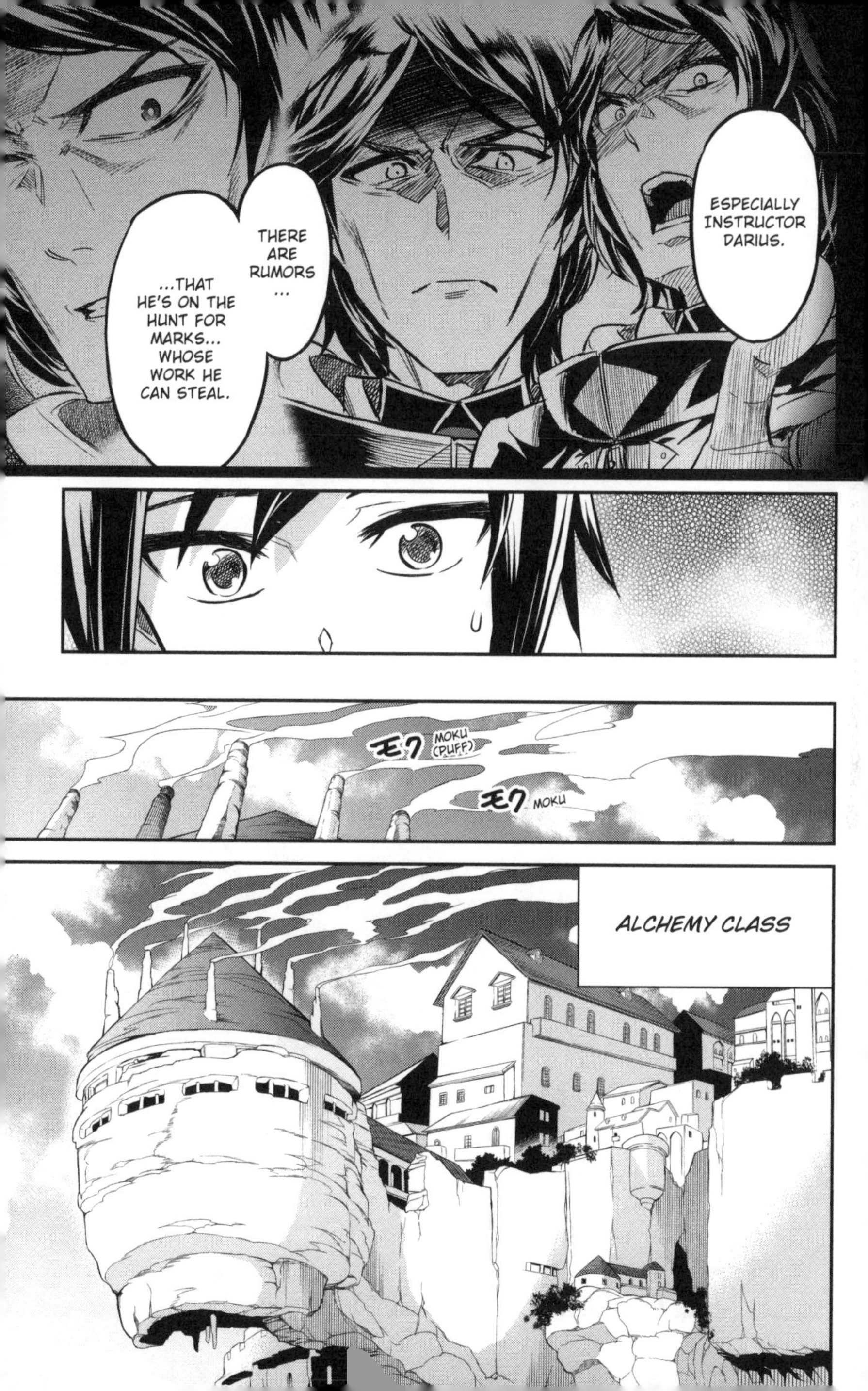
ESPECIALLY INSTRUCTOR DARIUS.
THERE ARE RUMORS...
...THAT HE'S ON THE HUNT FOR MARKS... WHOSE WORK HE CAN STEAL.
モク MOKU (PUFF)
モク MOKU
ALCHEMY CLASS

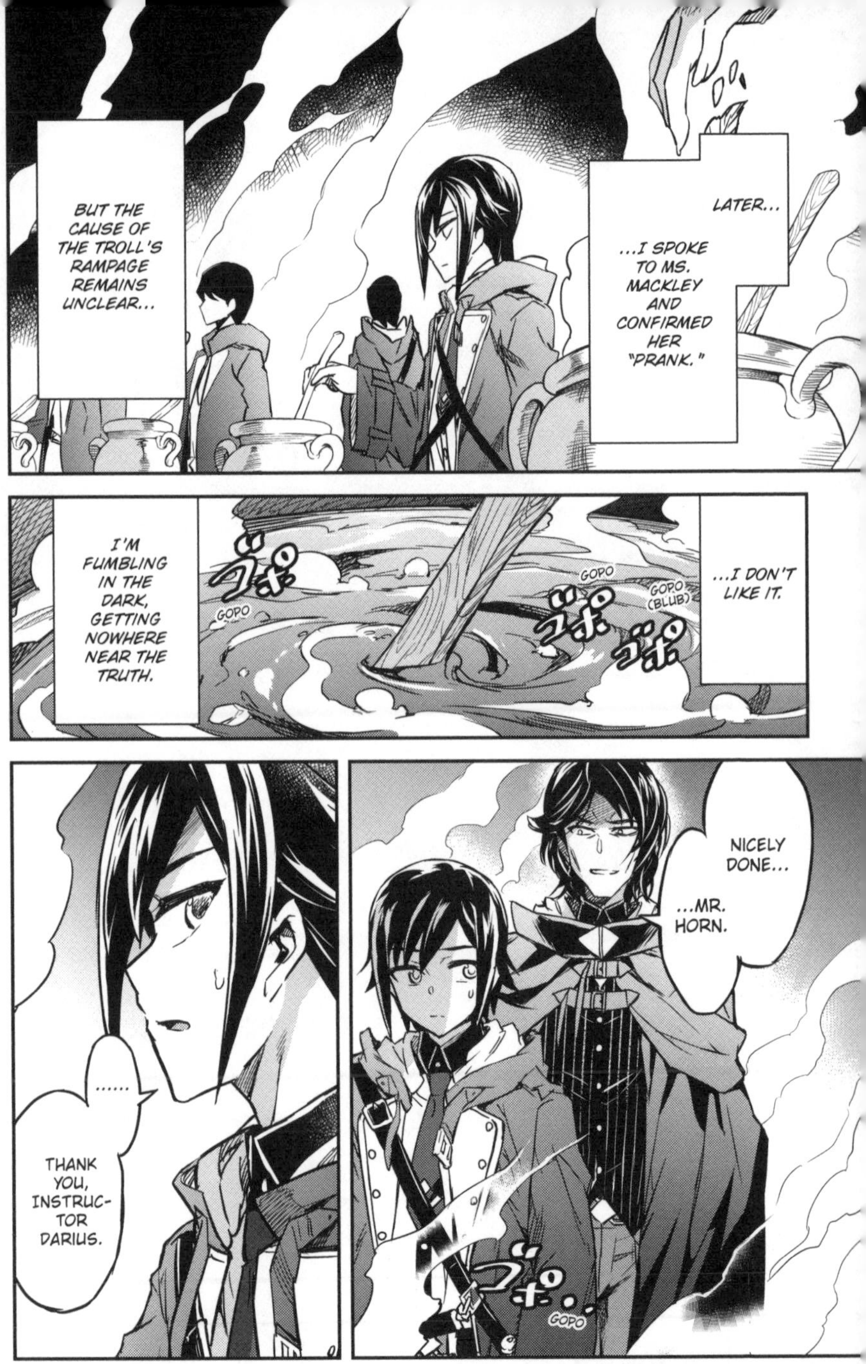
LATER...
...I SPOKE TO MS. MACKLEY AND CONFIRMED HER "PRANK."
BUT THE CAUSE OF THE TROLL'S RAMPAGE REMAINS UNCLEAR...
...I DON'T LIKE IT.
ゴポ
GOPO (BLUB)
ゴポ
GOPO
ゴポ
GOPO
I'M FUMBLING IN THE DARK, GETTING NOWHERE NEAR THE TRUTH.
NICELY DONE...
...MR. HORN.
ゴポ..
GOPO
......
THANK YOU, INSTRUCTOR DARIUS.

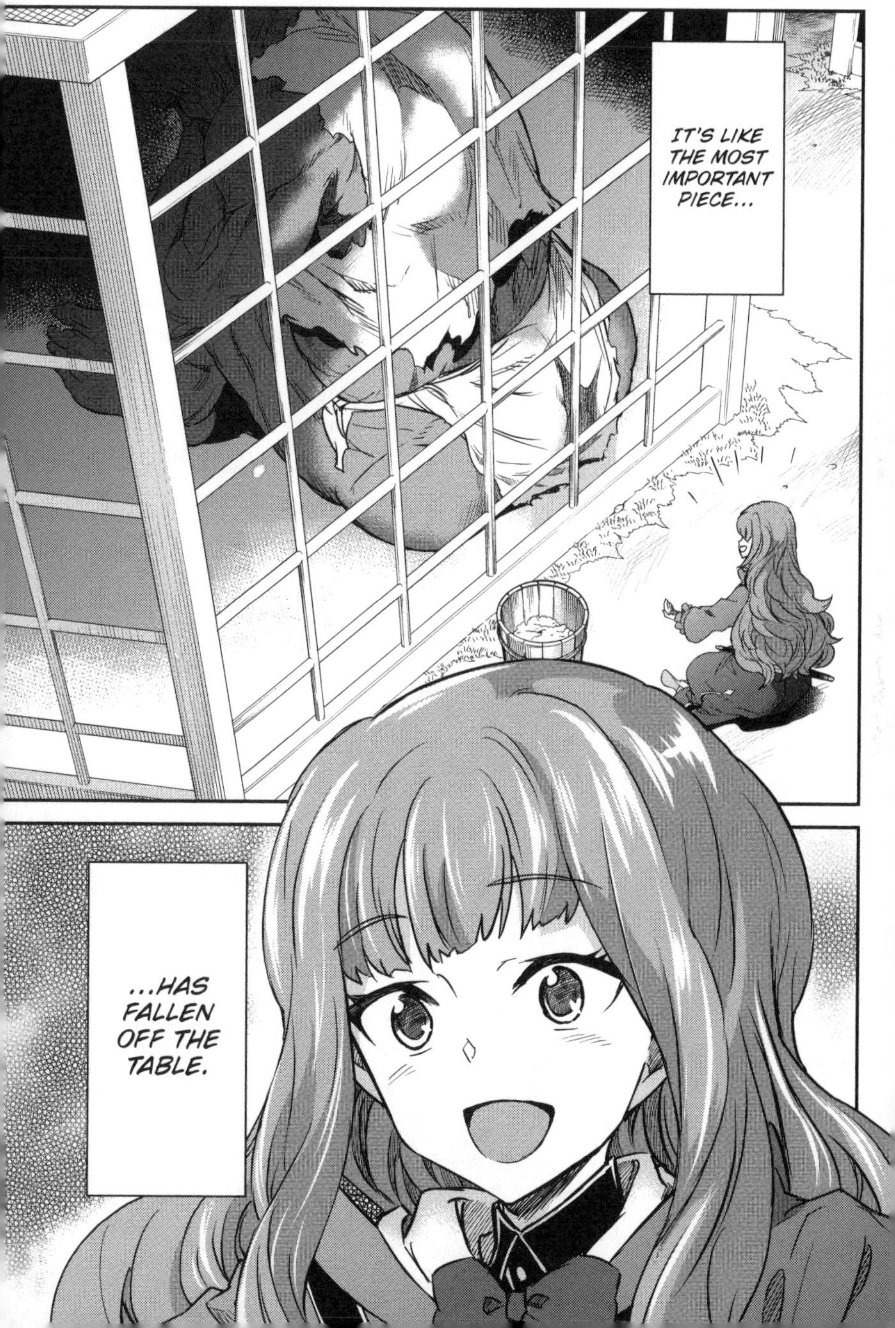
IT'S LIKE THE MOST IMPORTANT PIECE...
...HAS FALLEN OFF THE TABLE.

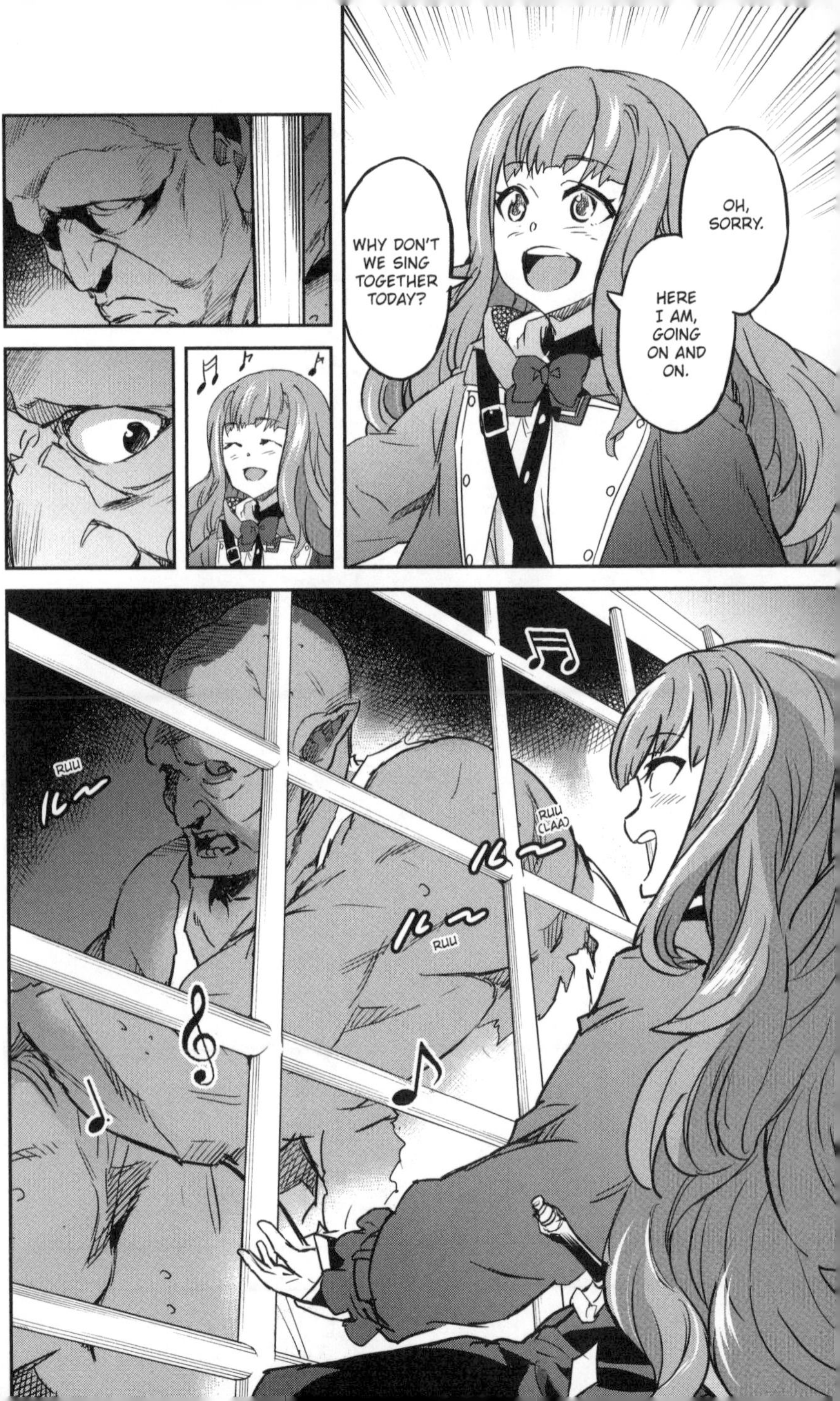
OH, SORRY.
HERE I AM, GOING ON AND ON.
WHY DON'T WE SING TOGETHER TODAY?
RUU (LAA)
ル~
ル~
RUU
RUU
ル~

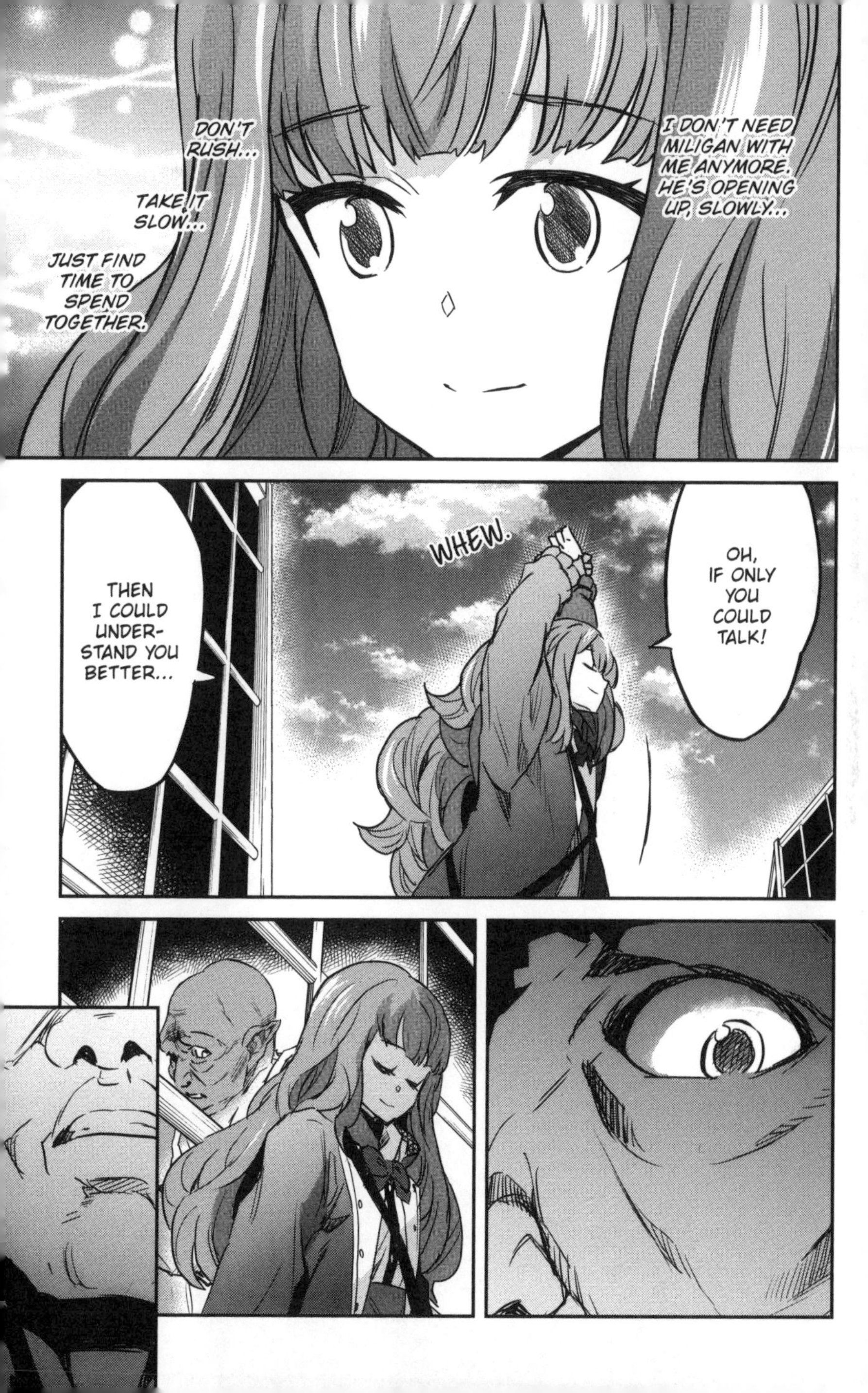
I DON'T NEED MILIGAN WITH ME ANYMORE. HE'S OPENING UP, SLOWLY...
DON'T RUSH...
TAKE IT SLOW...
JUST FIND TIME TO SPEND TOGETHER.
OH, IF ONLY YOU COULD TALK!
WHEW.
THEN I COULD UNDERSTAND YOU BETTER...

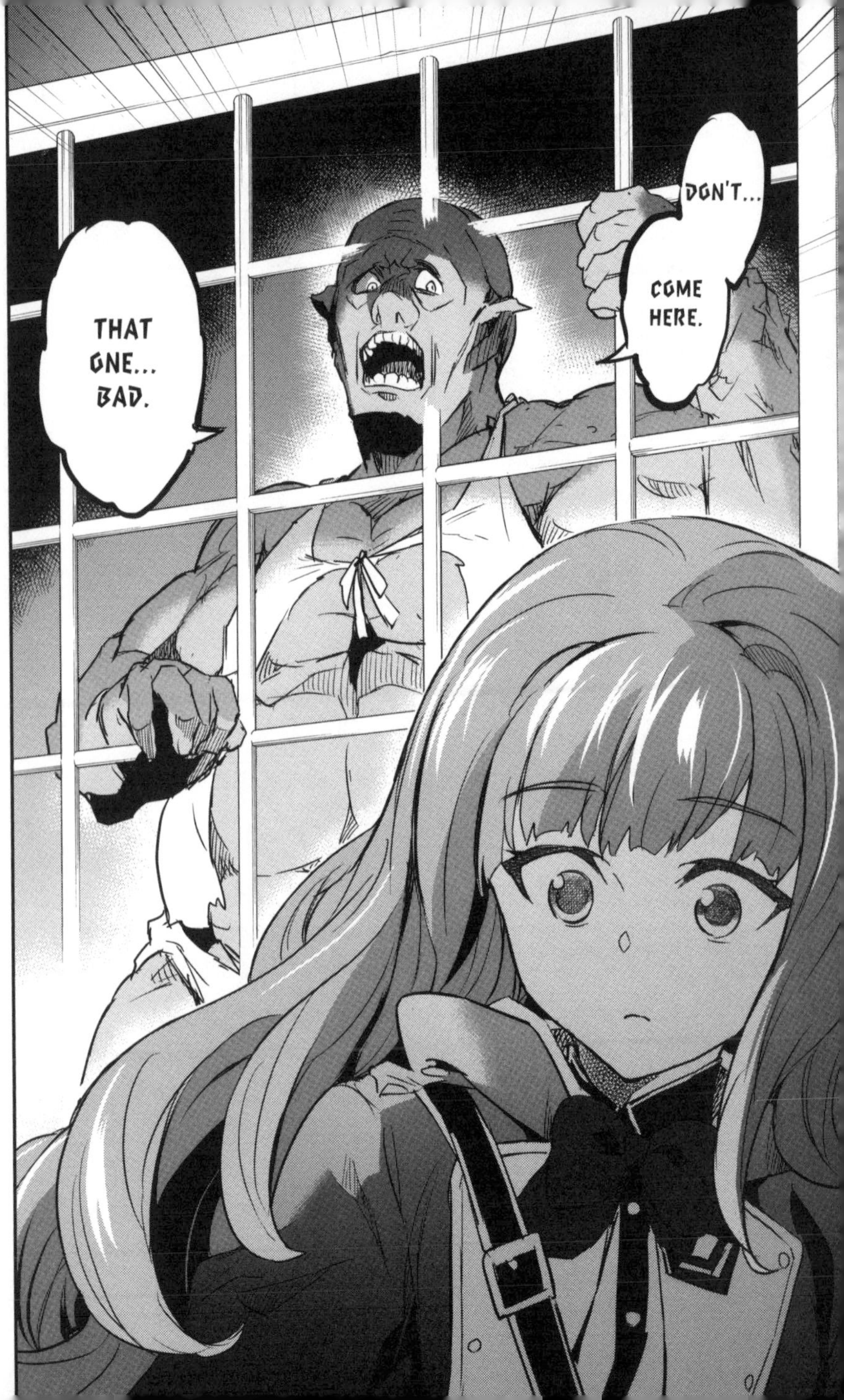
DON'T...
COME HERE.
THAT ONE... BAD.

STAY
AWAY.

NOT
SAFE.

YOU...

PACHI
(SPARK)

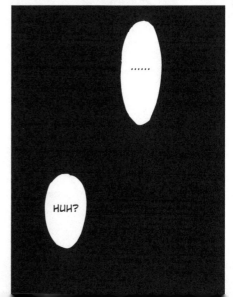

......

HUH?

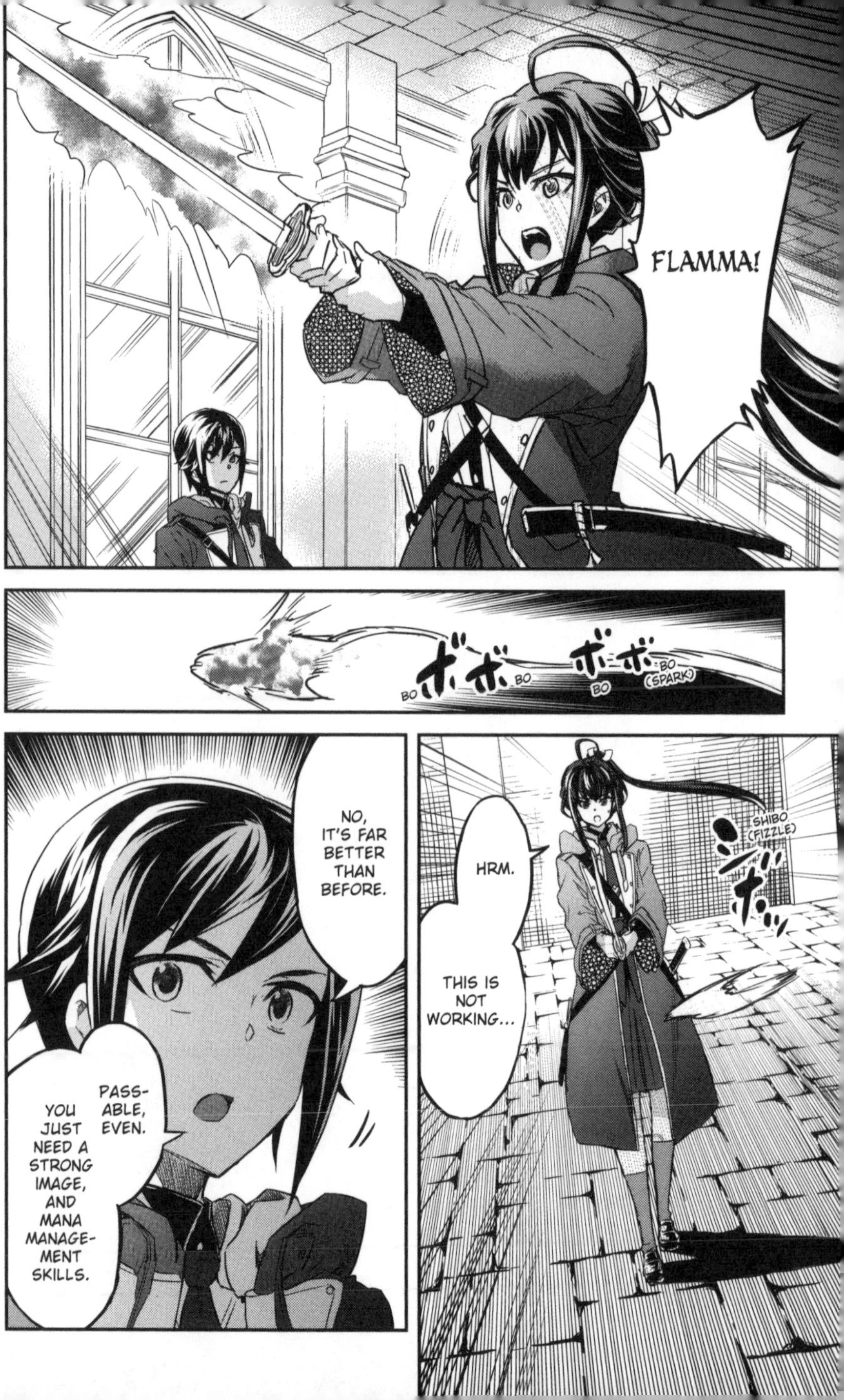
FLAMMA!
ボボ
BO
BO
ボボ
BO
BO
BO (SPARK)
シボ
SHIBO (FIZZLE)
HRM.
THIS IS NOT WORKING...
NO, IT'S FAR BETTER THAN BEFORE.
PASS-ABLE, EVEN.
YOU JUST NEED A STRONG IMAGE, AND MANA MANAGE-MENT SKILLS.

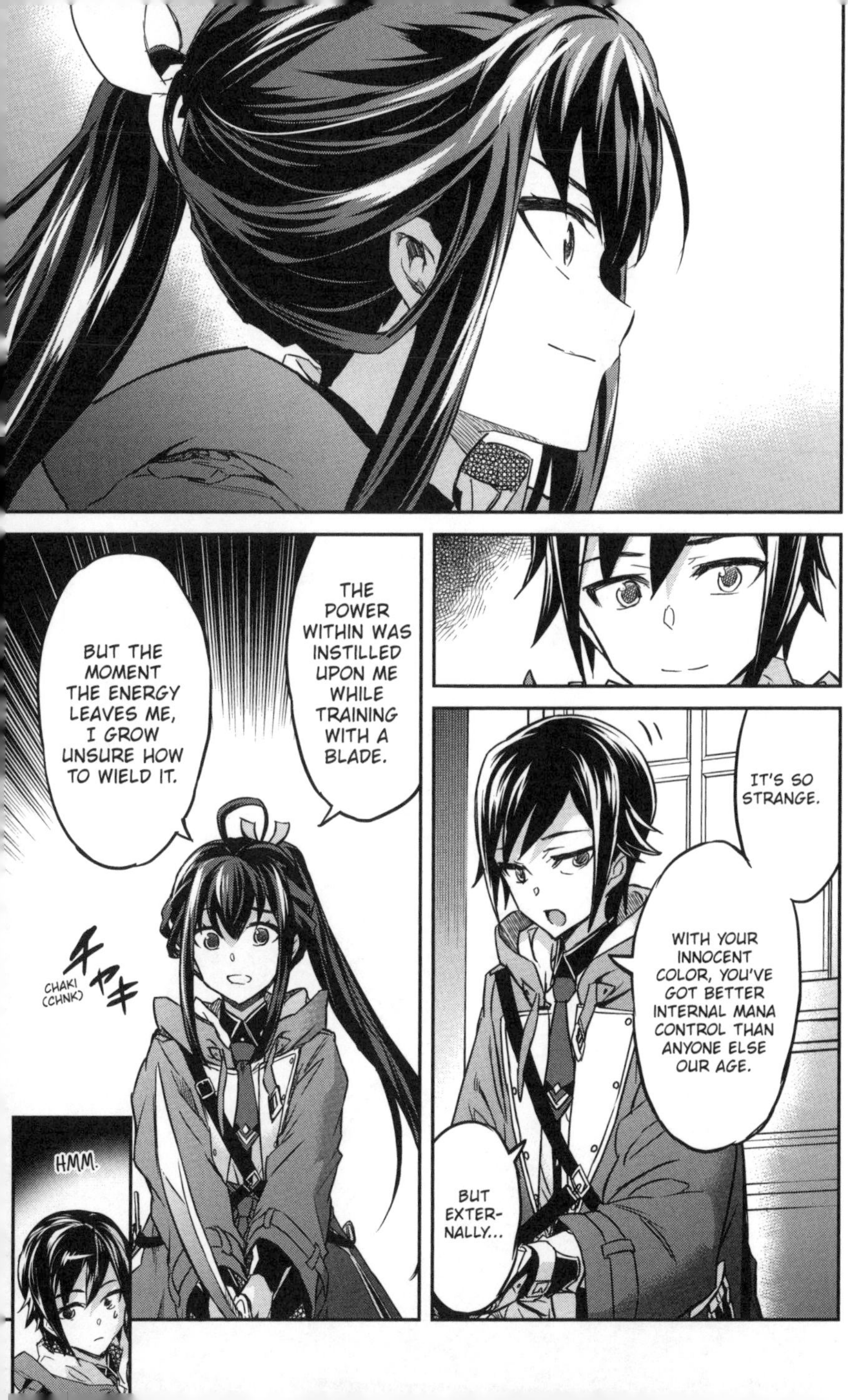
IT'S SO STRANGE.
WITH YOUR INNOCENT COLOR, YOU'VE GOT BETTER INTERNAL MANA CONTROL THAN ANYONE ELSE OUR AGE.
BUT EXTER-NALLY...
THE POWER WITHIN WAS INSTILLED UPON ME WHILE TRAINING WITH A BLADE.
BUT THE MOMENT THE ENERGY LEAVES ME, I GROW UNSURE HOW TO WIELD IT.
チャキ
CHAKI (CHNK)
HMM.

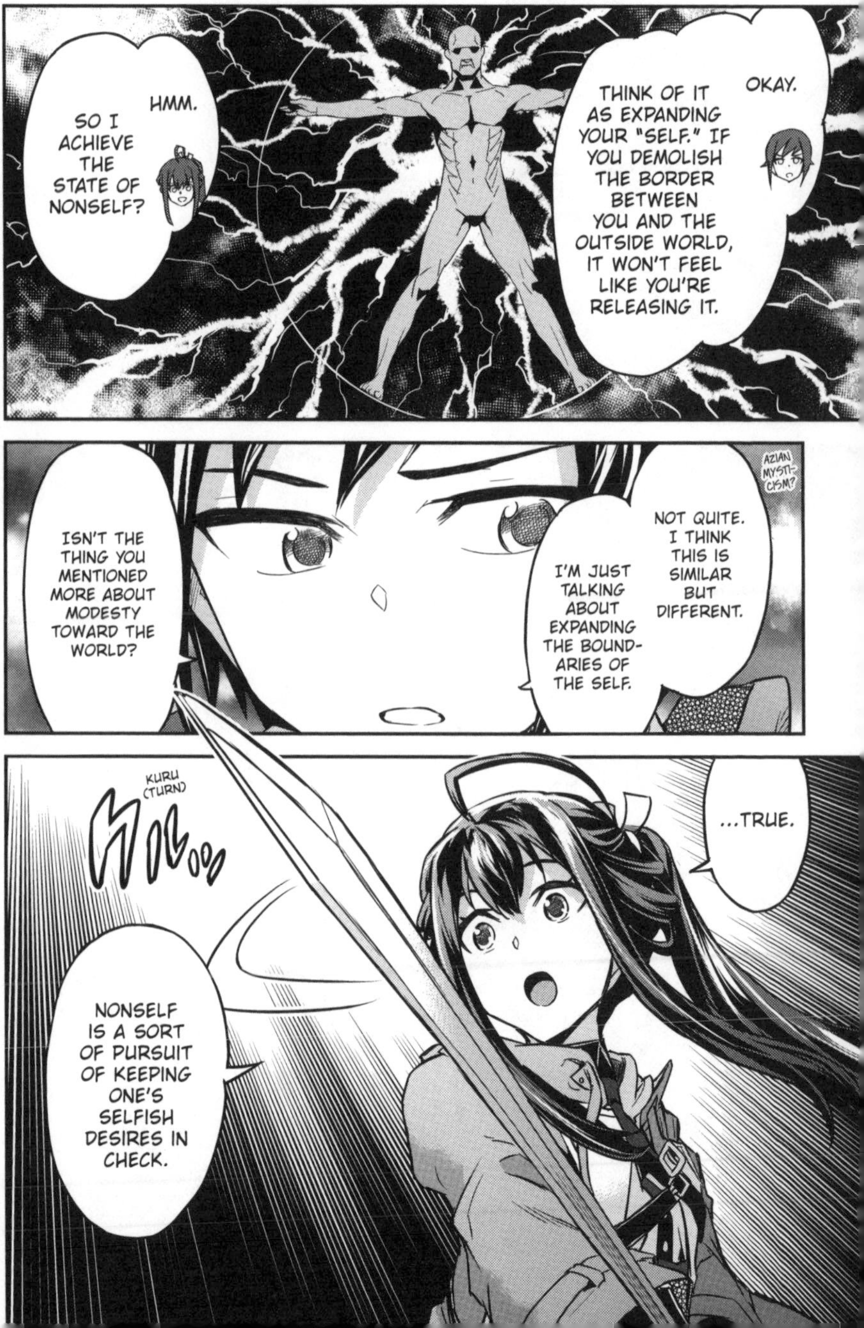
OKAY.
THINK OF IT AS EXPANDING YOUR "SELF." IF YOU DEMOLISH THE BORDER BETWEEN YOU AND THE OUTSIDE WORLD, IT WON'T FEEL LIKE YOU'RE RELEASING IT.
HMM.
SO I ACHIEVE THE STATE OF NONSELF?
AZIAN MYSTI-CISM?
NOT QUITE. I THINK THIS IS SIMILAR BUT DIFFERENT.
I'M JUST TALKING ABOUT EXPANDING THE BOUND-ARIES OF THE SELF.
ISN'T THE THING YOU MENTIONED MORE ABOUT MODESTY TOWARD THE WORLD?
...TRUE.
KURU (TURN)
NONSELF IS A SORT OF PURSUIT OF KEEPING ONE'S SELFISH DESIRES IN CHECK.

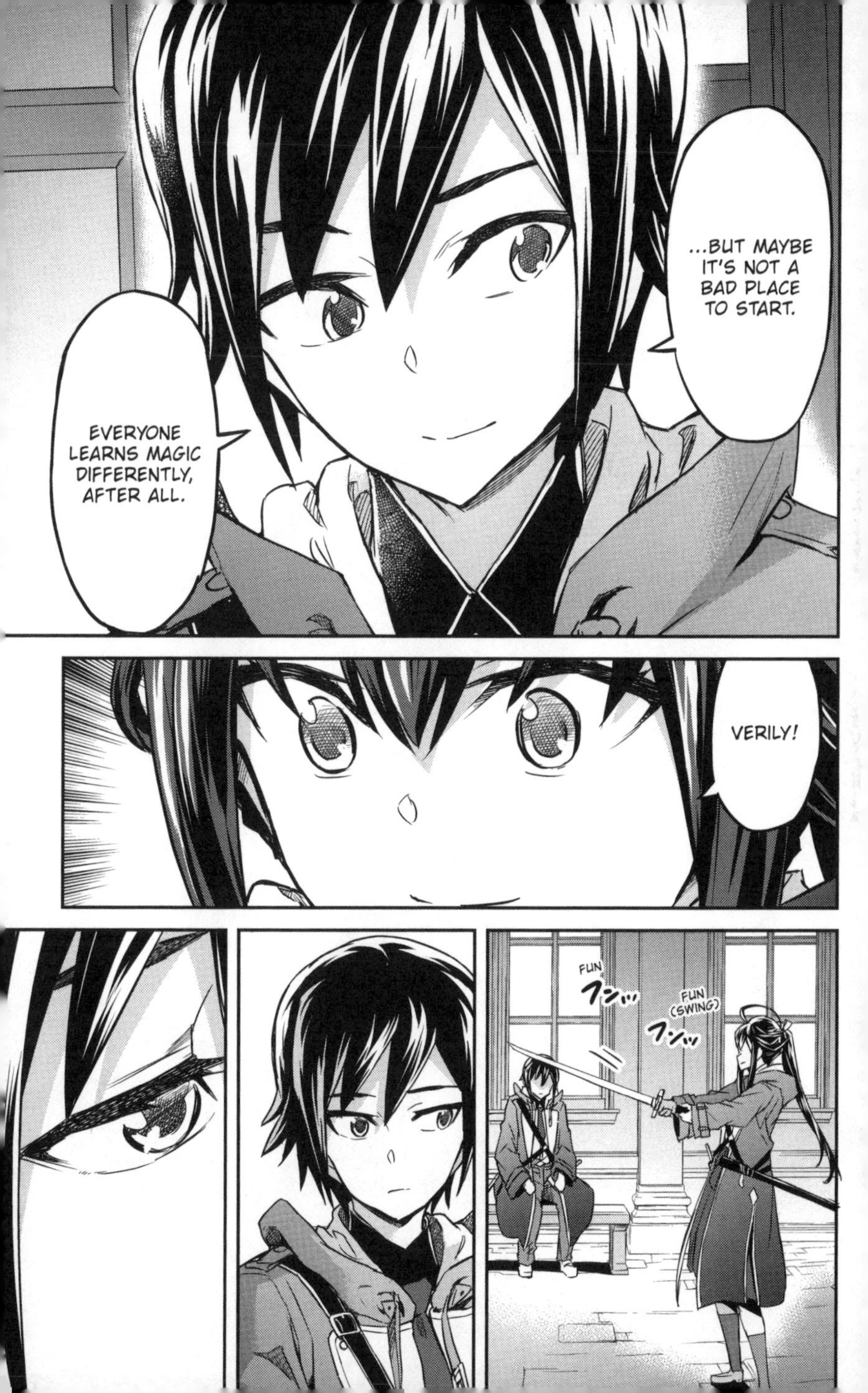
...BUT MAYBE IT'S NOT A BAD PLACE TO START.
EVERYONE LEARNS MAGIC DIFFERENTLY, AFTER ALL.
VERILY!
FUN
フンッ
FUN (SWING)
フンッ

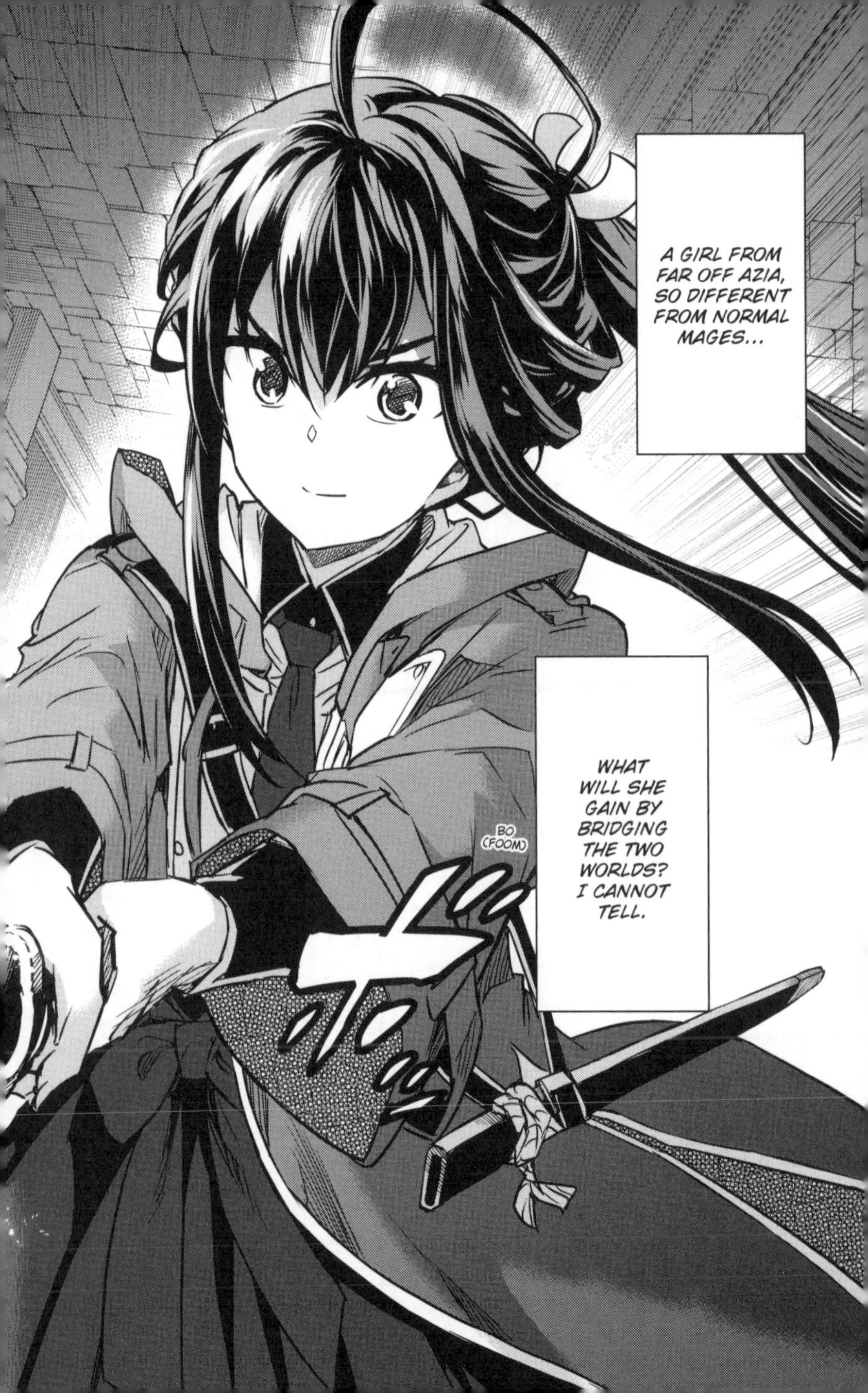
A GIRL FROM FAR OFF AZIA, SO DIFFERENT FROM NORMAL MAGES...
WHAT WILL SHE GAIN BY BRIDGING THE TWO WORLDS? I CANNOT TELL.
BO (FOOM)

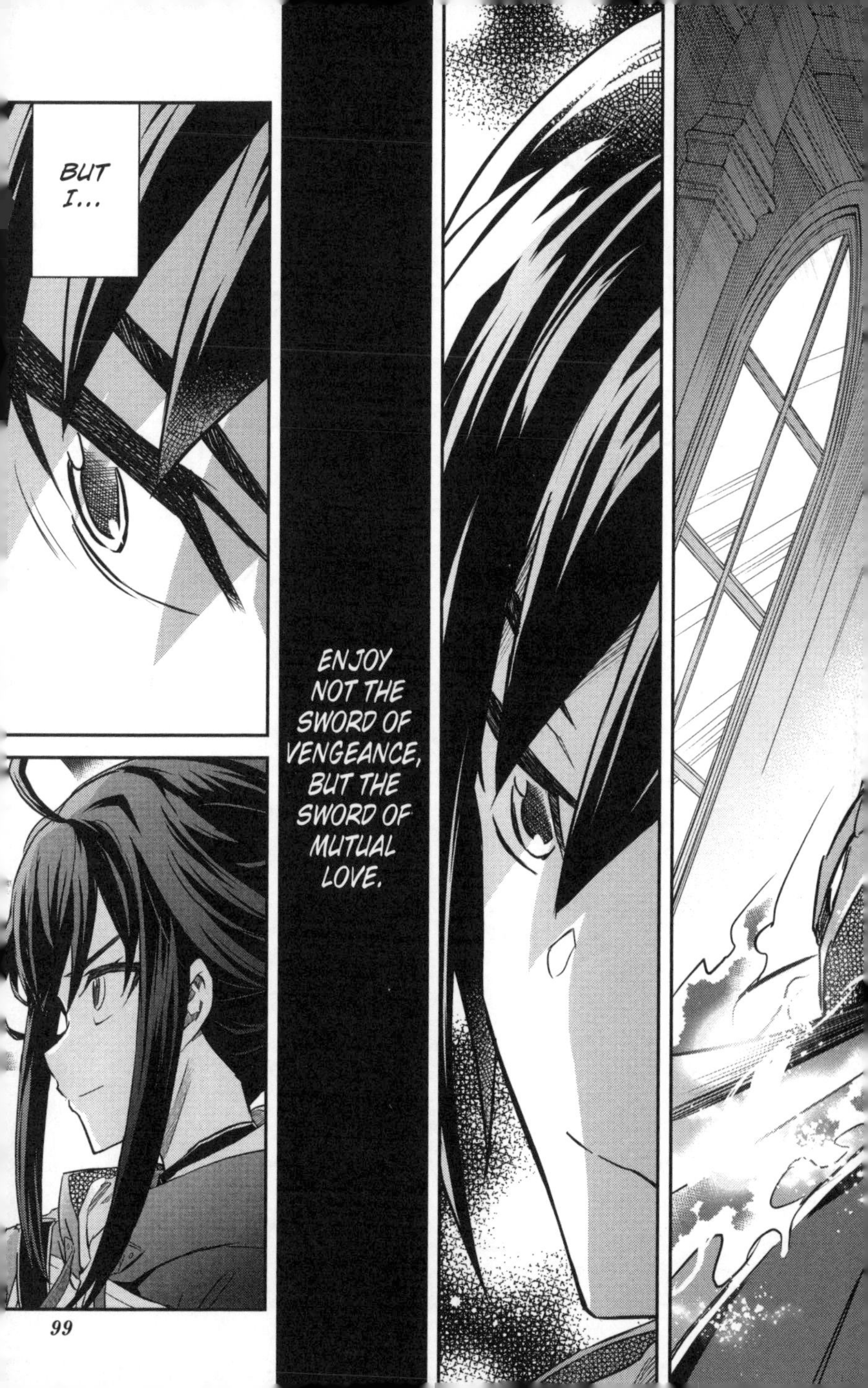
BUT I...
ENJOY NOT THE SWORD OF VENGEANCE, BUT THE SWORD OF MUTUAL LOVE.

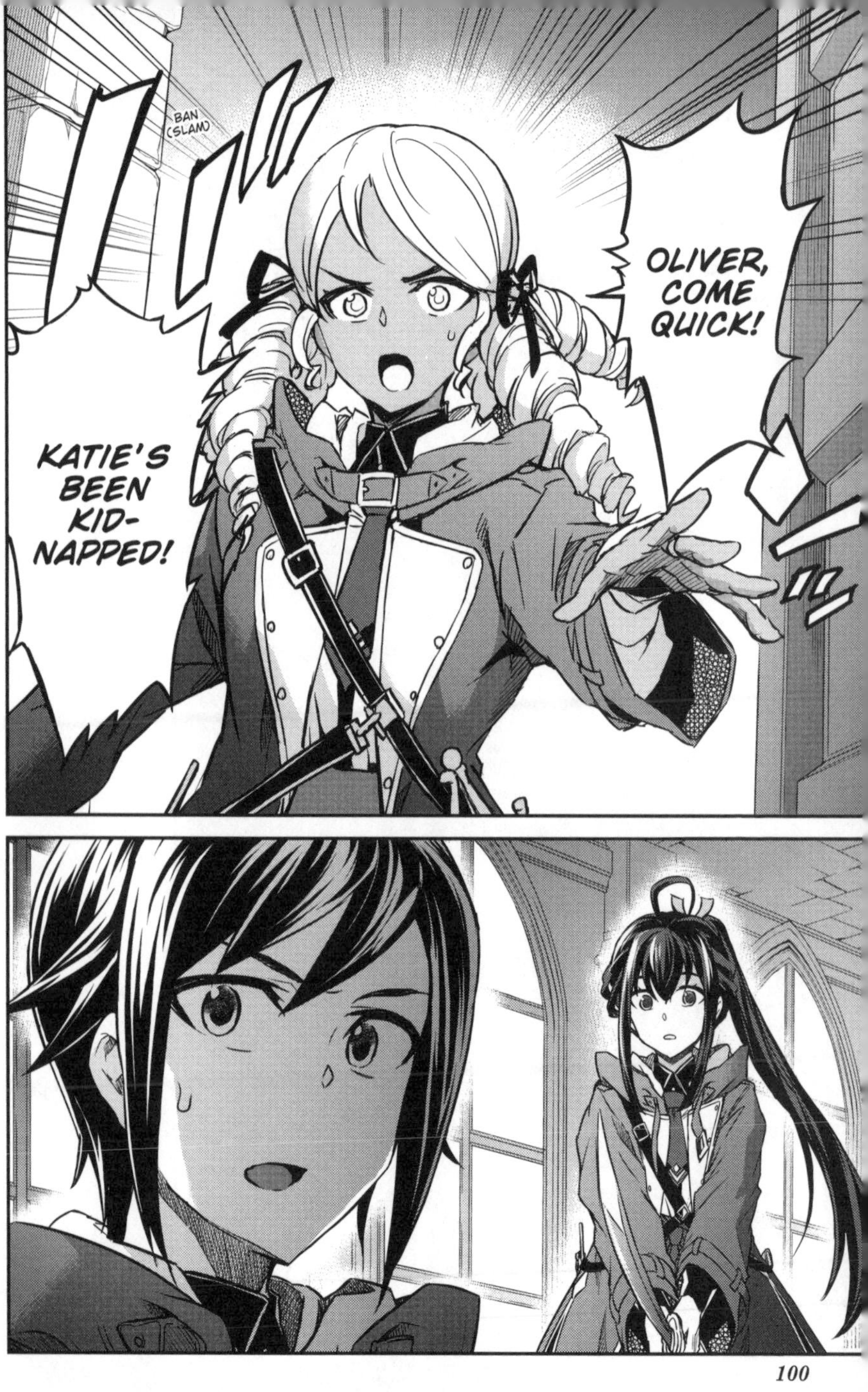
BAN (SLAM)
OLIVER, COME QUICK!
KATIE'S BEEN KID-NAPPED!

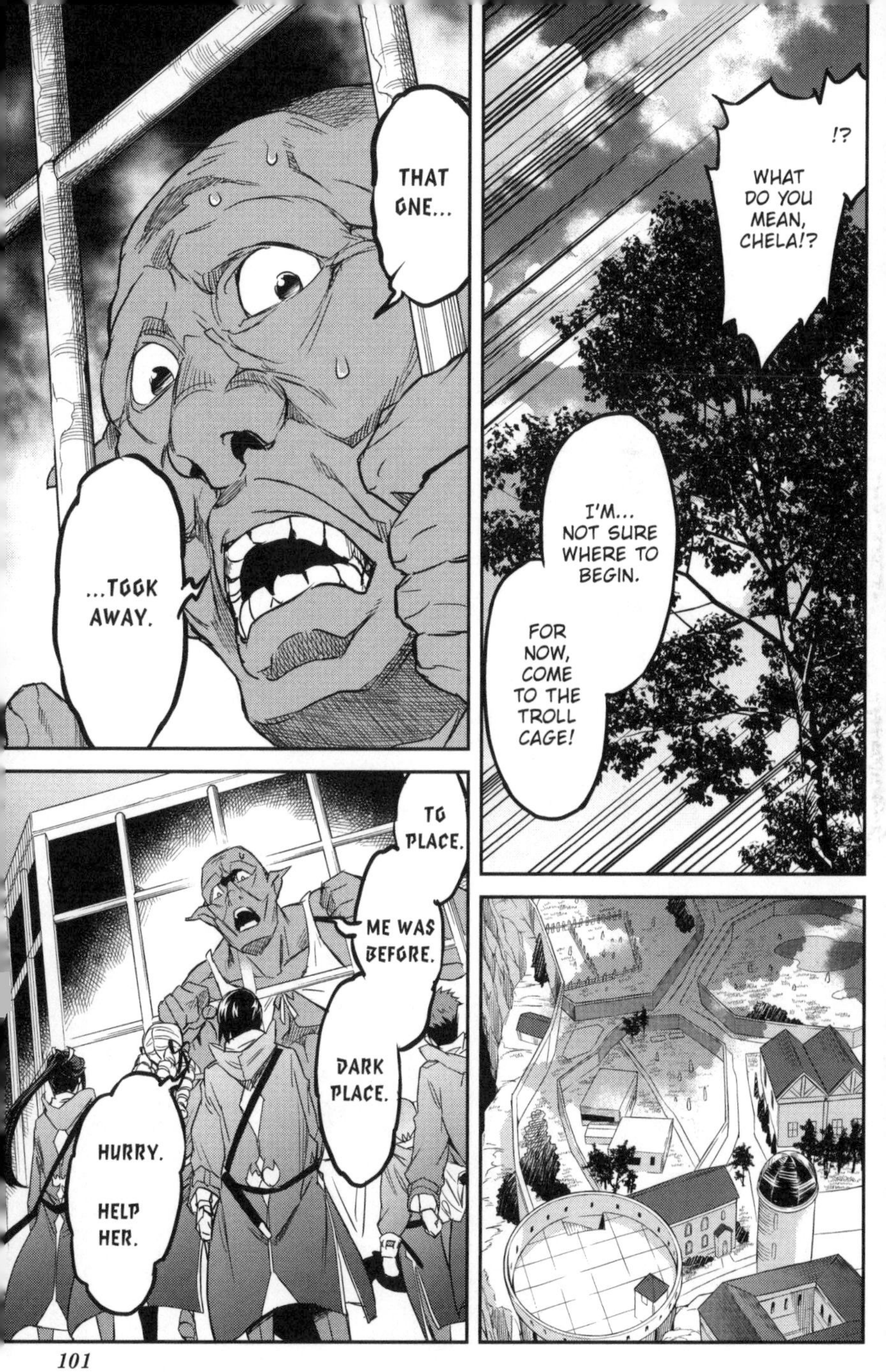
!?
WHAT DO YOU MEAN, CHELA!?
I'M... NOT SURE WHERE TO BEGIN.
FOR NOW, COME TO THE TROLL CAGE!
THAT ONE...
...TOOK AWAY.
TO PLACE.
ME WAS BEFORE.
DARK PLACE.
HURRY.
HELP HER.

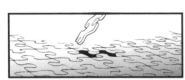

PACHI
(SNAP)

......

TH-THE TROLL IS TALKING ...!?

CHELA...

YOU KNOW **WHAT THIS MEANS,** DON'T YOU?

BA
(SHPP)

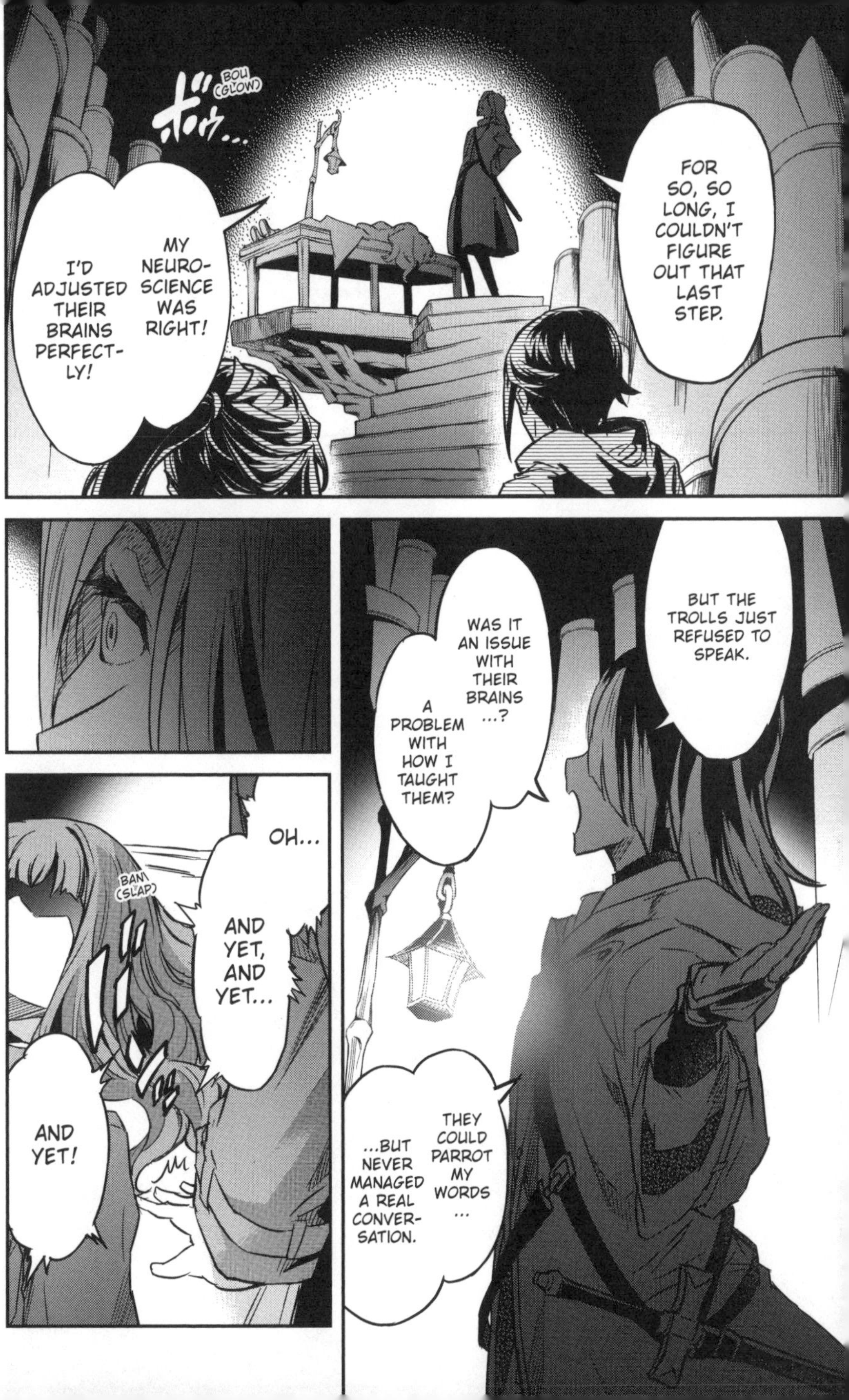
FOR SO, SO LONG, I COULDN'T FIGURE OUT THAT LAST STEP.
BOU (GLOW)
MY NEURO-SCIENCE WAS RIGHT!
I'D ADJUSTED THEIR BRAINS PERFECTLY!
BUT THE TROLLS JUST REFUSED TO SPEAK.
WAS IT AN ISSUE WITH THEIR BRAINS ...?
A PROBLEM WITH HOW I TAUGHT THEM?
THEY COULD PARROT MY WORDS ...
...BUT NEVER MANAGED A REAL CONVERSATION.
OH...
BAN (SLAP)
AND YET, AND YET...
AND YET!

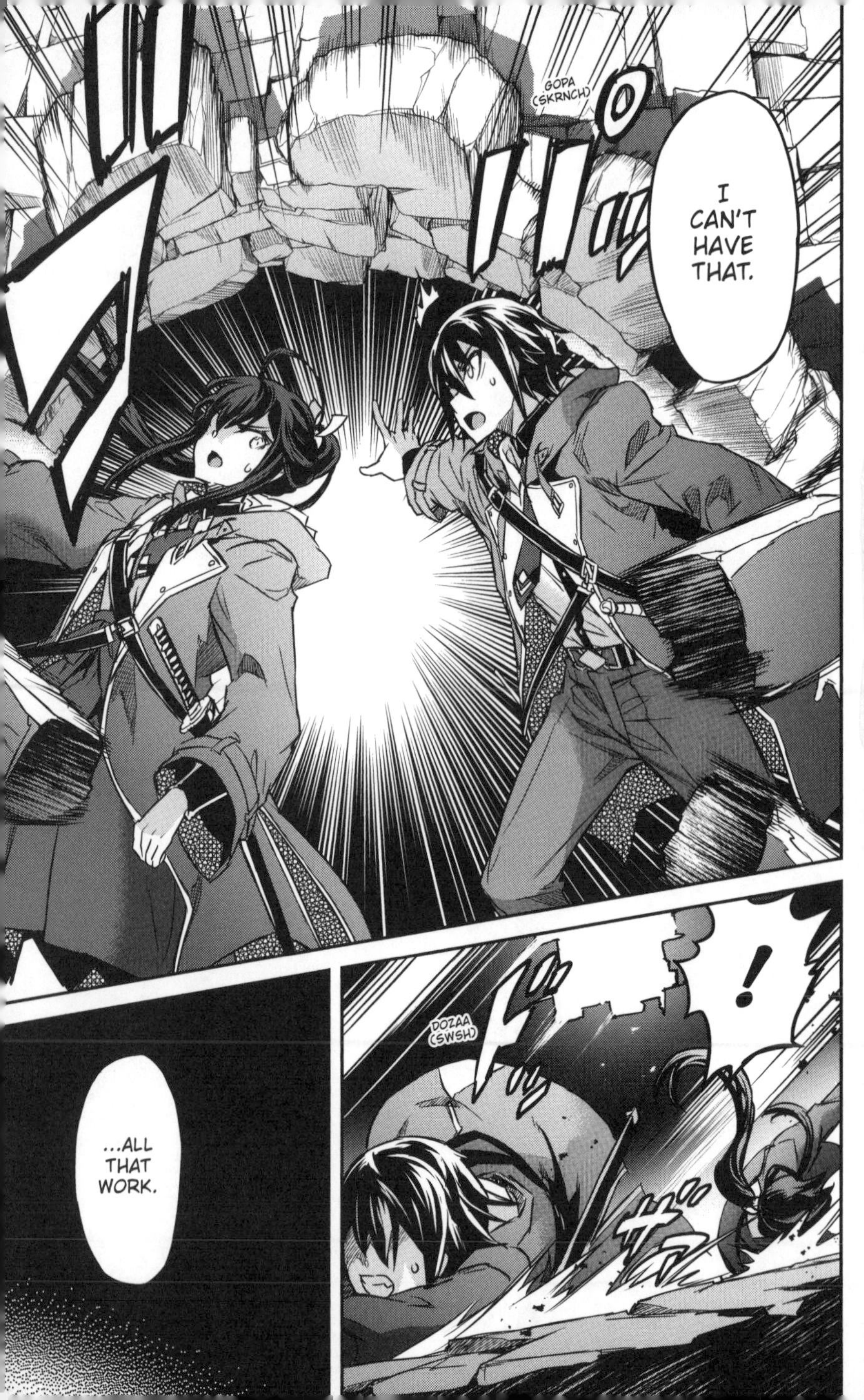
GOPA (SKRNCH)
I CAN'T HAVE THAT.
DOZAA (SWSH)
!
...ALL THAT WORK.

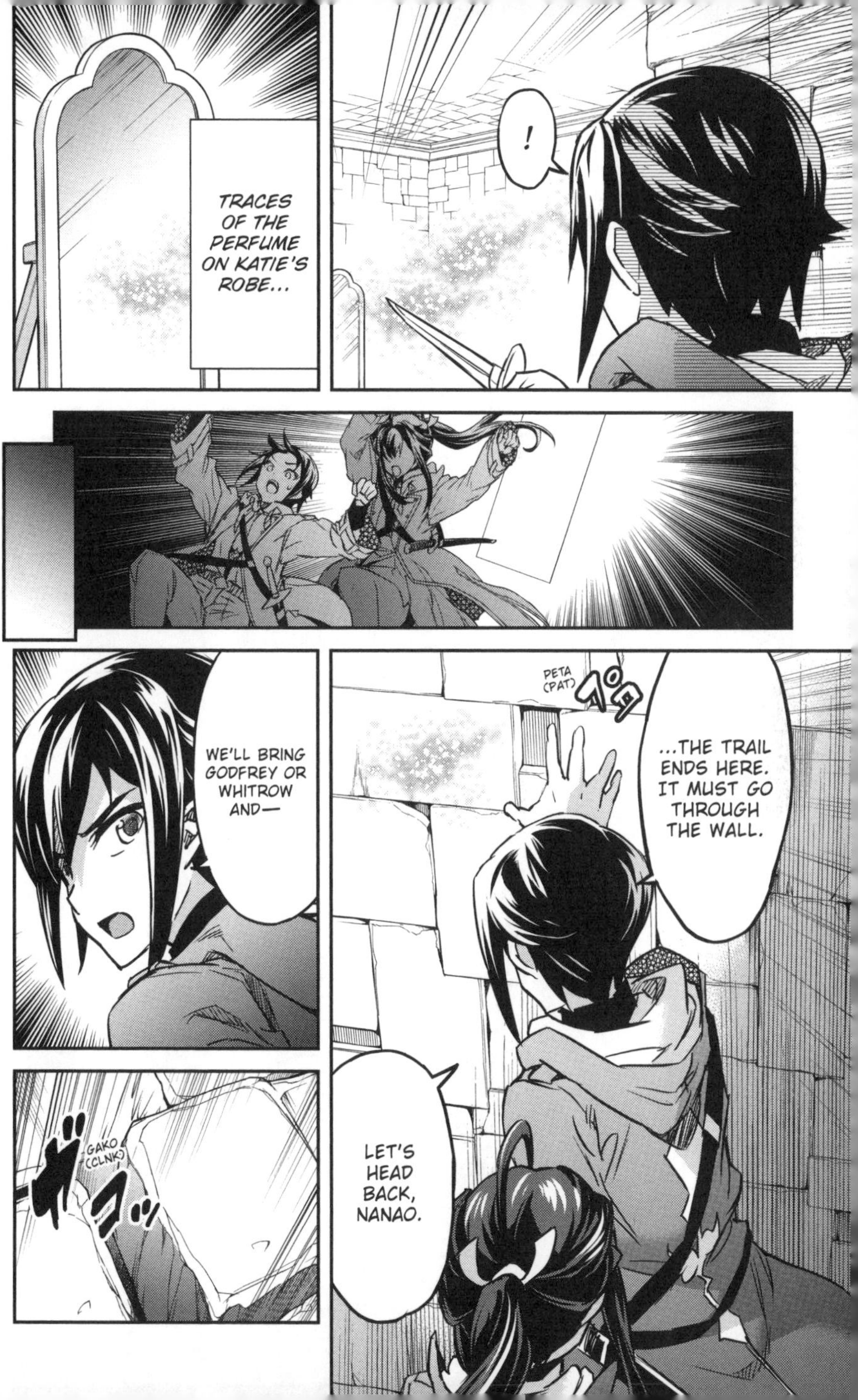
!
TRACES OF THE PERFUME ON KATIE'S ROBE...
PETA (PAT)
...THE TRAIL ENDS HERE. IT MUST GO THROUGH THE WALL.
LET'S HEAD BACK, NANAO.
WE'LL BRING GODFREY OR WHITROW AND—
GAKO (CLNK)

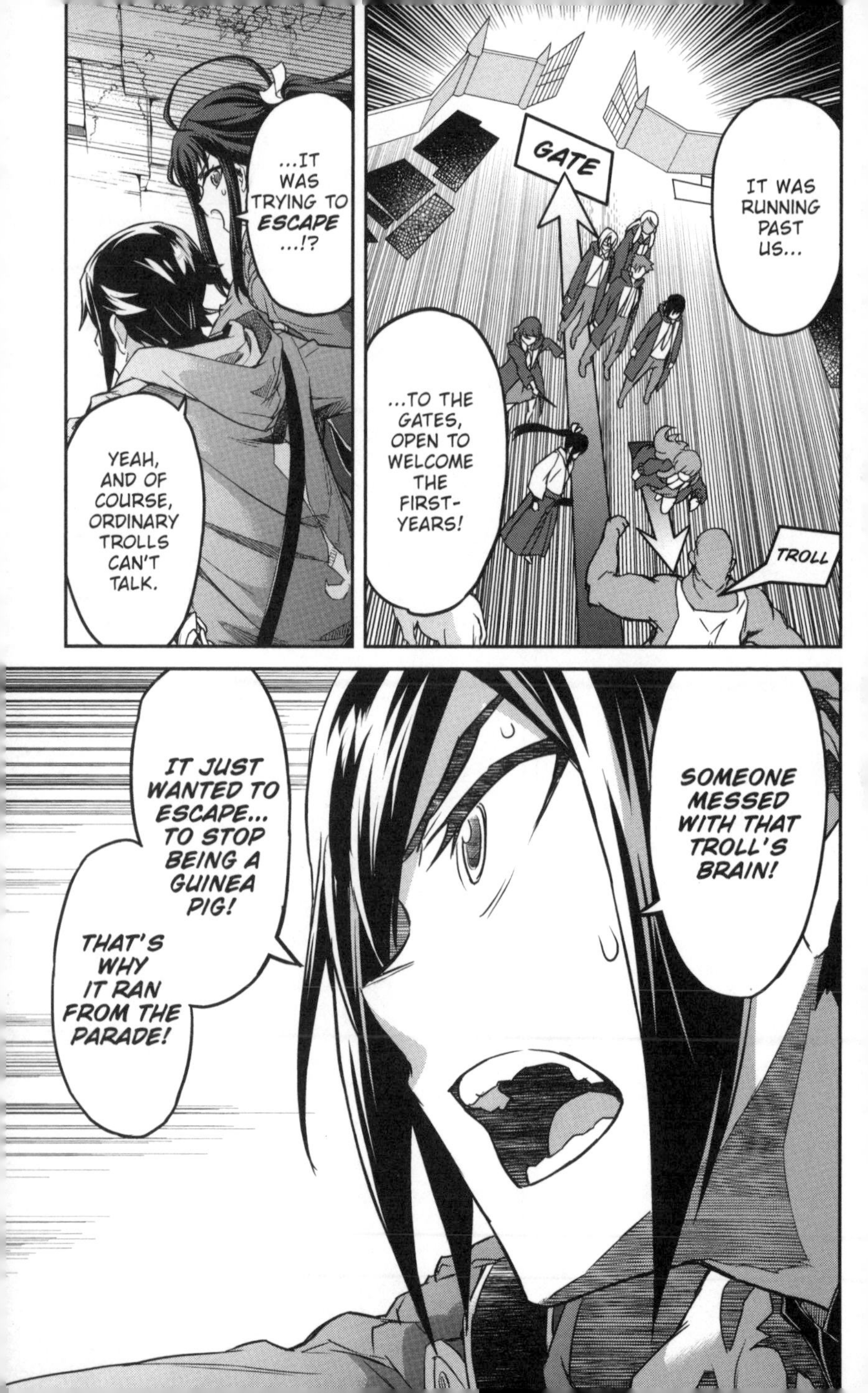
IT WAS RUNNING PAST US...
GATE
...TO THE GATES, OPEN TO WELCOME THE FIRST-YEARS!
TROLL
...IT WAS TRYING TO ESCAPE ...!?
YEAH, AND OF COURSE, ORDINARY TROLLS CAN'T TALK.
SOMEONE MESSED WITH THAT TROLL'S BRAIN!
IT JUST WANTED TO ESCAPE... TO STOP BEING A GUINEA PIG!
THAT'S WHY IT RAN FROM THE PARADE!

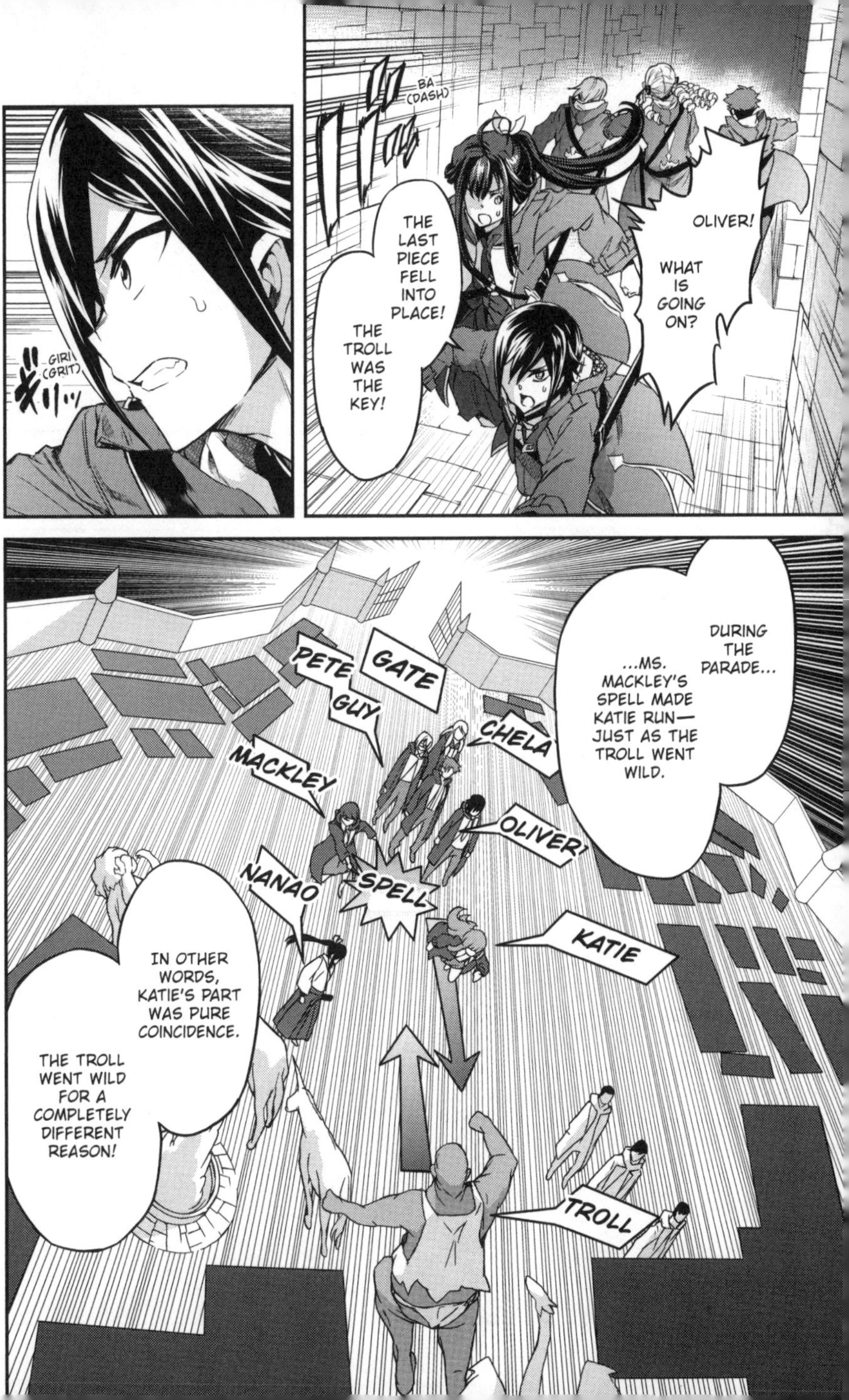
BA (DASH)
OLIVER!
WHAT IS GOING ON?
THE LAST PIECE FELL INTO PLACE!
THE TROLL WAS THE KEY!
GIRI (GRIT)
DURING THE PARADE...
...MS. MACKLEY'S SPELL MADE KATIE RUN— JUST AS THE TROLL WENT WILD.
GATE
PETE
GUY
CHELA
MACKLEY
OLIVER
NANAO
SPELL
KATIE
IN OTHER WORDS, KATIE'S PART WAS PURE COINCIDENCE.
THE TROLL WENT WILD FOR A COMPLETELY DIFFERENT REASON!
TROLL

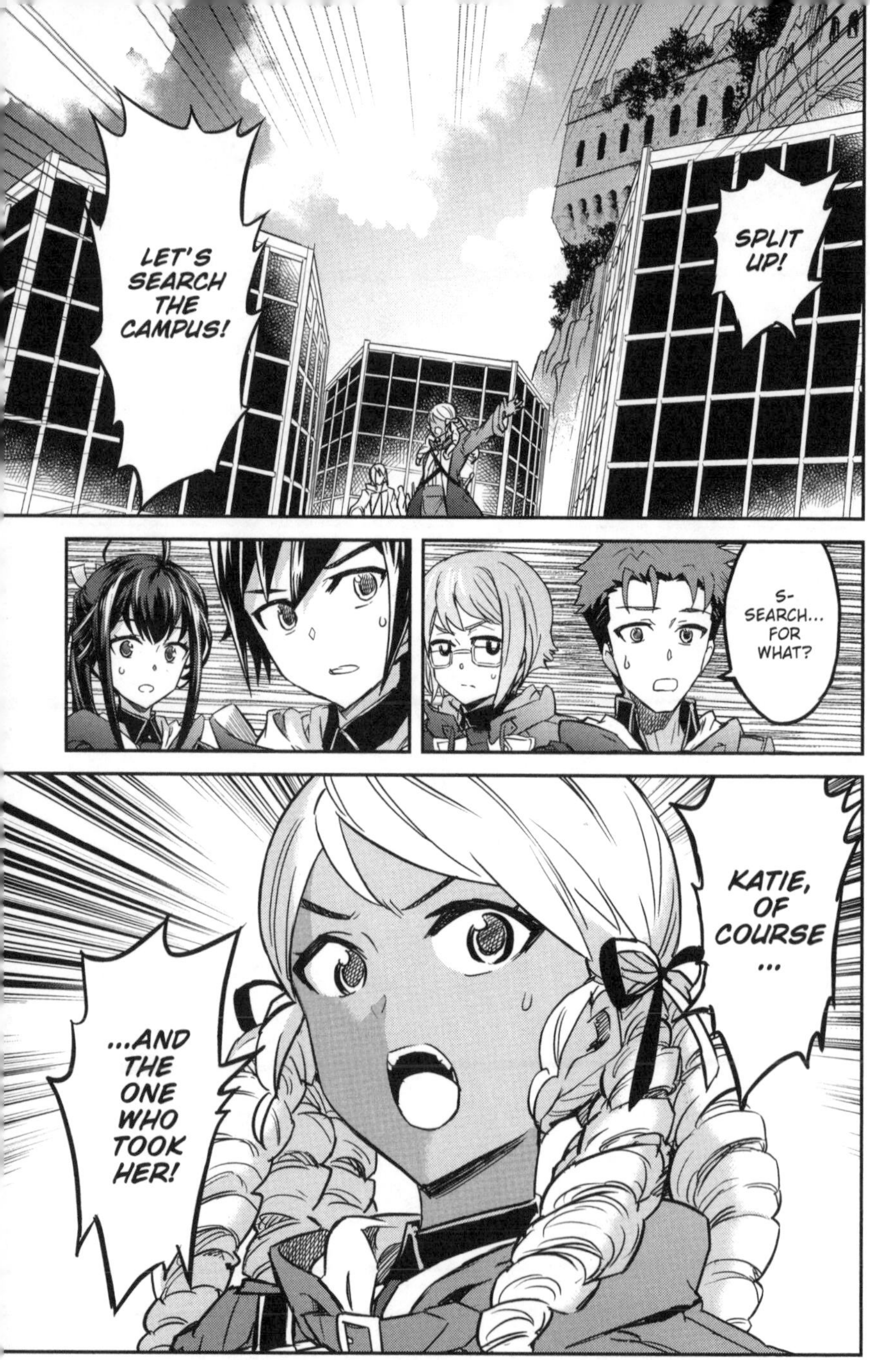
SPLIT UP!
LET'S SEARCH THE CAMPUS!
S-SEARCH... FOR WHAT?
KATIE, OF COURSE ...
...AND THE ONE WHO TOOK HER!

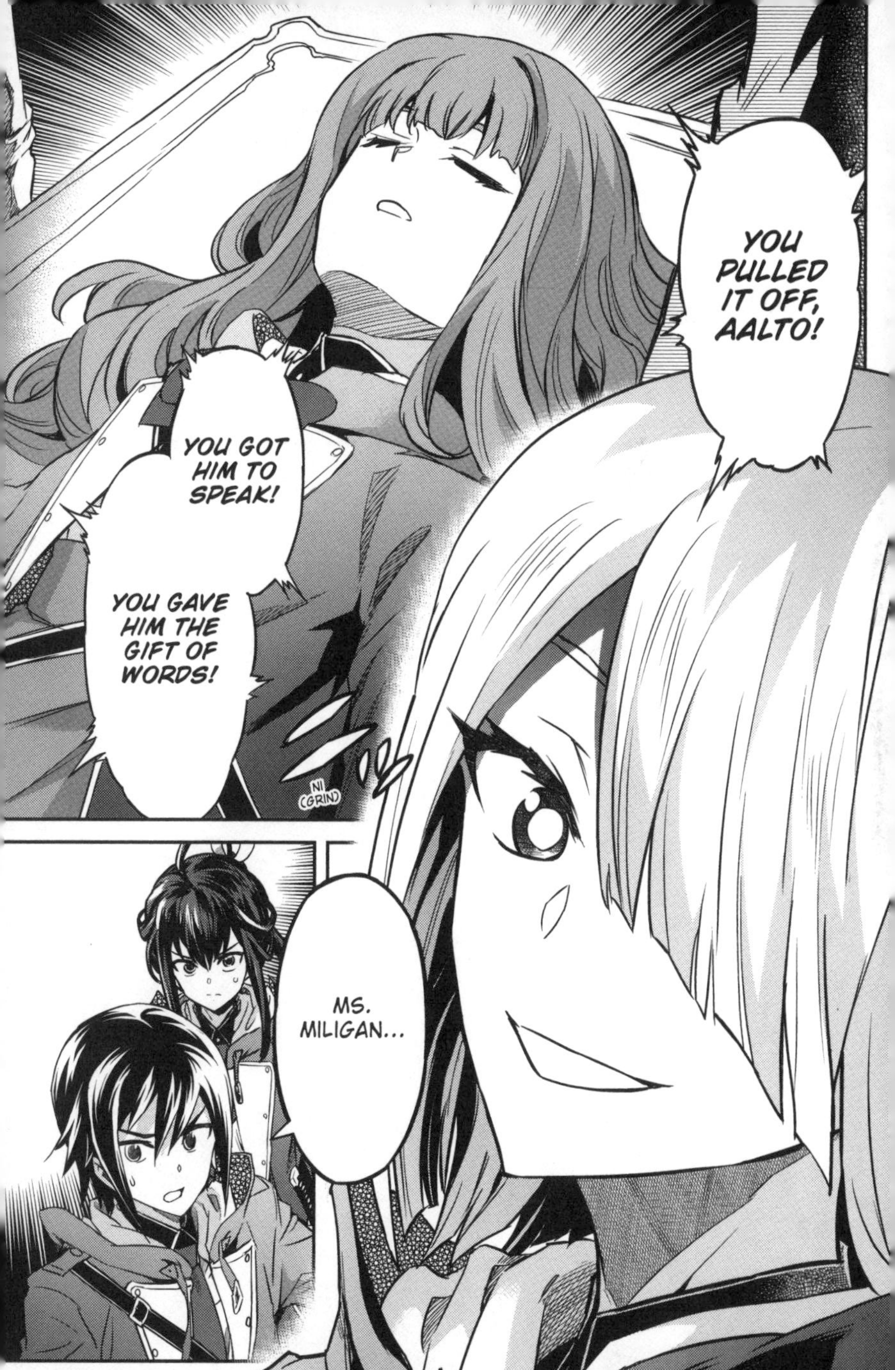
YOU PULLED IT OFF, AALTO!
YOU GOT HIM TO SPEAK!
YOU GAVE HIM THE GIFT OF WORDS!
NI (GRIN)
MS. MILIGAN...

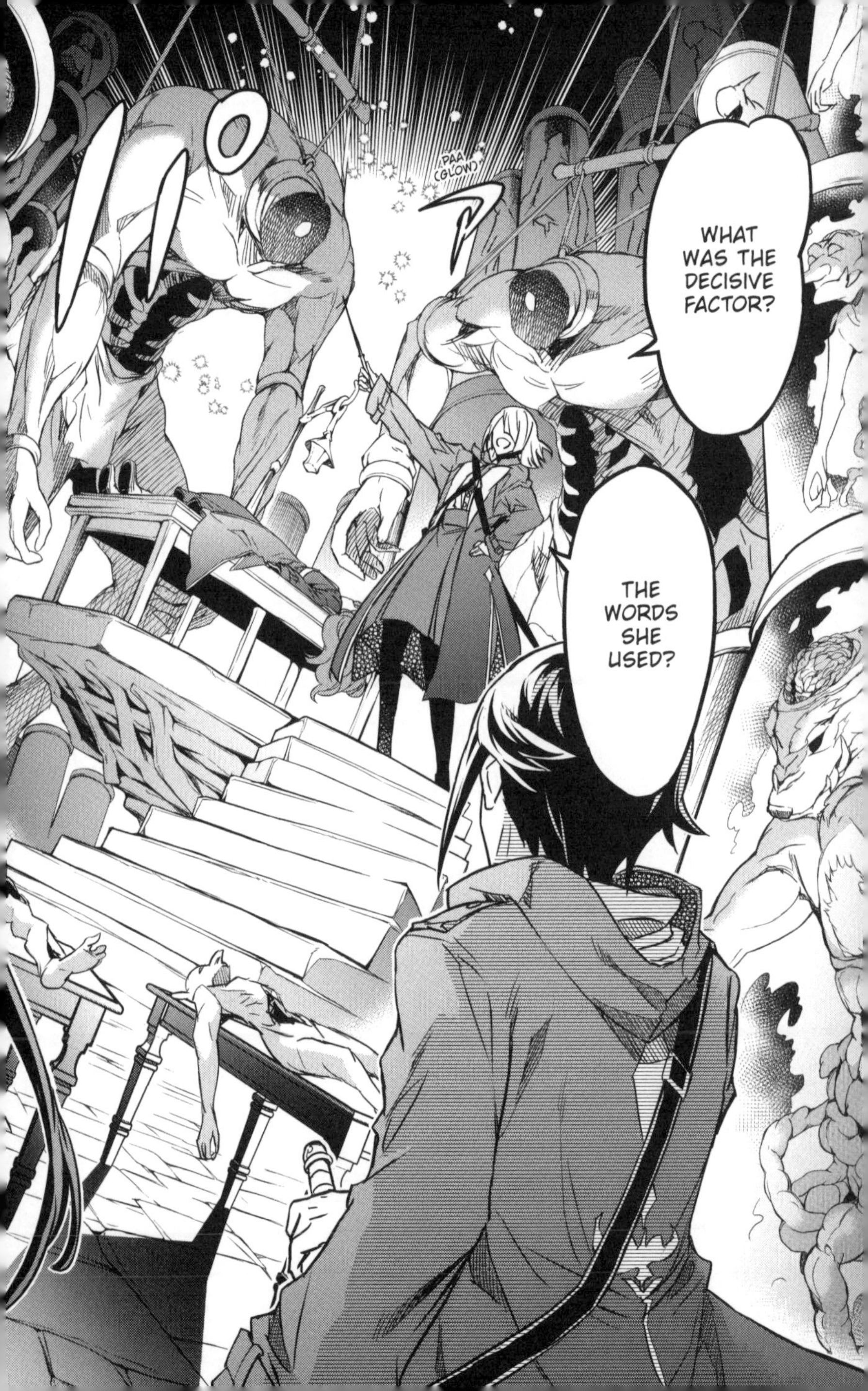
WHAT WAS THE DECISIVE FACTOR?
THE WORDS SHE USED?
PAA (GLOW)

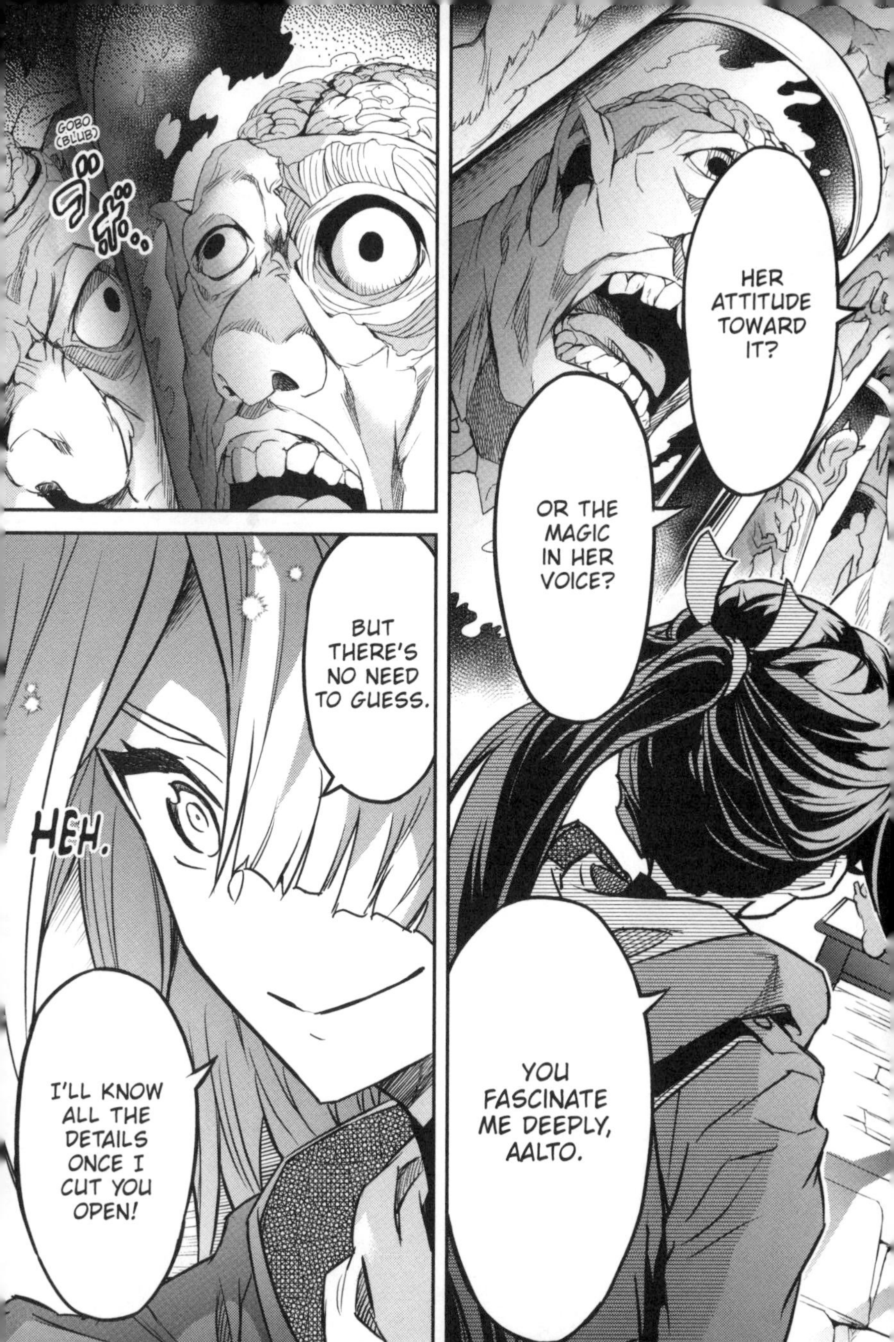
HER ATTITUDE TOWARD IT?
OR THE MAGIC IN HER VOICE?
YOU FASCINATE ME DEEPLY, AALTO.
GOBO (BLUB)
BUT THERE'S NO NEED TO GUESS.
HEH.
I'LL KNOW ALL THE DETAILS ONCE I CUT YOU OPEN!

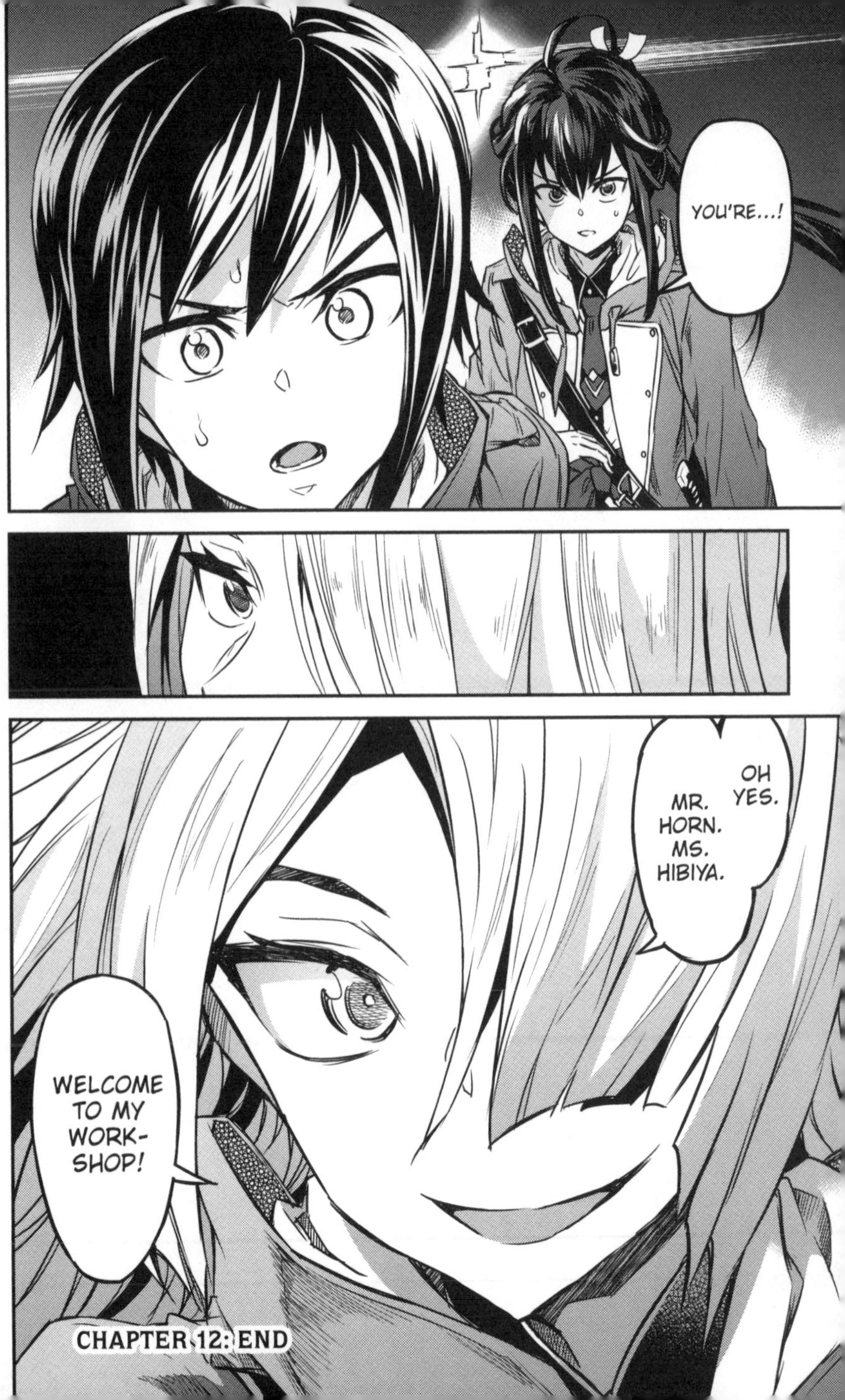
YOU'RE...!
OH YES.
MR. HORN. MS. HIBIYA.
WELCOME TO MY WORK-SHOP!
CHAPTER 12: END

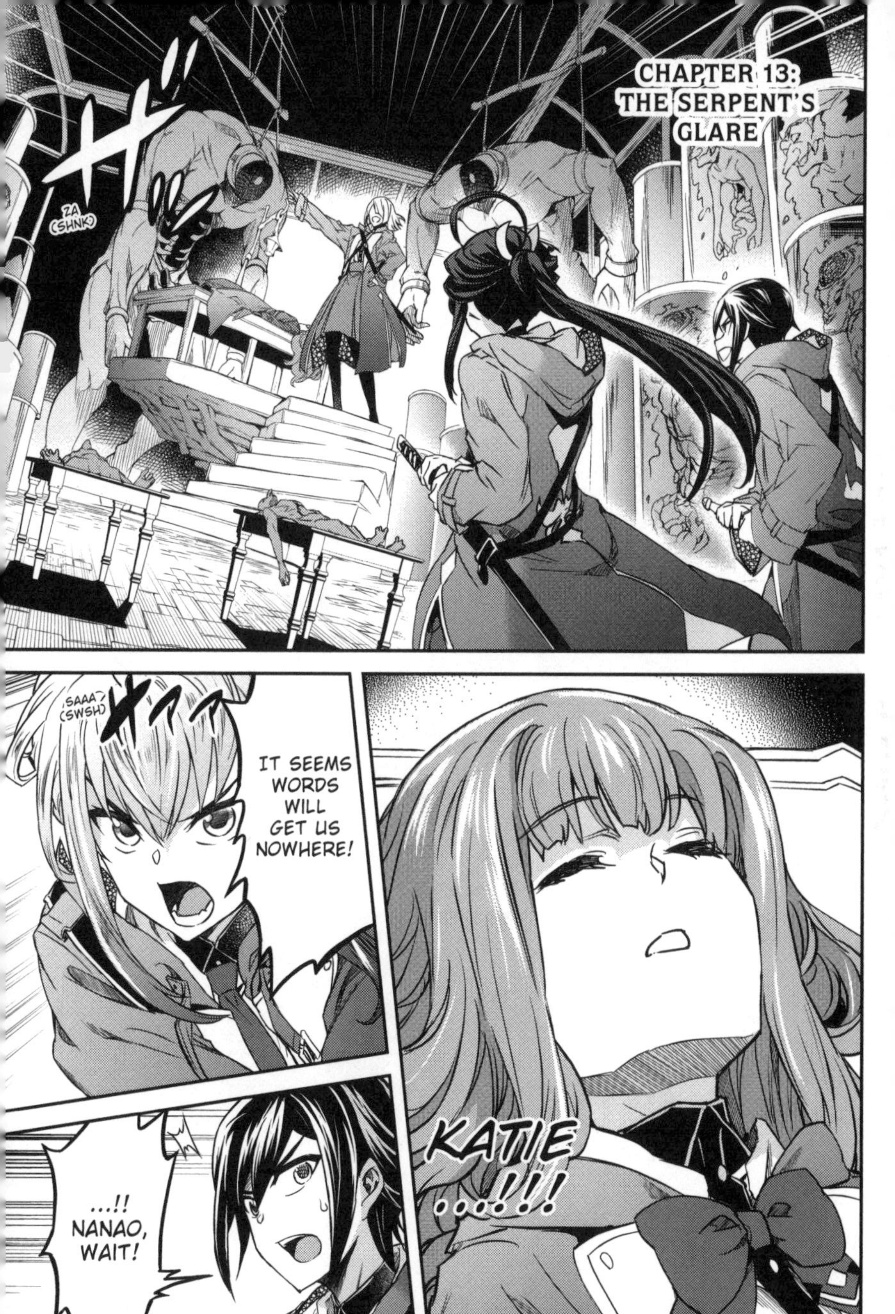
CHAPTER 13: THE SERPENT'S GLARE
ZA (SHNK)
KATIE...!!!
SAAA (SWSH)
IT SEEMS WORDS WILL GET US NOWHERE!
...!! NANAO, WAIT!

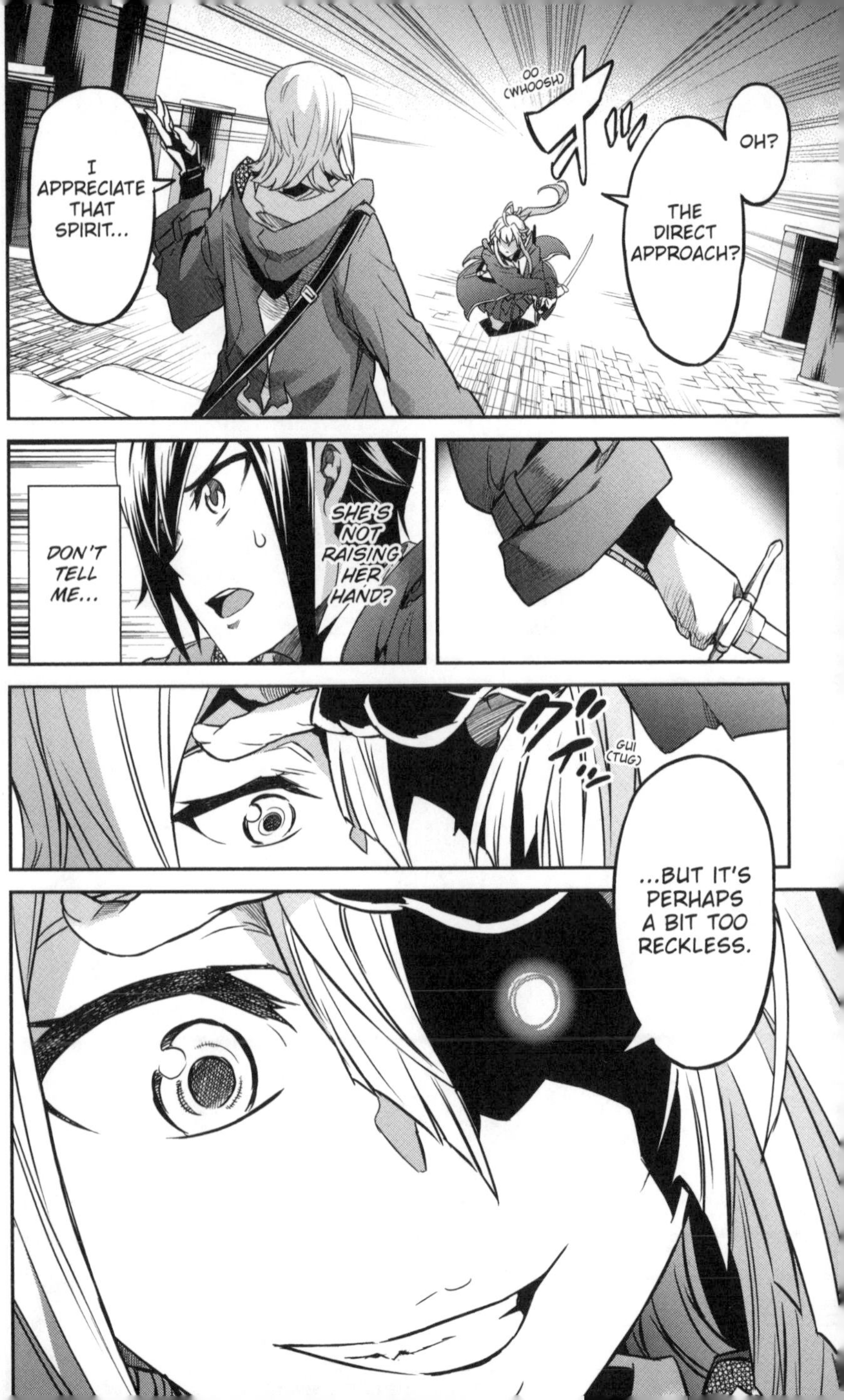
OH? THE DIRECT APPROACH?
OO (WHOOSH)
I APPRECIATE THAT SPIRIT...
SHE'S NOT RAISING HER HAND?
DON'T TELL ME...
GUI (TUG)
...BUT IT'S PERHAPS A BIT TOO RECKLESS.

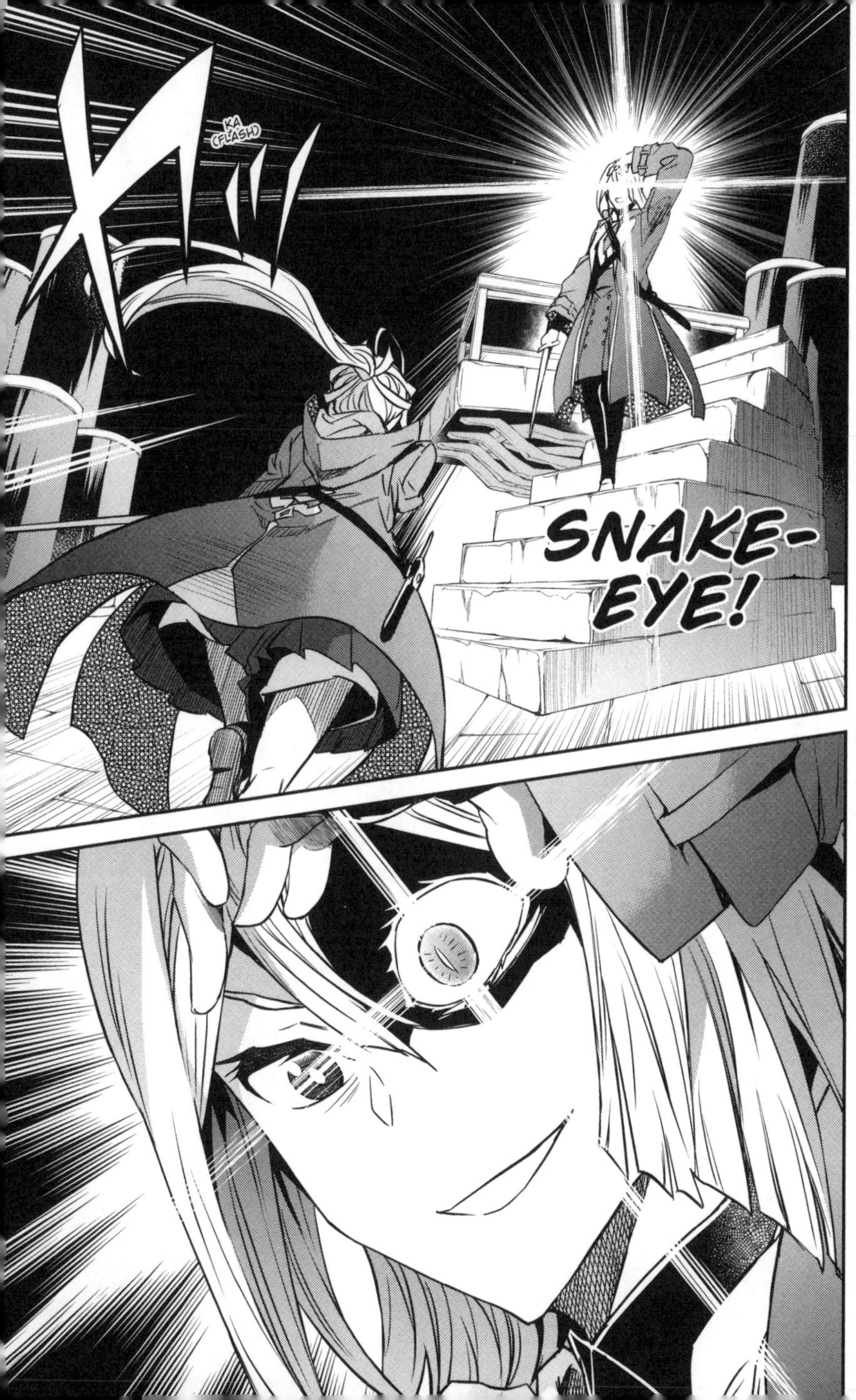
KA (FLASH)
SNAKE-EYE!

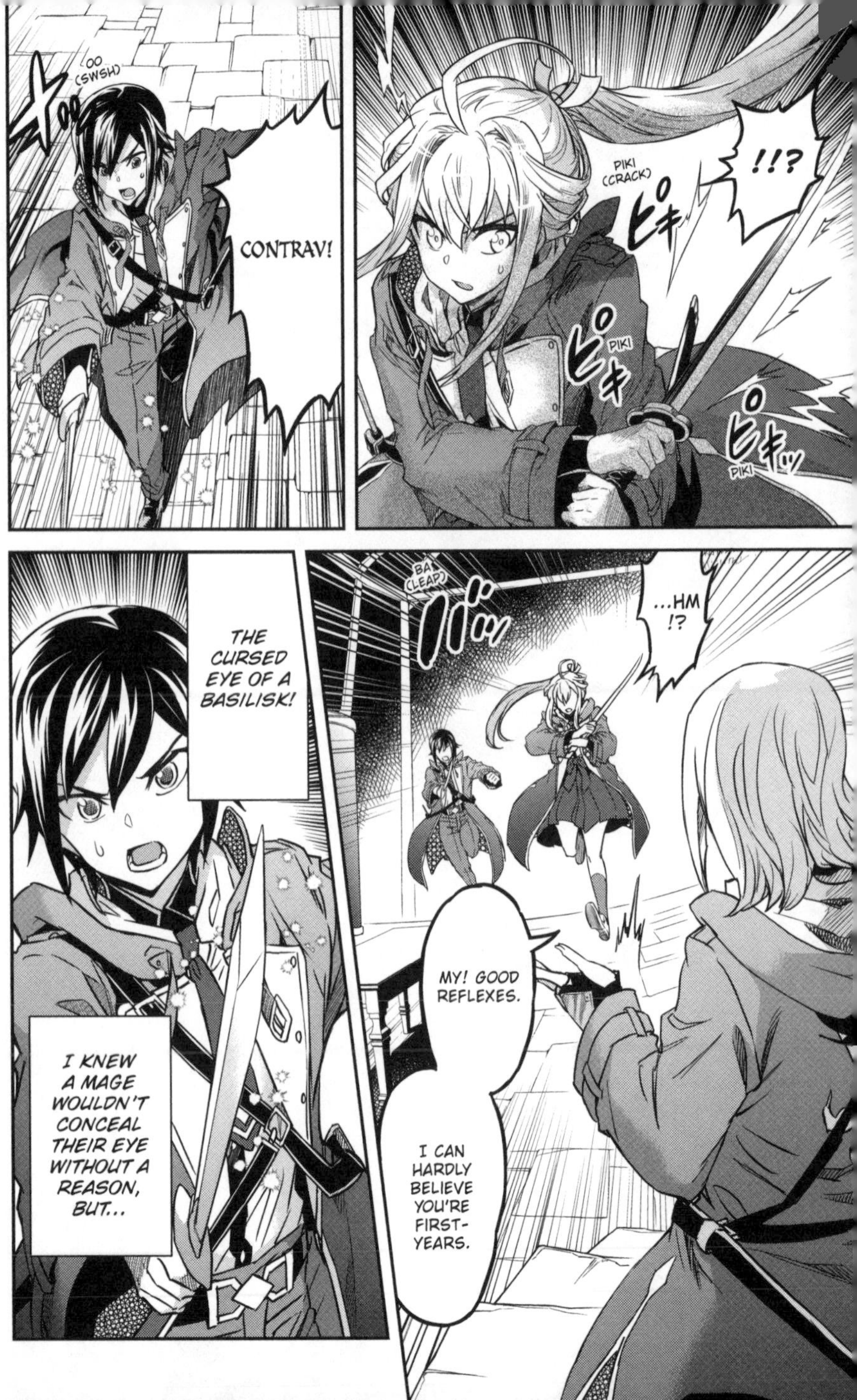
!!?
PIKI (CRACK)
PIKI
PIKI
OO (SWSH)
CONTRAV!
BA (LEAP)
...HM !?
MY! GOOD REFLEXES.
I CAN HARDLY BELIEVE YOU'RE FIRST-YEARS.
THE CURSED EYE OF A BASILISK!
I KNEW A MAGE WOULDN'T CONCEAL THEIR EYE WITHOUT A REASON, BUT...

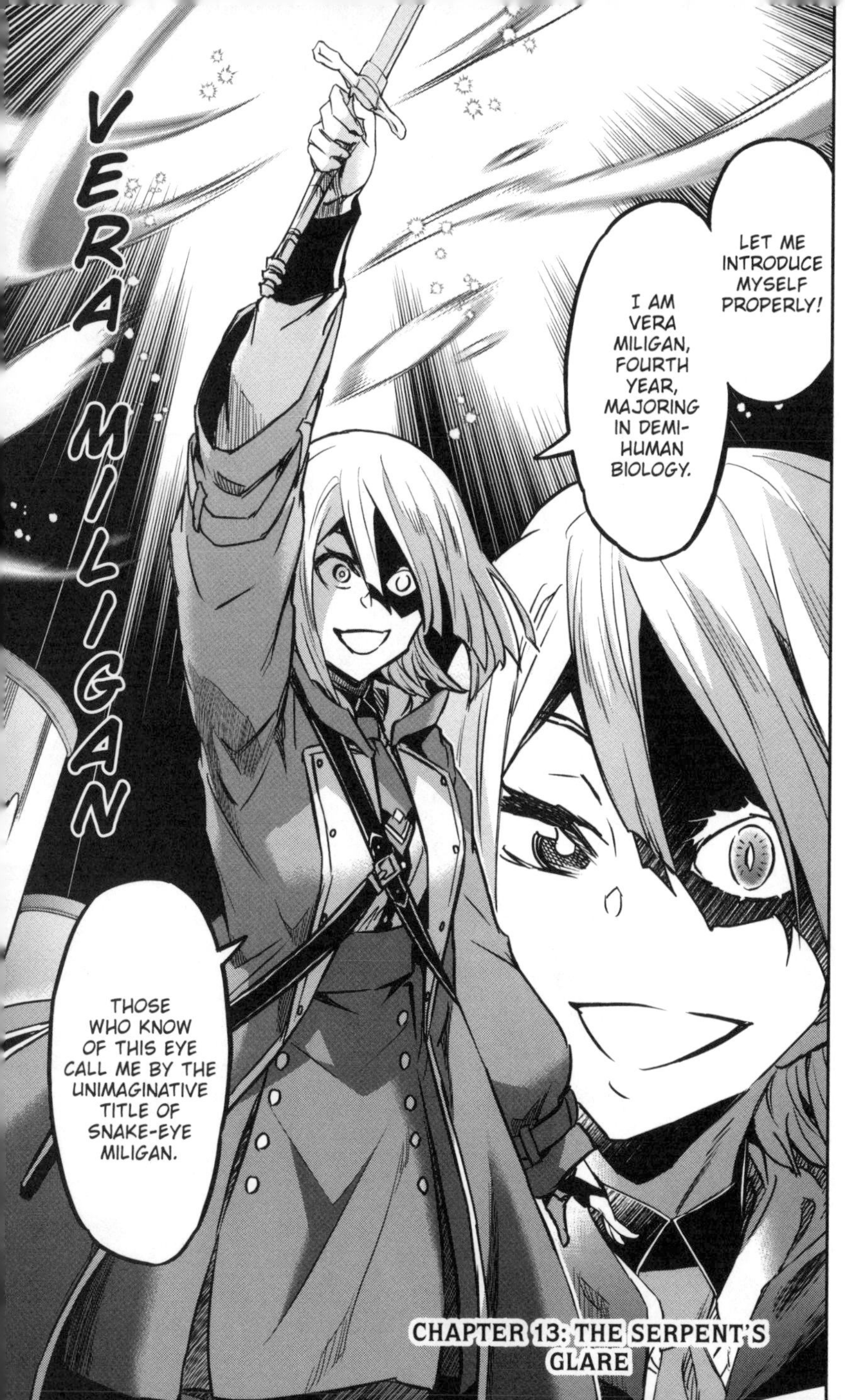
LET ME INTRODUCE MYSELF PROPERLY!
I AM VERA MILIGAN, FOURTH YEAR, MAJORING IN DEMI-HUMAN BIOLOGY.
VERA MILIGAN
THOSE WHO KNOW OF THIS EYE CALL ME BY THE UNIMAGINATIVE TITLE OF SNAKE-EYE MILIGAN.
CHAPTER 13: THE SERPENT'S GLARE

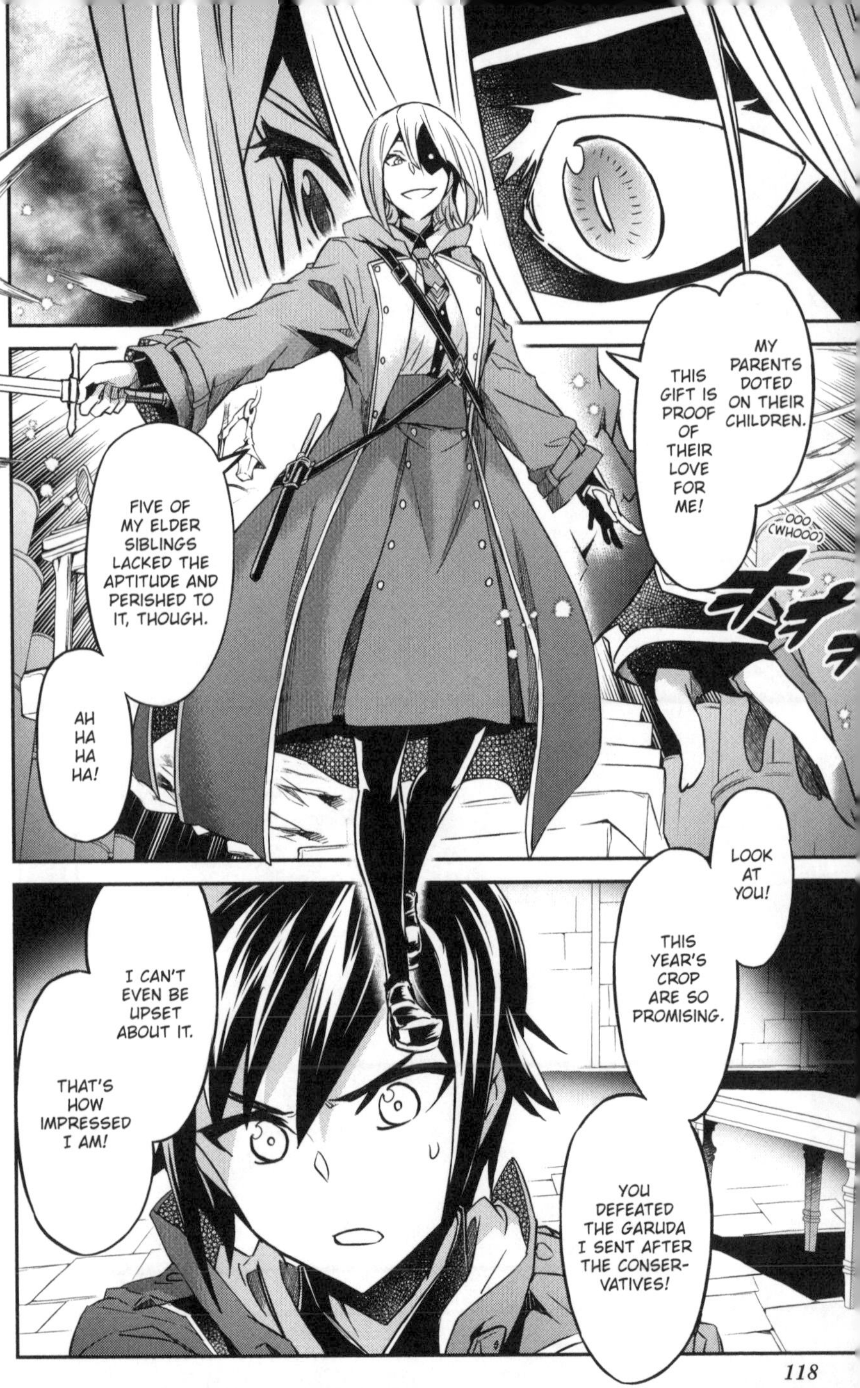
MY PARENTS DOTED ON THEIR CHILDREN.
THIS GIFT IS PROOF OF THEIR LOVE FOR ME!
-OOO (WHOOO)
FIVE OF MY ELDER SIBLINGS LACKED THE APTITUDE AND PERISHED TO IT, THOUGH.
AH HA HA HA!
LOOK AT YOU!
THIS YEAR'S CROP ARE SO PROMISING.
YOU DEFEATED THE GARUDA I SENT AFTER THE CONSER-VATIVES!
I CAN'T EVEN BE UPSET ABOUT IT.
THAT'S HOW IMPRESSED I AM!

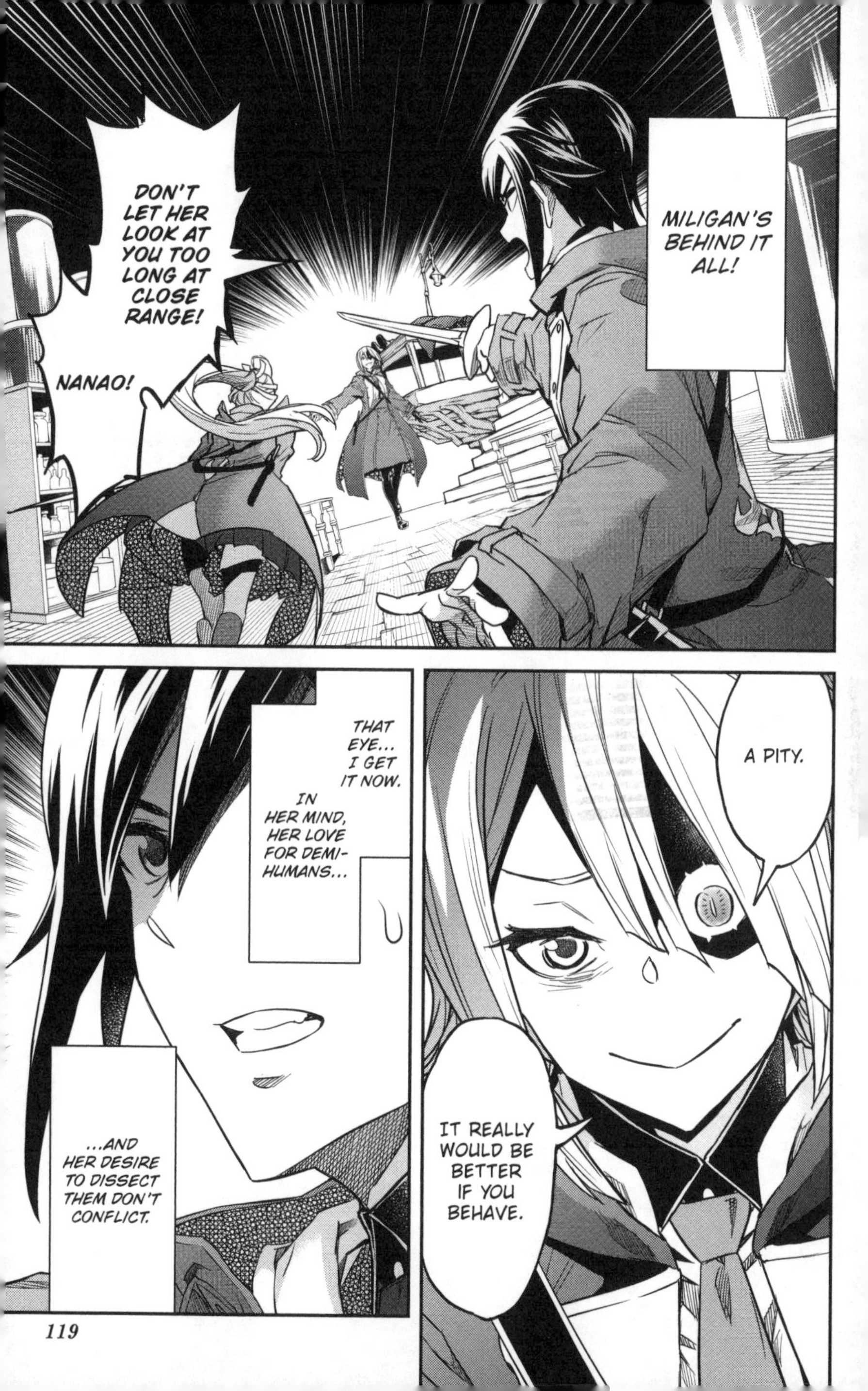
MILIGAN'S BEHIND IT ALL!
DON'T LET HER LOOK AT YOU TOO LONG AT CLOSE RANGE!
NANAO!
A PITY.
IT REALLY WOULD BE BETTER IF YOU BEHAVE.
THAT EYE... I GET IT NOW.
IN HER MIND, HER LOVE FOR DEMI-HUMANS...
...AND HER DESIRE TO DISSECT THEM DON'T CONFLICT.

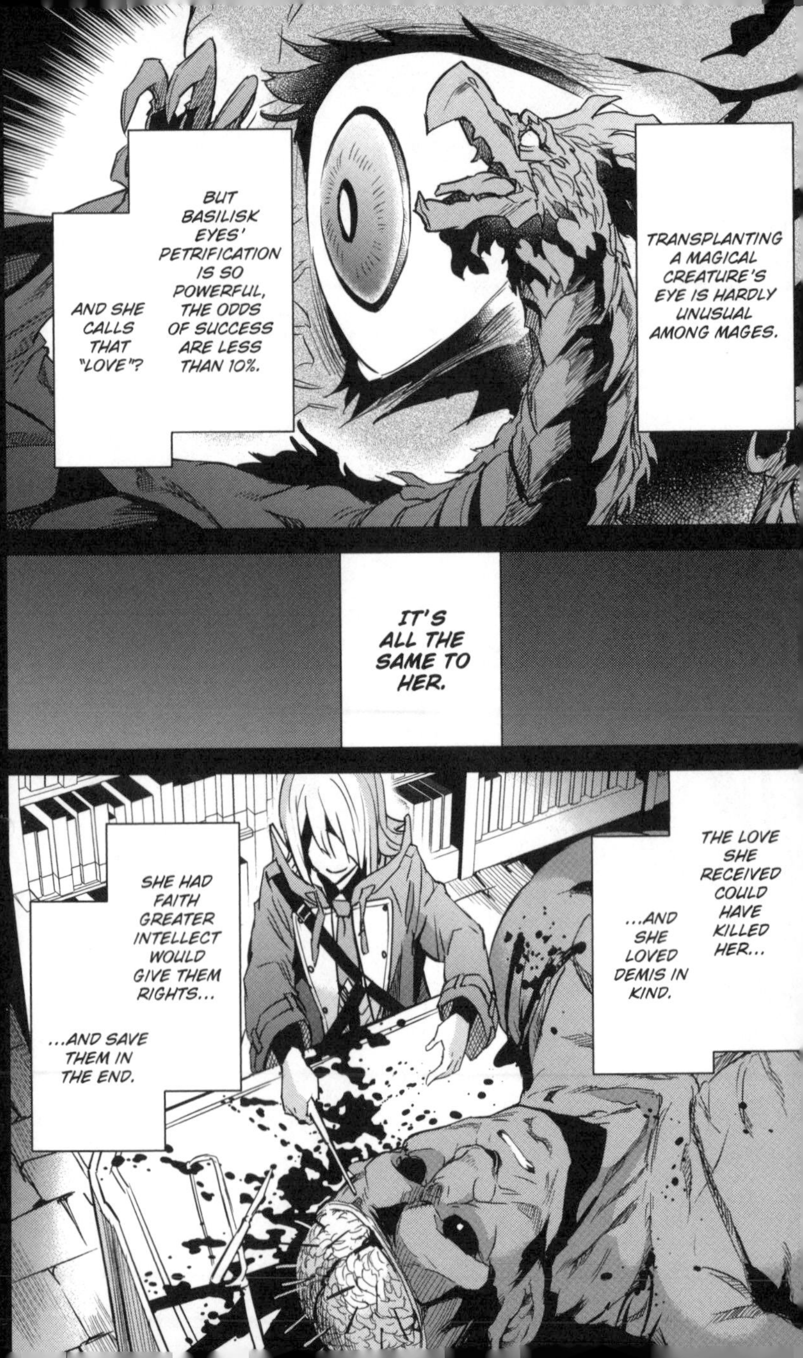
TRANSPLANTING A MAGICAL CREATURE'S EYE IS HARDLY UNUSUAL AMONG MAGES.
BUT BASILISK EYES' PETRIFICATION IS SO POWERFUL, THE ODDS OF SUCCESS ARE LESS THAN 10%.
AND SHE CALLS THAT "LOVE"?
IT'S ALL THE SAME TO HER.
THE LOVE SHE RECEIVED COULD HAVE KILLED HER...
...AND SHE LOVED DEMIS IN KIND.
SHE HAD FAITH GREATER INTELLECT WOULD GIVE THEM RIGHTS...
...AND SAVE THEM IN THE END.

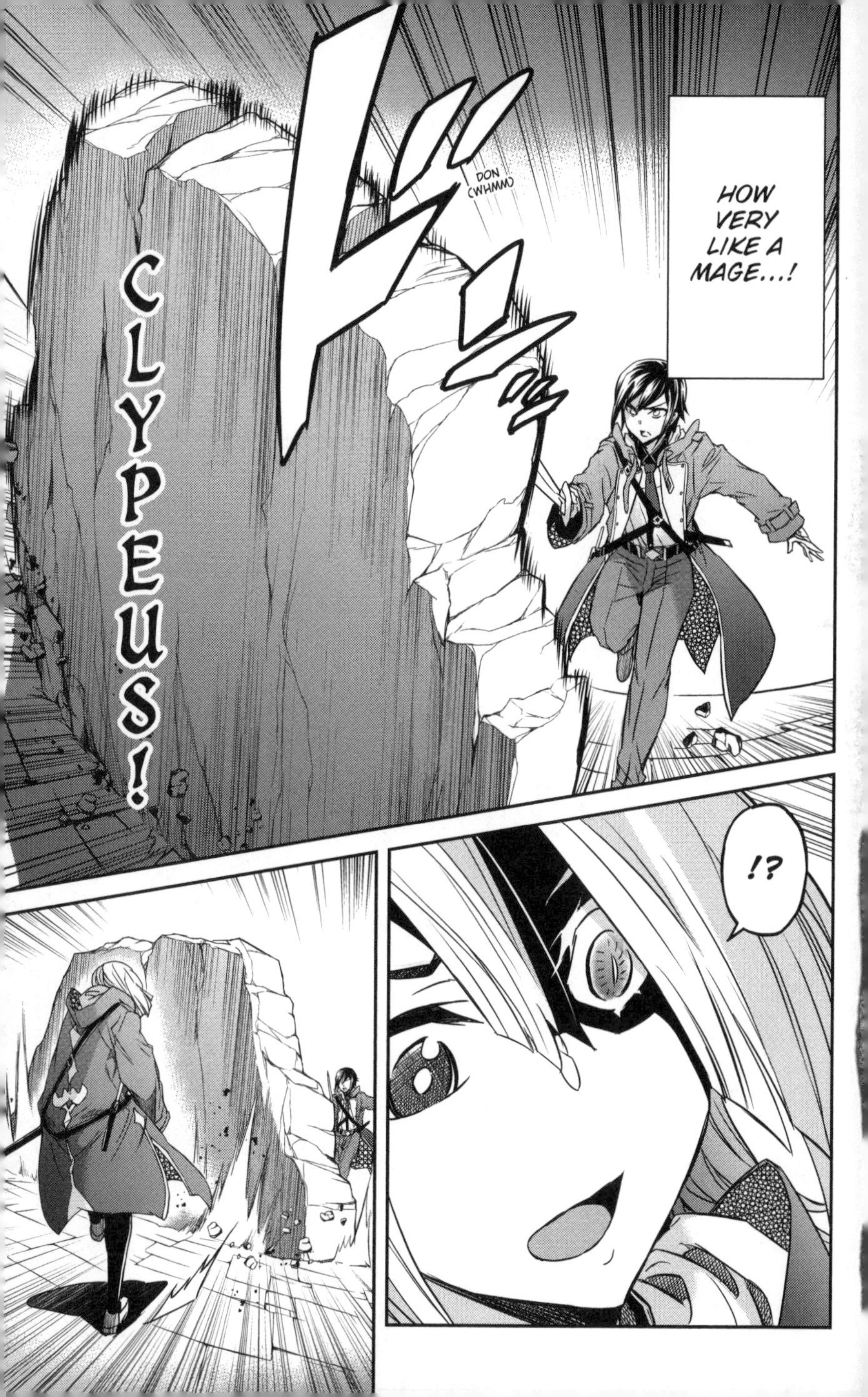
HOW VERY LIKE A MAGE...!
DON (WHMM)
CLYPEUS!
!?

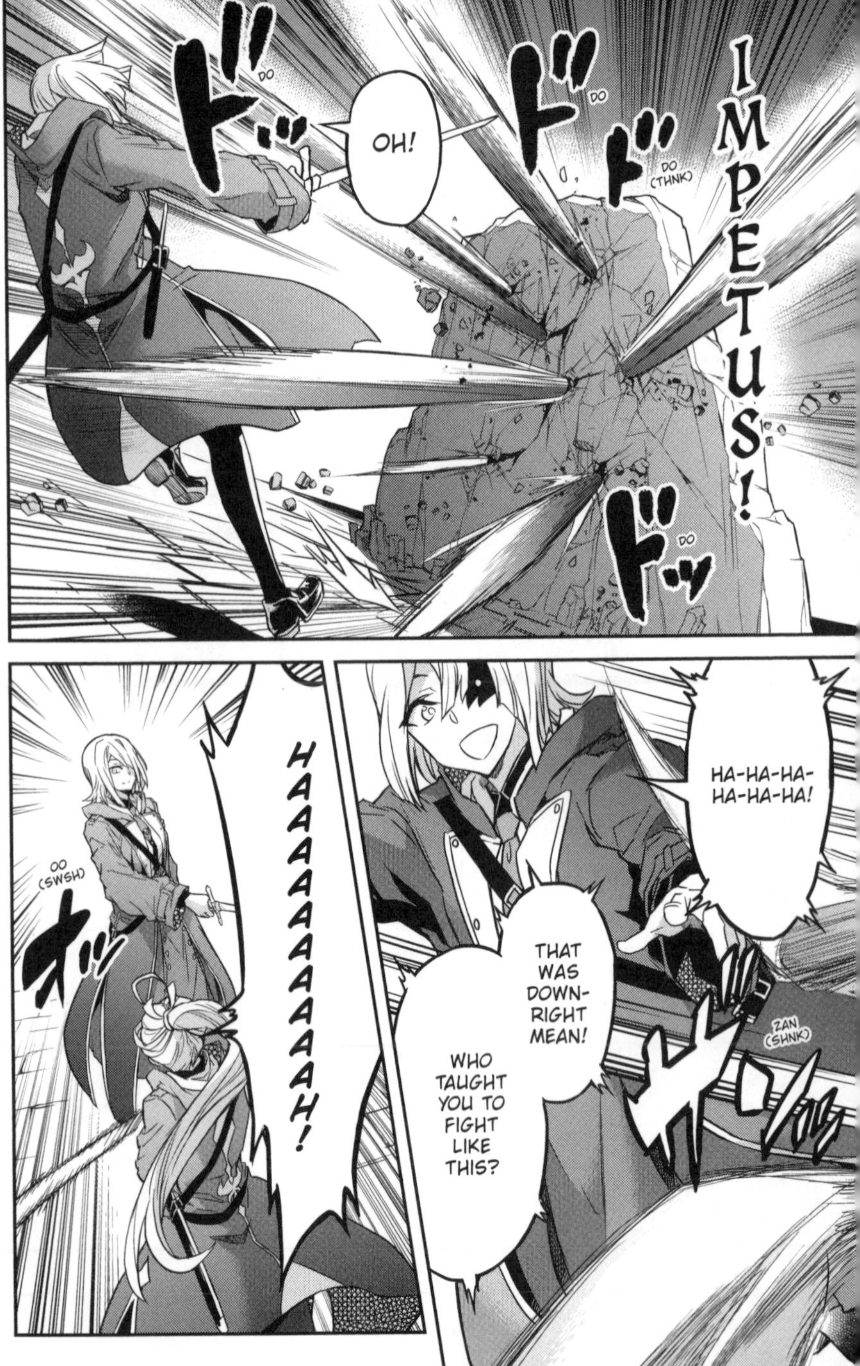

IMPETUS!
DO
DO (THNK)
OH!
DO
DO
HA-HA-HA-HA-HA-HA!
THAT WAS DOWN-RIGHT MEAN!
WHO TAUGHT YOU TO FIGHT LIKE THIS?
ZAN (SHNK)
HAAAAAAAAAAAAAH!
OO (SWSH)

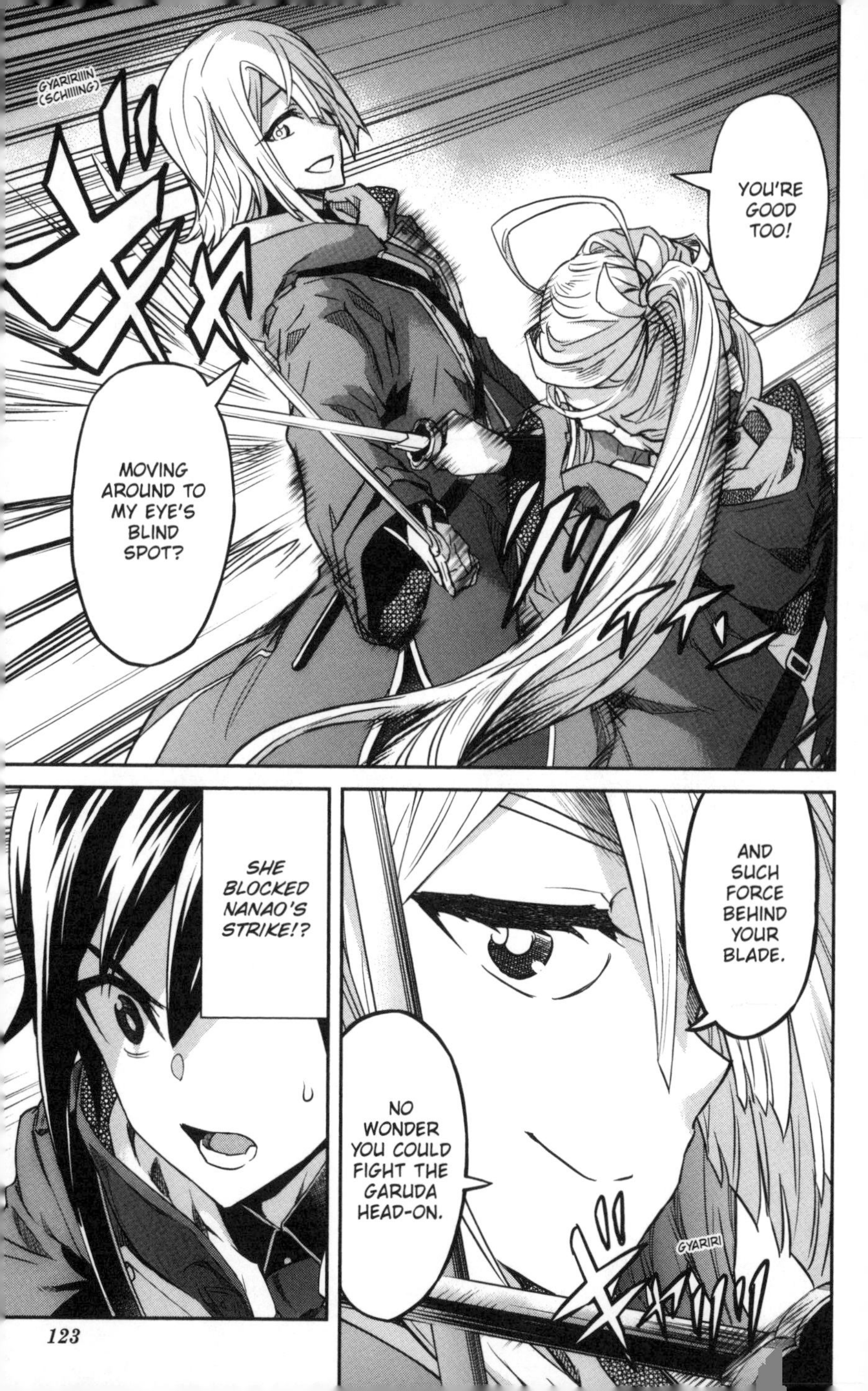

YOU'RE GOOD TOO!
GYARIRIIN (SCHIIIING)
MOVING AROUND TO MY EYE'S BLIND SPOT?
AND SUCH FORCE BEHIND YOUR BLADE.
NO WONDER YOU COULD FIGHT THE GARUDA HEAD-ON.
GYARIRI
SHE BLOCKED NANAO'S STRIKE!?

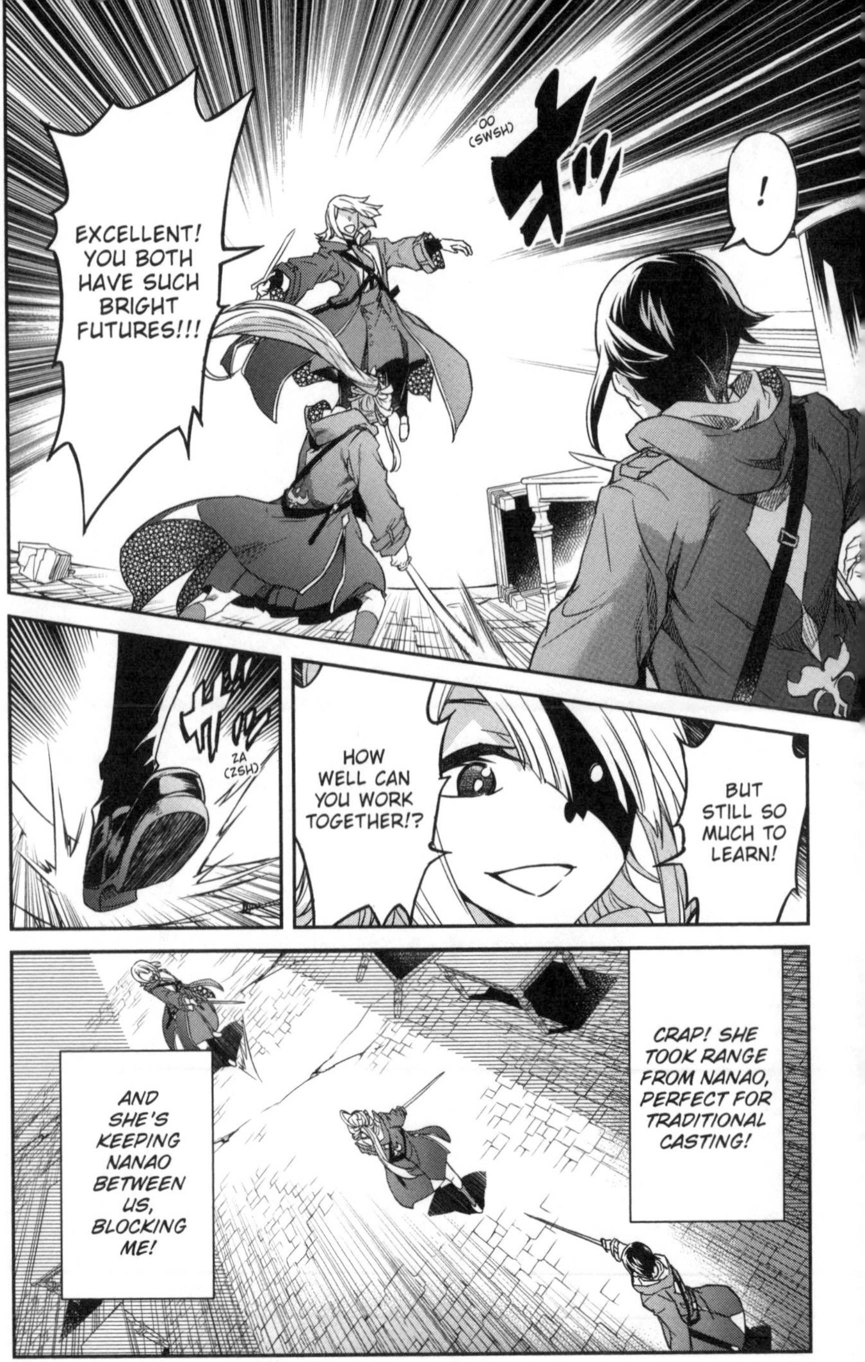
!
OO (SWSH)
EXCELLENT! YOU BOTH HAVE SUCH BRIGHT FUTURES!!!
BUT STILL SO MUCH TO LEARN!
HOW WELL CAN YOU WORK TOGETHER!?
ZA (ZSH)
CRAP! SHE TOOK RANGE FROM NANAO, PERFECT FOR TRADITIONAL CASTING!
AND SHE'S KEEPING NANAO BETWEEN US, BLOCKING ME!

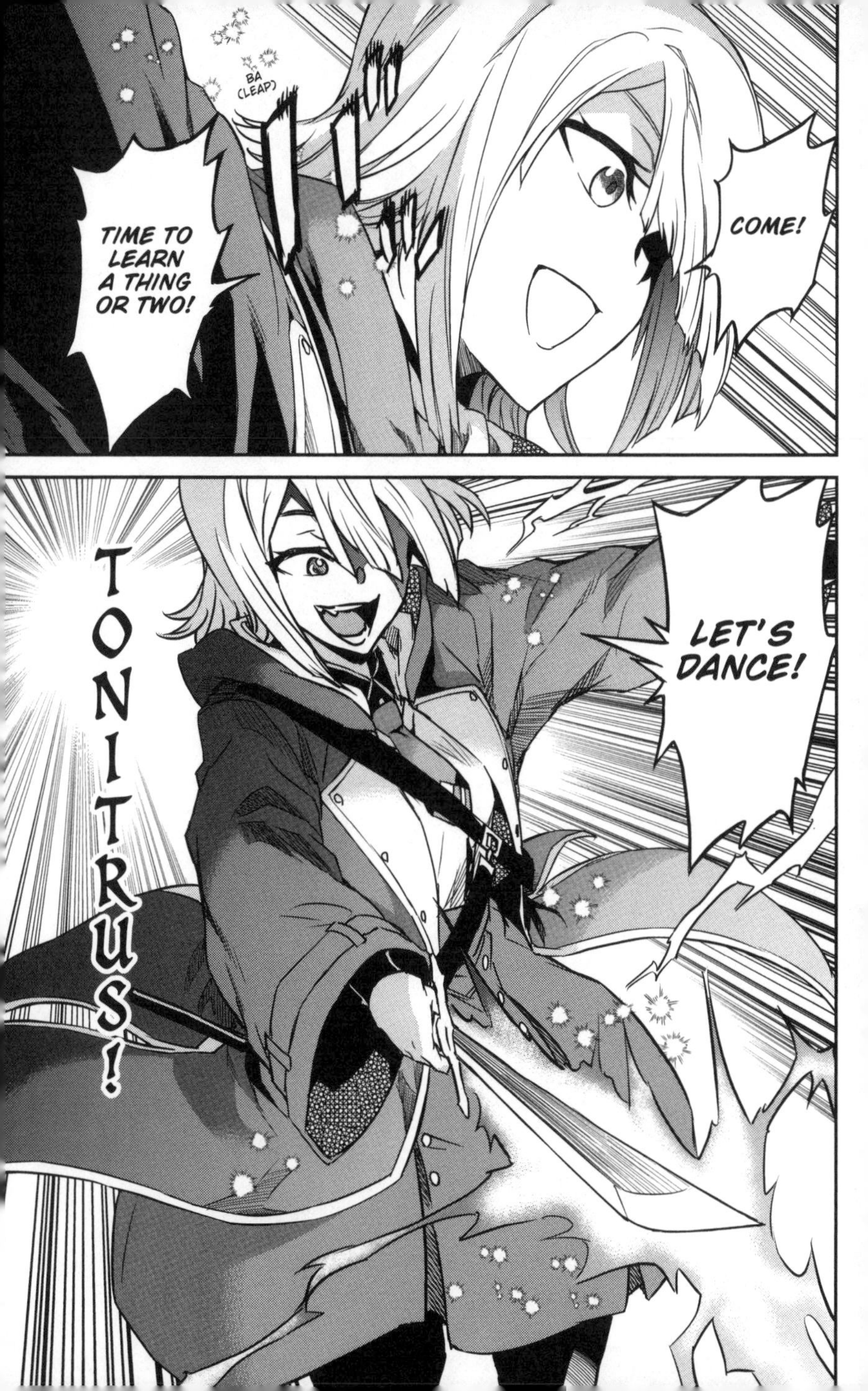
COME!
BA (LEAP)
TIME TO LEARN A THING OR TWO!
LET'S DANCE!
TONITRUS!

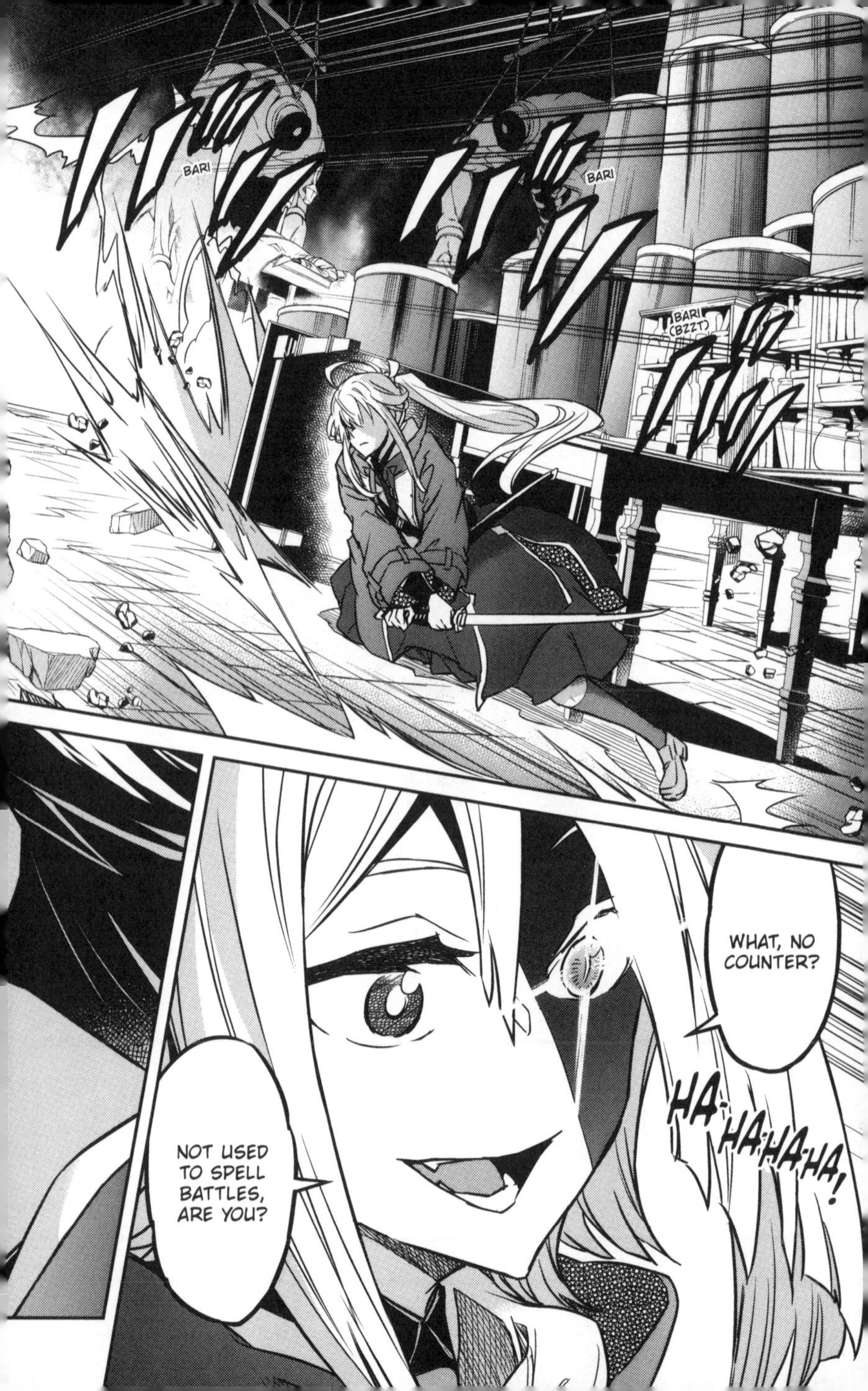
BARI
BARI
BARI (BZZT)
WHAT, NO COUNTER?
HA-HA-HA-HA-HA!
NOT USED TO SPELL BATTLES, ARE YOU?

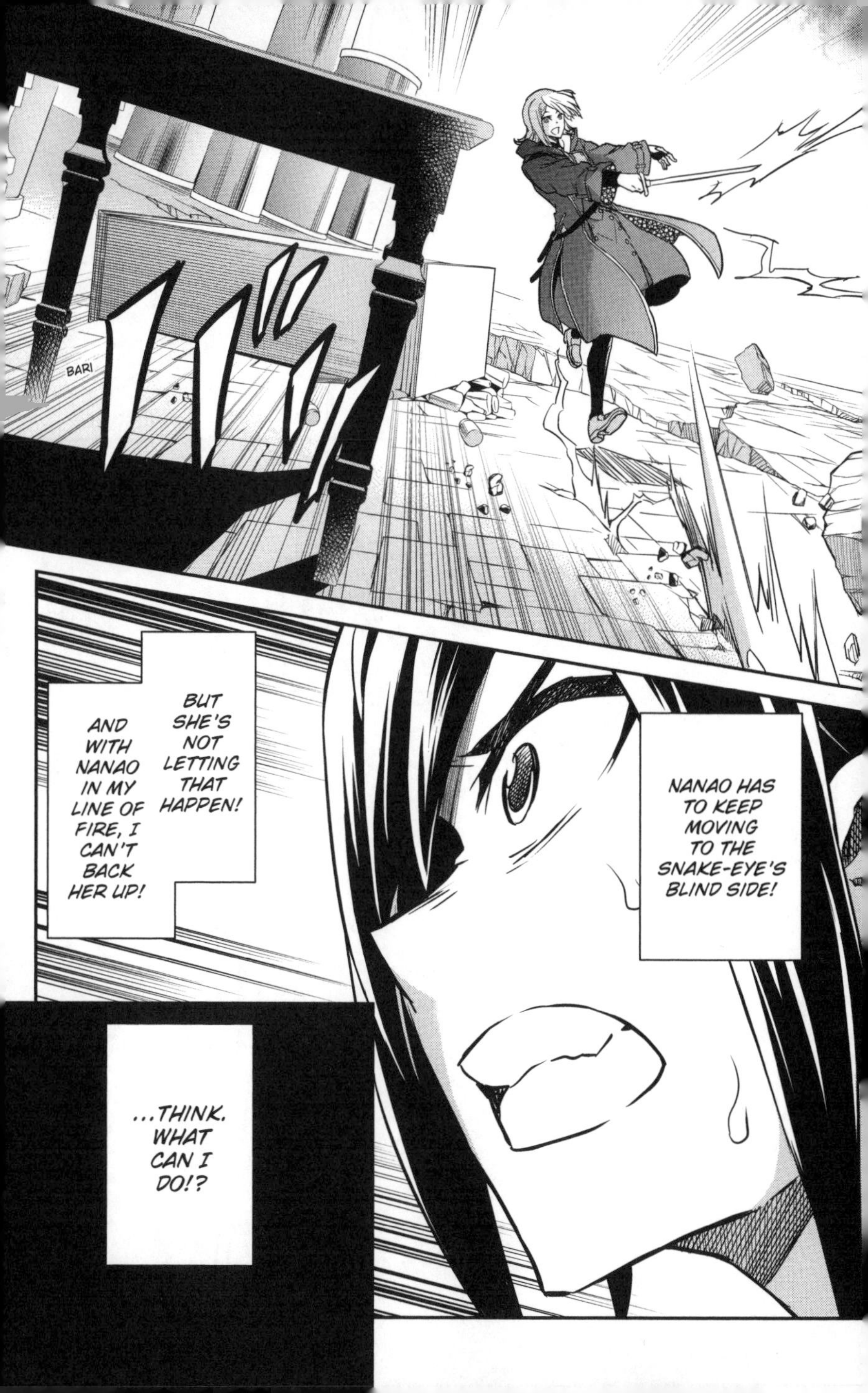
BARI
NANAO HAS TO KEEP MOVING TO THE SNAKE-EYE'S BLIND SIDE!
BUT SHE'S NOT LETTING THAT HAPPEN!
AND WITH NANAO IN MY LINE OF FIRE, I CAN'T BACK HER UP!
...THINK. WHAT CAN I DO!?

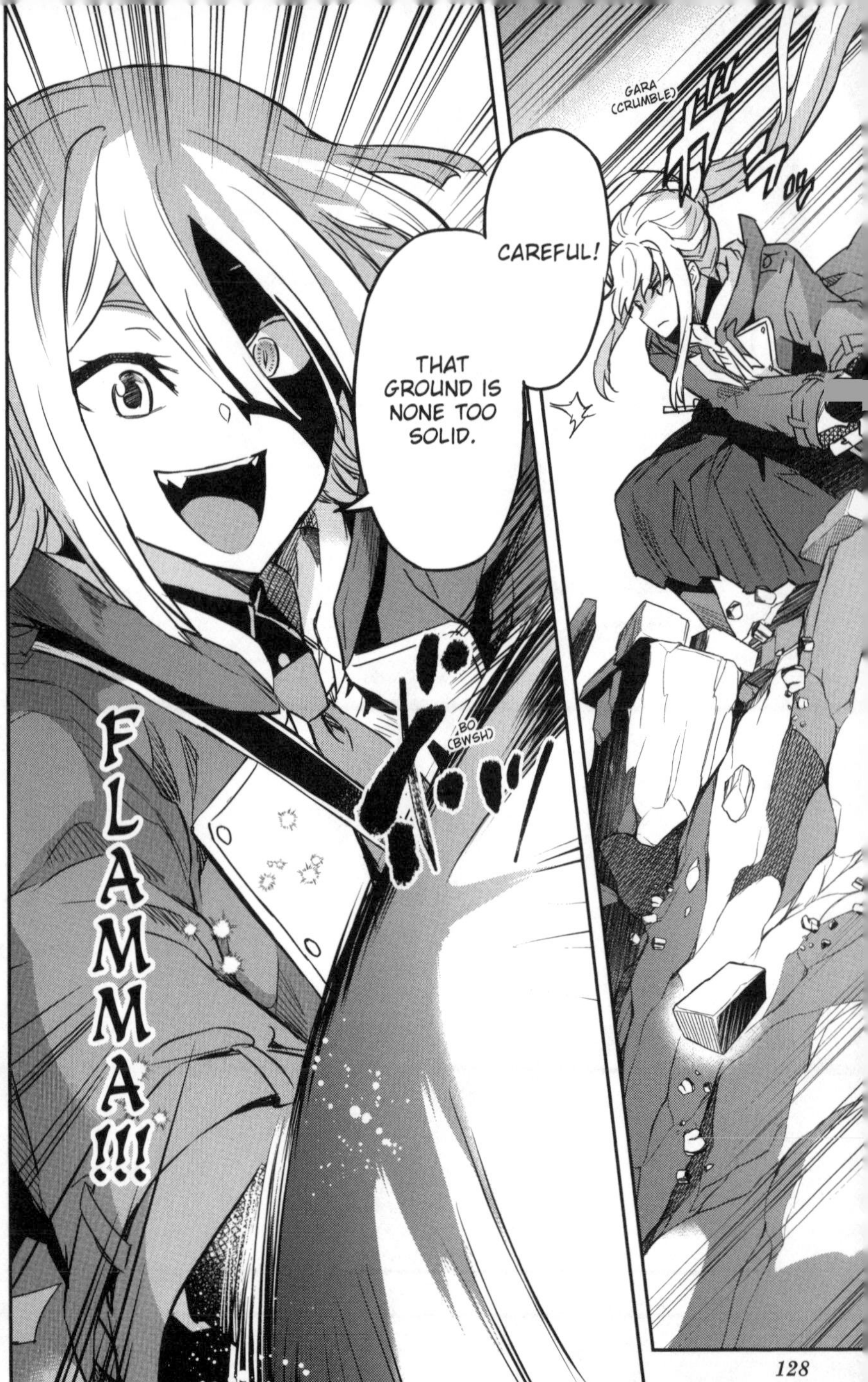
GARA (CRUMBLE)
CAREFUL!
THAT GROUND IS NONE TOO SOLID.
BO (BWSH)
FLAMMA!!!

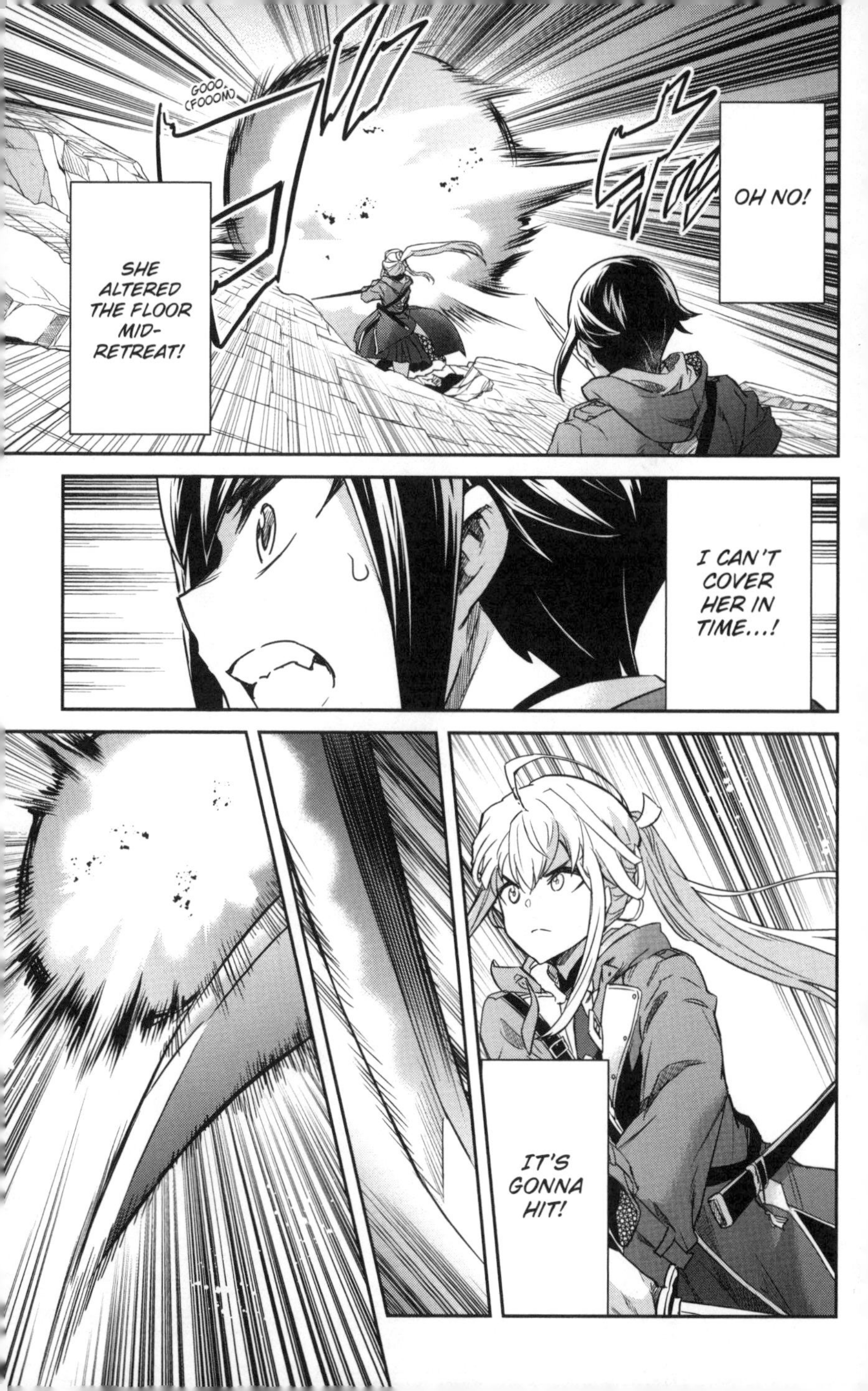
OH NO!
GOOO (FOOOM)
SHE ALTERED THE FLOOR MID-RETREAT!
I CAN'T COVER HER IN TIME...!
IT'S GONNA HIT!

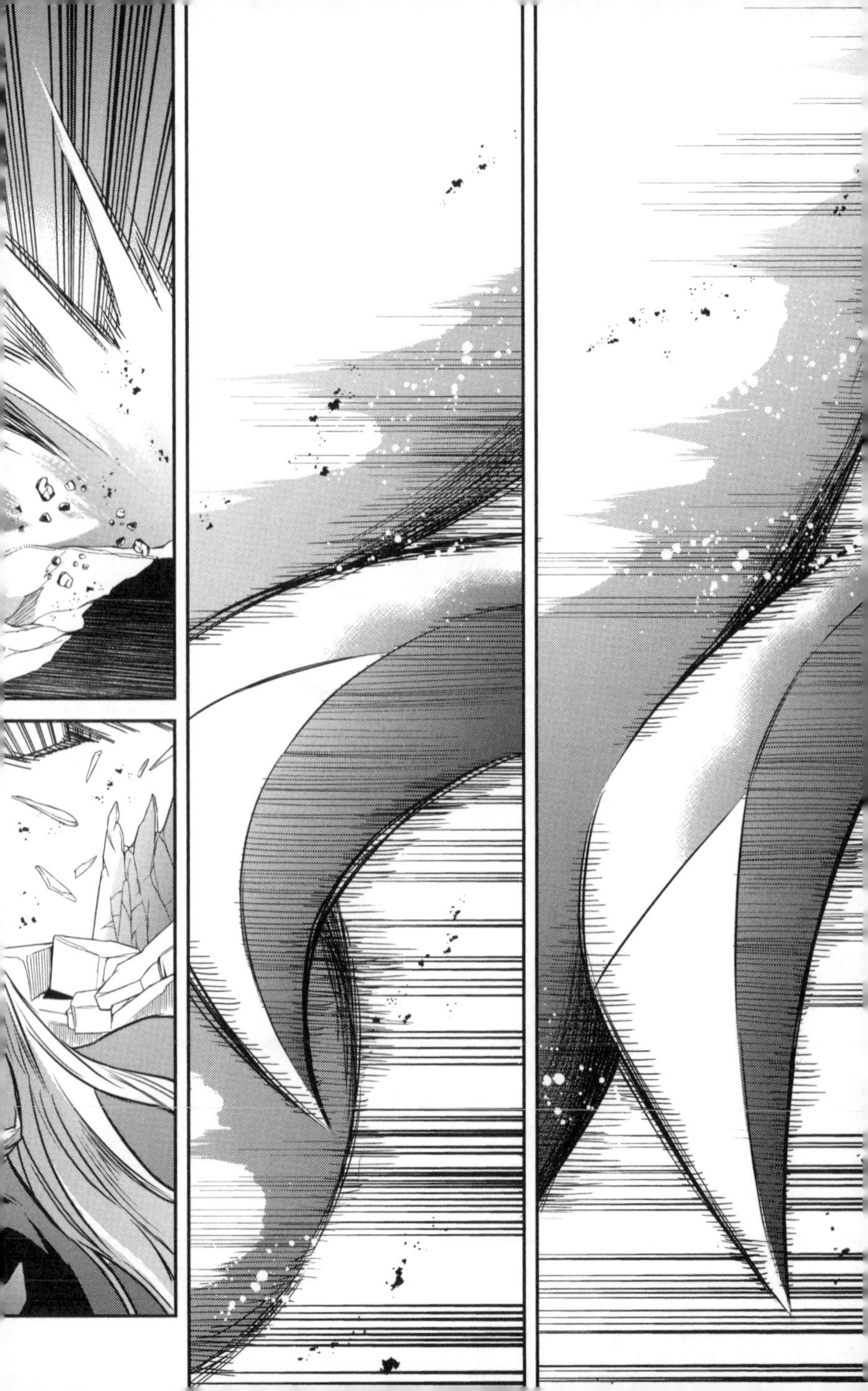

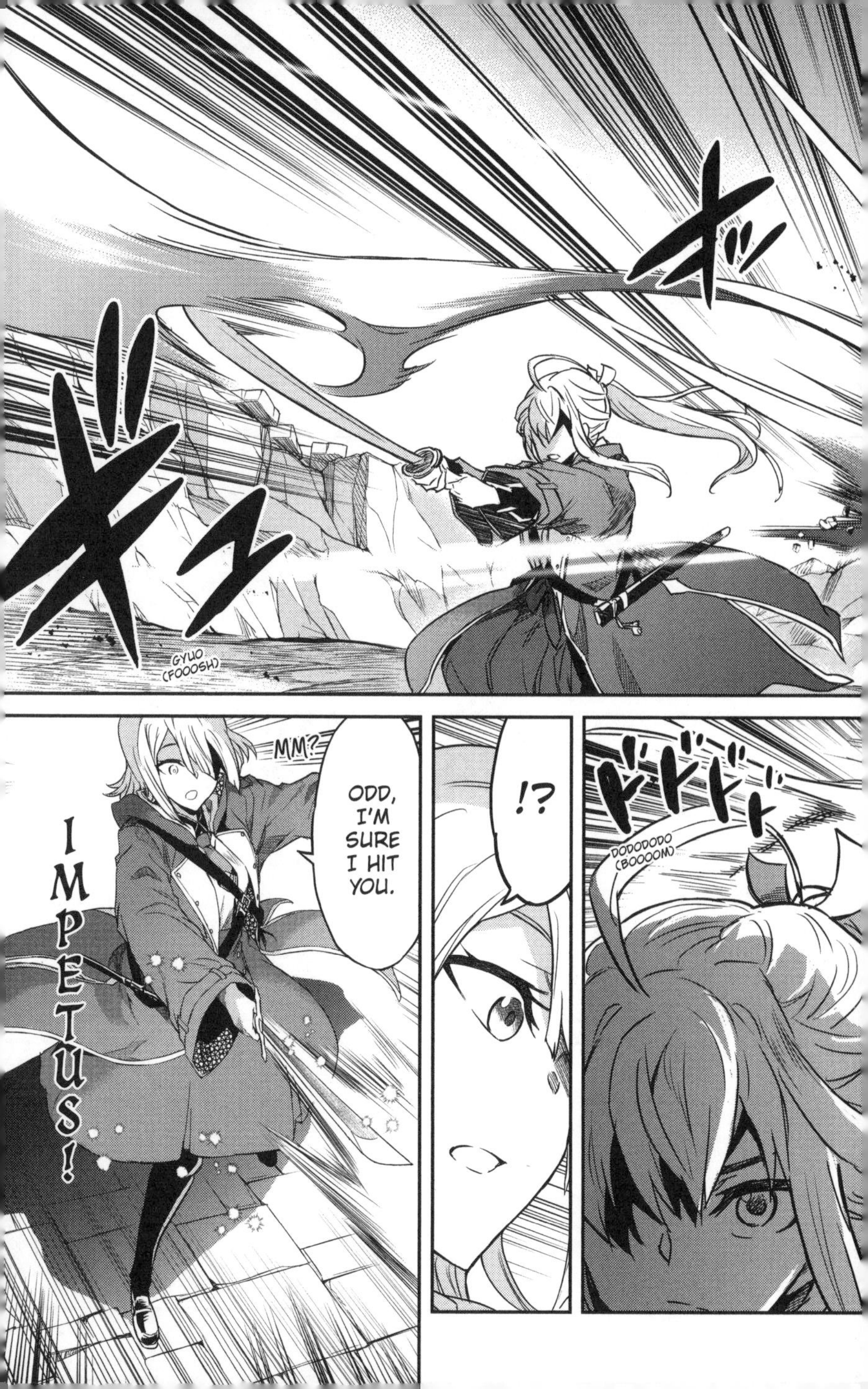

GYUO (FOOOSH)
DODODODO (BOOOOM)
!?
MM?
ODD, I'M SURE I HIT YOU.
IMPETUS!

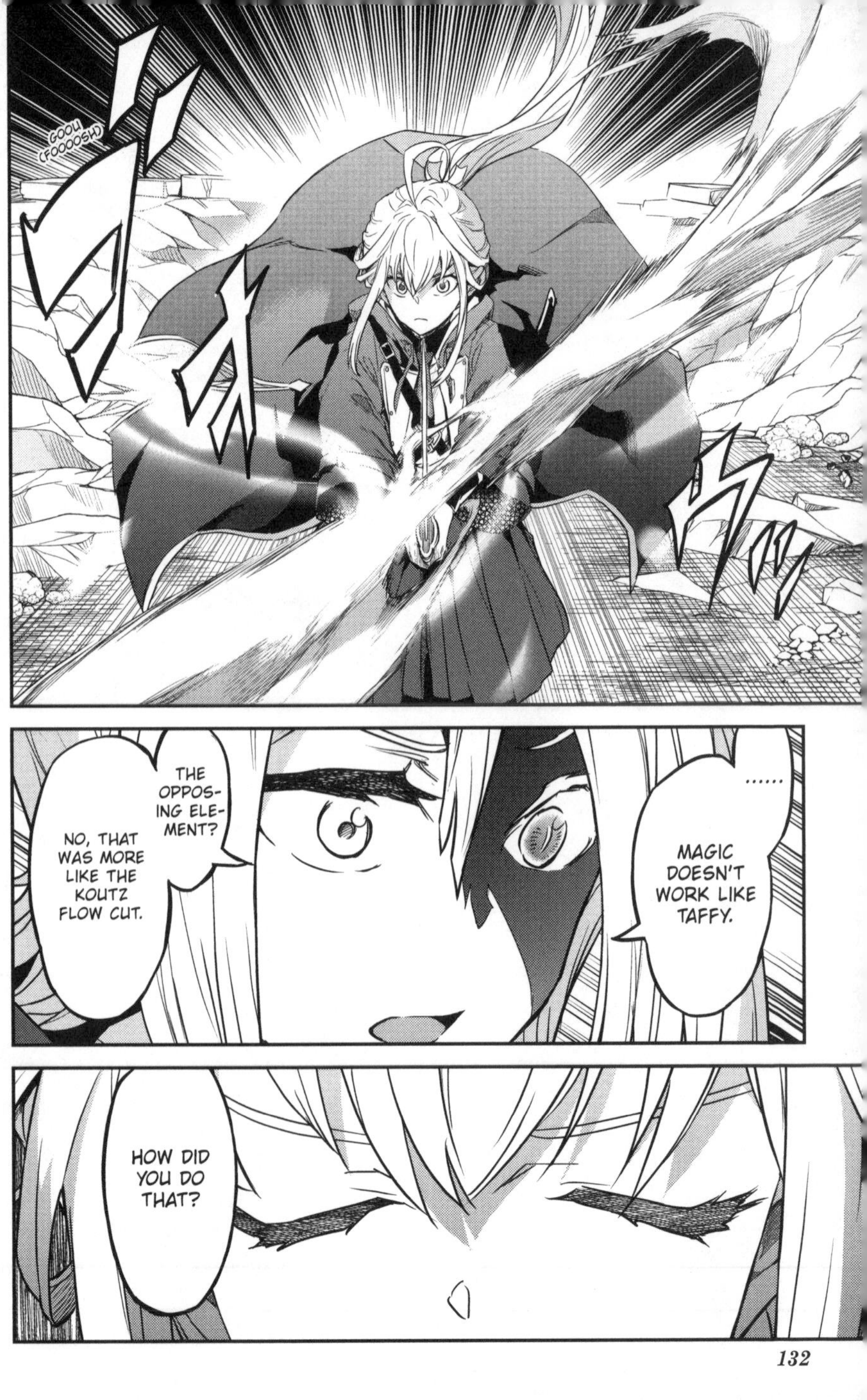
GOOU (FOOOOSH)
...... MAGIC DOESN'T WORK LIKE TAFFY.
THE OPPOSING ELEMENT?
NO, THAT WAS MORE LIKE THE KOUTZ FLOW CUT.
HOW DID YOU DO THAT?

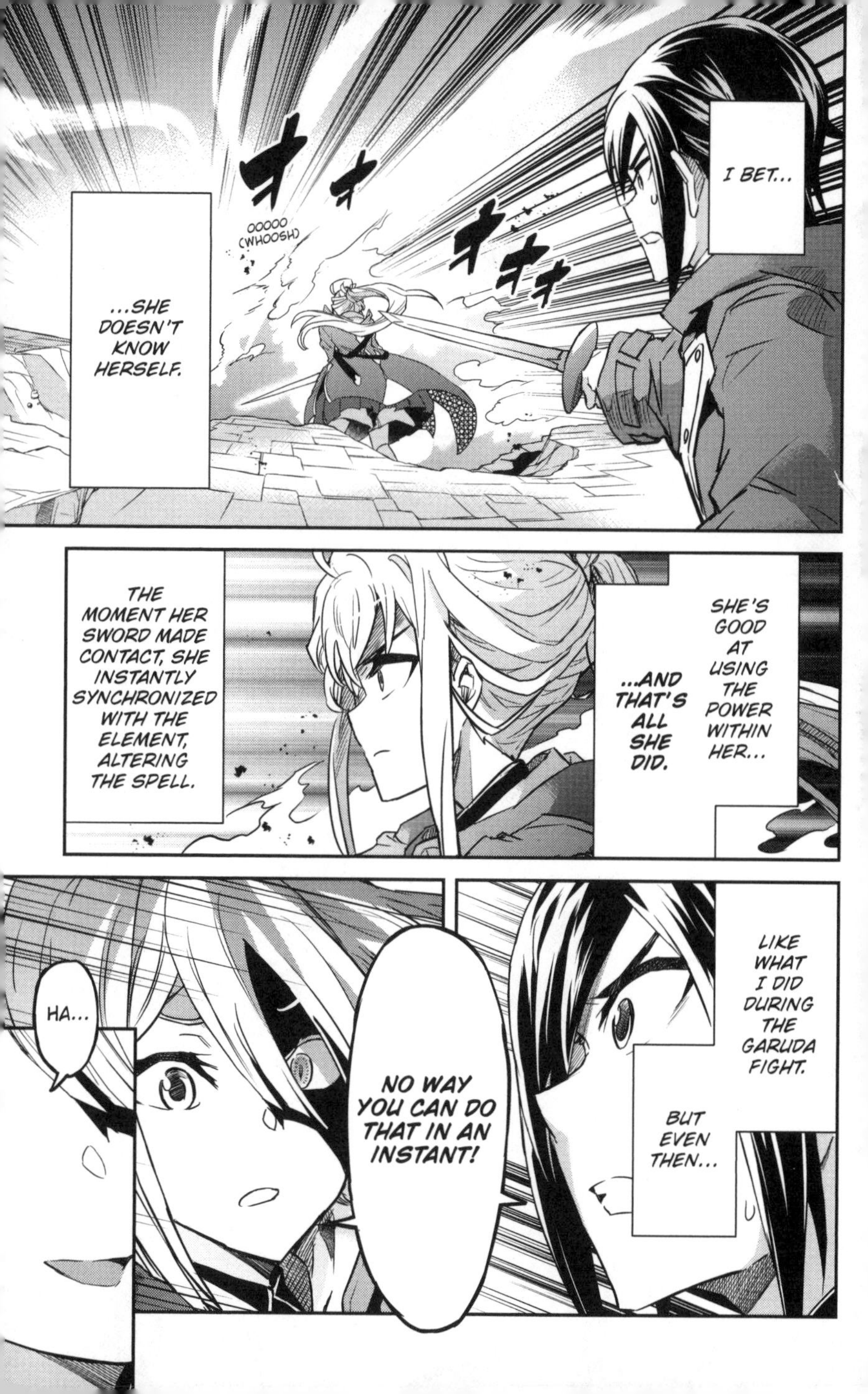
I BET...
OOOOO (WHOOSH)
...SHE DOESN'T KNOW HERSELF.
SHE'S GOOD AT USING THE POWER WITHIN HER...
...AND THAT'S ALL SHE DID.
THE MOMENT HER SWORD MADE CONTACT, SHE INSTANTLY SYNCHRONIZED WITH THE ELEMENT, ALTERING THE SPELL.
LIKE WHAT I DID DURING THE GARUDA FIGHT.
BUT EVEN THEN...
NO WAY YOU CAN DO THAT IN AN INSTANT!
HA...

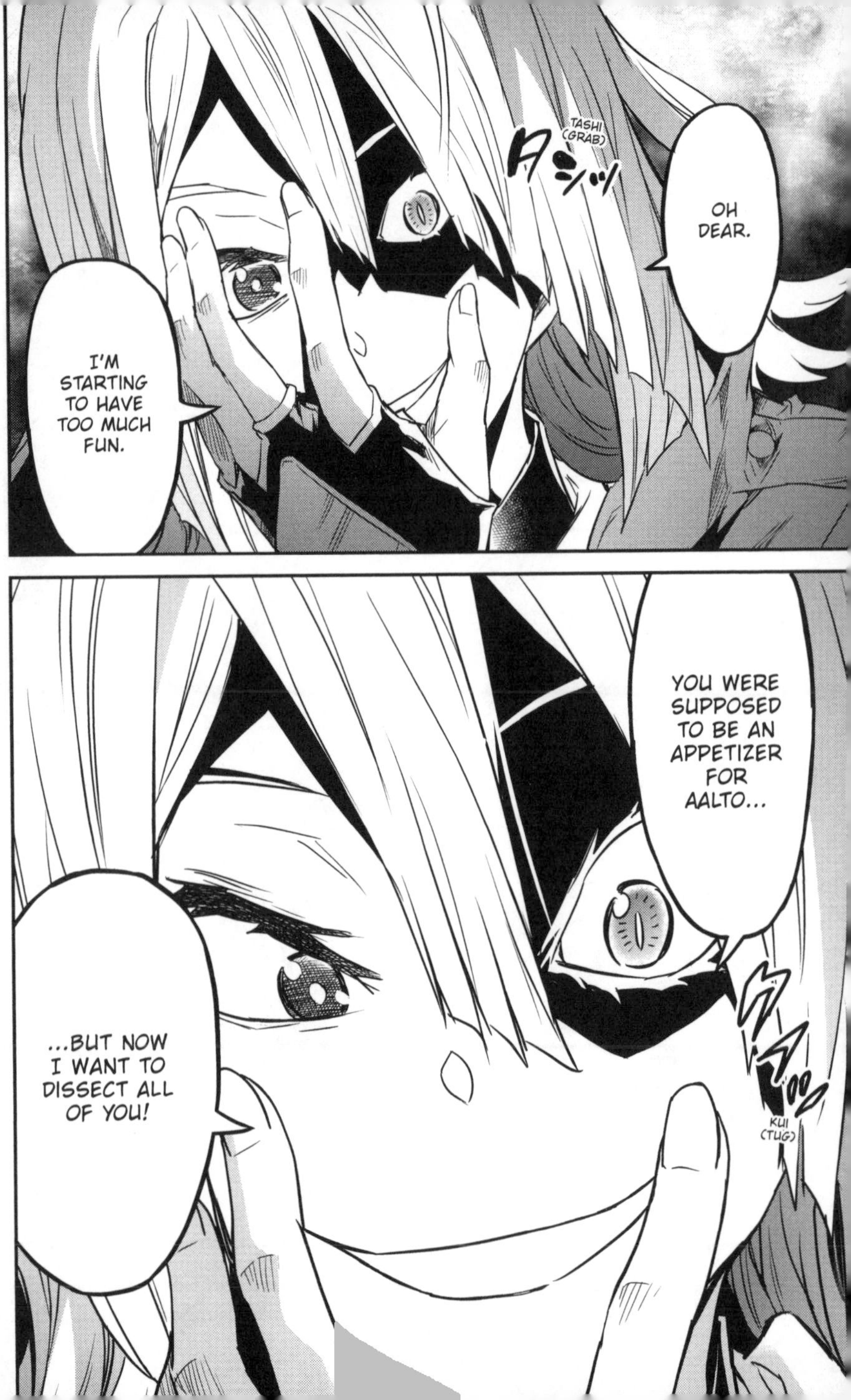
OH DEAR.
TASHI (GRAB)
I'M STARTING TO HAVE TOO MUCH FUN.
YOU WERE SUPPOSED TO BE AN APPETIZER FOR AALTO...
KUI (TUG)
...BUT NOW I WANT TO DISSECT ALL OF YOU!

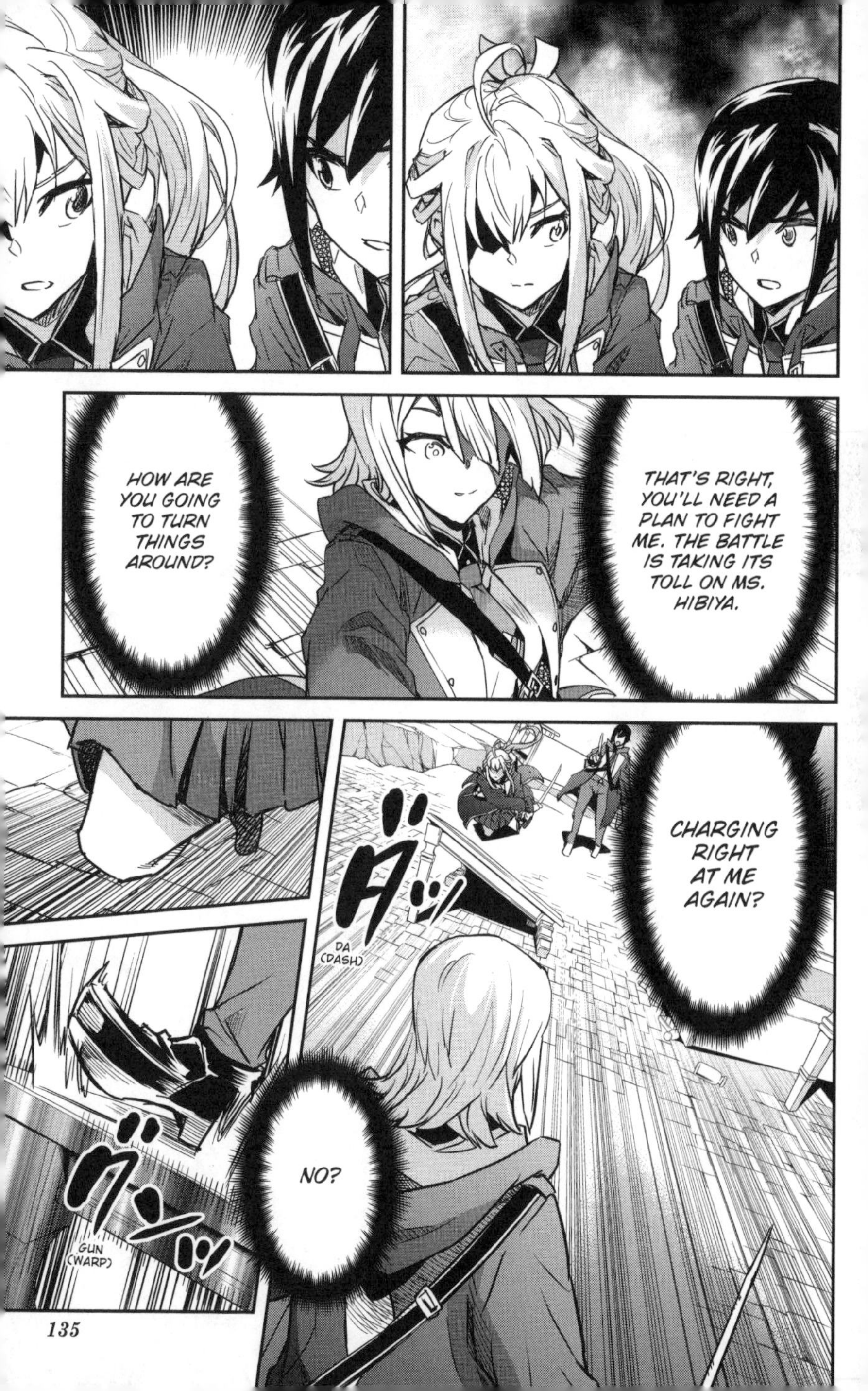

THAT'S RIGHT, YOU'LL NEED A PLAN TO FIGHT ME. THE BATTLE IS TAKING ITS TOLL ON MS. HIBIYA.
HOW ARE YOU GOING TO TURN THINGS AROUND?
CHARGING RIGHT AT ME AGAIN?
DA (DASH)
NO?
GUN (WARP)

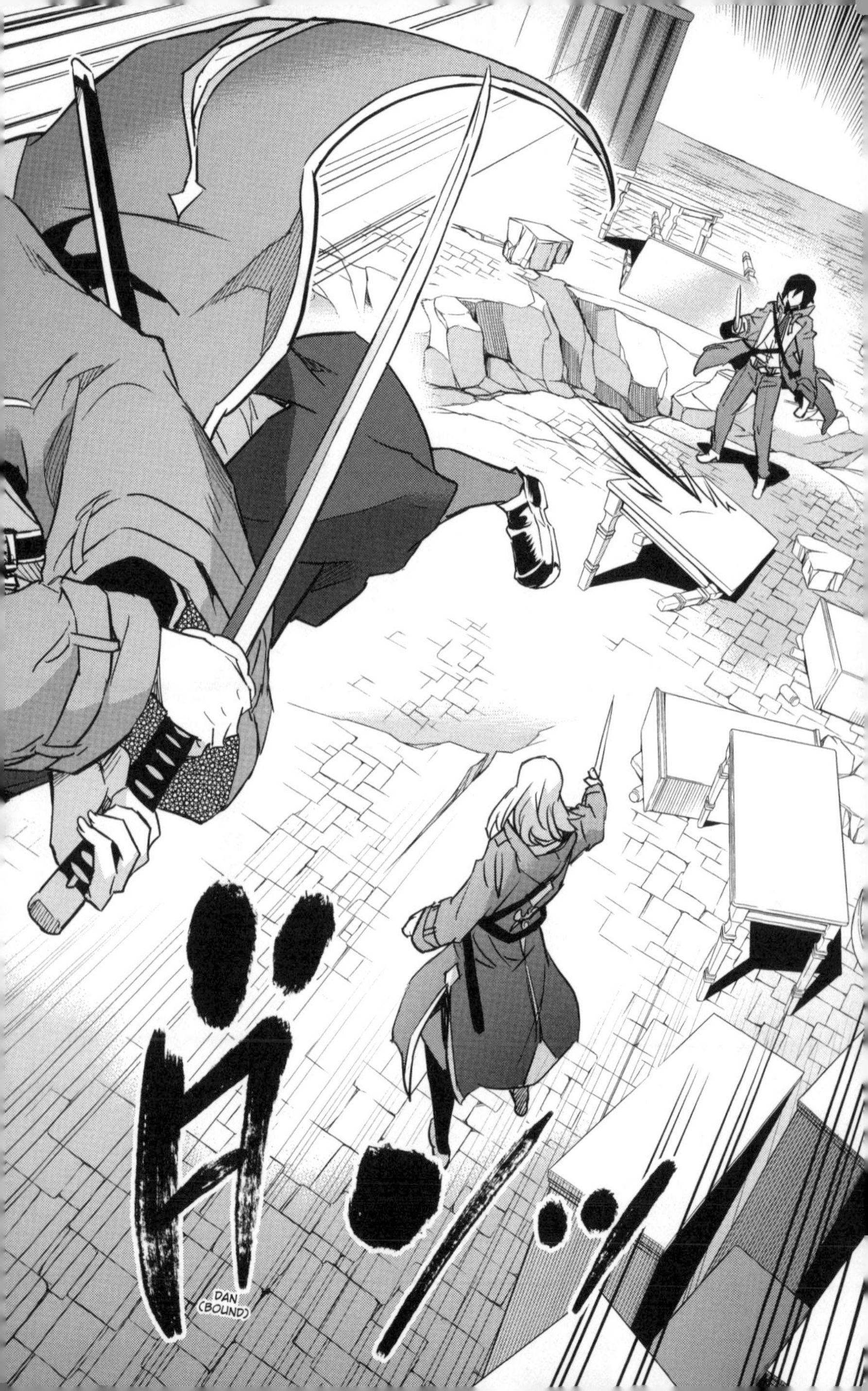
DAN (BOUND)

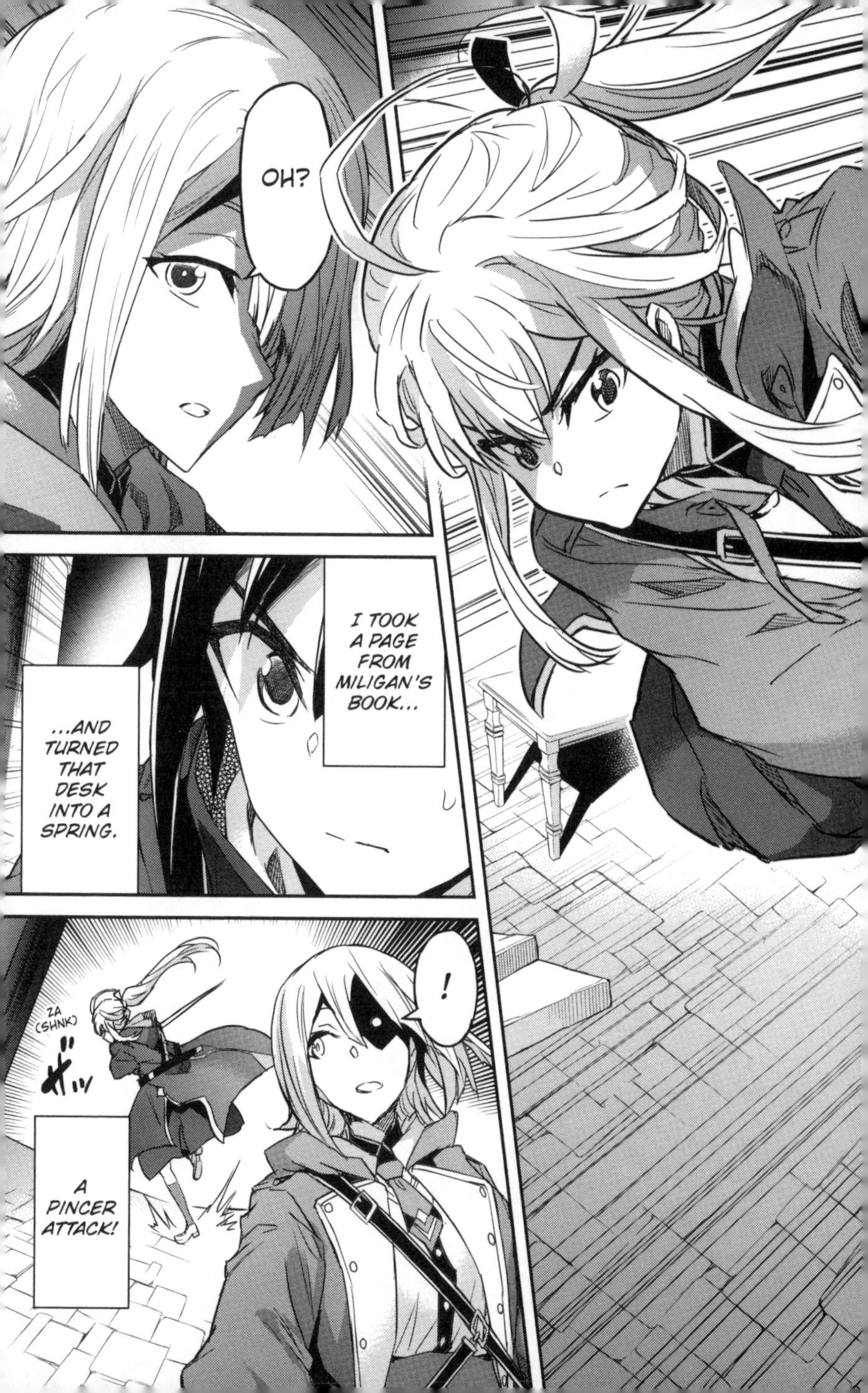
OH?
I TOOK A PAGE FROM MILIGAN'S BOOK...
...AND TURNED THAT DESK INTO A SPRING.
!
ZA (SHNK)
A PINCER ATTACK!

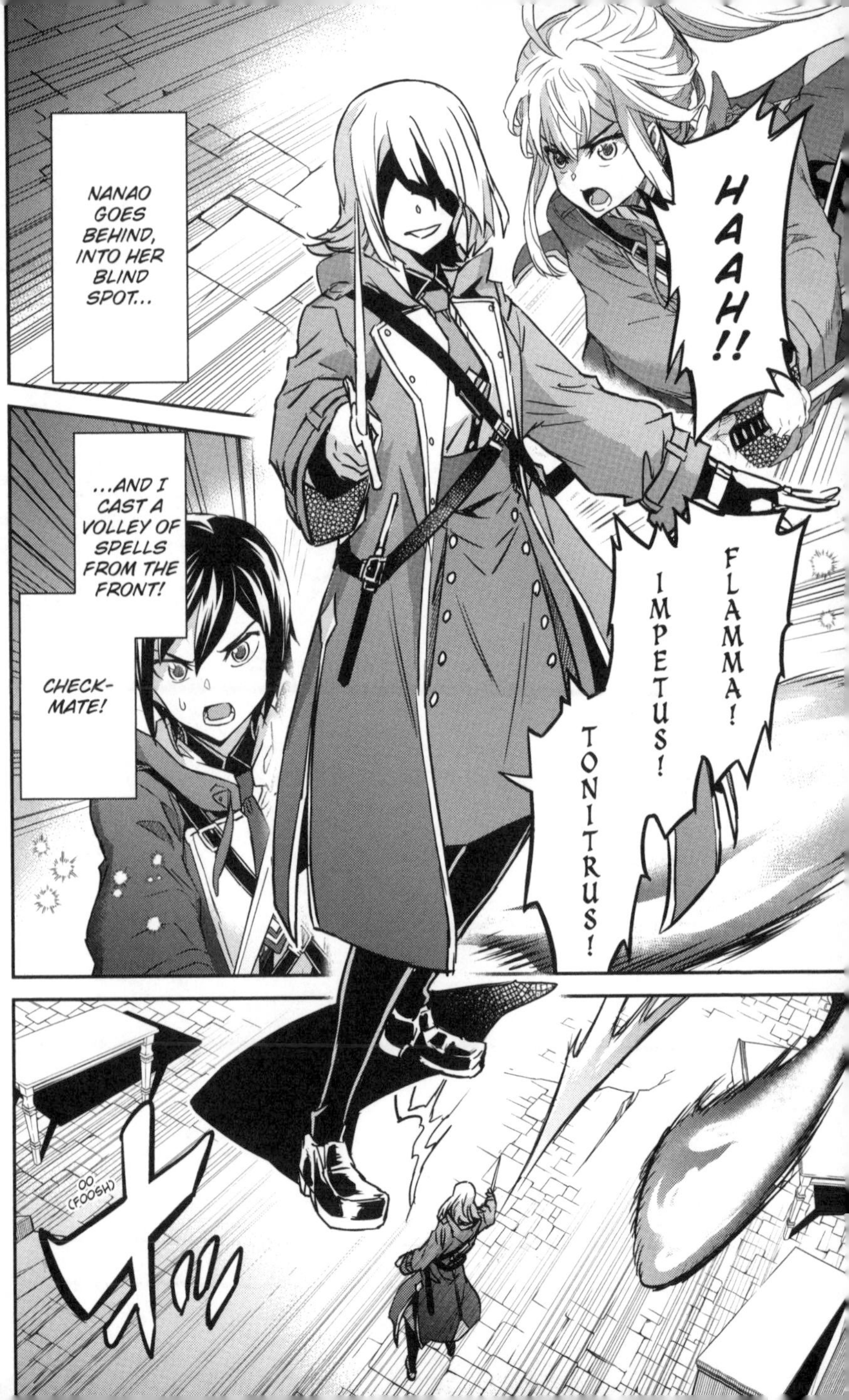
HAAAH!!
NANAO GOES BEHIND, INTO HER BLIND SPOT...
FLAMMA!
IMPETUS!
TONITRUS!
...AND I CAST A VOLLEY OF SPELLS FROM THE FRONT!
CHECK-MATE!
OO (FOOSH)

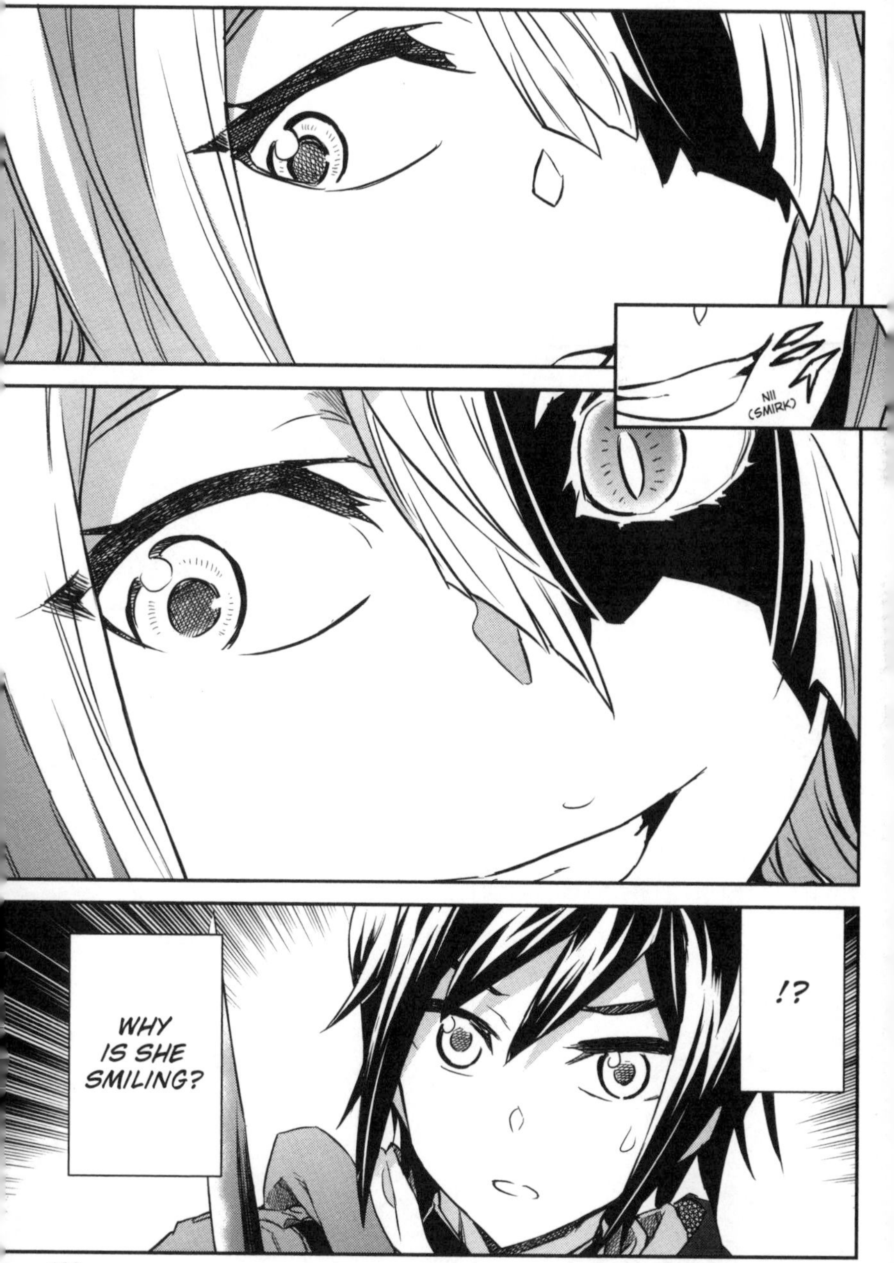
NII
(SMIRK)
!?
WHY IS SHE SMILING?

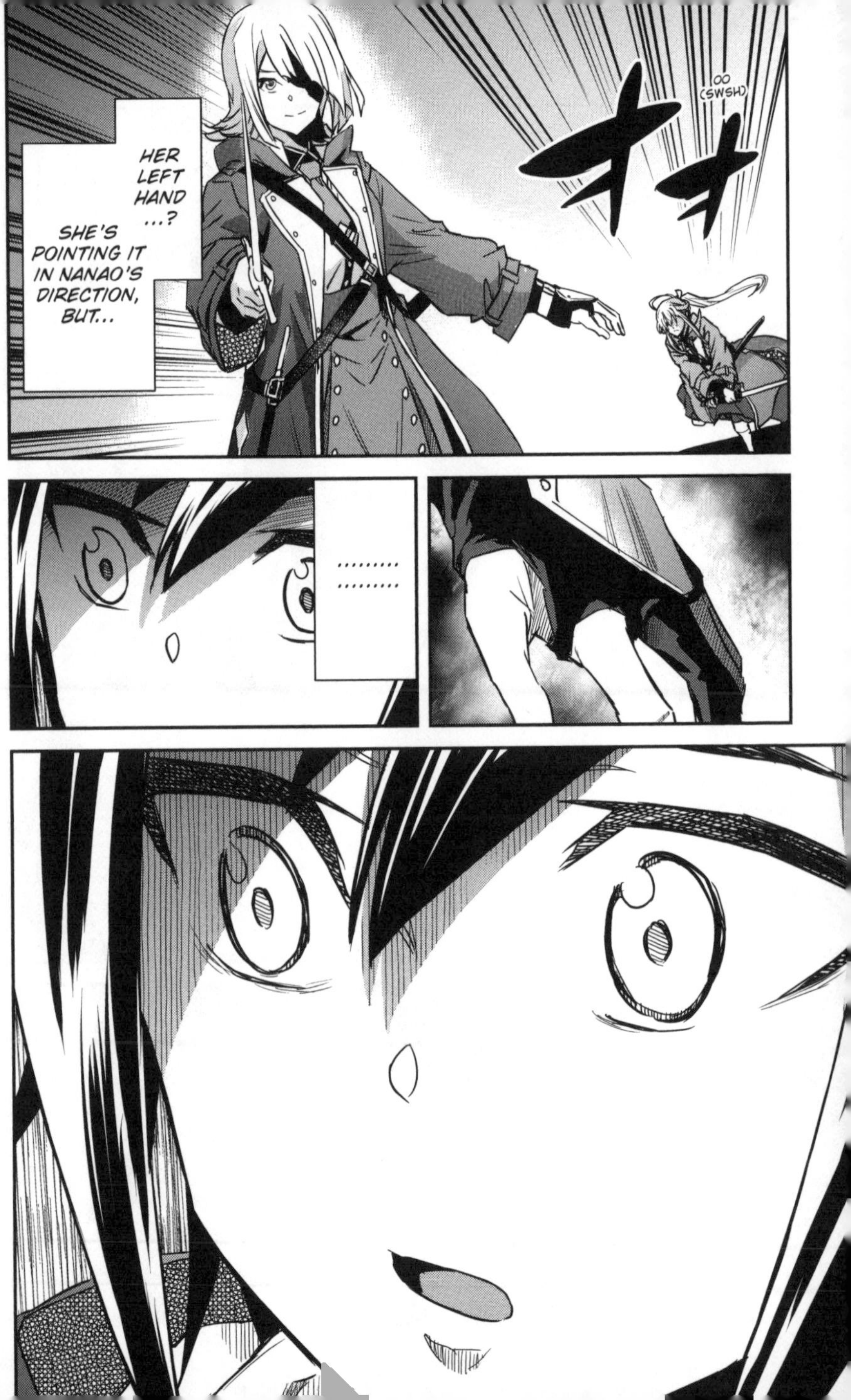
OO (SWSH)
HER LEFT HAND...?
SHE'S POINTING IT IN NANAO'S DIRECTION, BUT...
....
....

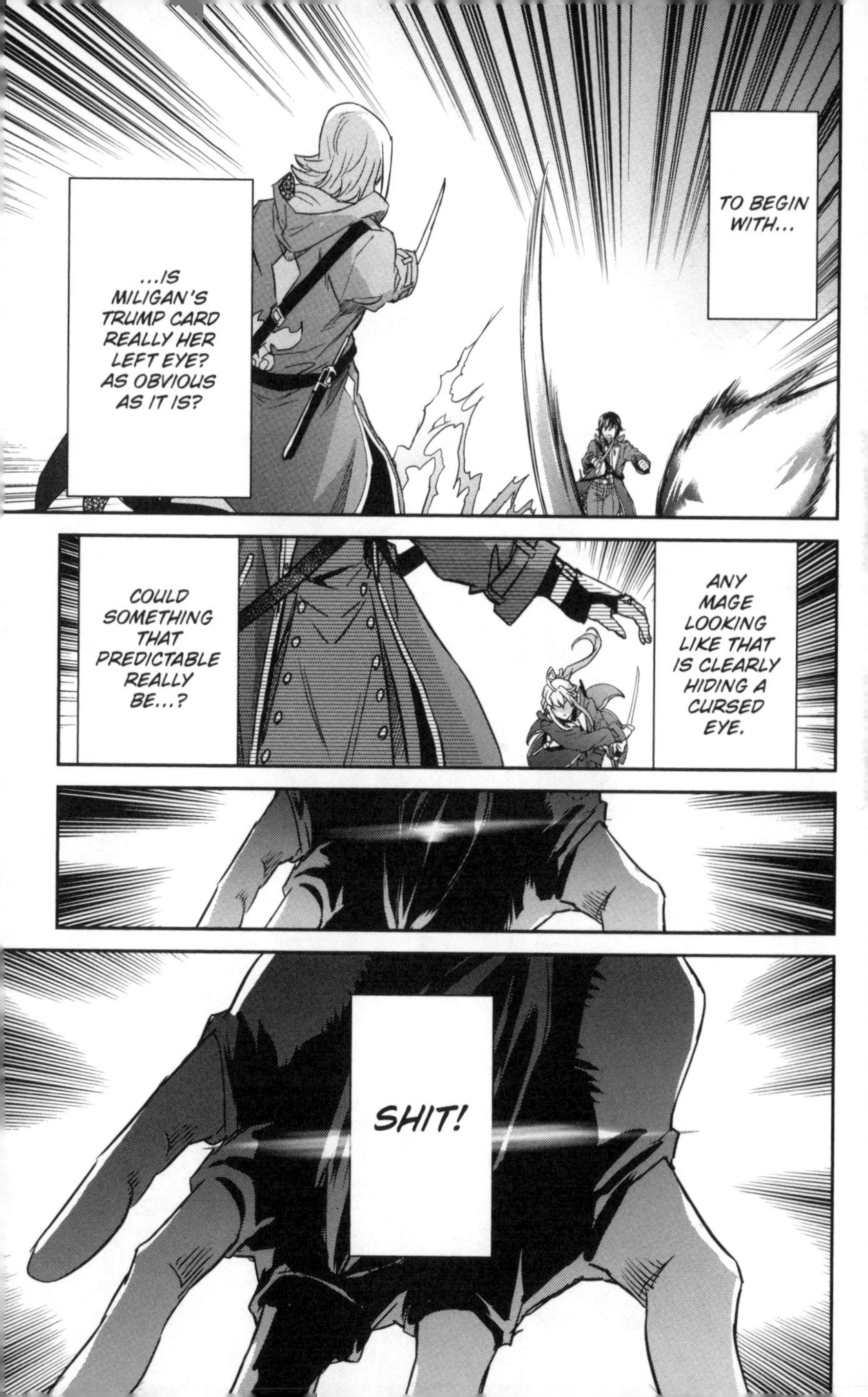
TO BEGIN WITH...
...IS MILIGAN'S TRUMP CARD REALLY HER LEFT EYE? AS OBVIOUS AS IT IS?
ANY MAGE LOOKING LIKE THAT IS CLEARLY HIDING A CURSED EYE.
COULD SOMETHING THAT PREDICTABLE REALLY BE...?
SHIT!

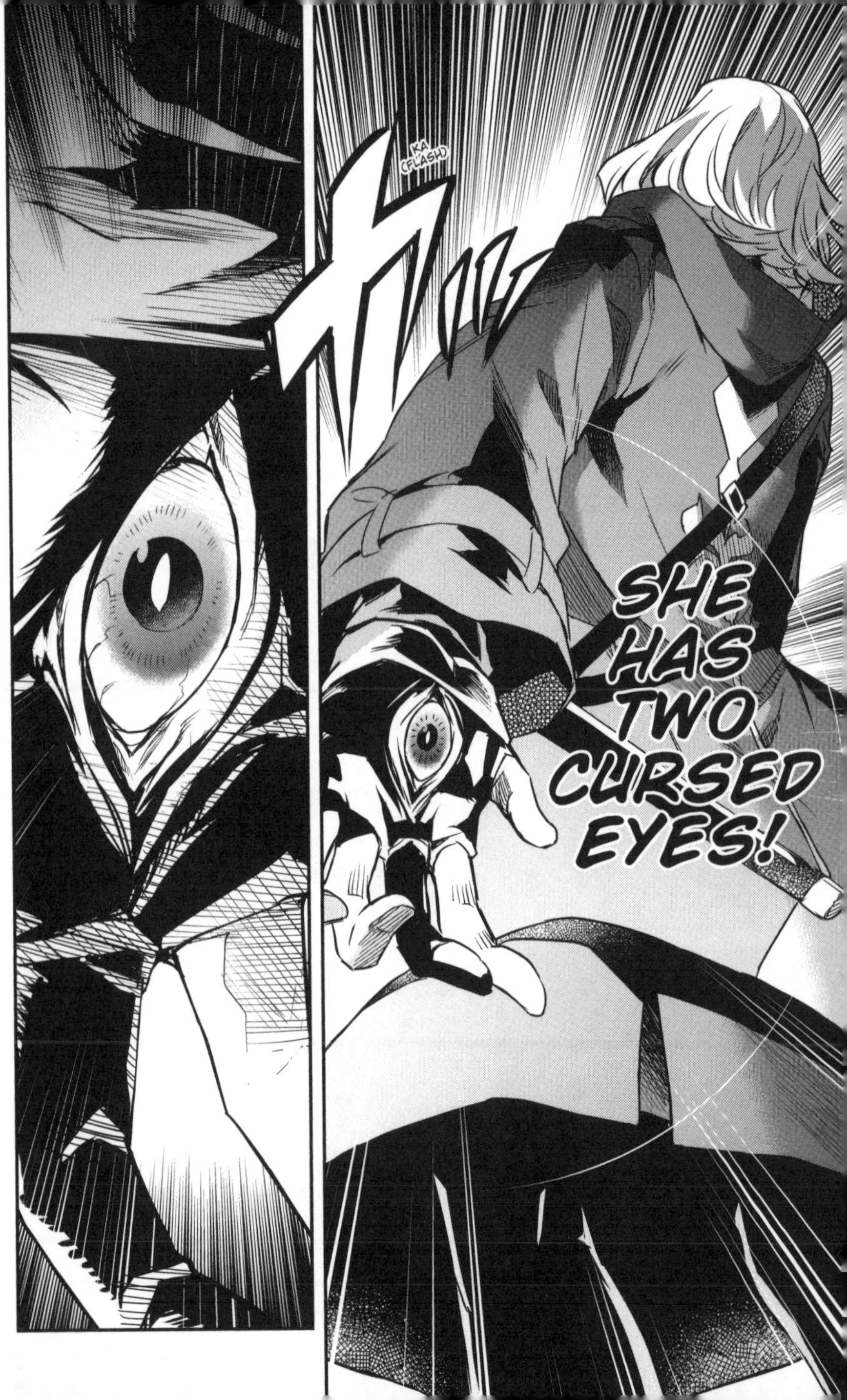
KA (FLASH)
SHE HAS TWO CURSED EYES!

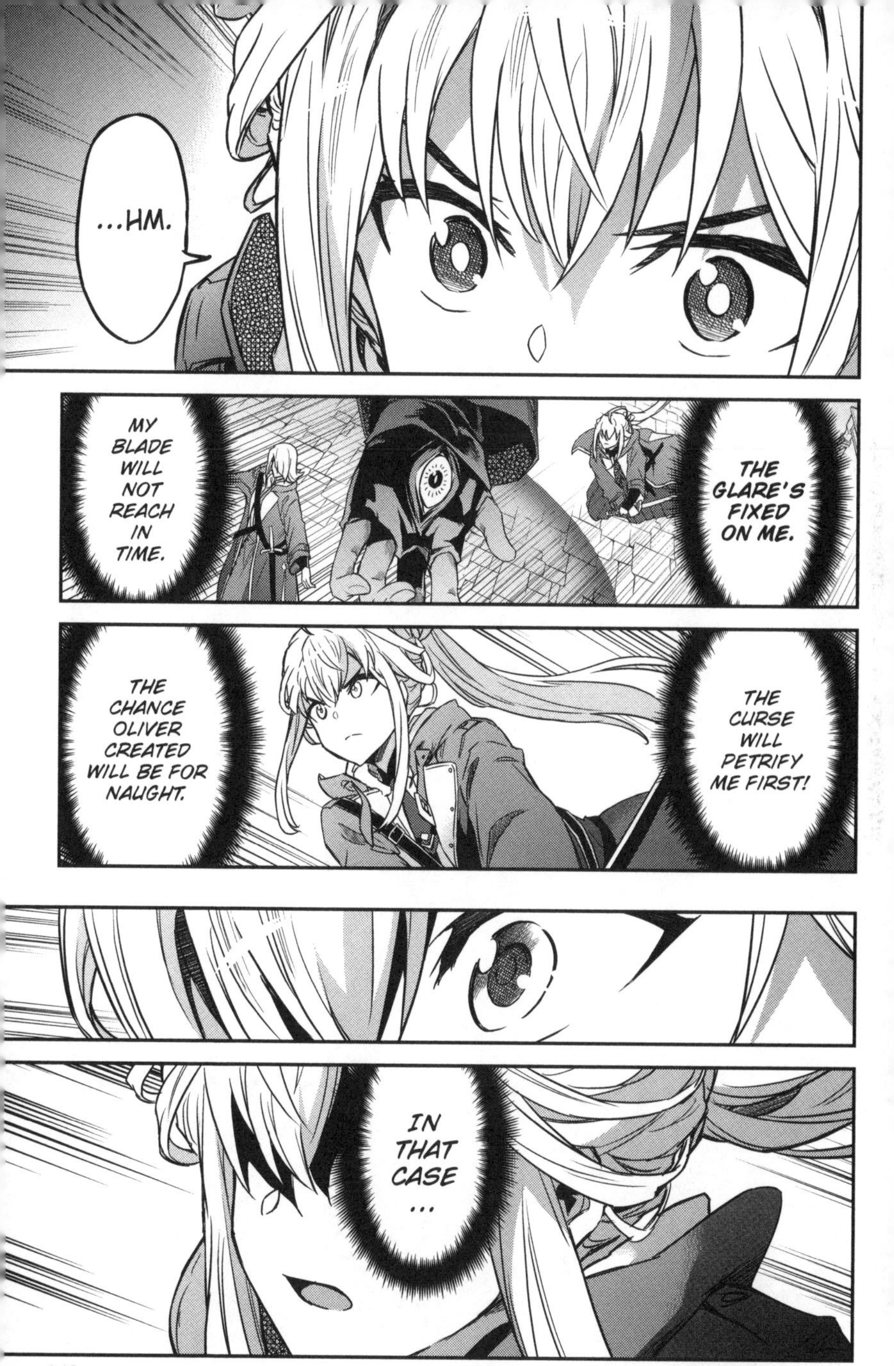
...HM.
THE GLARE'S FIXED ON ME.
MY BLADE WILL NOT REACH IN TIME.
THE CURSE WILL PETRIFY ME FIRST!
THE CHANCE OLIVER CREATED WILL BE FOR NAUGHT.
IN THAT CASE ...

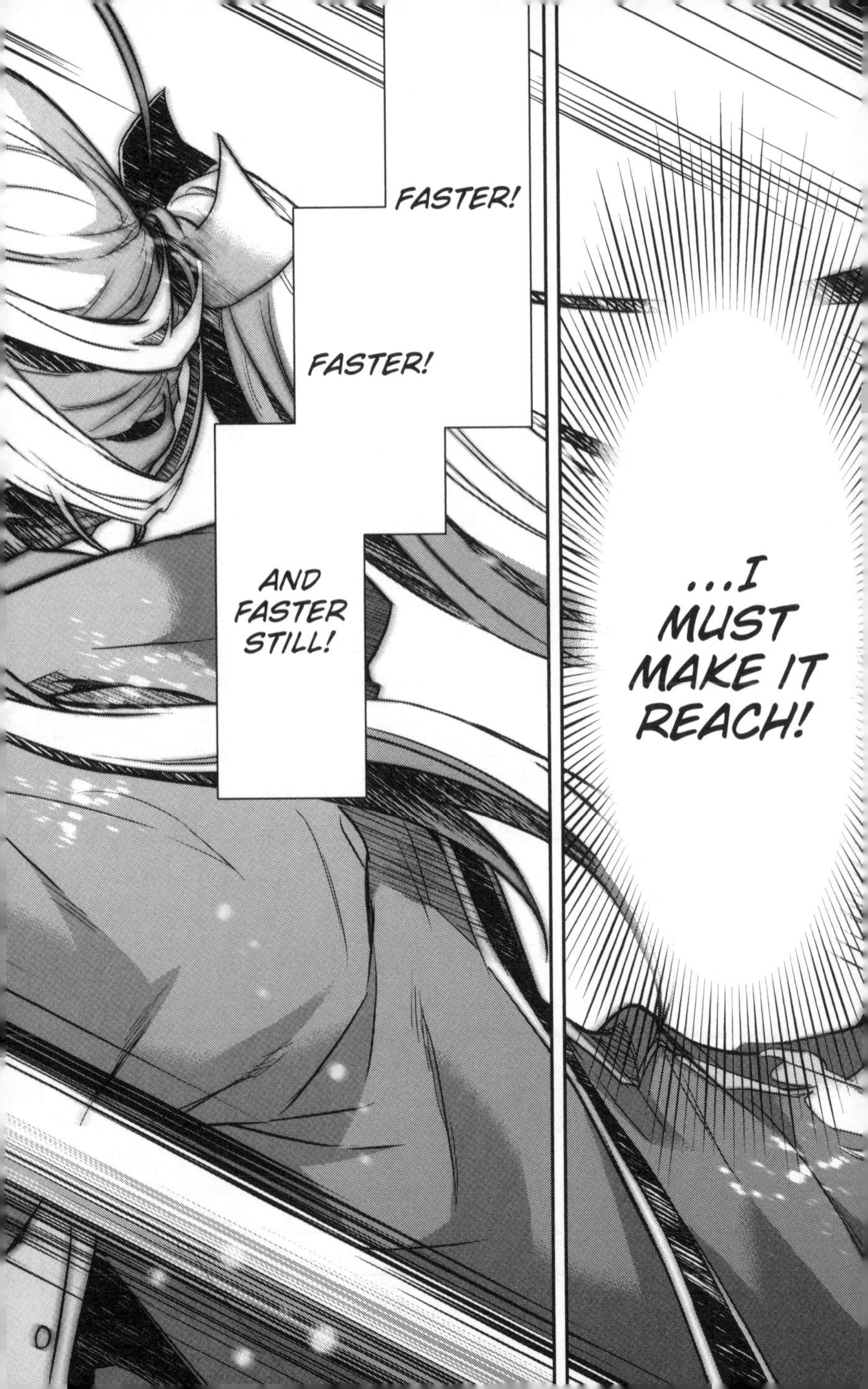
...I MUST MAKE IT REACH!
FASTER!
FASTER!
AND FASTER STILL!

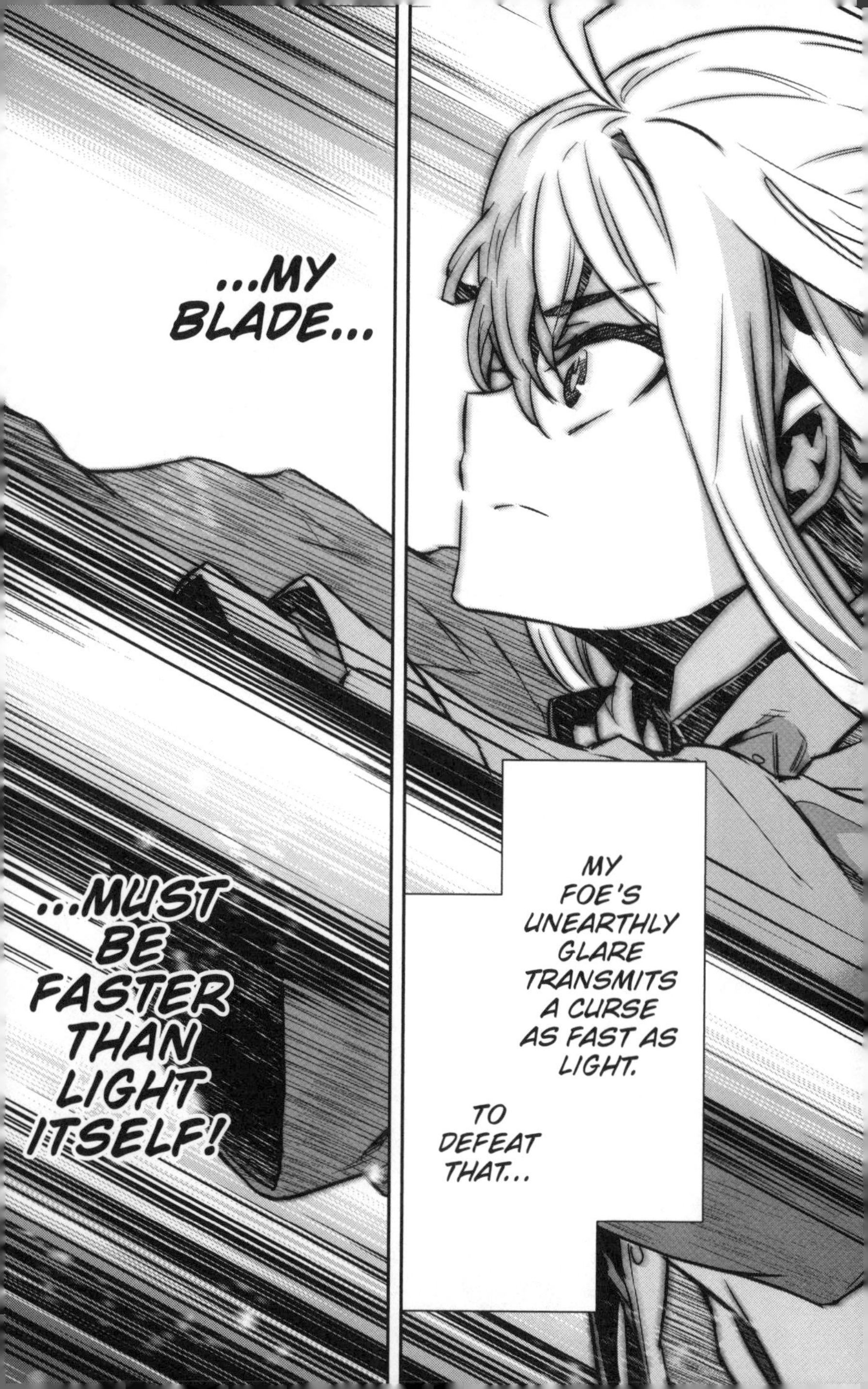
MY FOE'S UNEARTHLY GLARE TRANSMITS A CURSE AS FAST AS LIGHT.
TO DEFEAT THAT...
...MY BLADE...
...MUST BE FASTER THAN LIGHT ITSELF!

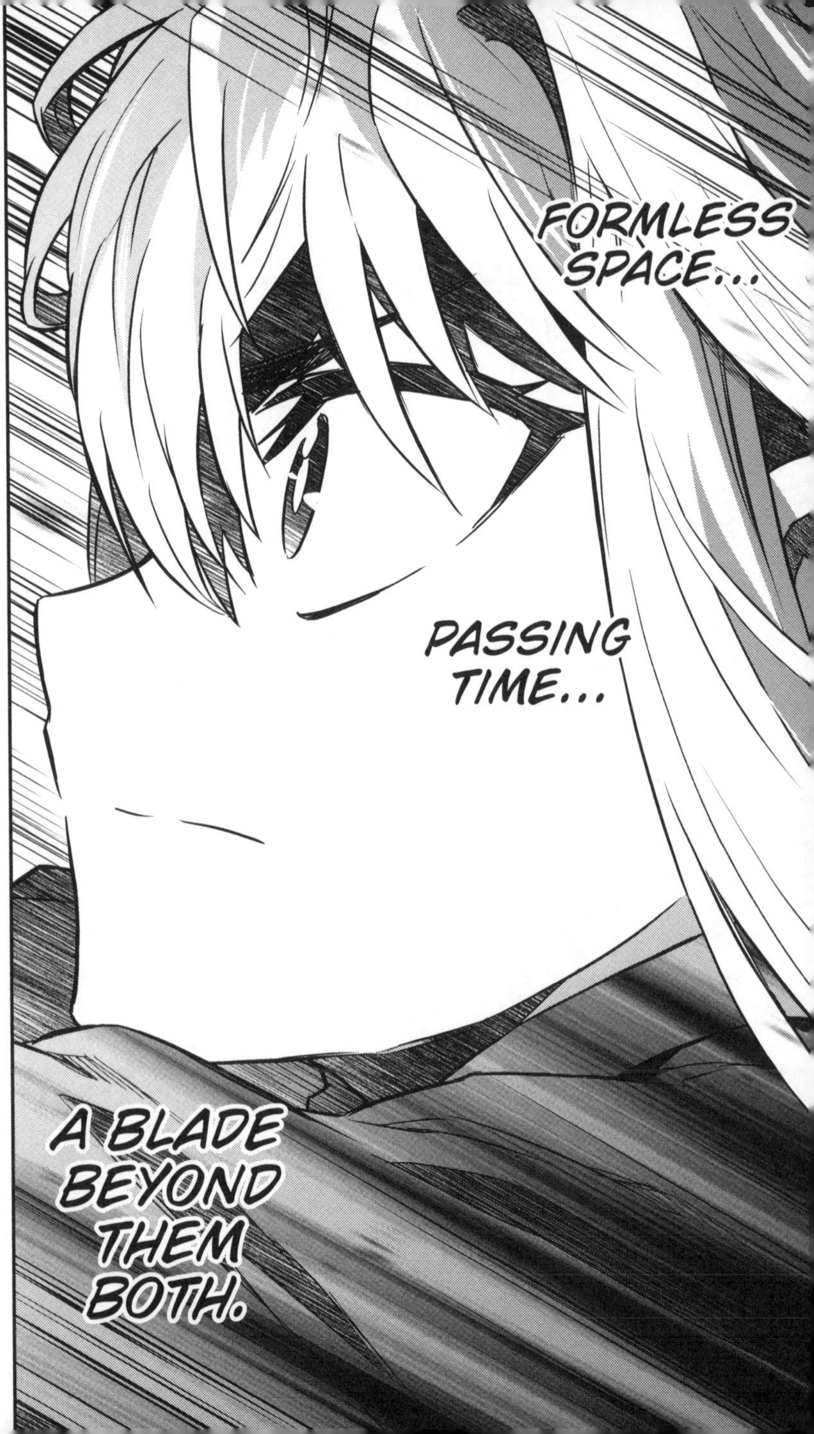
FORMLESS SPACE...
PASSING TIME...
A BLADE BEYOND THEM BOTH.

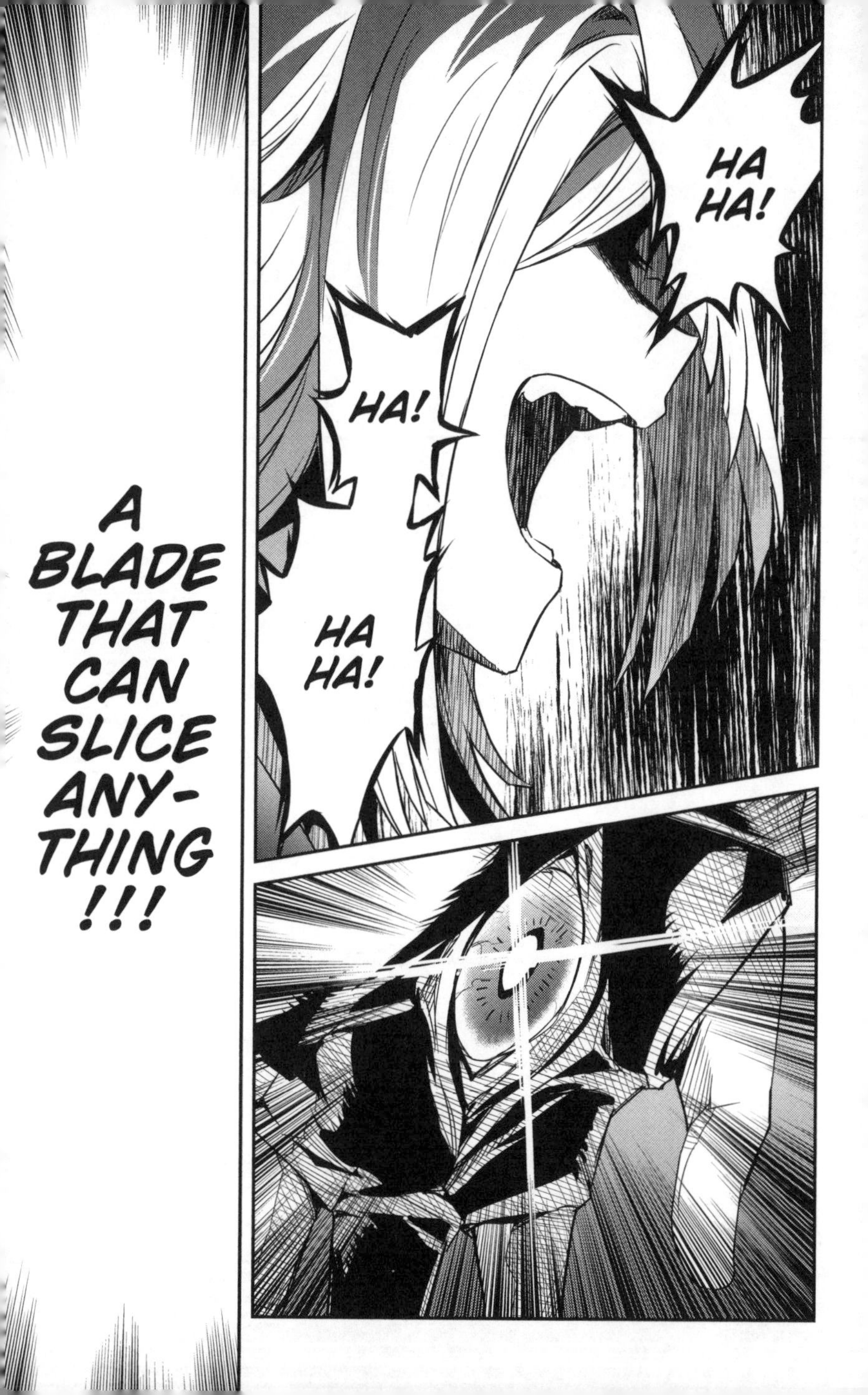
HA HA!
HA!
HA HA!
A BLADE THAT CAN SLICE ANY-THING!!!

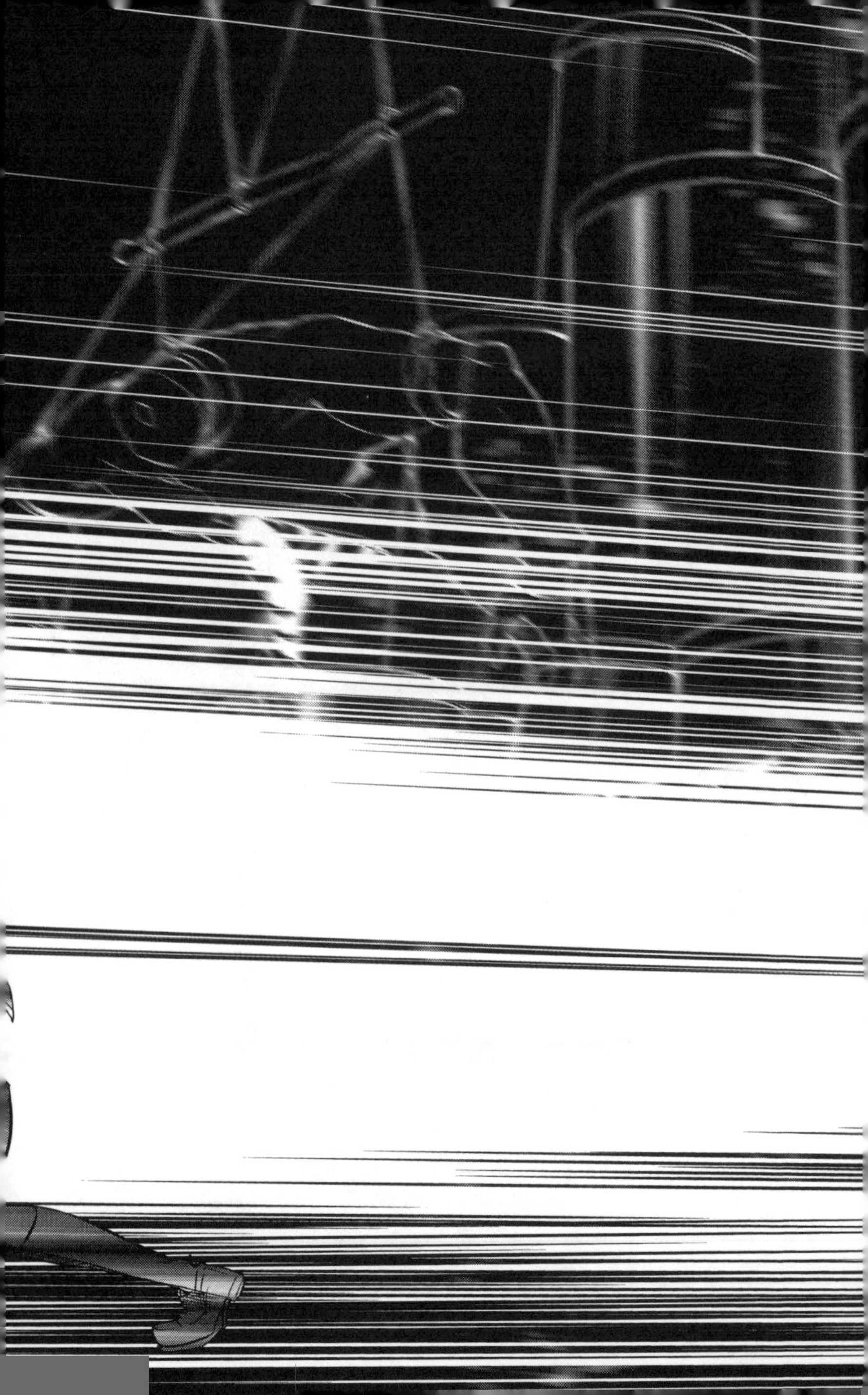

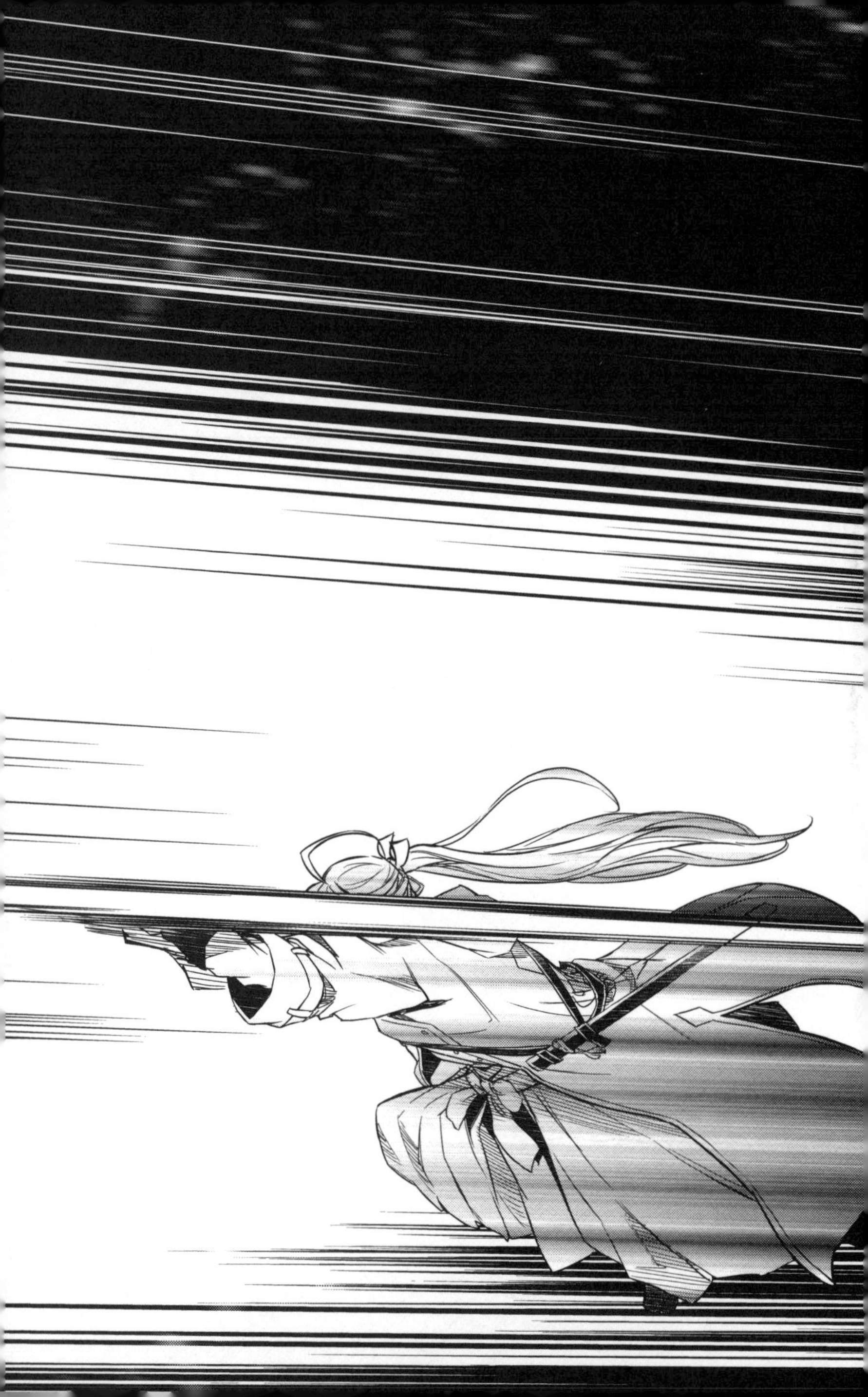

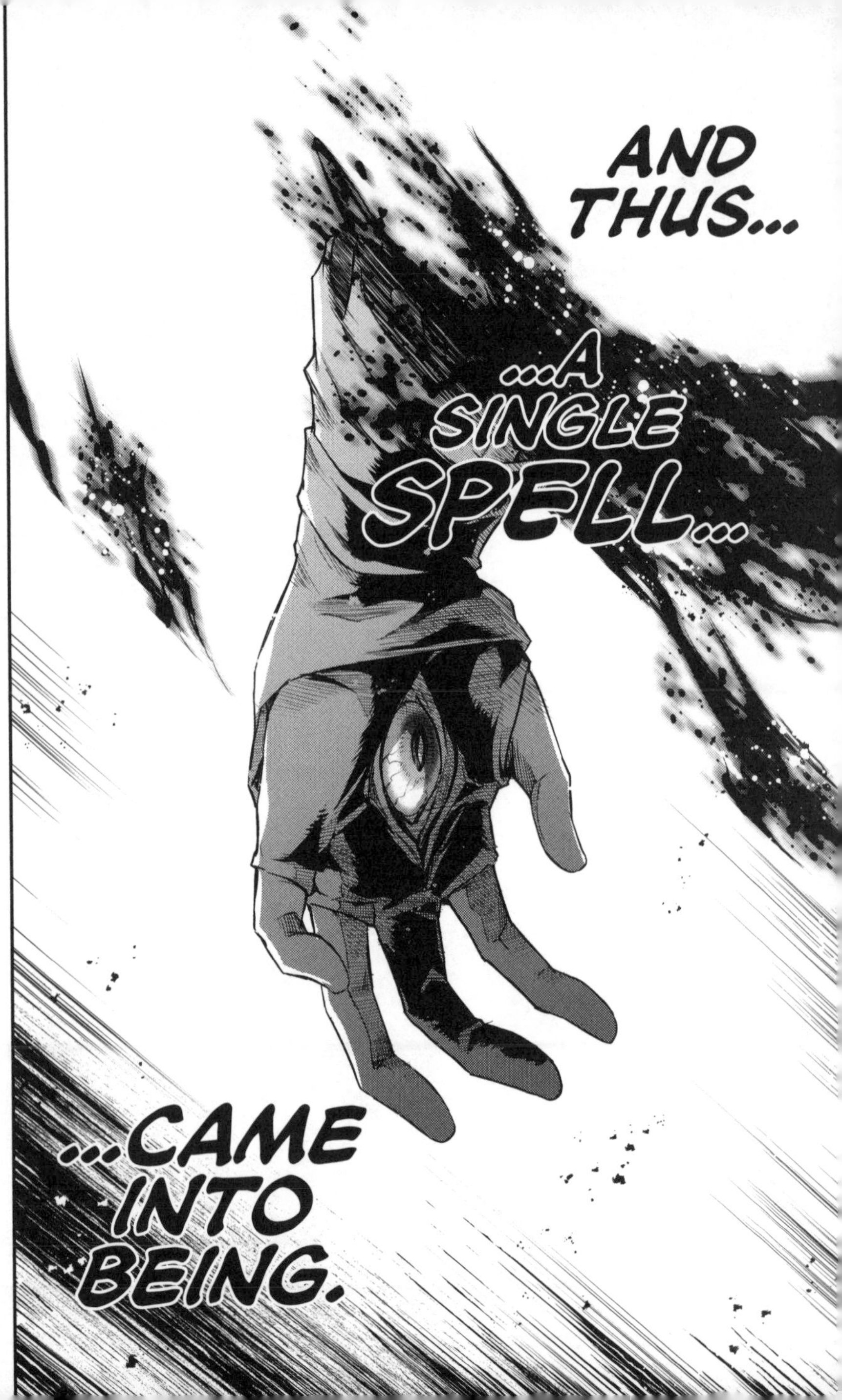
AND THUS...
...A SINGLE SPELL...
...CAME INTO BEING.

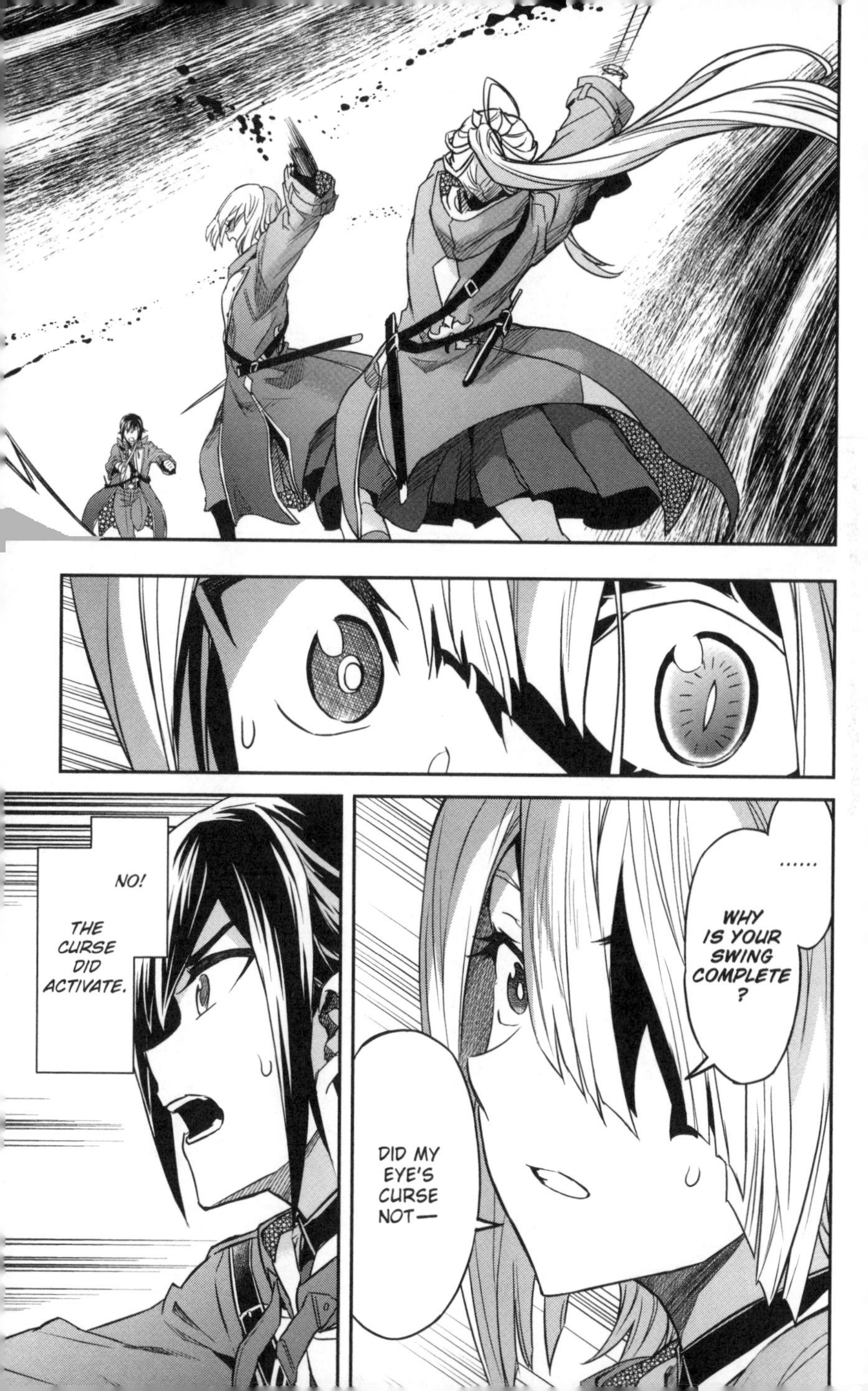
......
WHY IS YOUR SWING COMPLETE?
DID MY EYE'S CURSE NOT—
NO!
THE CURSE DID ACTIVATE.

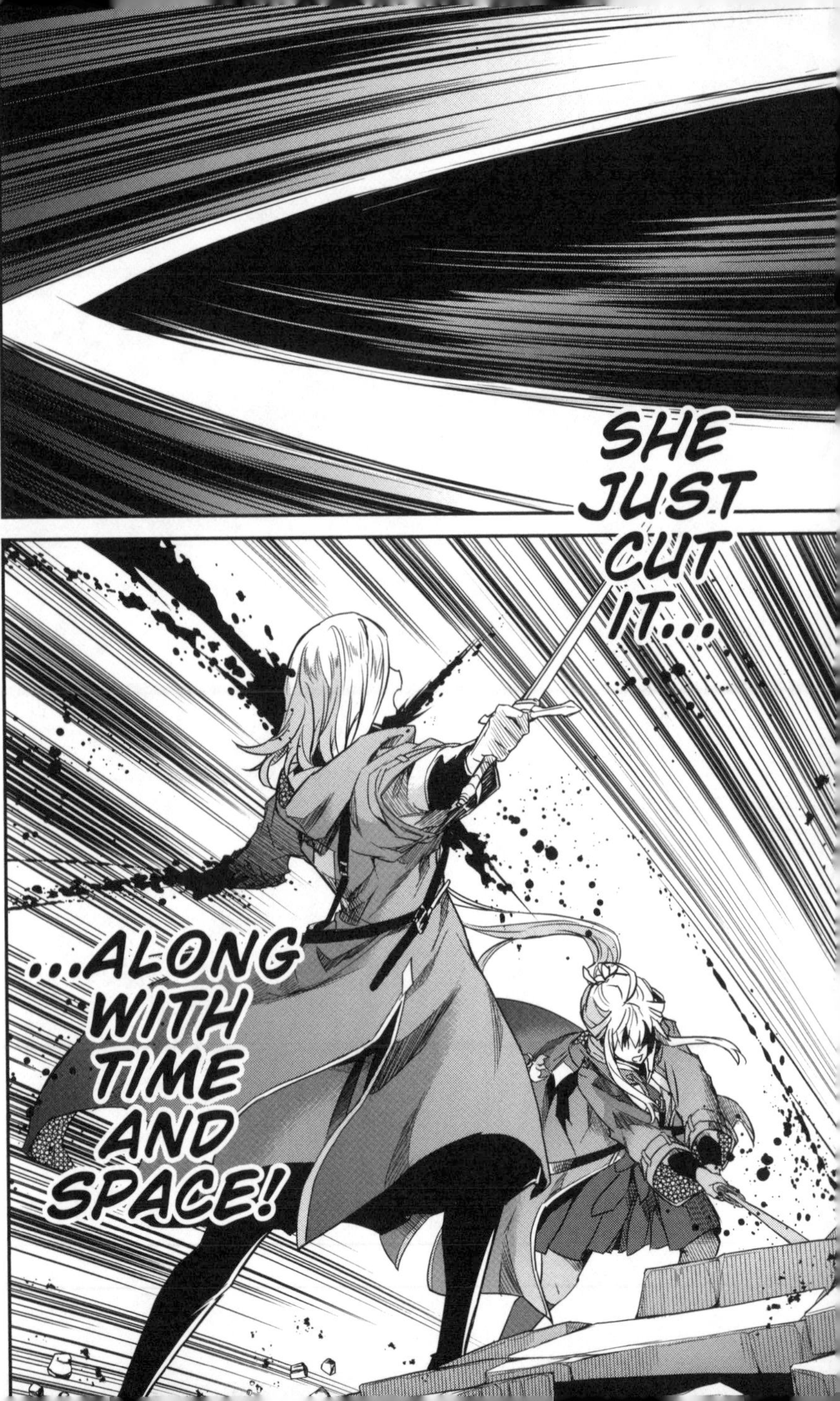
SHE JUST CUT IT...
...ALONG WITH TIME AND SPACE!

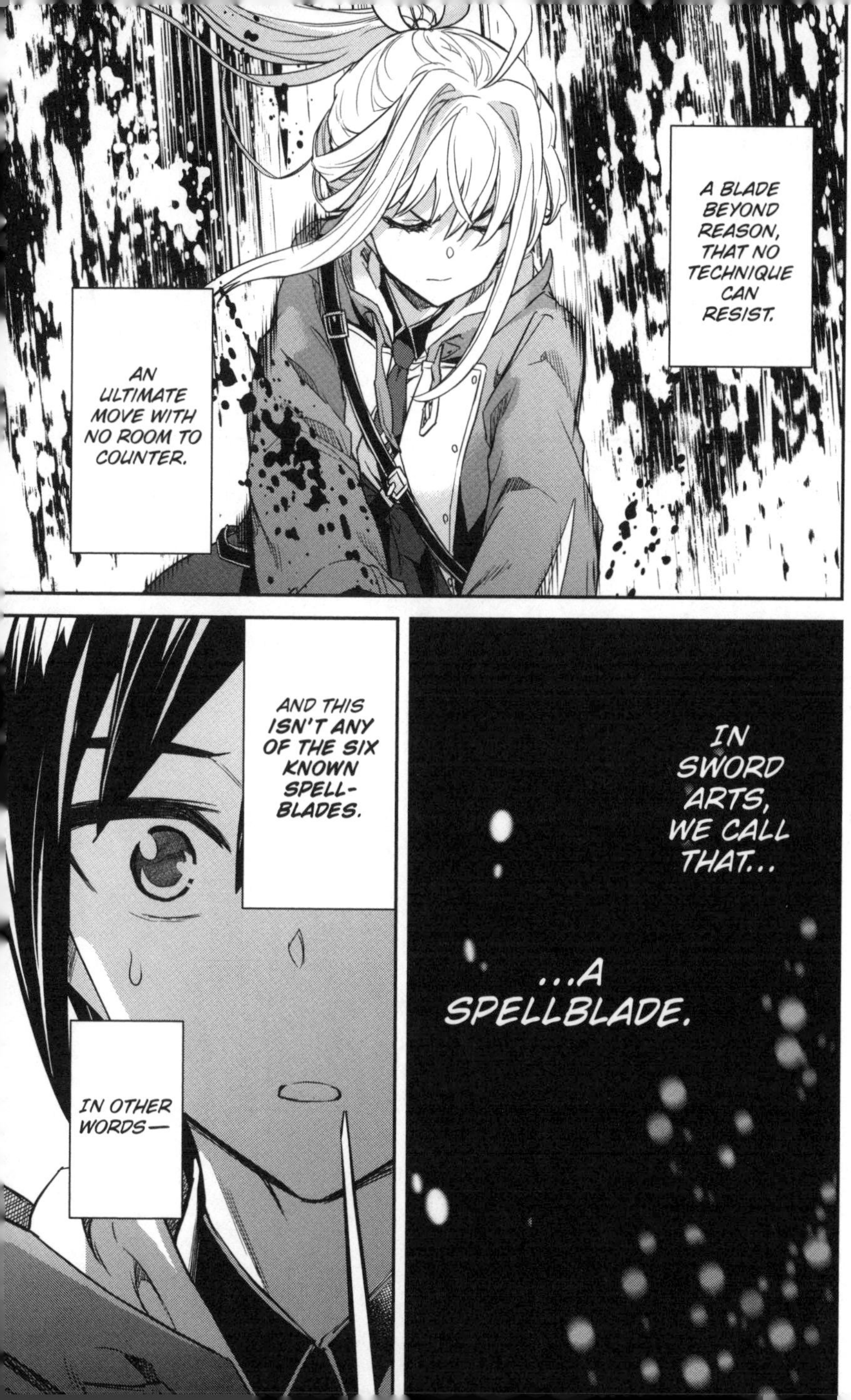

A BLADE BEYOND REASON, THAT NO TECHNIQUE CAN RESIST.
AN ULTIMATE MOVE WITH NO ROOM TO COUNTER.
IN SWORD ARTS, WE CALL THAT...
...A SPELLBLADE.
AND THIS ISN'T ANY OF THE SIX KNOWN SPELL-BLADES.
IN OTHER WORDS—

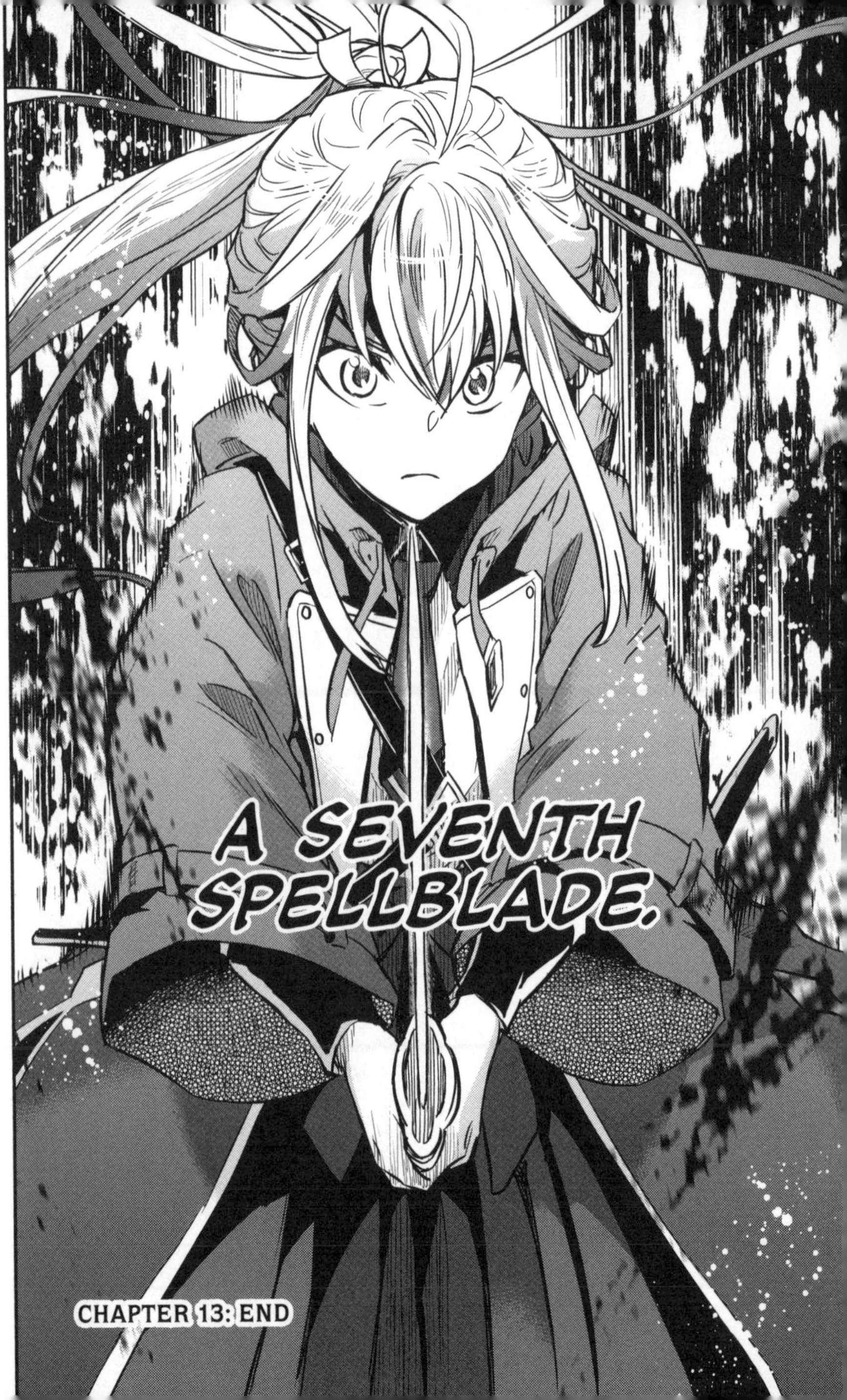
A SEVENTH SPELLBLADE.
CHAPTER 13: END

CHAPTER 14: EPILOGUE I

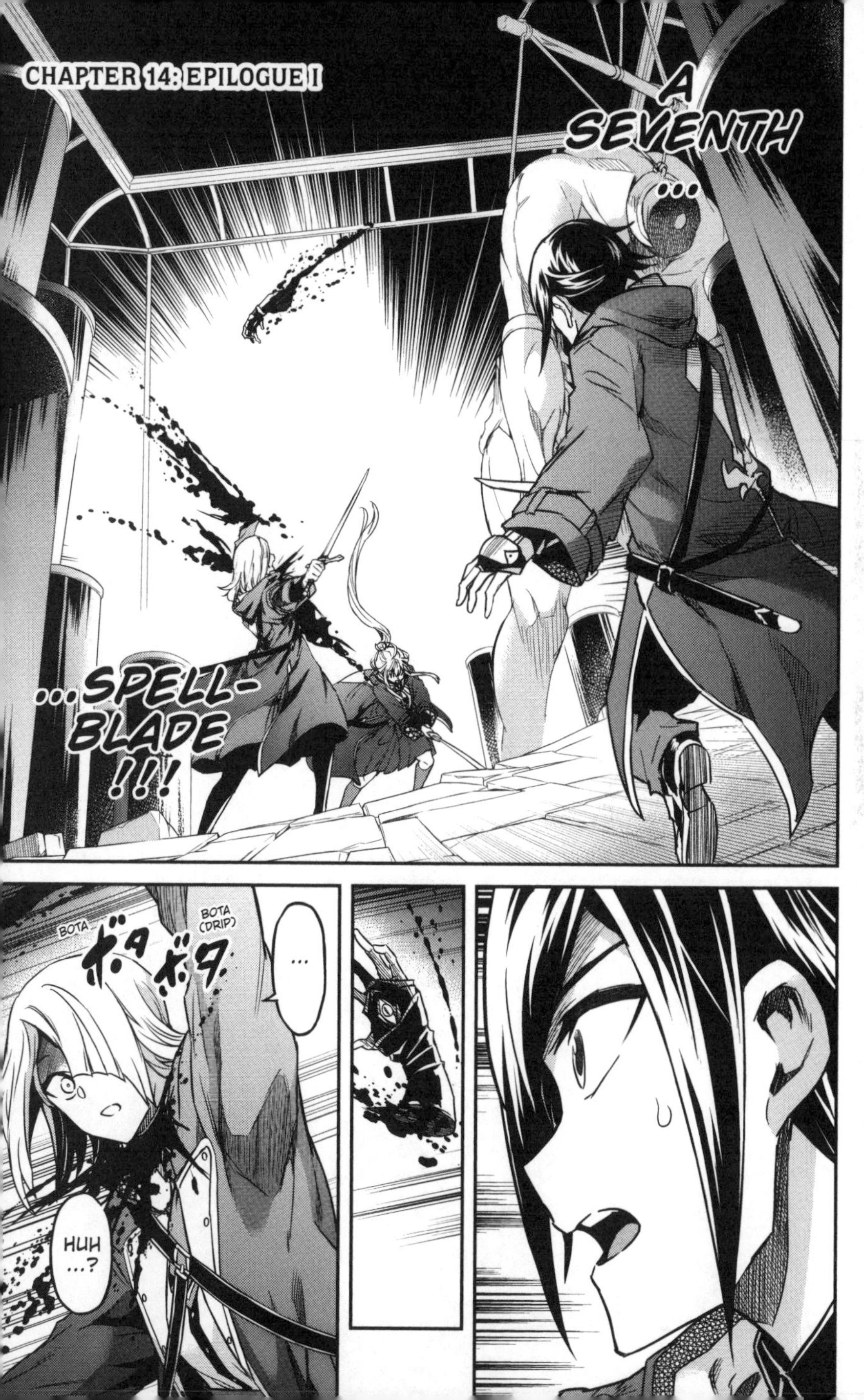
A SEVENTH
...
...SPELL-BLADE!!!
...
BOTA (DRIP)
BOTA
HUH ...?

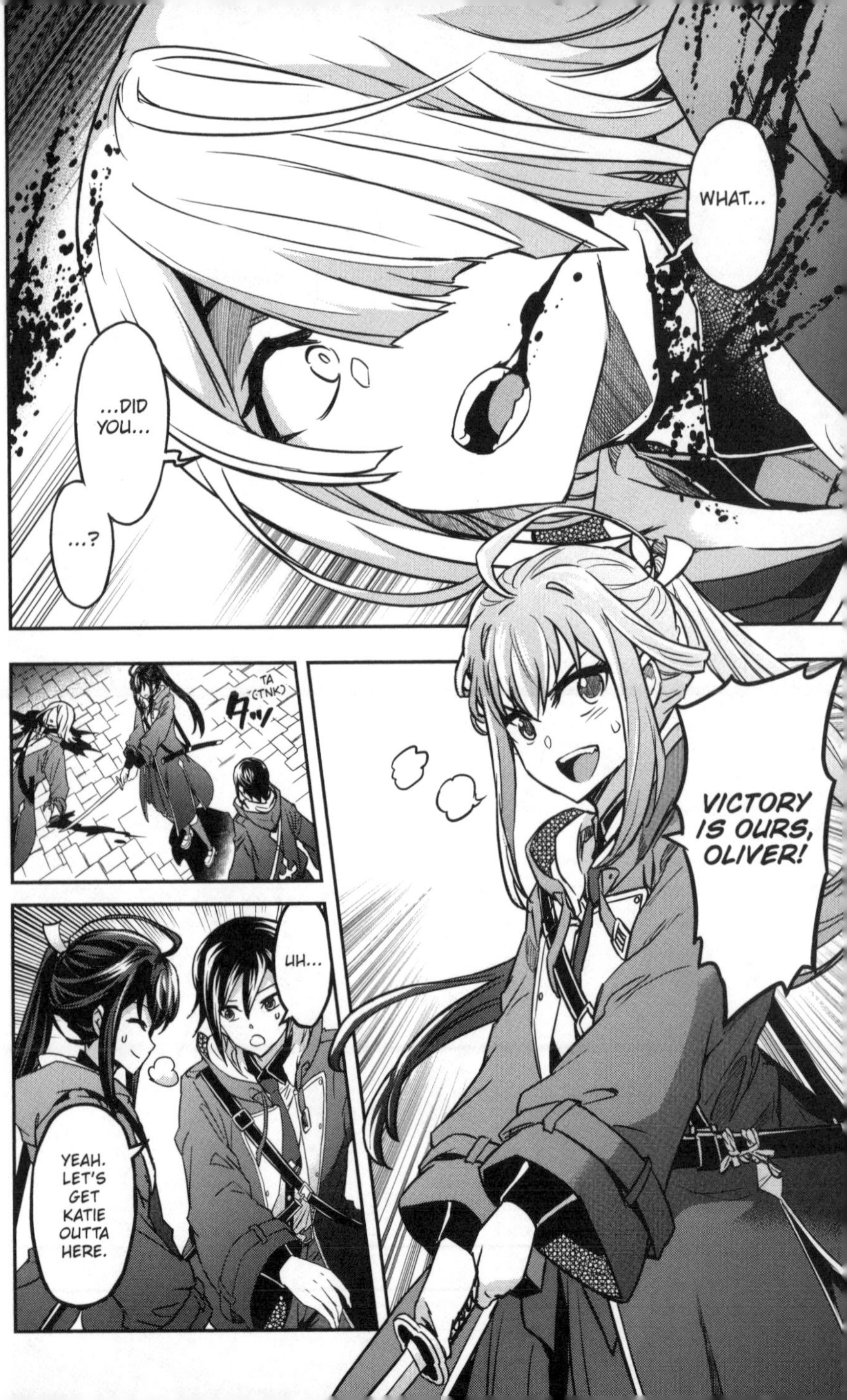
WHAT...
...DID YOU...
...?
VICTORY IS OURS, OLIVER!
タッ
TA (TNK)
UH...
YEAH. LET'S GET KATIE OUTTA HERE.

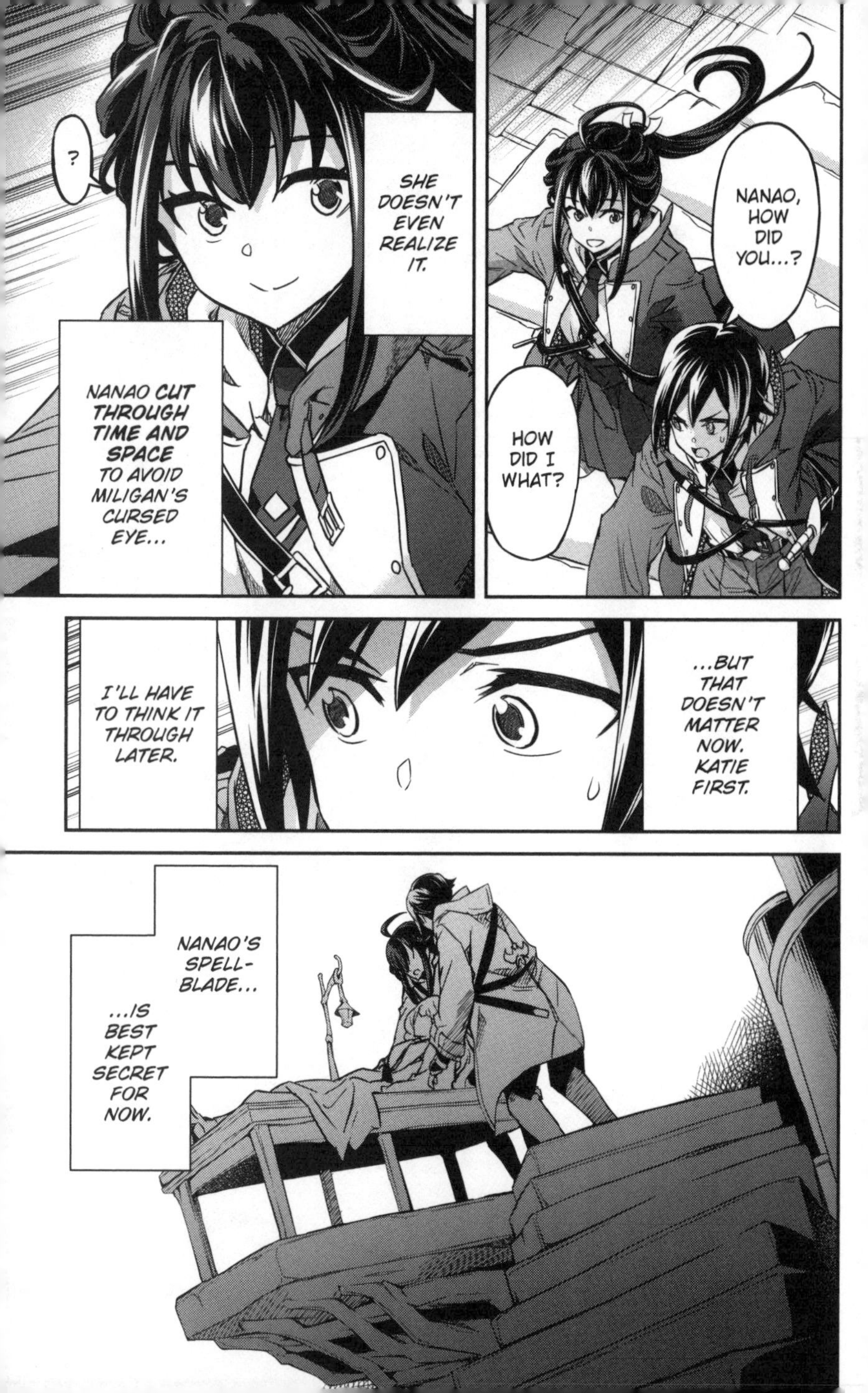
NANAO, HOW DID YOU...?
HOW DID I WHAT?
SHE DOESN'T EVEN REALIZE IT.
?
NANAO CUT THROUGH TIME AND SPACE TO AVOID MILIGAN'S CURSED EYE...
...BUT THAT DOESN'T MATTER NOW. KATIE FIRST.
I'LL HAVE TO THINK IT THROUGH LATER.
NANAO'S SPELL-BLADE...
...IS BEST KEPT SECRET FOR NOW.

CHAPTER 14: EPILOGUE I

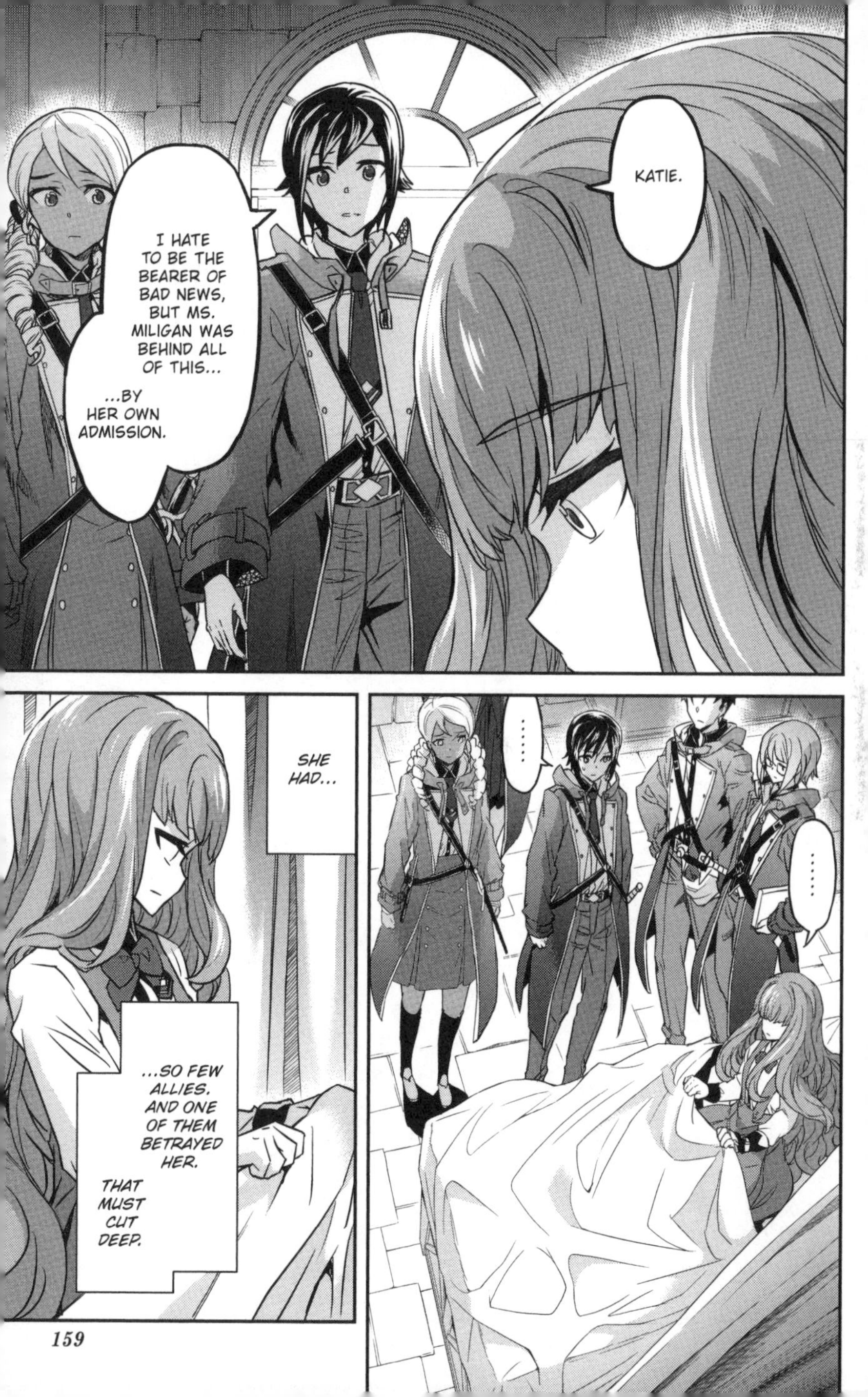
KATIE.
I HATE TO BE THE BEARER OF BAD NEWS, BUT MS. MILIGAN WAS BEHIND ALL OF THIS...
...BY HER OWN ADMISSION.
......
......
SHE HAD...
...SO FEW ALLIES. AND ONE OF THEM BETRAYED HER.
THAT MUST CUT DEEP.

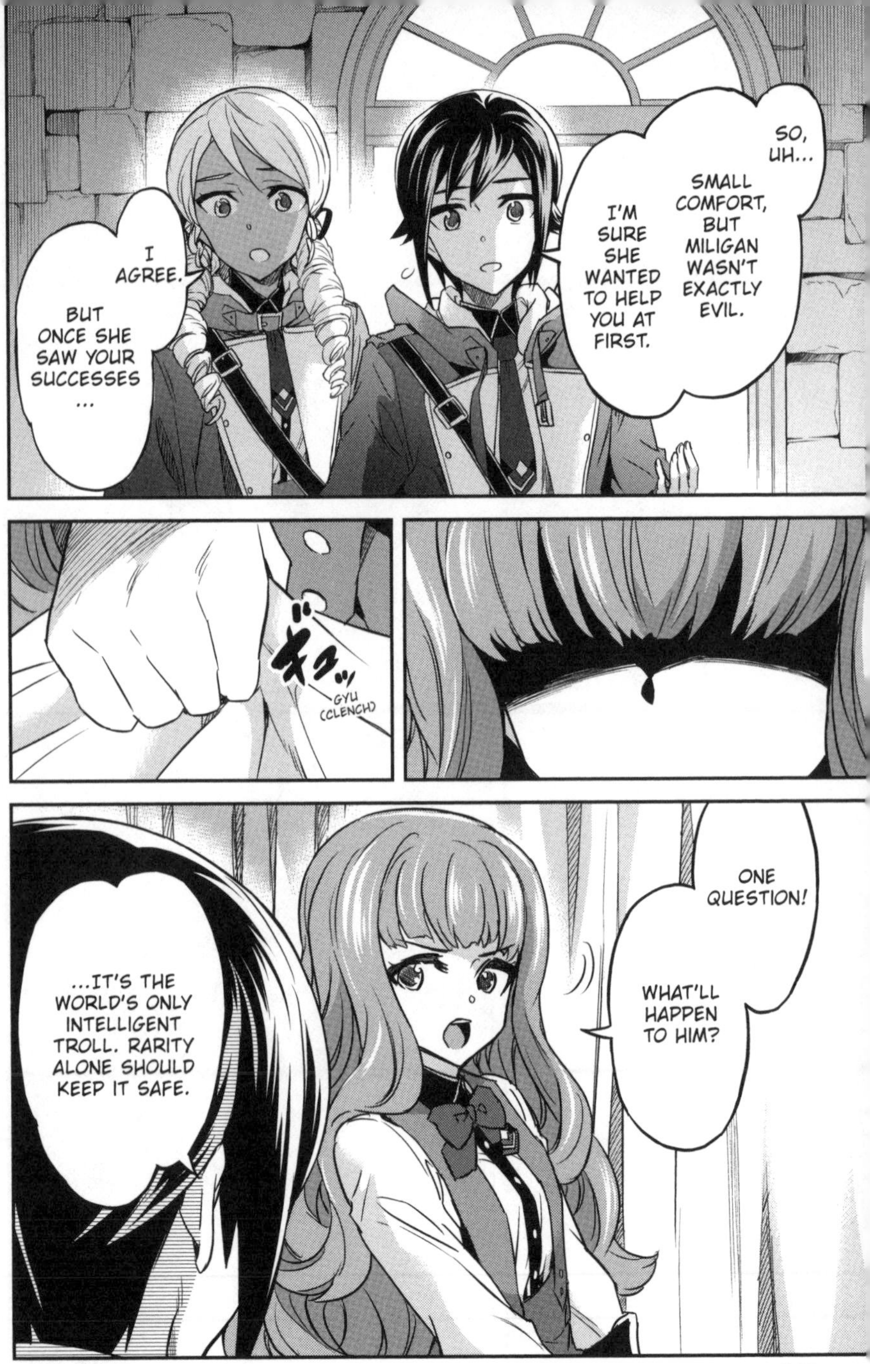
SO, UH... SMALL COMFORT, BUT MILIGAN WASN'T EXACTLY EVIL.
I'M SURE SHE WANTED TO HELP YOU AT FIRST.
I AGREE.
BUT ONCE SHE SAW YOUR SUCCESSES...
ギュッ
GYU (CLENCH)
ONE QUESTION!
WHAT'LL HAPPEN TO HIM?
...IT'S THE WORLD'S ONLY INTELLIGENT TROLL. RARITY ALONE SHOULD KEEP IT SAFE.

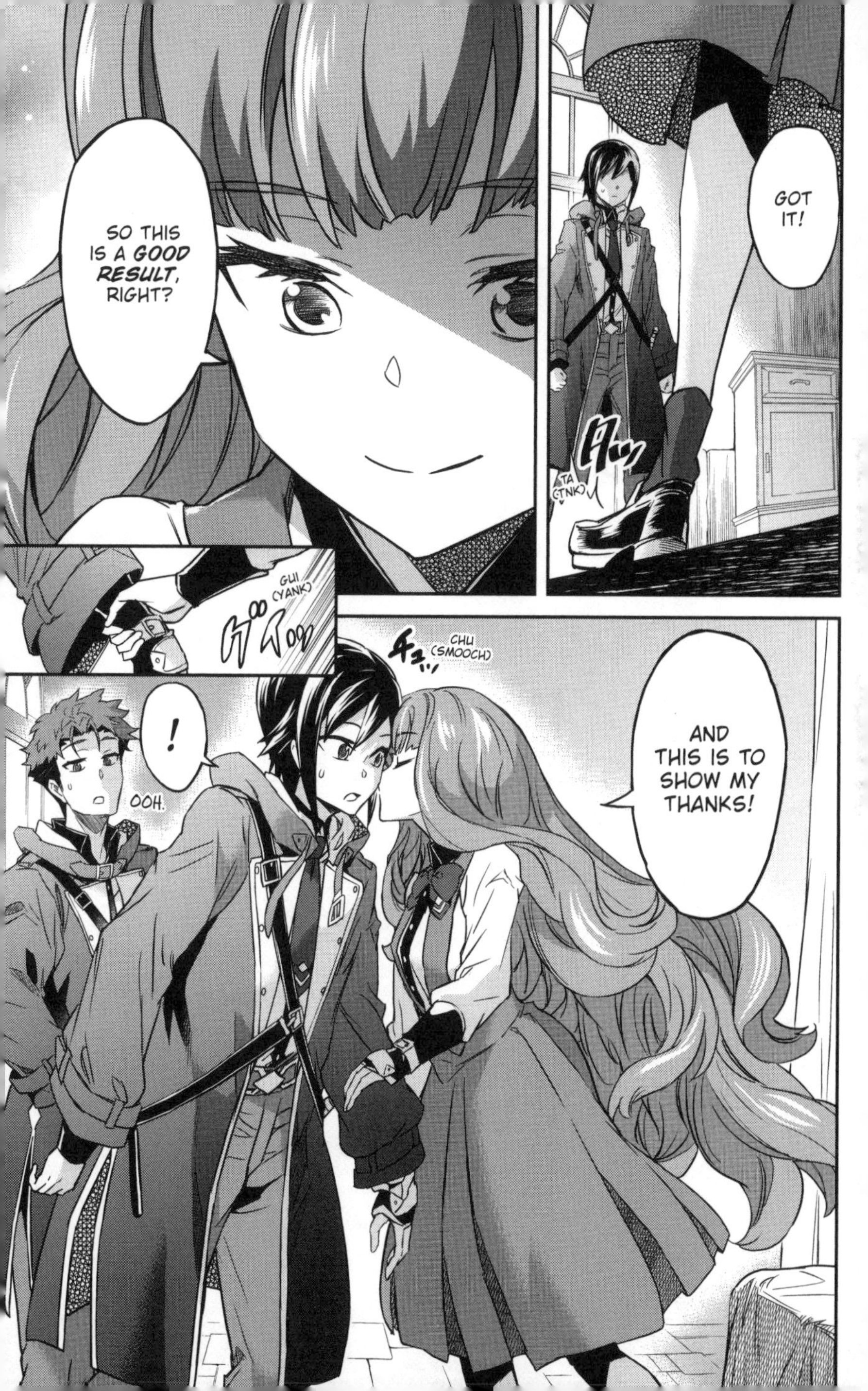
GOT IT!
TA (TNK)
SO THIS IS A ***GOOD RESULT***, RIGHT?
GUI (YANK)
CHU (SMOOCH)
AND THIS IS TO SHOW MY THANKS!
!
OOH.

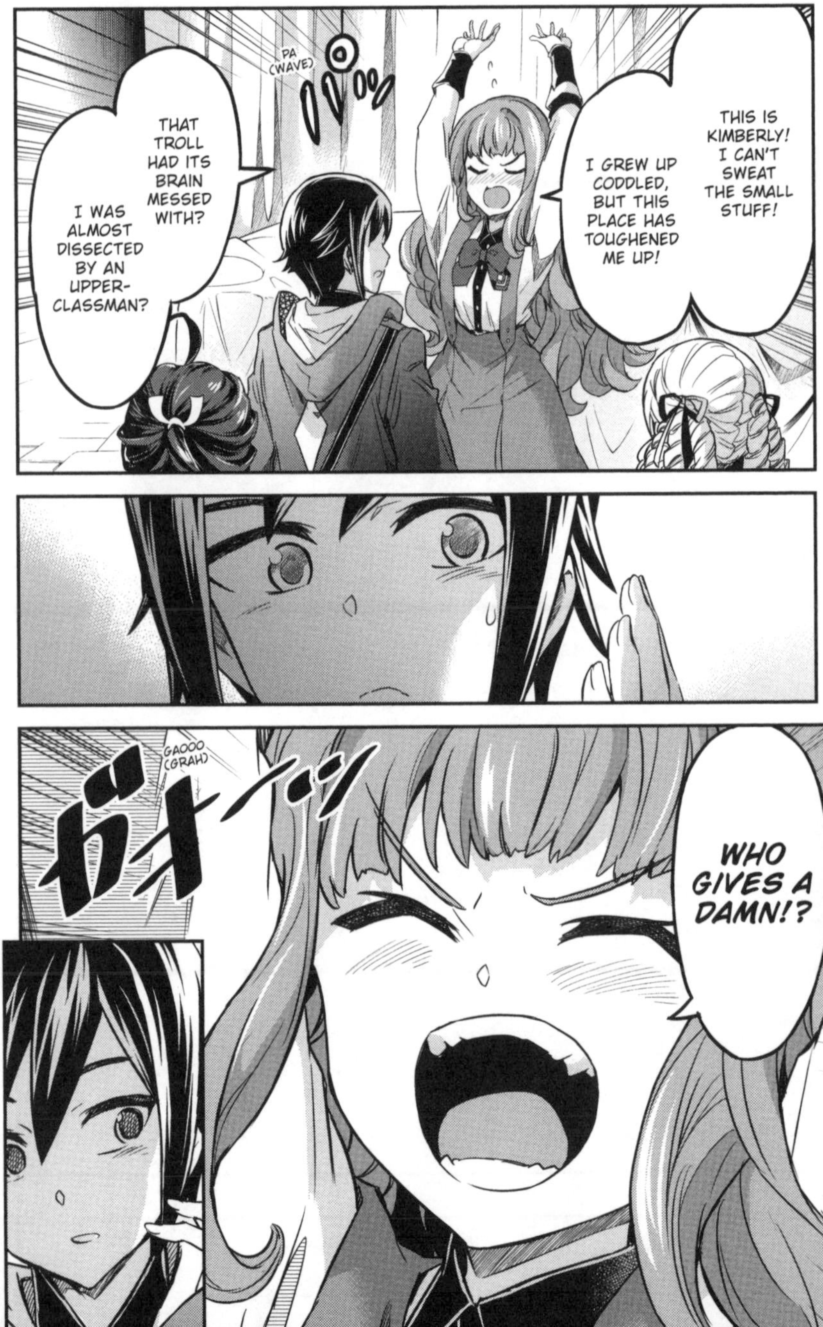
THIS IS KIMBERLY! I CAN'T SWEAT THE SMALL STUFF!
I GREW UP CODDLED, BUT THIS PLACE HAS TOUGHENED ME UP!
PA (WAVE)
THAT TROLL HAD ITS BRAIN MESSED WITH?
I WAS ALMOST DISSECTED BY AN UPPER-CLASSMAN?
WHO GIVES A DAMN!?
GAOOO (GRAH)

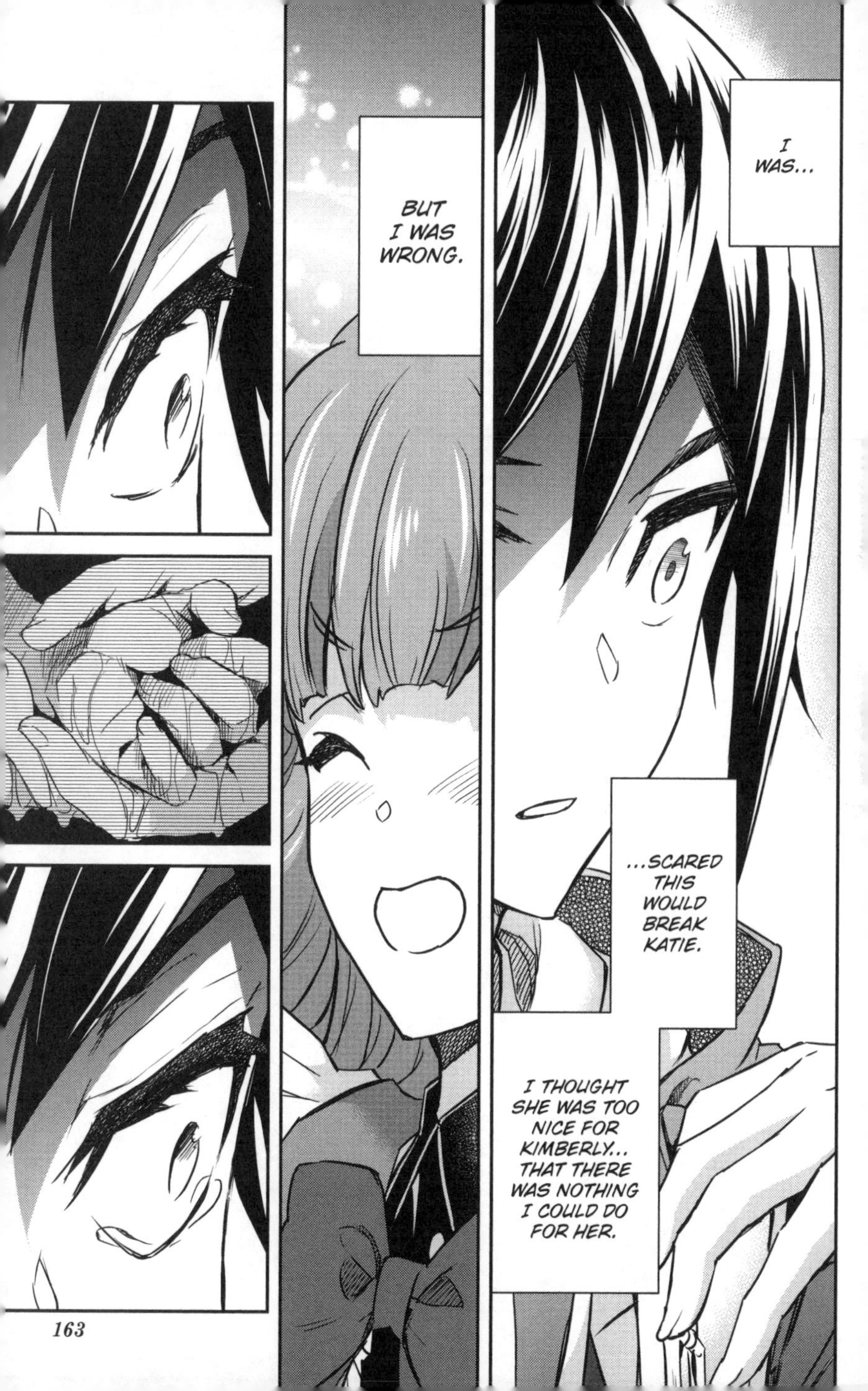
I WAS...
...SCARED THIS WOULD BREAK KATIE.
I THOUGHT SHE WAS TOO NICE FOR KIMBERLY... THAT THERE WAS NOTHING I COULD DO FOR HER.
BUT I WAS WRONG.

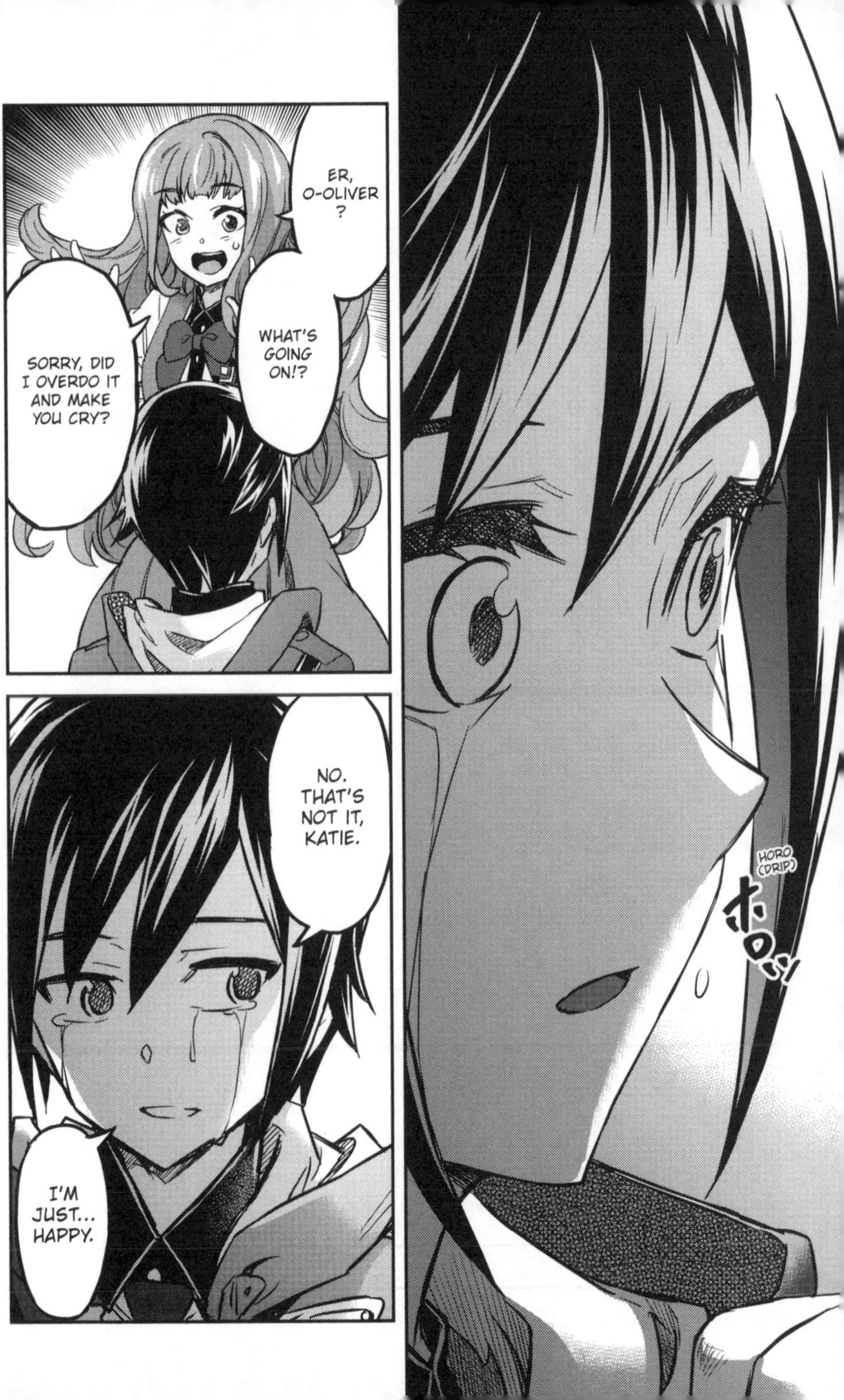
HORO (DRIP)
ER, O-OLIVER?
WHAT'S GOING ON!?
SORRY, DID I OVERDO IT AND MAKE YOU CRY?
NO. THAT'S NOT IT, KATIE.
I'M JUST... HAPPY.

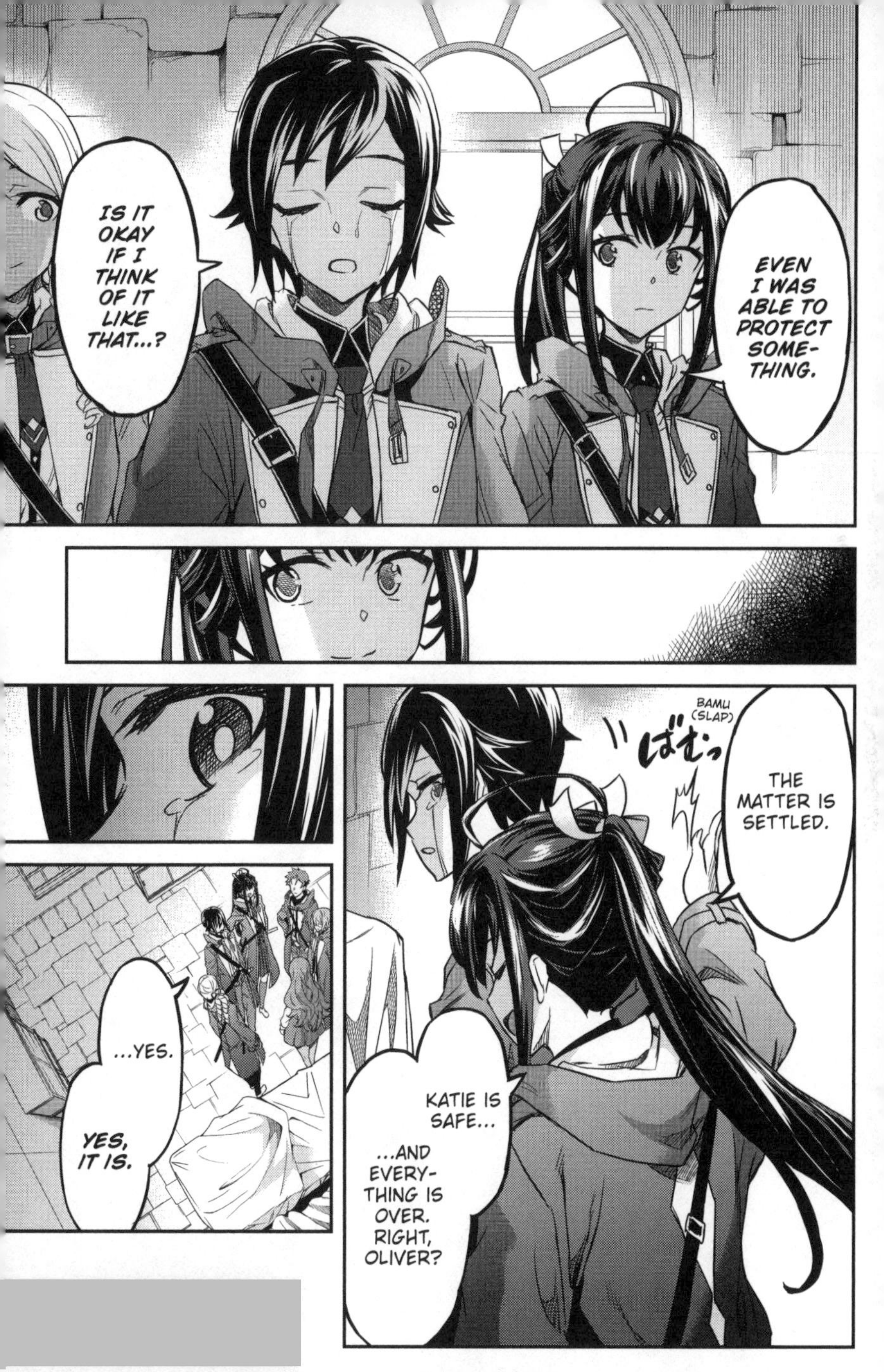
EVEN I WAS ABLE TO PROTECT SOME-THING.
IS IT OKAY IF I THINK OF IT LIKE THAT...?
BAMU (SLAP)
ばむっ
THE MATTER IS SETTLED.
KATIE IS SAFE...
...AND EVERY-THING IS OVER. RIGHT, OLIVER?
...YES.
YES, IT IS.

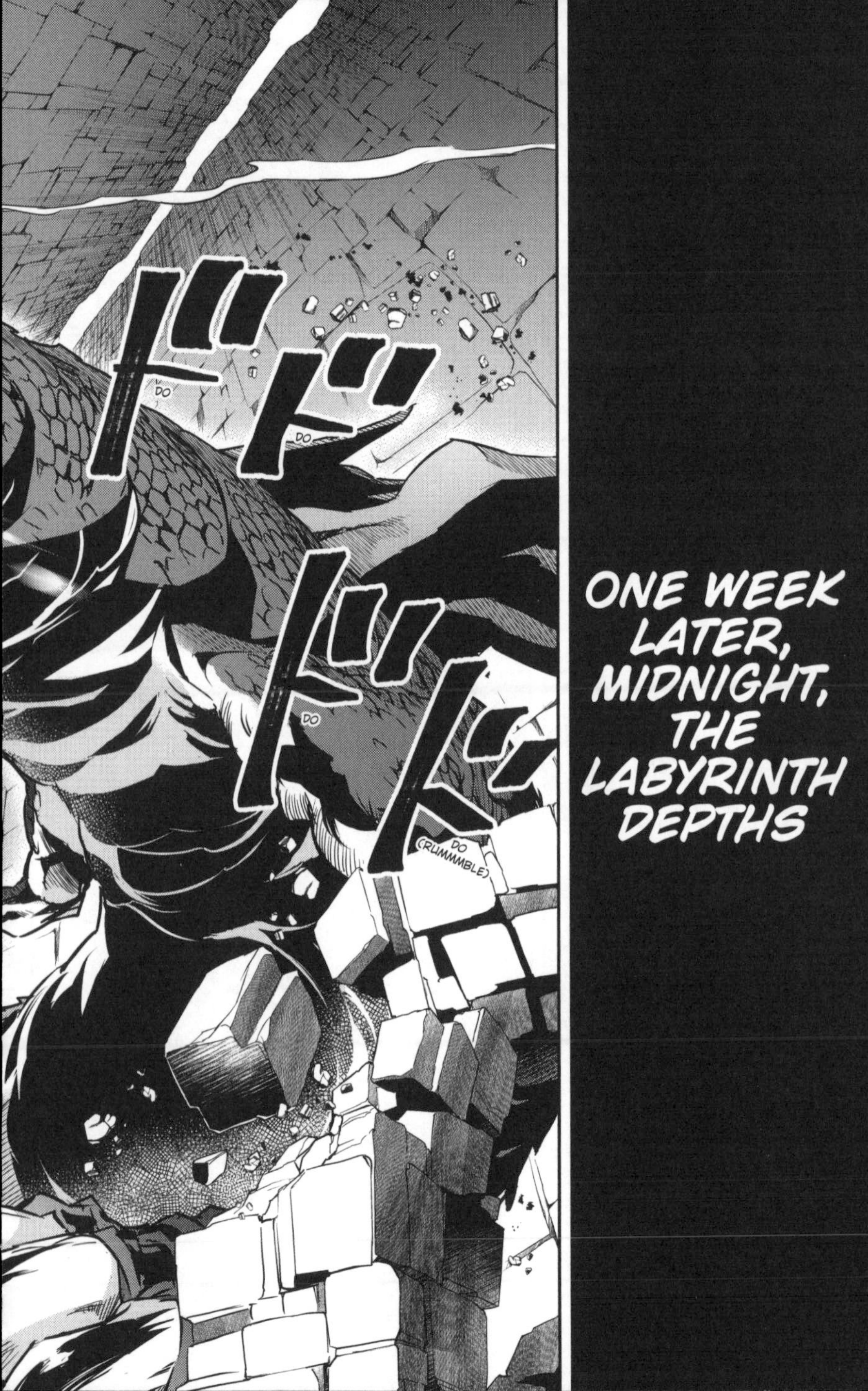
ONE WEEK LATER, MIDNIGHT, THE LABYRINTH DEPTHS
ドド
DO
DO
ドド
DO
DO
(RUMMMBLE)

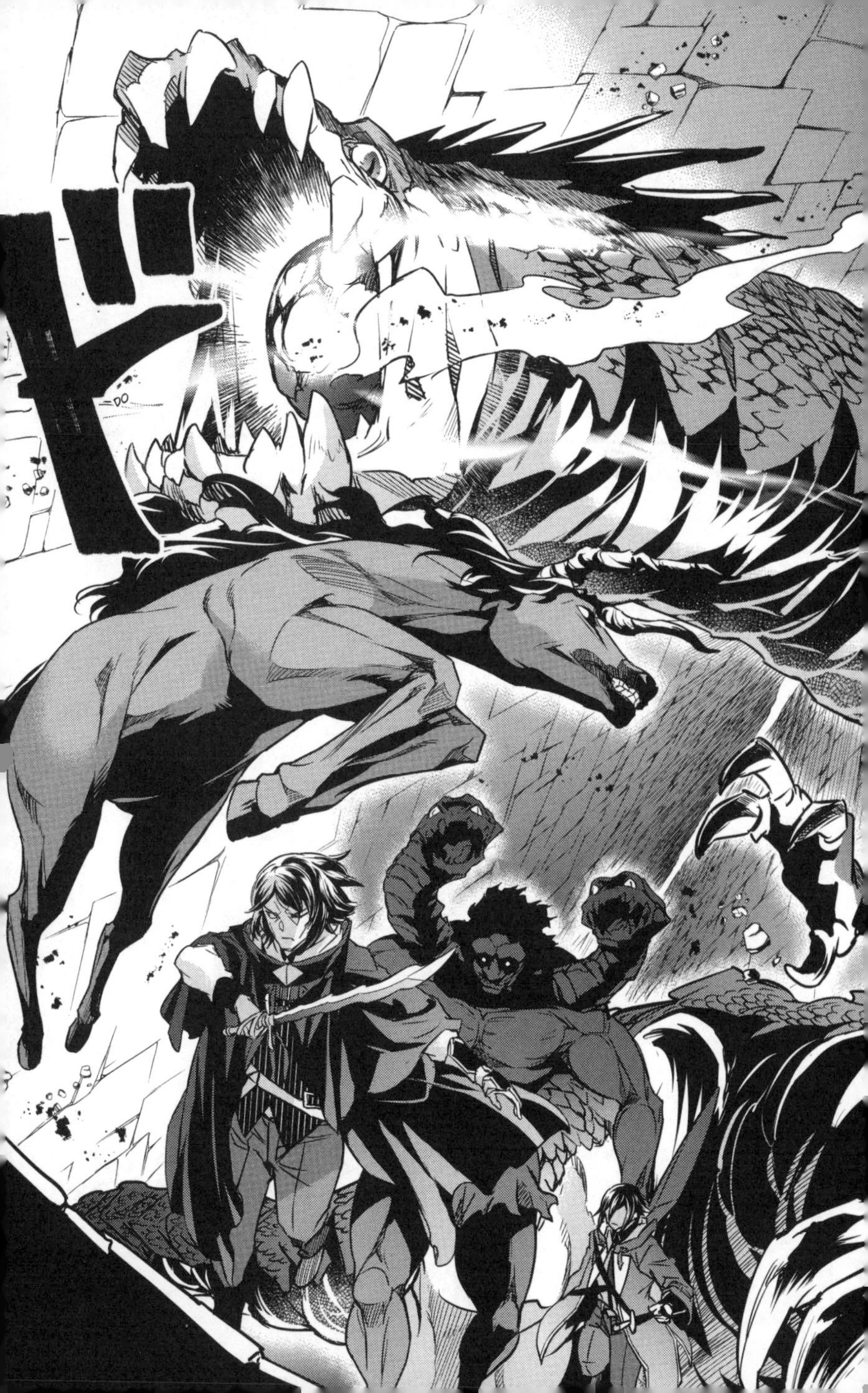

ド
DO

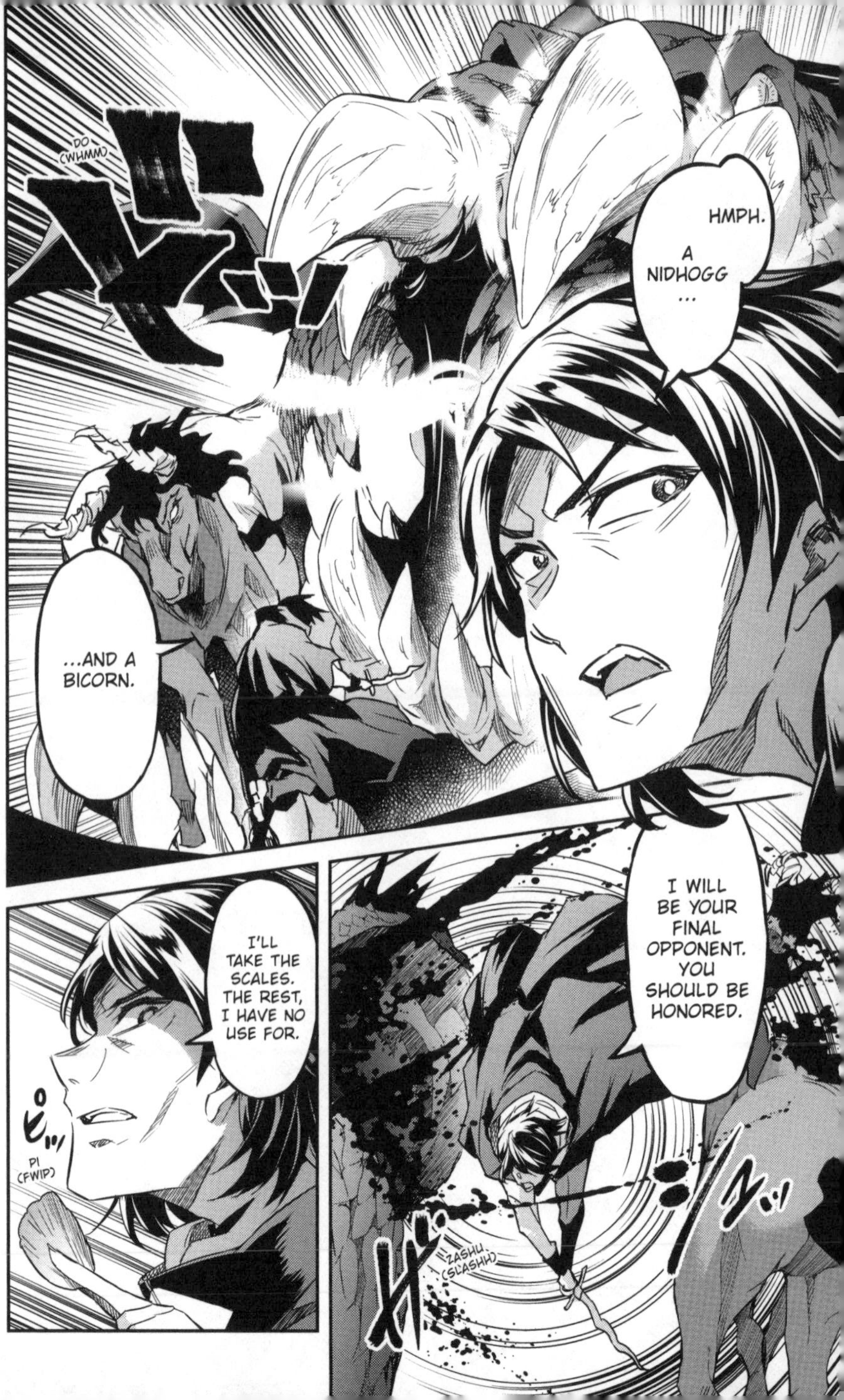
HMPH.
A NIDHOGG ...
DO (WHMM)
...AND A BICORN.
I WILL BE YOUR FINAL OPPONENT. YOU SHOULD BE HONORED.
ZASHU (SLASHH)
I'LL TAKE THE SCALES. THE REST, I HAVE NO USE FOR.
PI (FWIP)

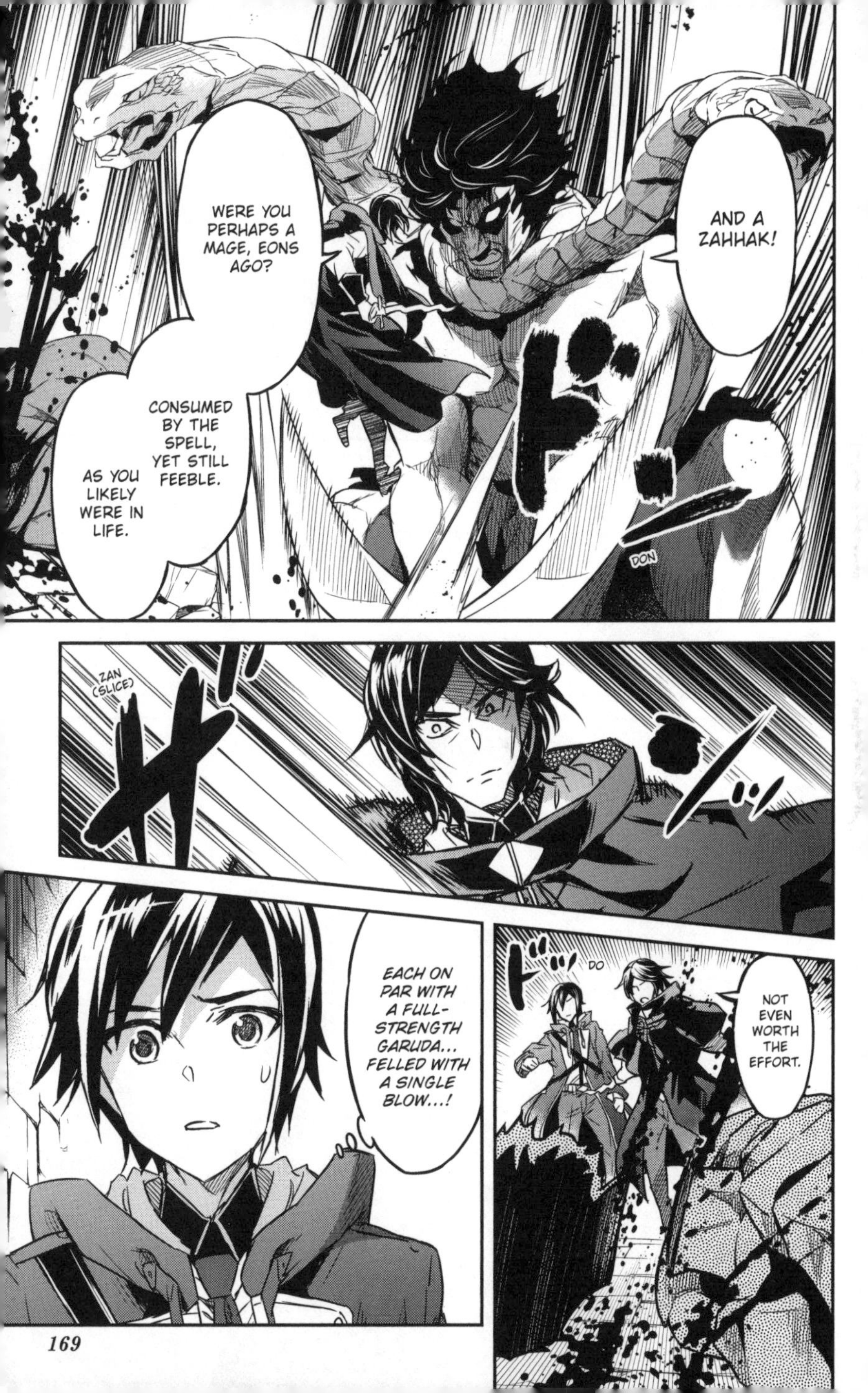
AND A ZAHHAK!
WERE YOU PERHAPS A MAGE, EONS AGO?
CONSUMED BY THE SPELL, YET STILL FEEBLE.
AS YOU LIKELY WERE IN LIFE.
DON
ZAN (SLICE)
DO
NOT EVEN WORTH THE EFFORT.
EACH ON PAR WITH A FULL-STRENGTH GARUDA... FELLED WITH A SINGLE BLOW...!

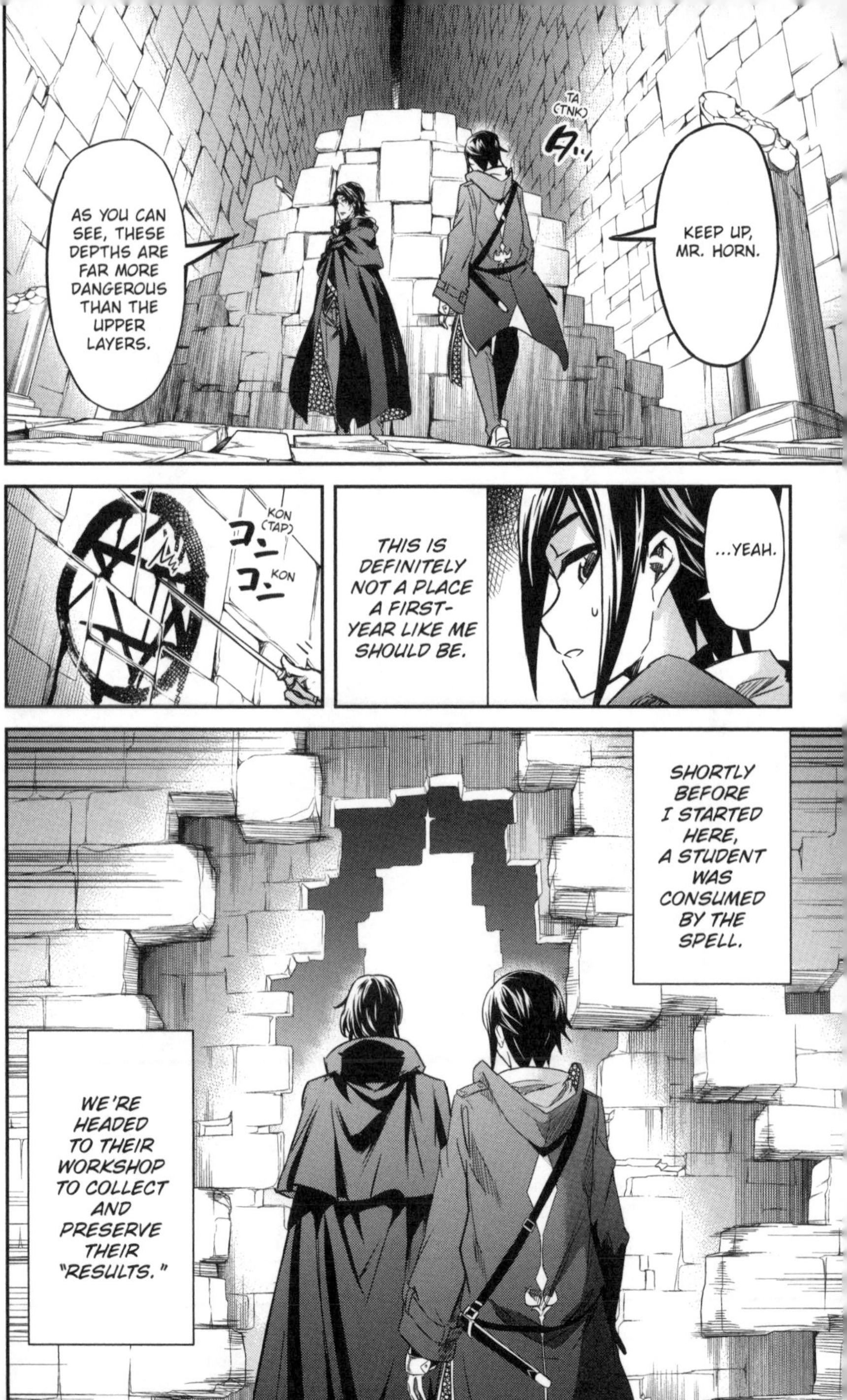
TA (TNK)
KEEP UP, MR. HORN.
AS YOU CAN SEE, THESE DEPTHS ARE FAR MORE DANGEROUS THAN THE UPPER LAYERS.
...YEAH.
THIS IS DEFINITELY NOT A PLACE A FIRST-YEAR LIKE ME SHOULD BE.
KON (TAP)
KON
SHORTLY BEFORE I STARTED HERE, A STUDENT WAS CONSUMED BY THE SPELL.
WE'RE HEADED TO THEIR WORKSHOP TO COLLECT AND PRESERVE THEIR "RESULTS."

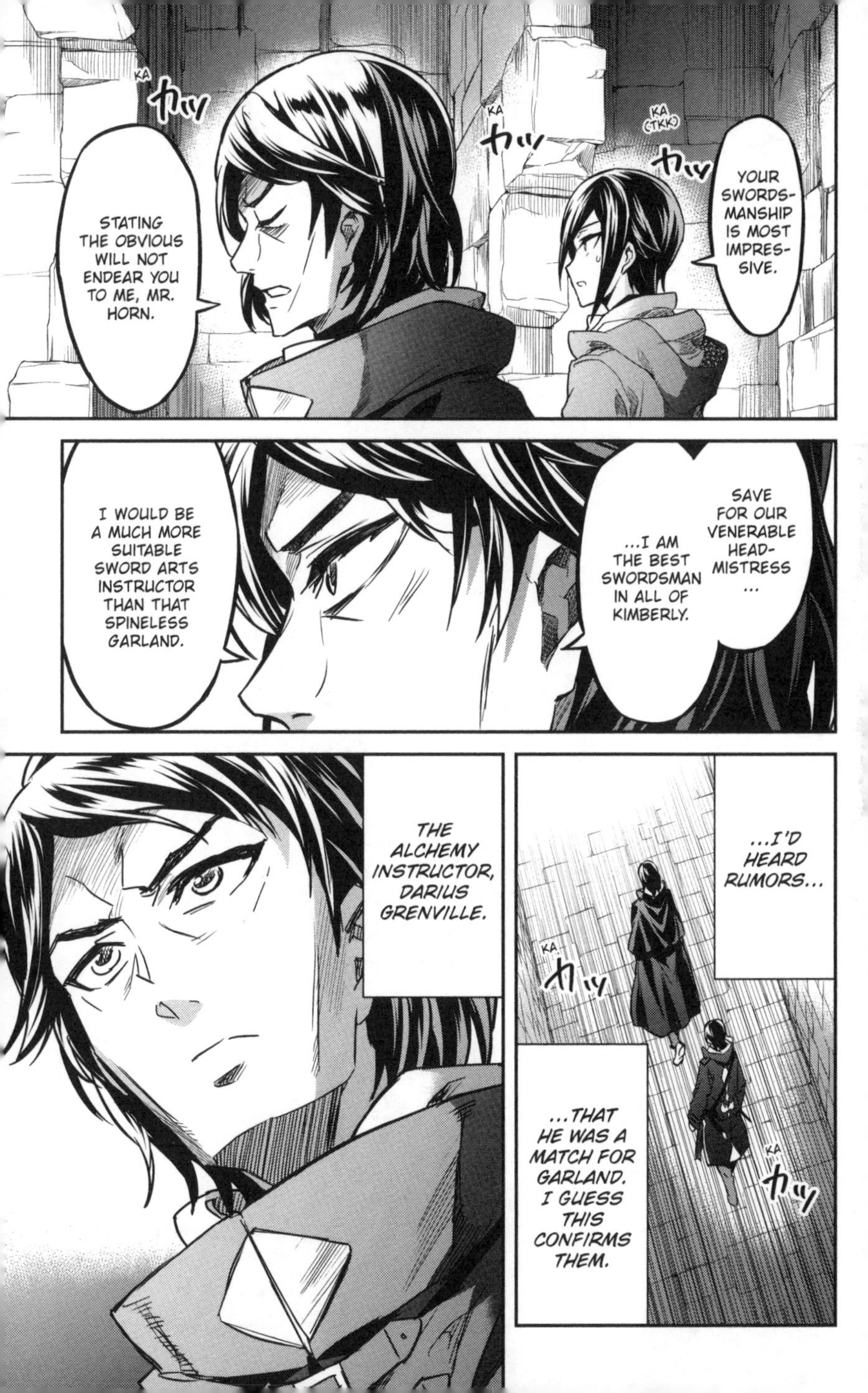
KA (TKK)
カッ
YOUR SWORDSMANSHIP IS MOST IMPRESSIVE.
KA
カッ
KA
カッ
STATING THE OBVIOUS WILL NOT ENDEAR YOU TO ME, MR. HORN.
SAVE FOR OUR VENERABLE HEADMISTRESS ...
...I AM THE BEST SWORDSMAN IN ALL OF KIMBERLY.
I WOULD BE A MUCH MORE SUITABLE SWORD ARTS INSTRUCTOR THAN THAT SPINELESS GARLAND.
...I'D HEARD RUMORS...
KA
カッ
...THAT HE WAS A MATCH FOR GARLAND. I GUESS THIS CONFIRMS THEM.
KA
カッ
THE ALCHEMY INSTRUCTOR, DARIUS GRENVILLE.

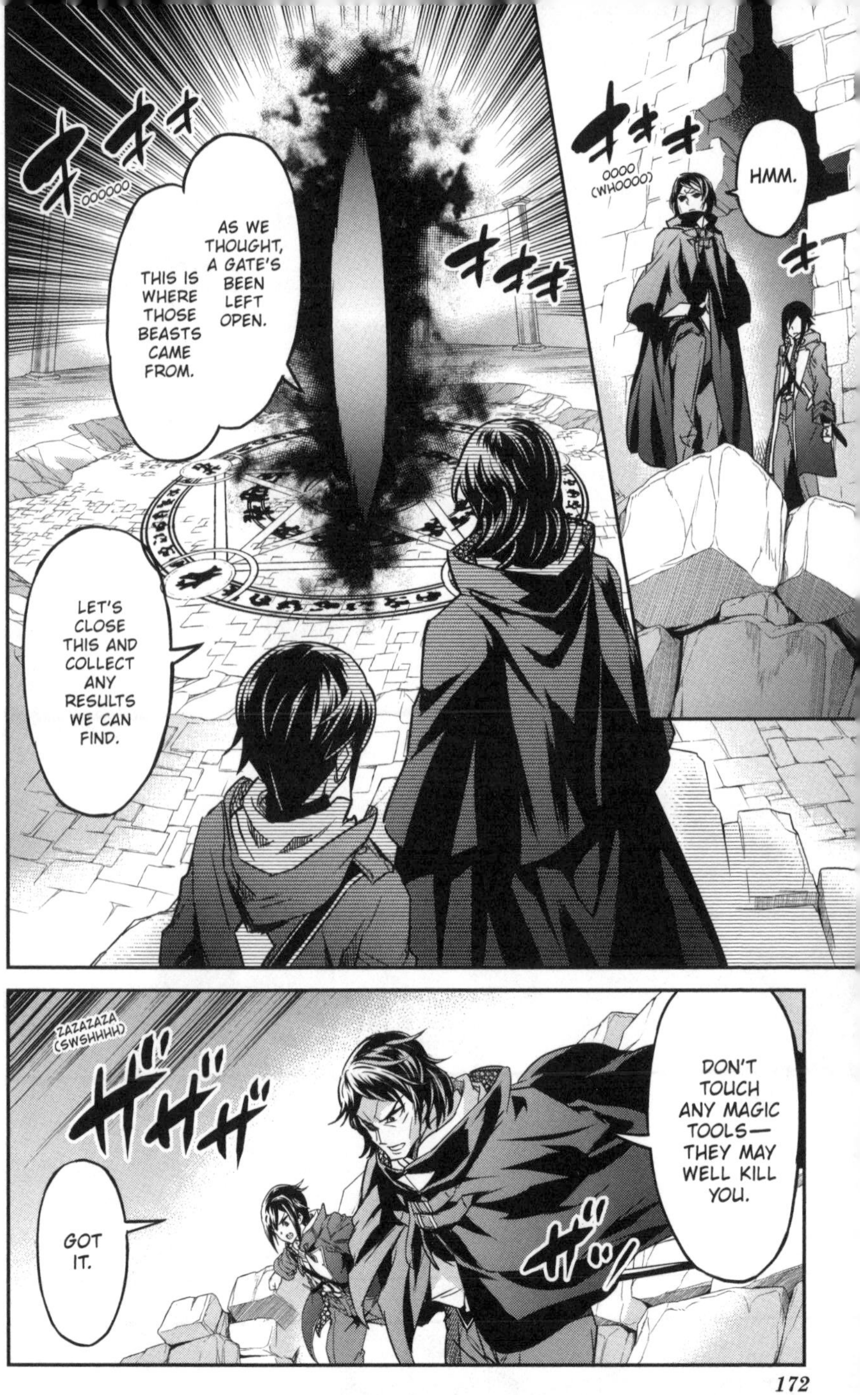
OOOO (WHOOOO)
HMM.
OOOOOO
AS WE THOUGHT, A GATE'S BEEN LEFT OPEN.
THIS IS WHERE THOSE BEASTS CAME FROM.
LET'S CLOSE THIS AND COLLECT ANY RESULTS WE CAN FIND.
DON'T TOUCH ANY MAGIC TOOLS— THEY MAY WELL KILL YOU.
ZAZAZAZA (SWSHHHH)
GOT IT.

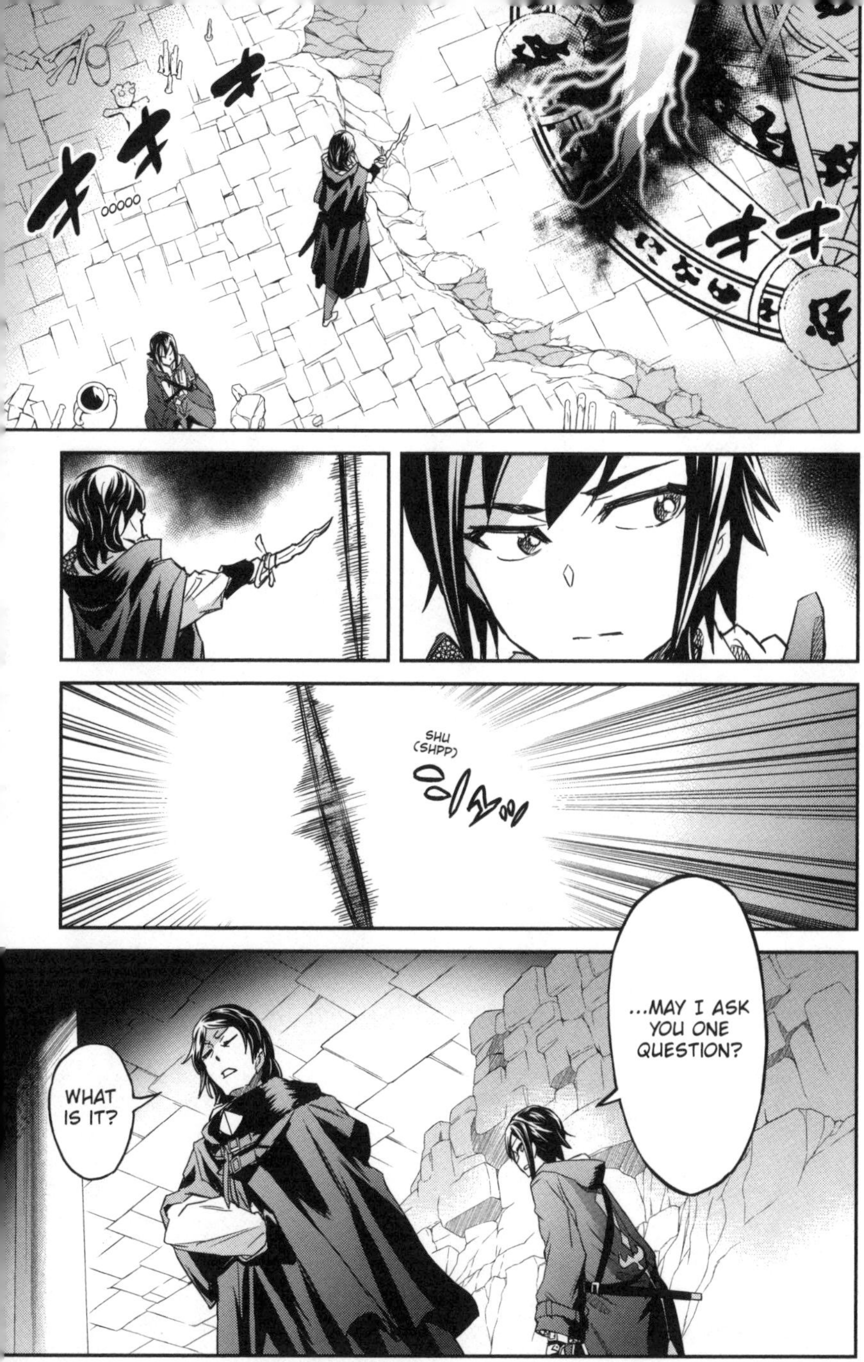
OOOOO
SHU
(SHPP)
...MAY I ASK YOU ONE QUESTION?
WHAT IS IT?

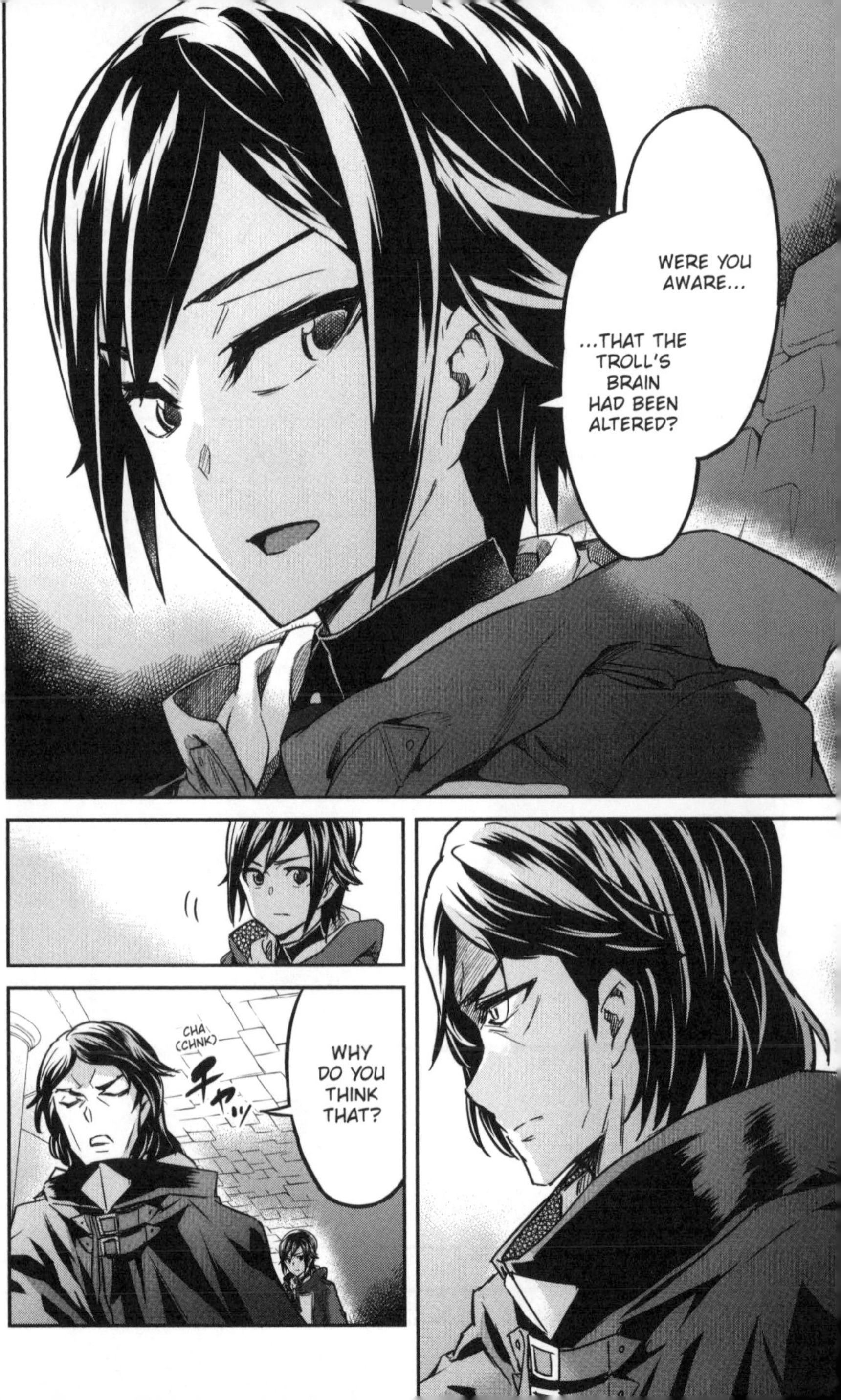
WERE YOU AWARE...
...THAT THE TROLL'S BRAIN HAD BEEN ALTERED?
WHY DO YOU THINK THAT?
CHA (CHNK)
チャッ

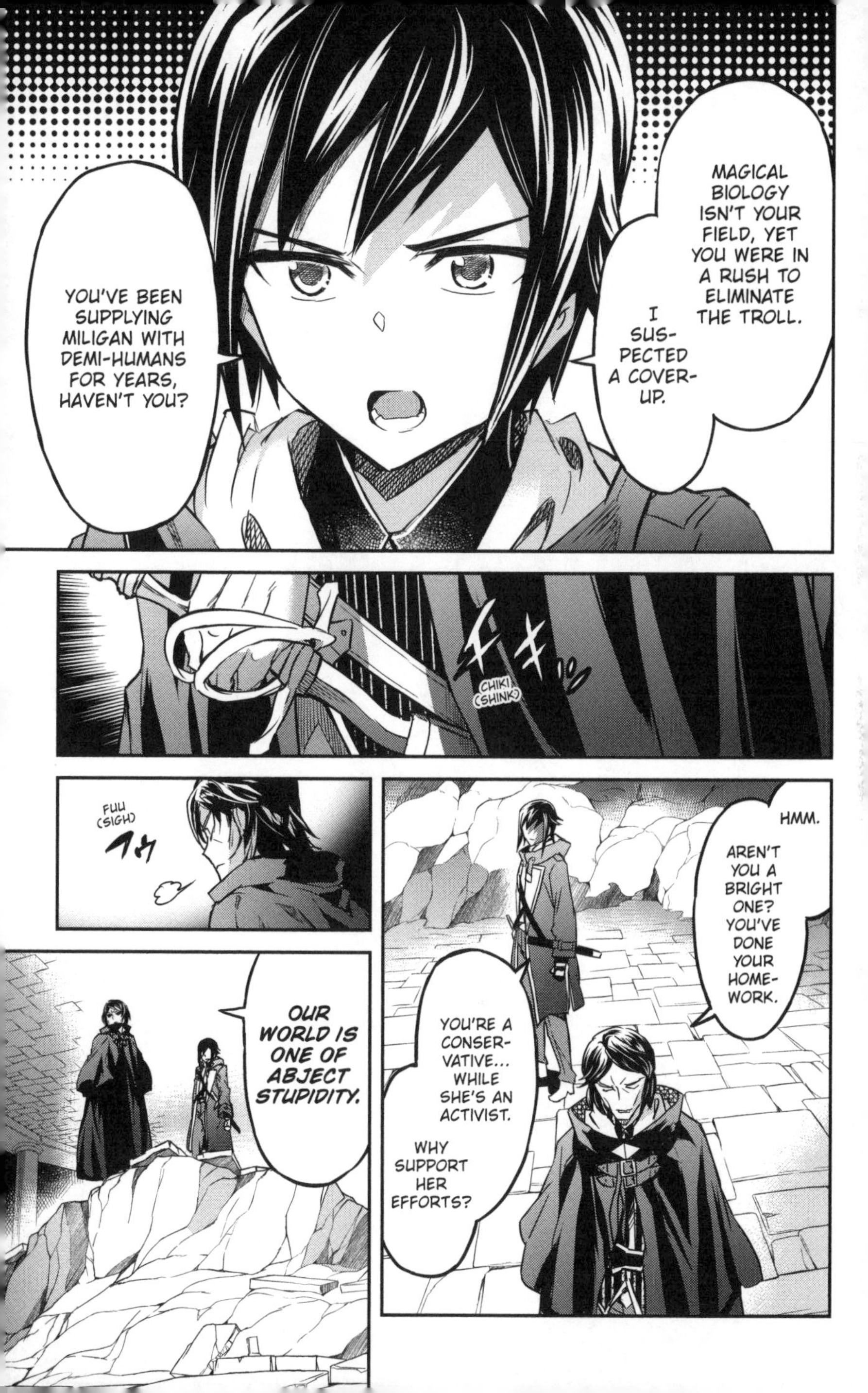
MAGICAL BIOLOGY ISN'T YOUR FIELD, YET YOU WERE IN A RUSH TO ELIMINATE THE TROLL.
I SUSPECTED A COVER-UP.
YOU'VE BEEN SUPPLYING MILIGAN WITH DEMI-HUMANS FOR YEARS, HAVEN'T YOU?
CHIKI (SHINK)
HMM.
AREN'T YOU A BRIGHT ONE? YOU'VE DONE YOUR HOMEWORK.
YOU'RE A CONSERVATIVE... WHILE SHE'S AN ACTIVIST.
WHY SUPPORT HER EFFORTS?
FUU (SIGH)
OUR WORLD IS ONE OF ABJECT STUPIDITY.

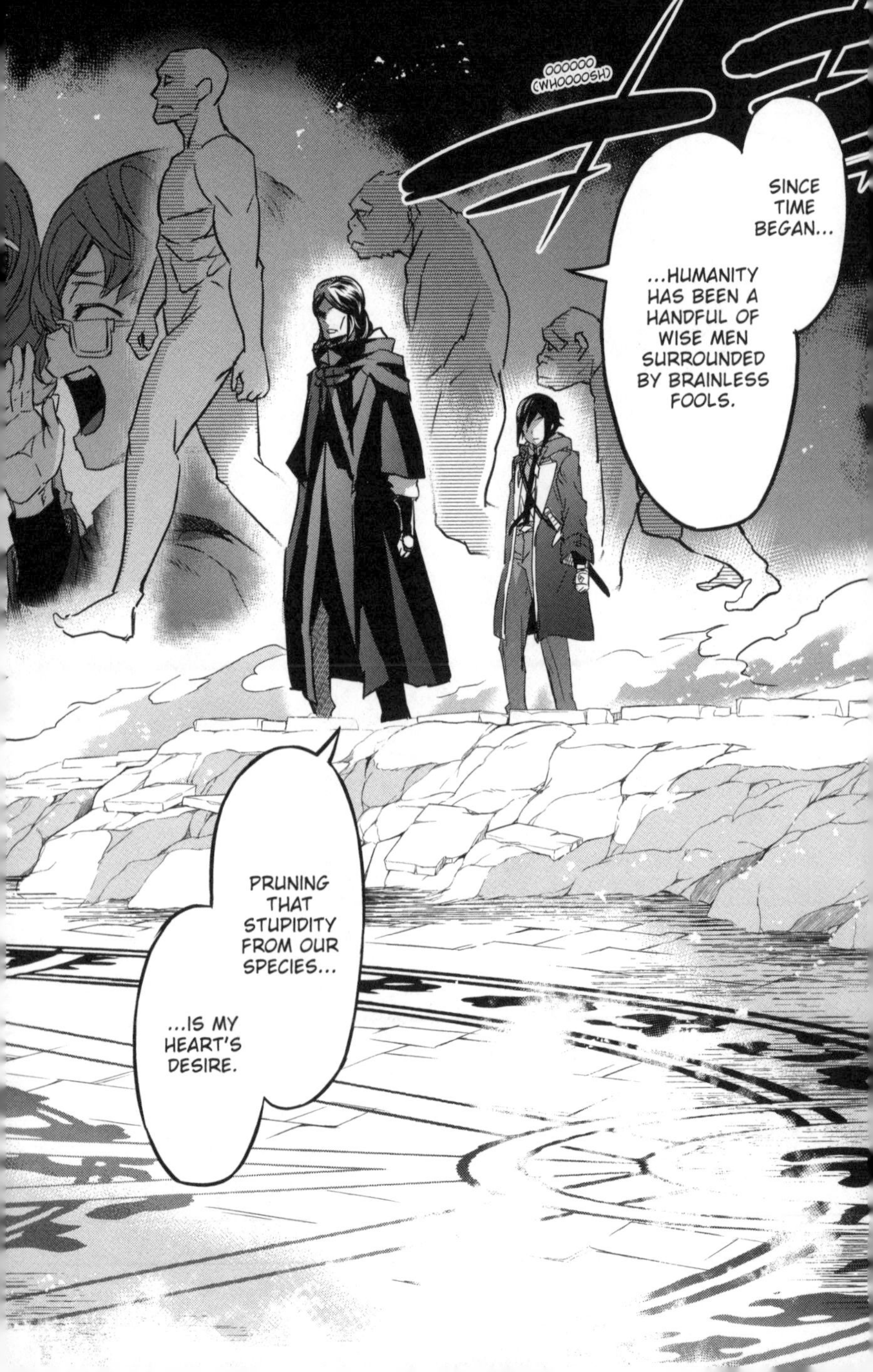

OOOOOO (WHOOOOSH)
SINCE TIME BEGAN...
...HUMANITY HAS BEEN A HANDFUL OF WISE MEN SURROUNDED BY BRAINLESS FOOLS.
PRUNING THAT STUPIDITY FROM OUR SPECIES...
...IS MY HEART'S DESIRE.

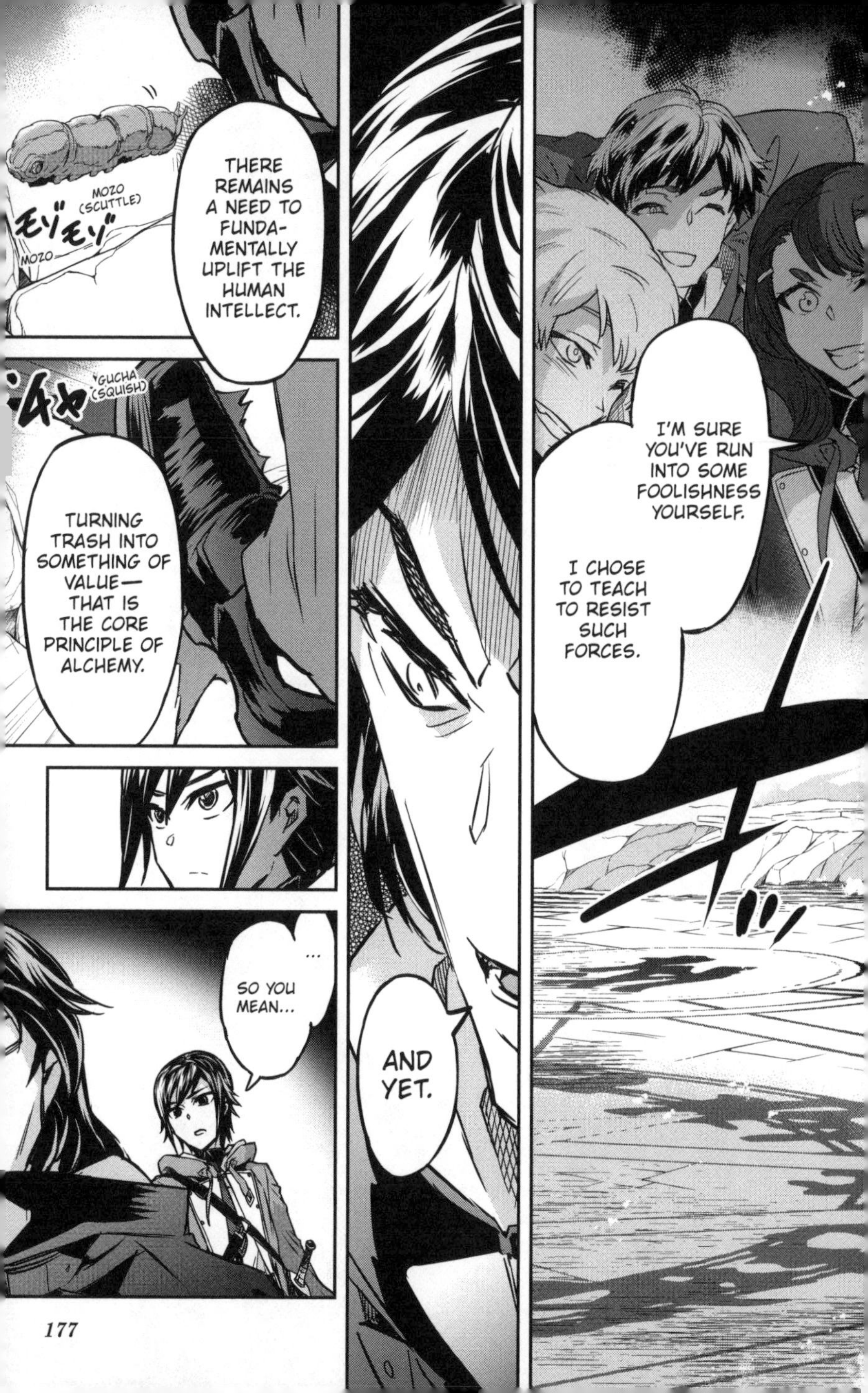

I'M SURE YOU'VE RUN INTO SOME FOOLISHNESS YOURSELF.
I CHOSE TO TEACH TO RESIST SUCH FORCES.
AND YET.
モゾモゾ
MOZO MOZO (SCUTTLE)
THERE REMAINS A NEED TO FUNDAMENTALLY UPLIFT THE HUMAN INTELLECT.
グチャ
GUCHA (SQUISH)
TURNING TRASH INTO SOMETHING OF VALUE—THAT IS THE CORE PRINCIPLE OF ALCHEMY.
...
SO YOU MEAN...

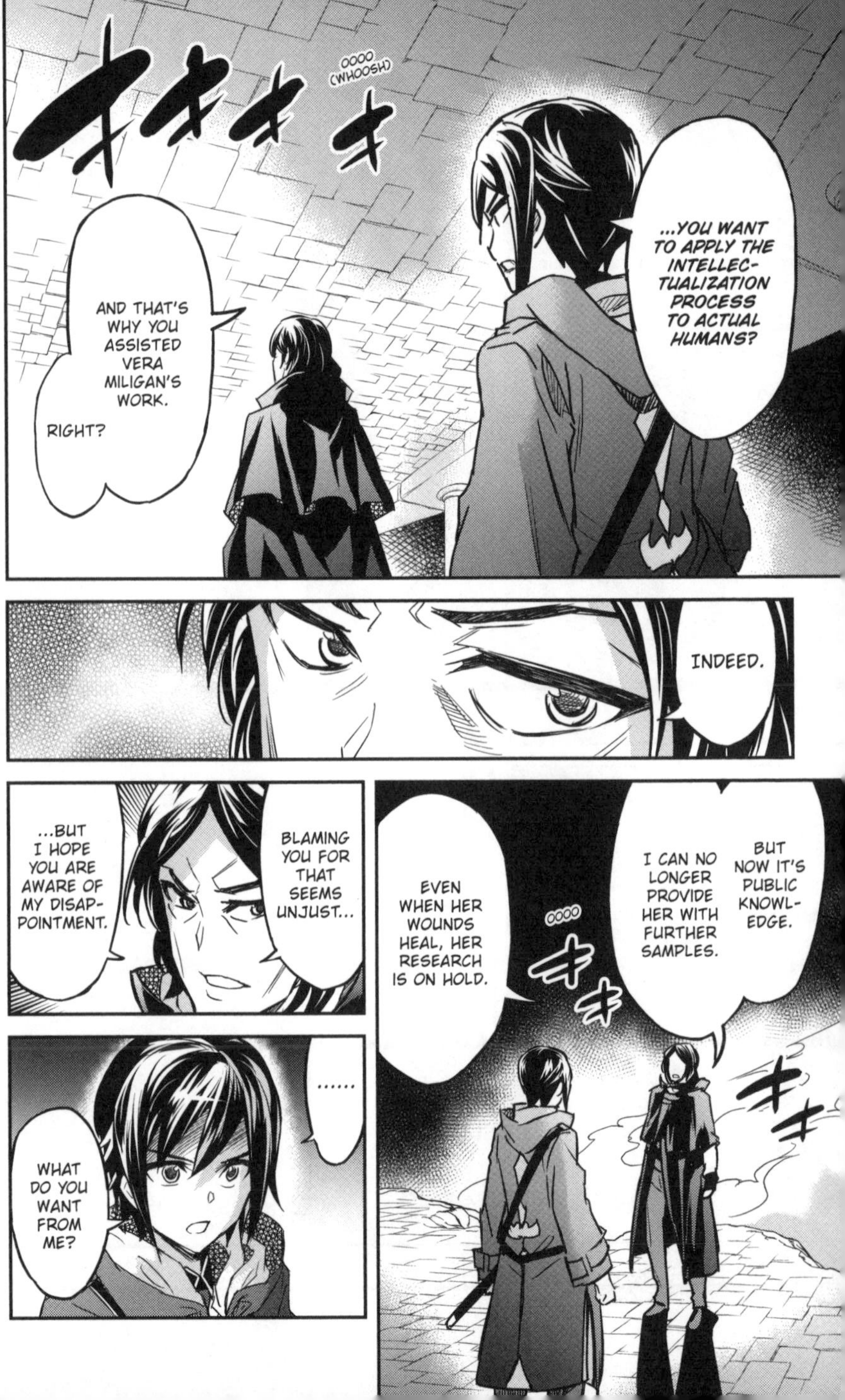
...YOU WANT TO APPLY THE INTELLEC-TUALIZATION PROCESS TO ACTUAL HUMANS?
OOOO (WHOOSH)
AND THAT'S WHY YOU ASSISTED VERA MILIGAN'S WORK.
RIGHT?
INDEED.
BUT NOW IT'S PUBLIC KNOWL-EDGE.
I CAN NO LONGER PROVIDE HER WITH FURTHER SAMPLES.
OOOO
EVEN WHEN HER WOUNDS HEAL, HER RESEARCH IS ON HOLD.
BLAMING YOU FOR THAT SEEMS UNJUST...
...BUT I HOPE YOU ARE AWARE OF MY DISAP-POINTMENT.
......
WHAT DO YOU WANT FROM ME?

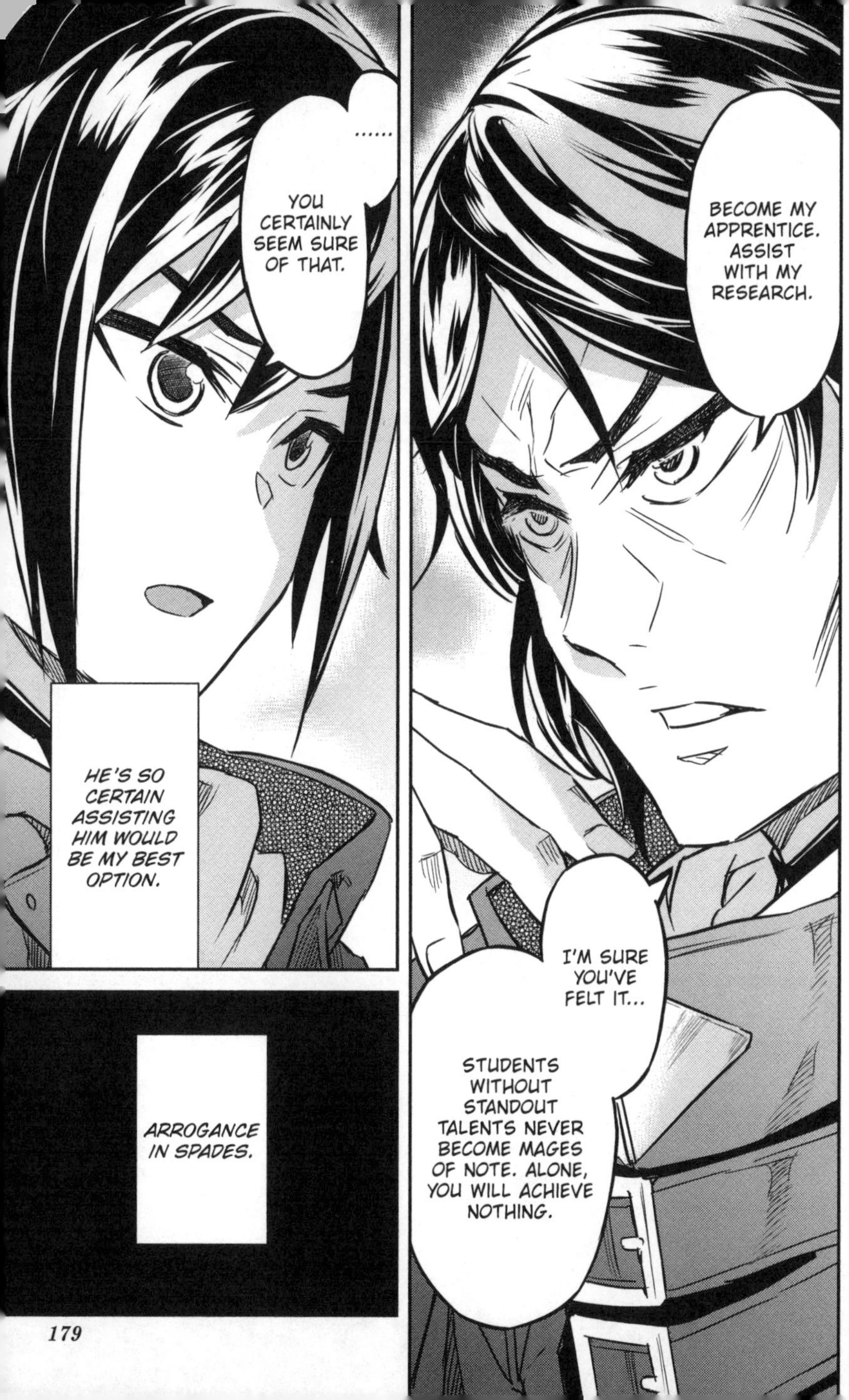
BECOME MY APPRENTICE. ASSIST WITH MY RESEARCH.
I'M SURE YOU'VE FELT IT...
STUDENTS WITHOUT STANDOUT TALENTS NEVER BECOME MAGES OF NOTE. ALONE, YOU WILL ACHIEVE NOTHING.
......
YOU CERTAINLY SEEM SURE OF THAT.
HE'S SO CERTAIN ASSISTING HIM WOULD BE MY BEST OPTION.
ARROGANCE IN SPADES.

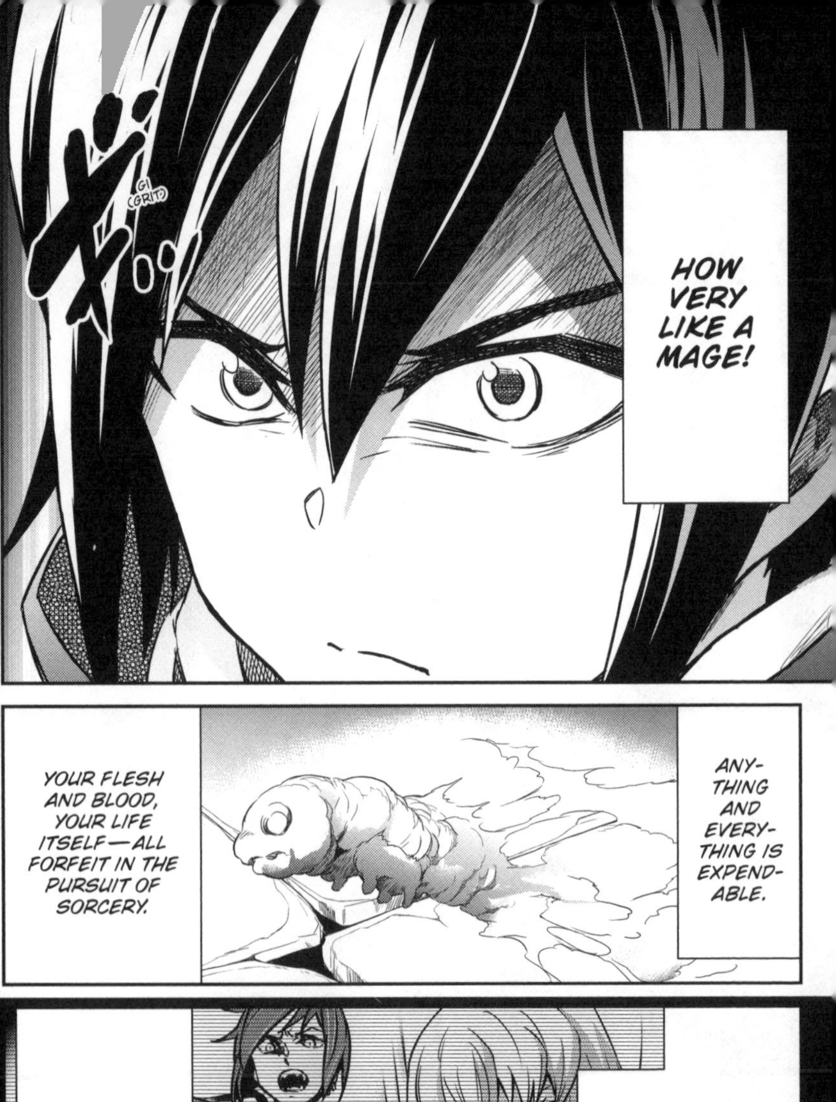
HOW VERY LIKE A MAGE!
GI (GRIT)
ANY-THING AND EVERY-THING IS EXPEND-ABLE.
YOUR FLESH AND BLOOD, YOUR LIFE ITSELF—ALL FORFEIT IN THE PURSUIT OF SORCERY.
THAT IS HOW A MAGE OUGHT TO BE.
AND WHY THEY CANNOT ACCEPT...
...THAT THERE IS ANY VALUE IN KINDNESS.

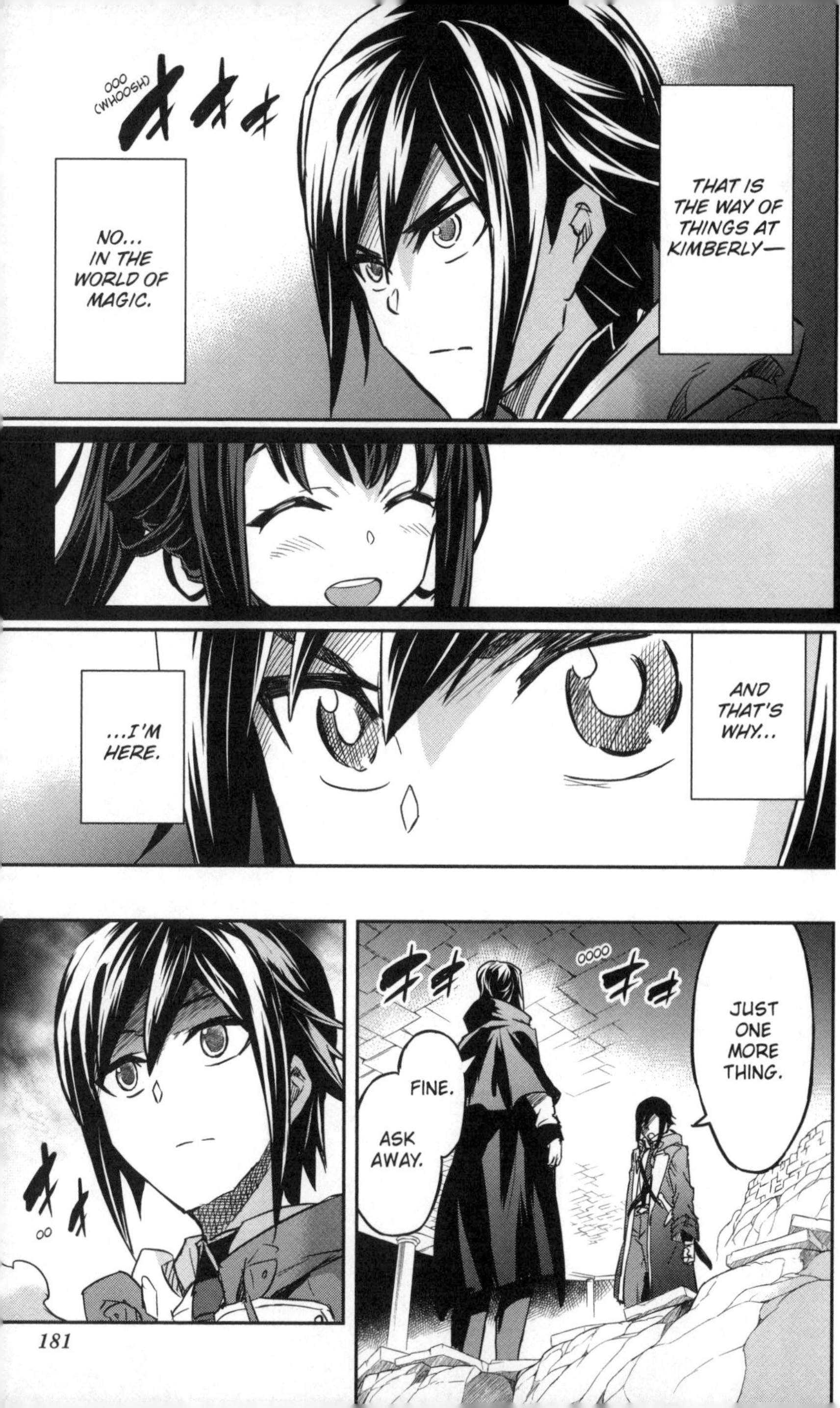
THAT IS THE WAY OF THINGS AT KIMBERLY—
OOO (WHOOSH)
NO... IN THE WORLD OF MAGIC.
AND THAT'S WHY...
...I'M HERE.
JUST ONE MORE THING.
OOOO
FINE.
ASK AWAY.
OO

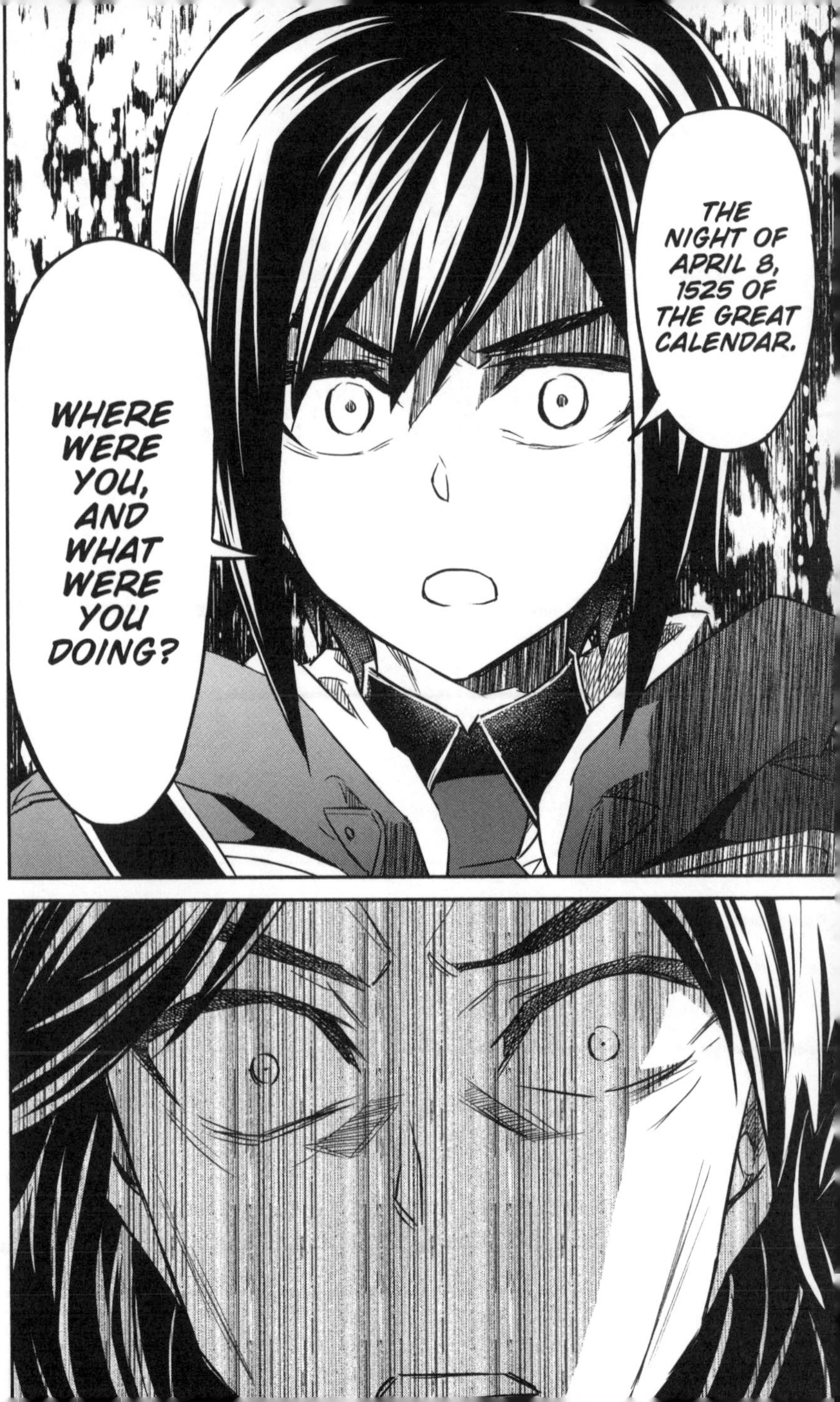
THE NIGHT OF APRIL 8, 1525 OF THE GREAT CALENDAR.
WHERE WERE YOU, AND WHAT WERE YOU DOING?

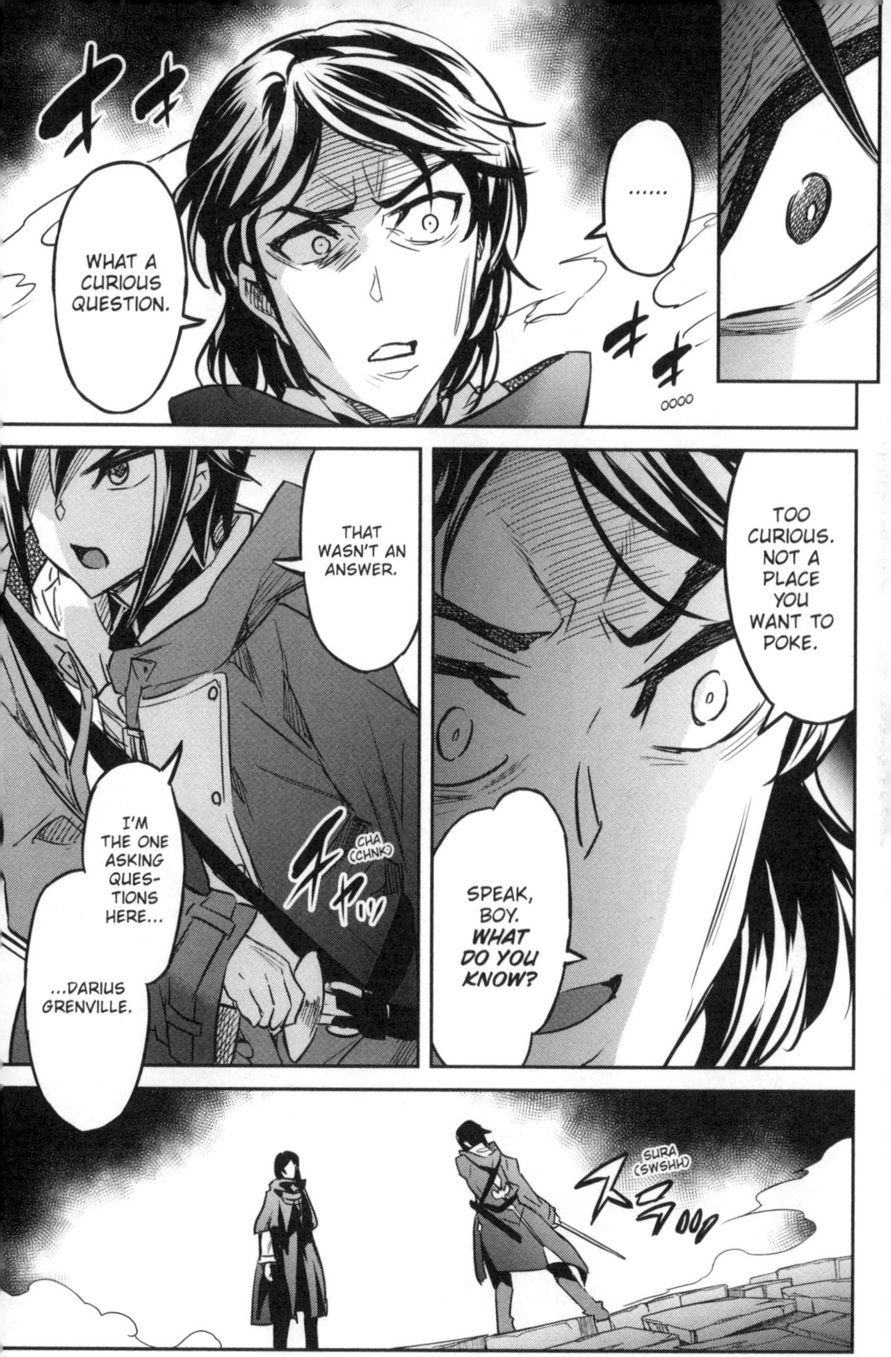
......
OOOO
WHAT A CURIOUS QUESTION.
TOO CURIOUS. NOT A PLACE YOU WANT TO POKE.
SPEAK, BOY. ***WHAT DO YOU KNOW?***
THAT WASN'T AN ANSWER.
CHA (CHNK)
I'M THE ONE ASKING QUES-TIONS HERE...
...DARIUS GRENVILLE.
SURA (SWSHH)

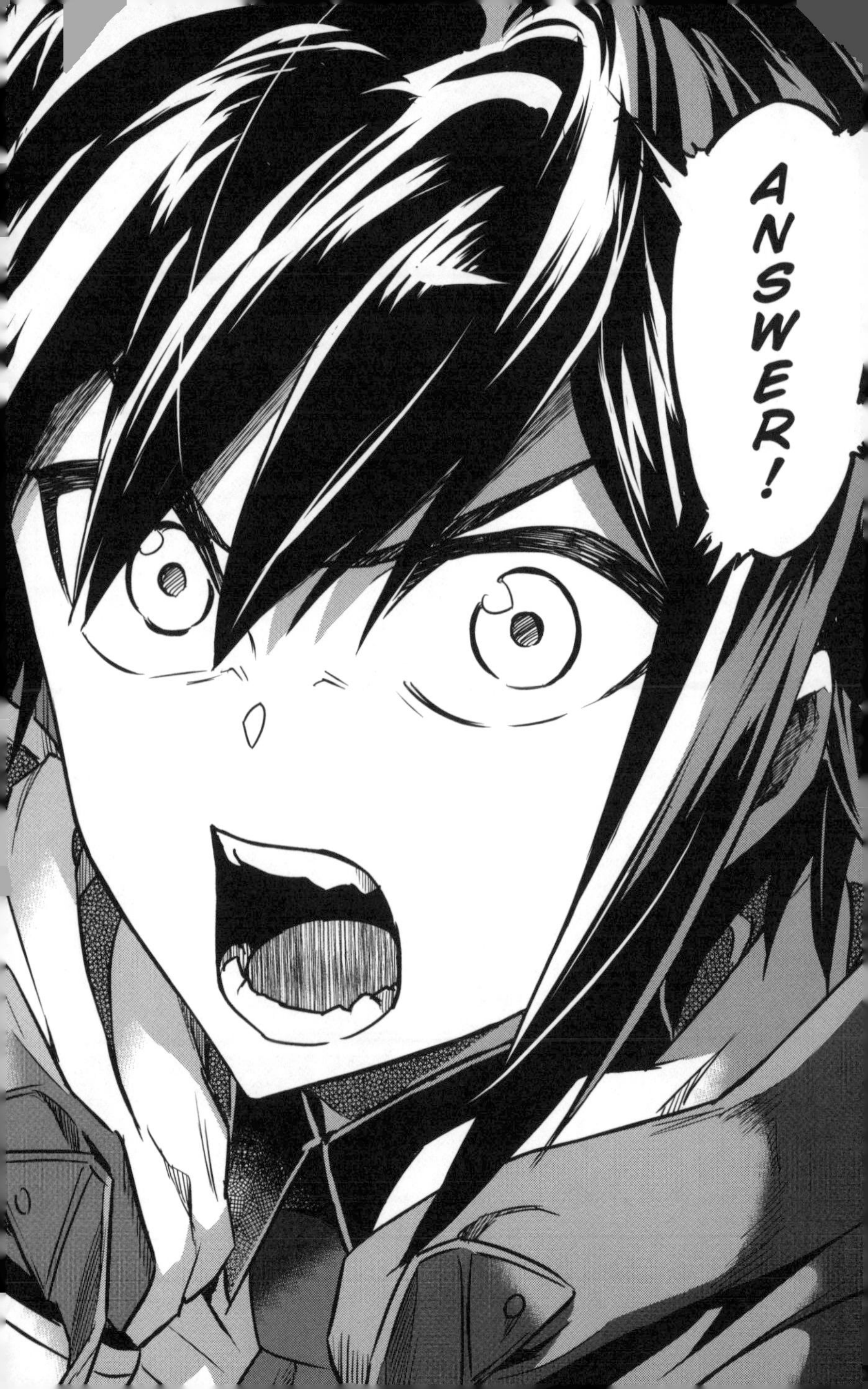
ANSWER!

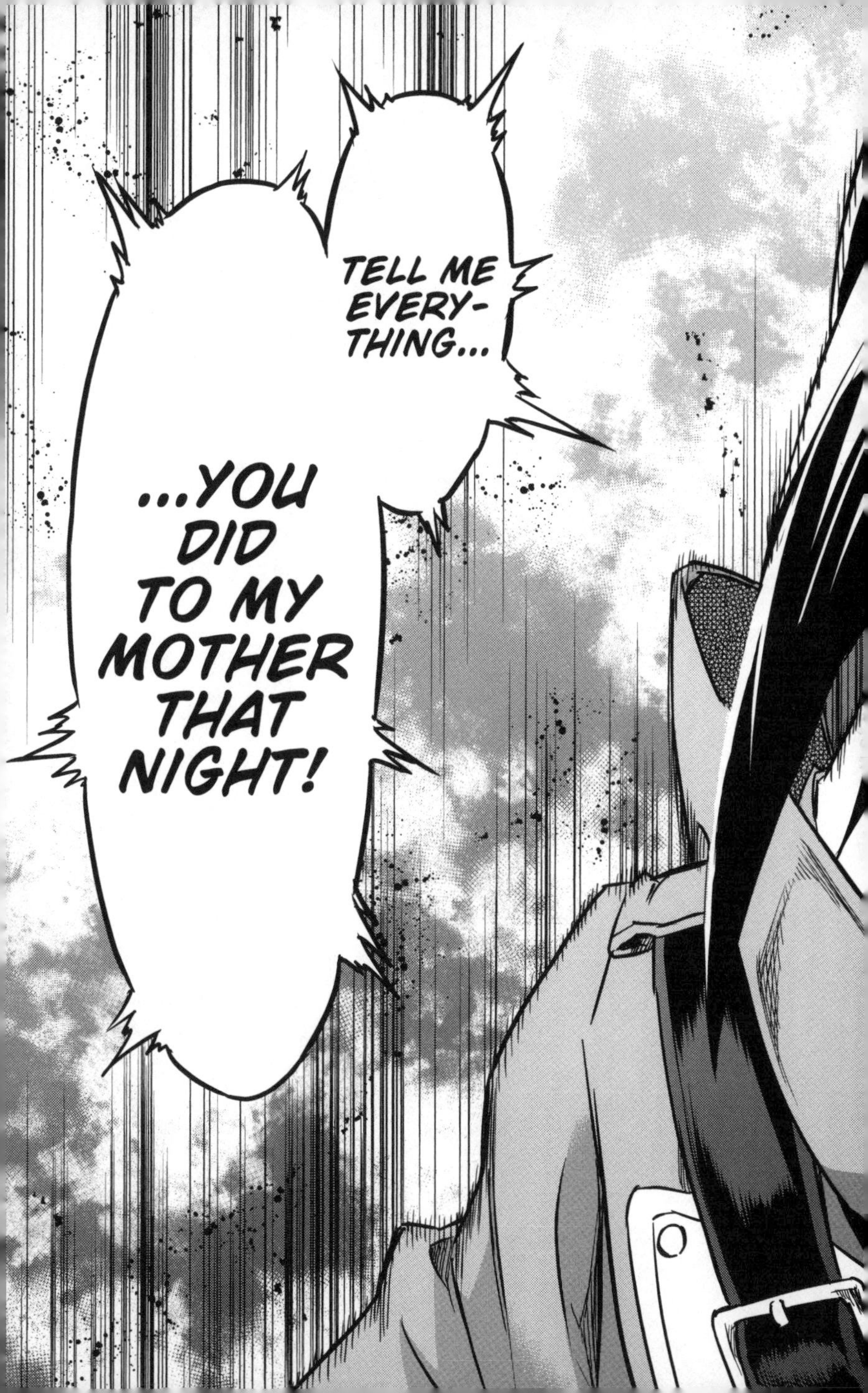
TELL ME EVERYTHING...
...YOU DID TO MY MOTHER THAT NIGHT!

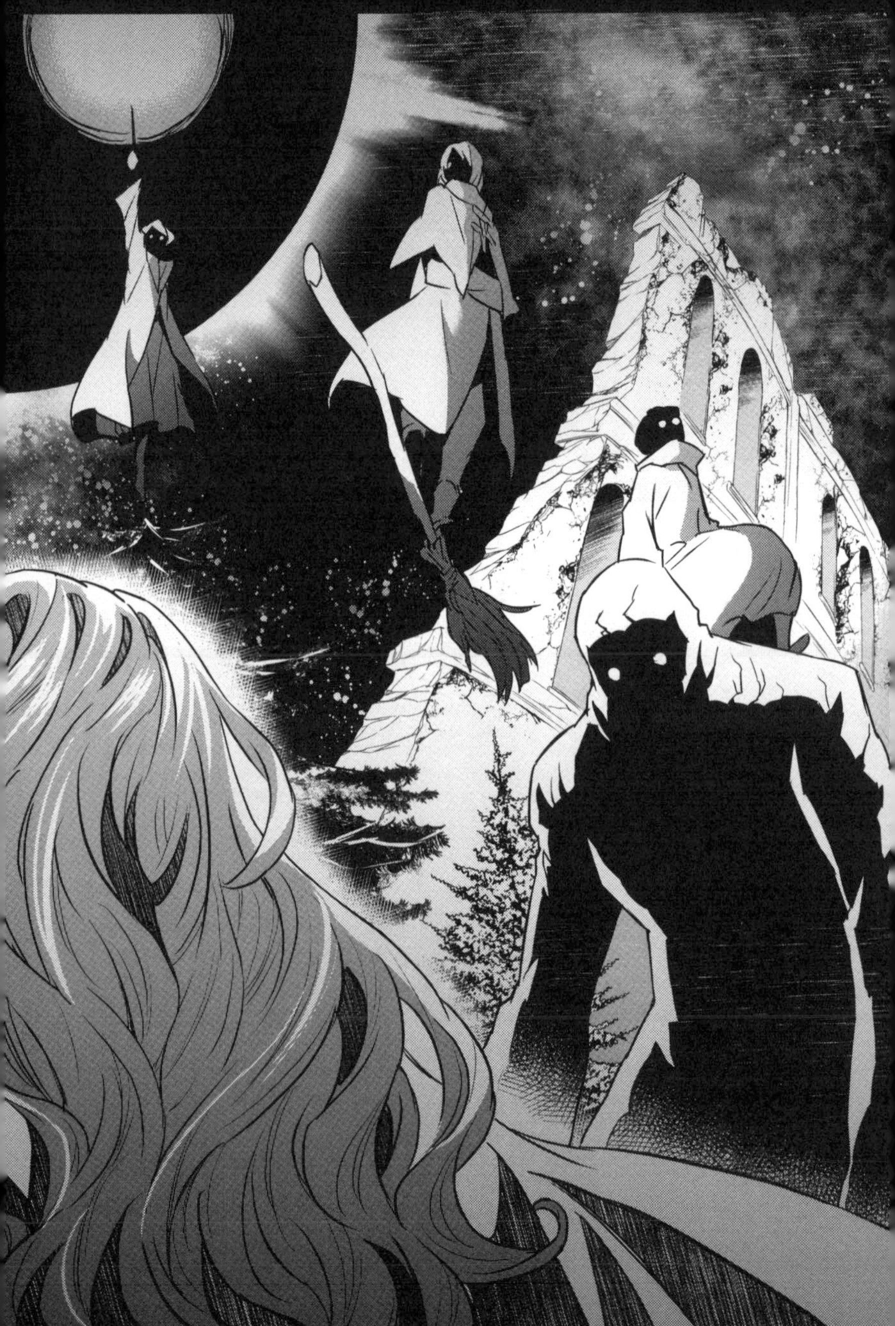

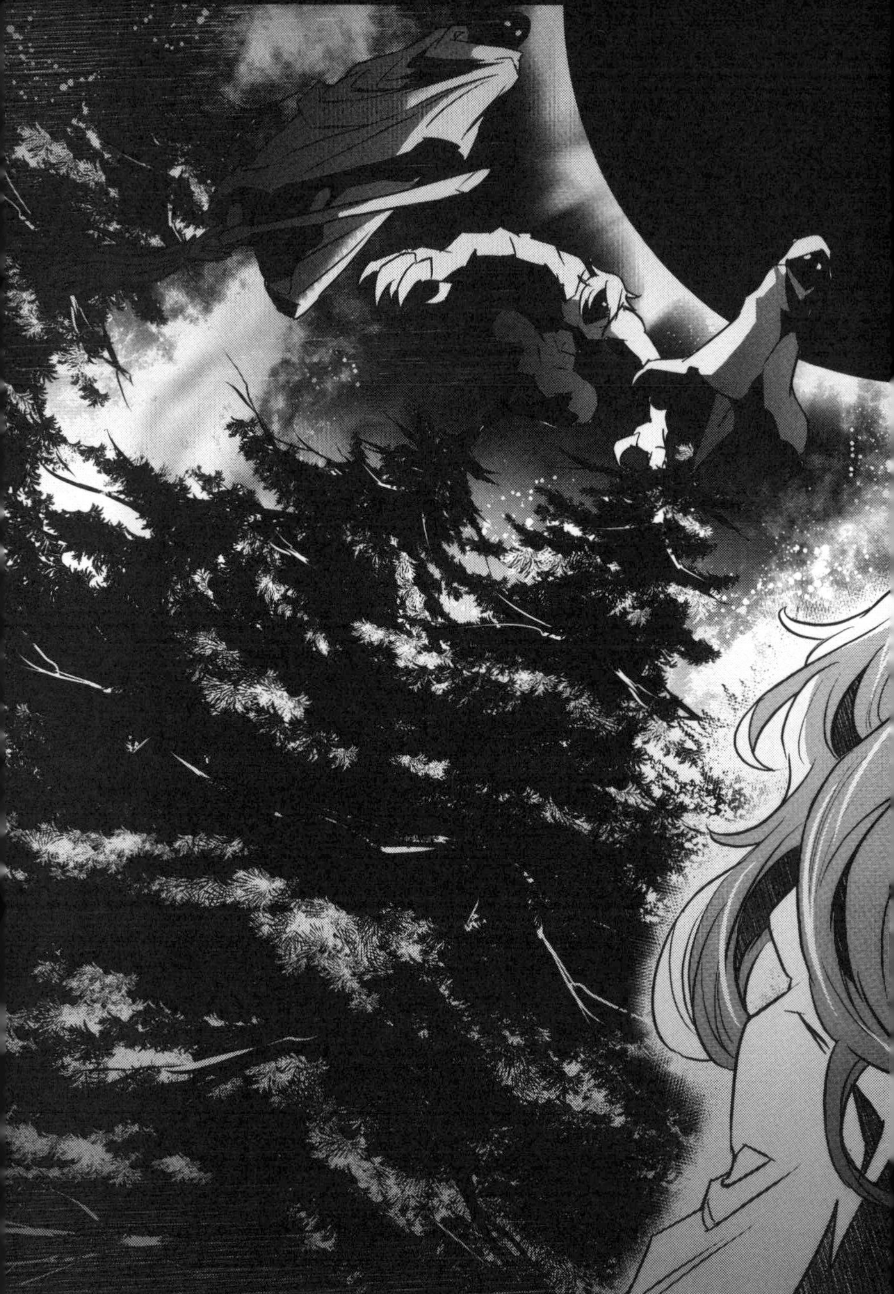

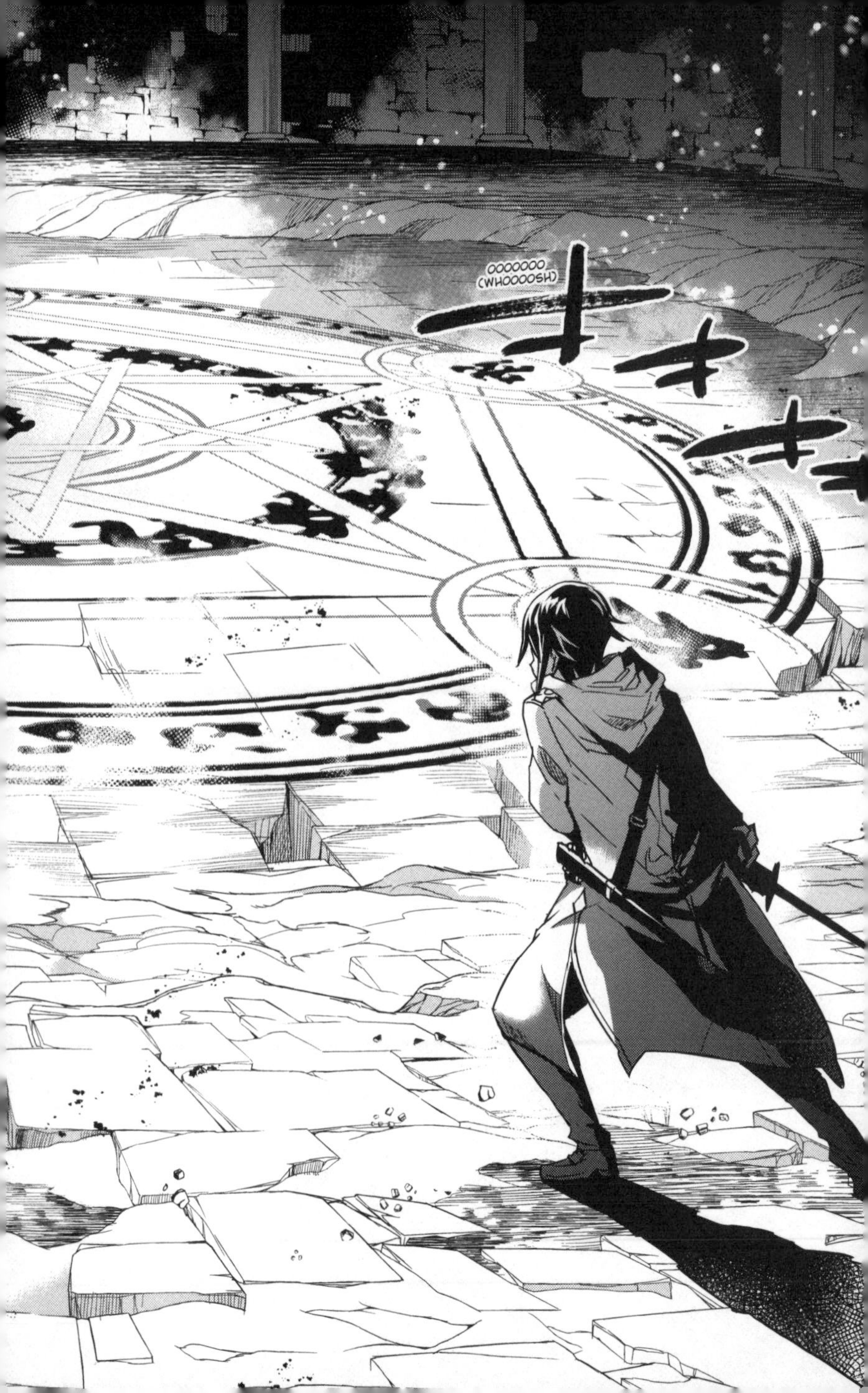
OOOOOOO
(WHOOOOSH)

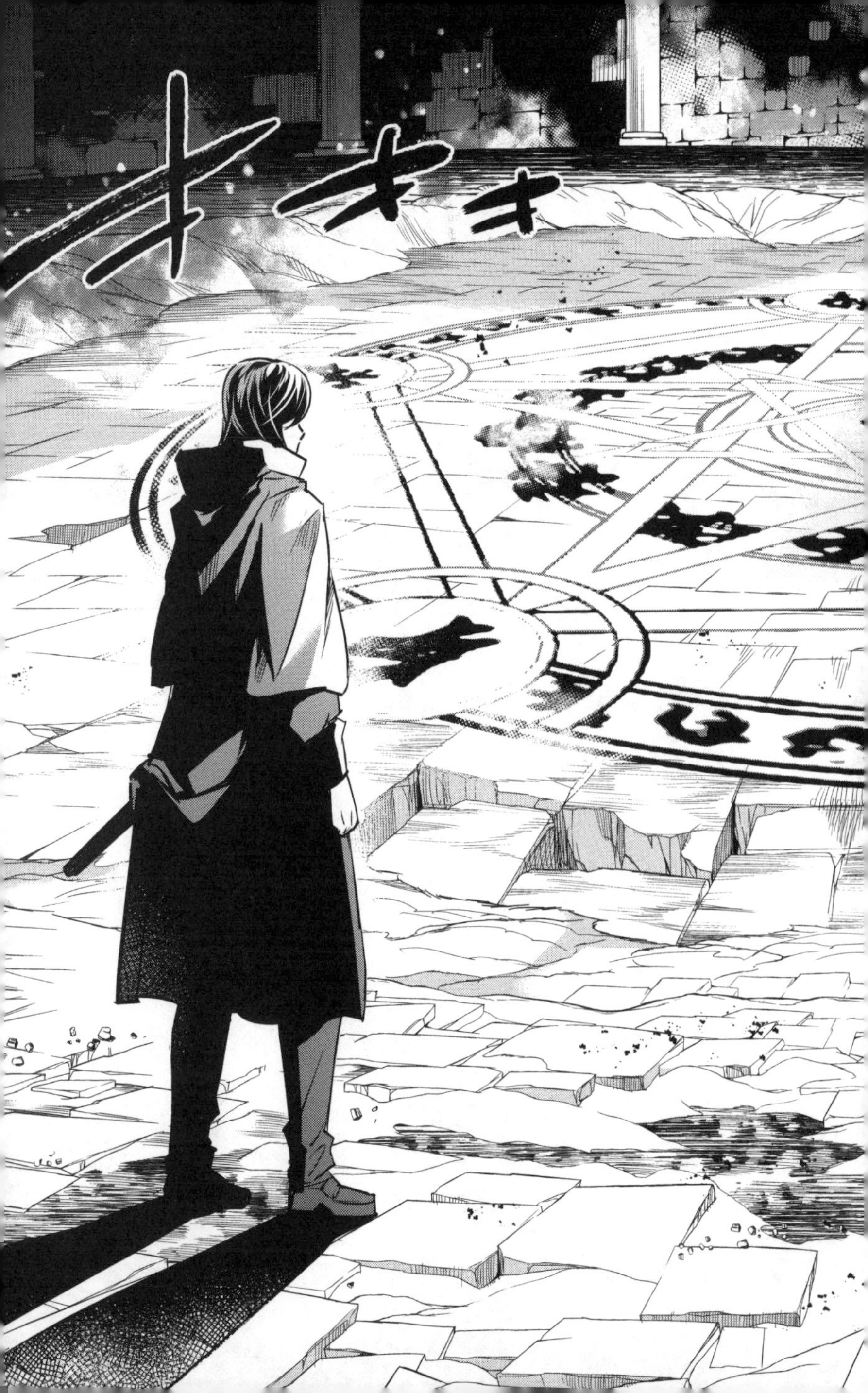
キキキ

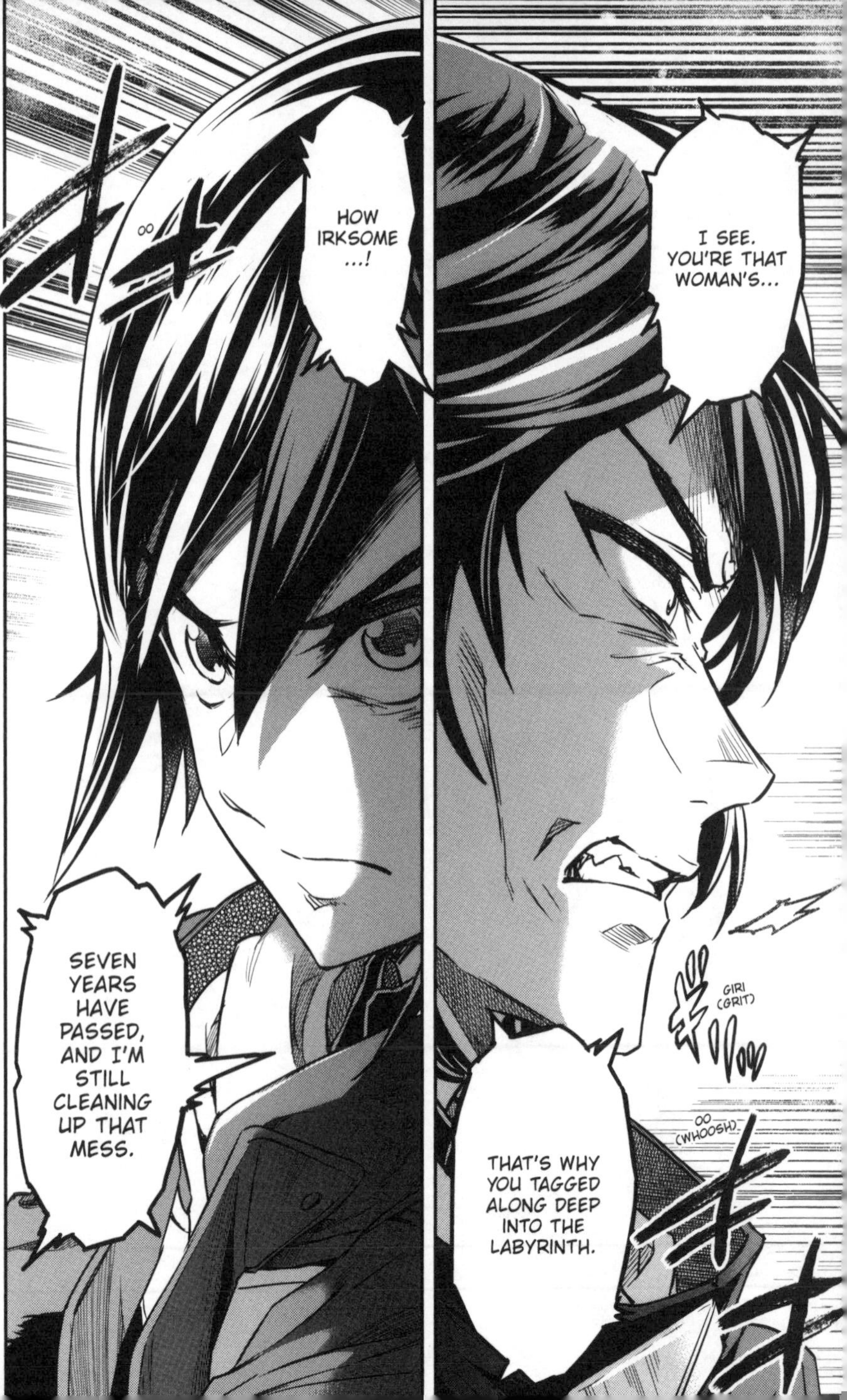
I SEE. YOU'RE THAT WOMAN'S...
GIRI (GRIT)
THAT'S WHY YOU TAGGED ALONG DEEP INTO THE LABYRINTH.
OO (WHOOSH)
OO
HOW IRKSOME ...!
SEVEN YEARS HAVE PASSED, AND I'M STILL CLEANING UP THAT MESS.

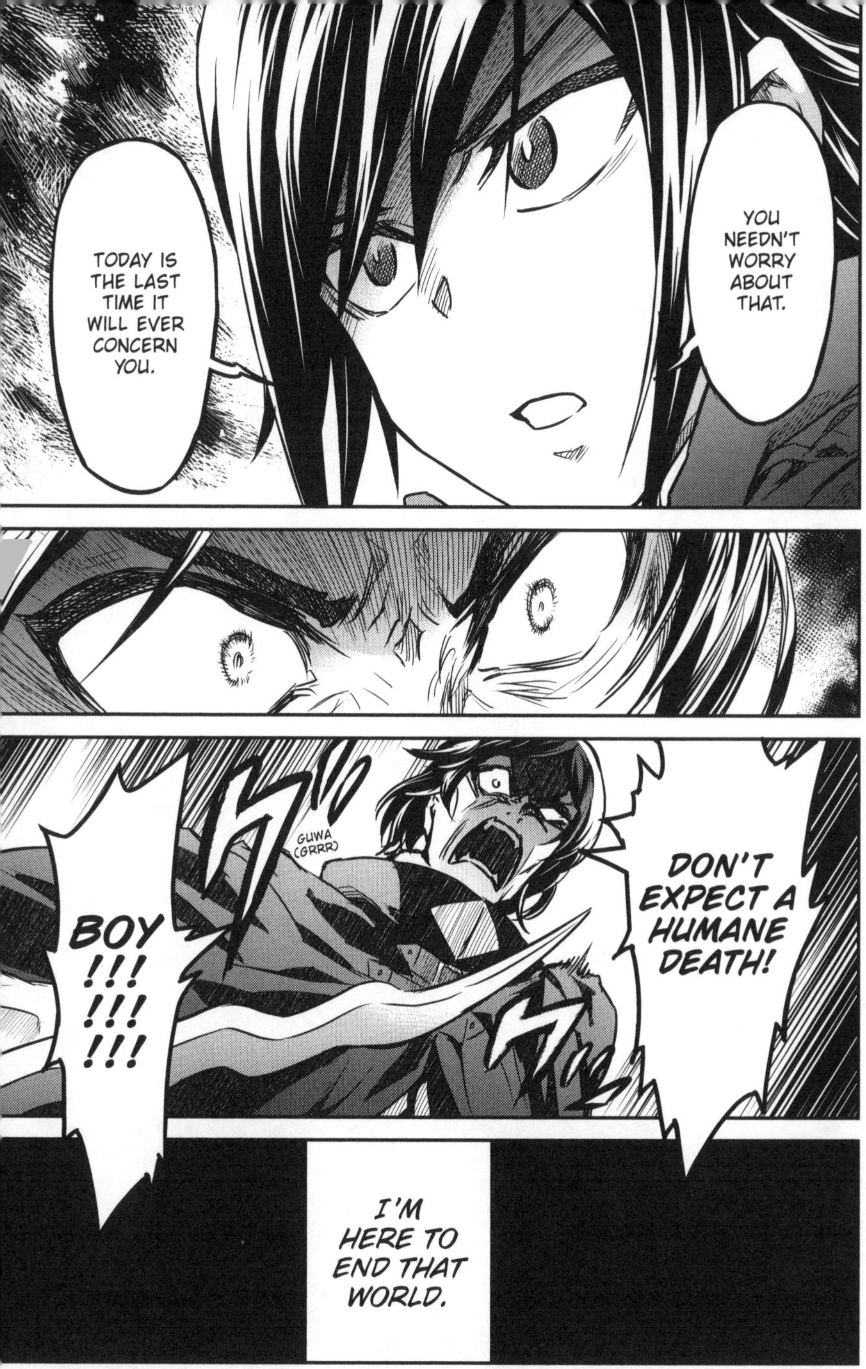
YOU NEEDN'T WORRY ABOUT THAT.
TODAY IS THE LAST TIME IT WILL EVER CONCERN YOU.
DON'T EXPECT A HUMANE DEATH!
GUWA (GRRR)
BOY!!!!!!!!!
I'M HERE TO END THAT WORLD.

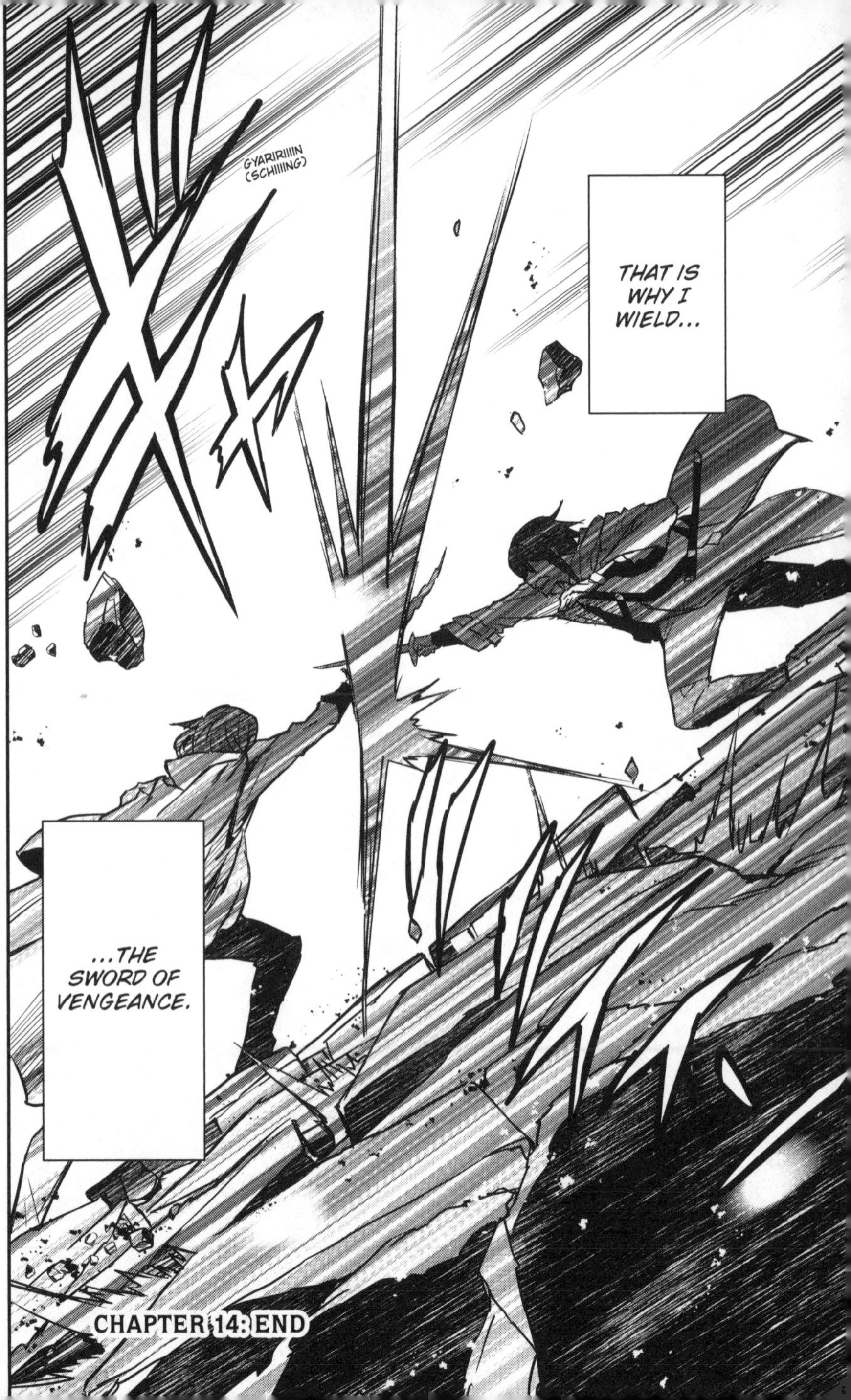

THAT IS WHY I WIELD...
GYARIRIIIIN (SCHIIIING)
...THE SWORD OF VENGEANCE.
CHAPTER 14: END

To Be Continued...

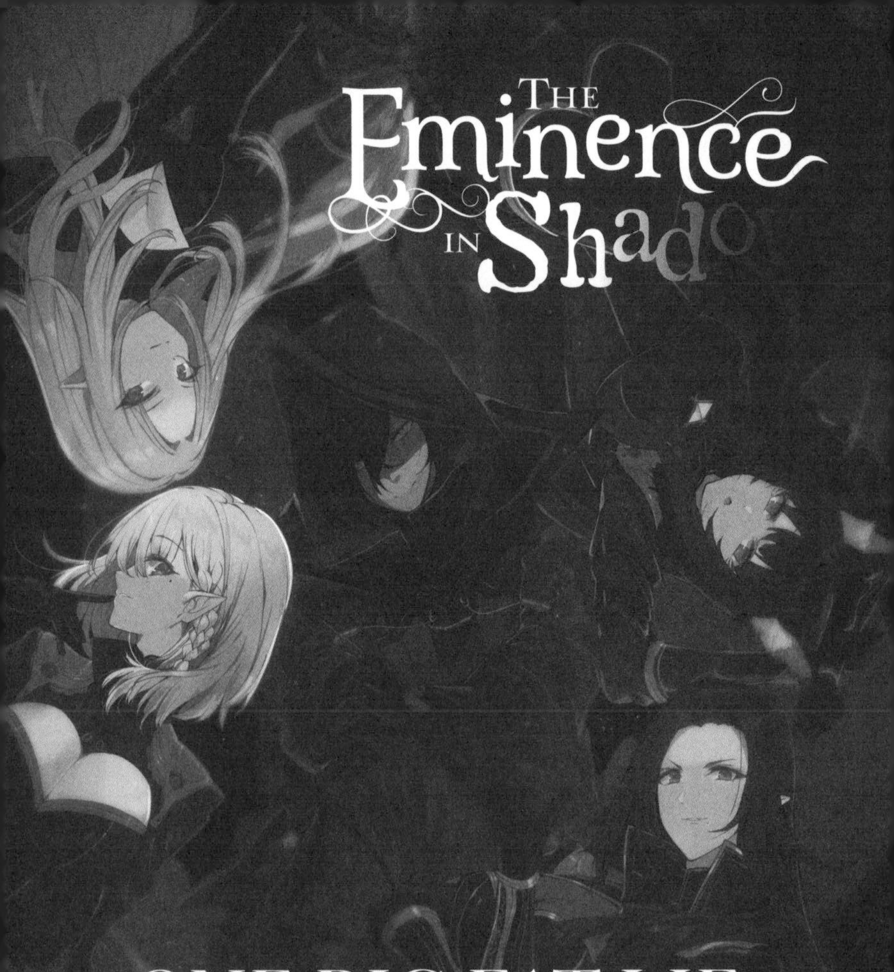
THE
Eminence
IN Shado

Reign of the Seven Spellblades

Sakae Esuno ORIGINAL STORY **Bokuto Uno** CHARACTER DESIGN **Ruria Miyuki**

3

TRANSLATION
Andrew Cunningham

LETTERING
Brandon Bovia

NANATSU NO MAKEN GA SHIHAISURU Vol.3
©Sakae Esuno 2020
©Bokuto Uno 2020
First published in Japan in 2020 by KADOKAWA CORPORATION, Tokyo. English translation rights arranged with KADOKAWA CORPORATION, Tokyo through TUTTLE-MORI AGENCY, INC., Tokyo.

English translation © 2022 by Yen Press, LLC

Yen Press
150 West 30th Street, 19th Floor
New York, NY 10001

Visit us at yenpress.com • facebook.com/yenpress
twitter.com/yenpress • yenpress.tumblr.com
instagram.com/yenpress

First Yen Press Edition: May 2022

Yen Press is an imprint of Yen Press, LLC.
The Yen Press name and logo are trademarks of Yen Press, LLC.

The publisher is not responsible for websites (or their content) that are not owned by the publisher.

Library of Congress Control Number: 2021943178

ISBNs: 978-1-9753-3667-7 (paperback)
978-1-9753-3668-4 (ebook)

1 3 5 7 9 10 8 6 4 2

LSC-C

Printed in the United States of America

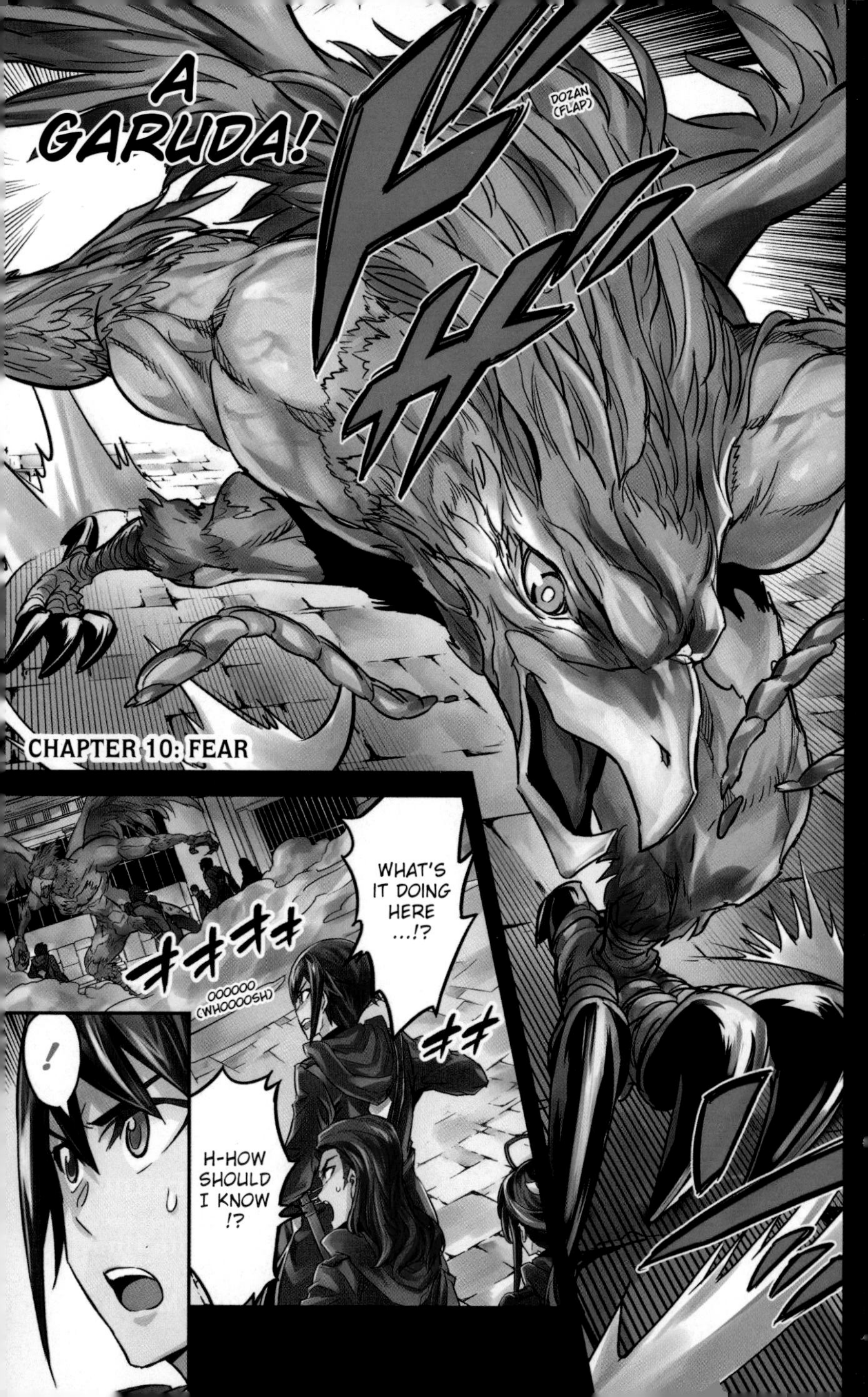
DOZAN (FLAP)
A GARUDA!
CHAPTER 10: FEAR
WHAT'S IT DOING HERE ...!?
オオオオ
オオ
OOOOOO (WHOOOOSH)
H-HOW SHOULD I KNOW !?
!

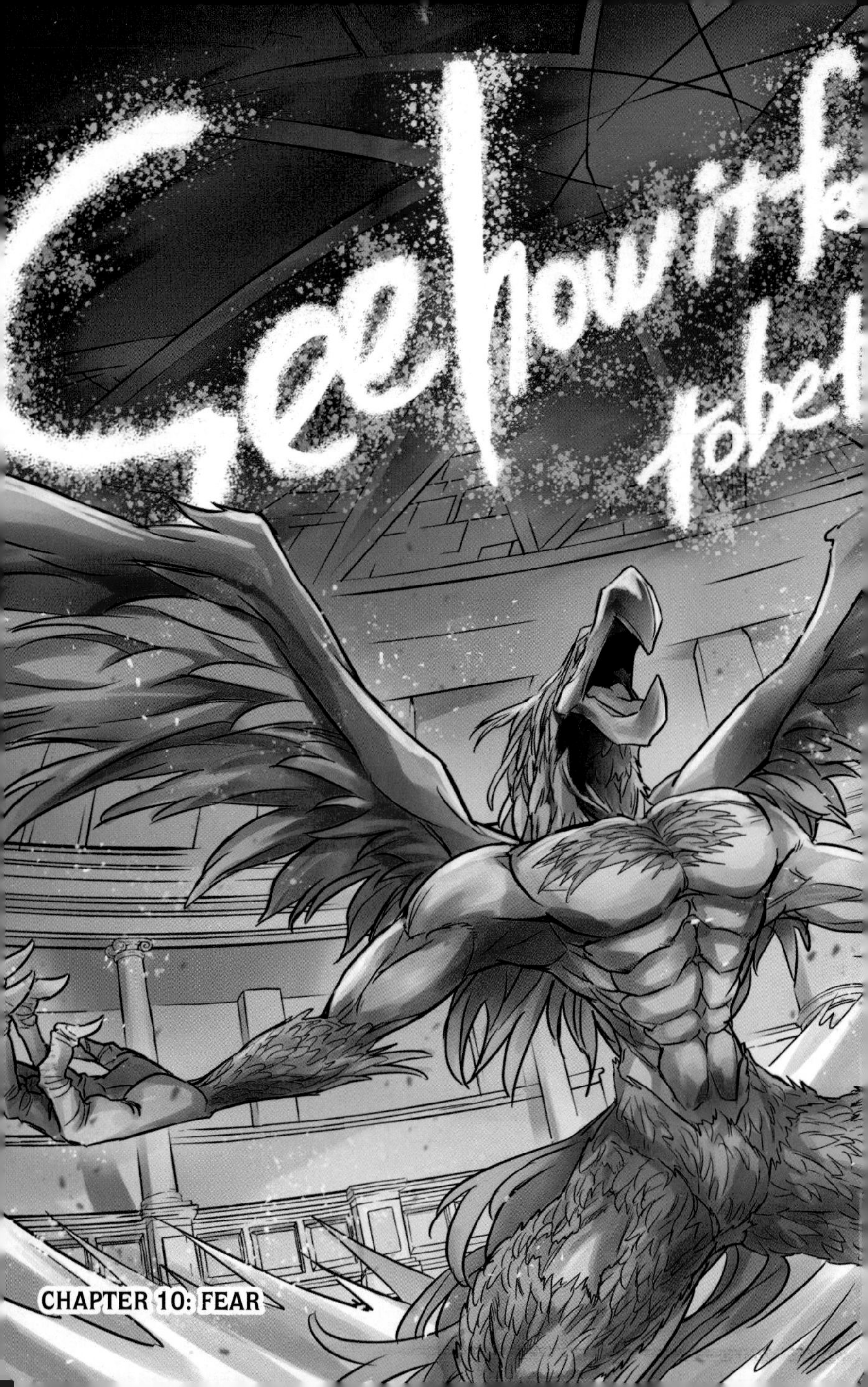
CHAPTER 10: FEAR

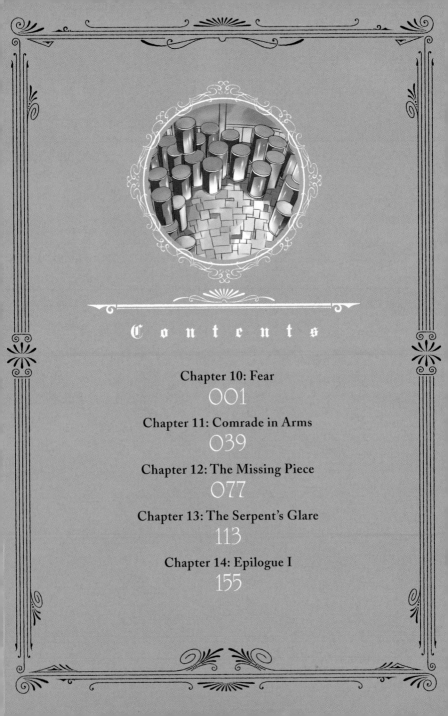

Contents